THE ELY TESTAMENT

THE ELY TESTAMENT

Philip Gooden

severn House

This first world edition published 2011
in Great Britain and in the USA by
SEVERN HOUSE PUBLISHERS LTD of
9–15 High Street, Sutton, Surrey, England, SM1 1DF.
Trade paperback edition first published
in Great Britain and the USA 2012 by
SEVERN HOUSE PUBLISHERS LTD.

British Library Cataloguing in Publication Data

Gooden, Philip.
  The Ely testament.
  1. Ansell, Tom (Fictitious character) – Fiction.
  2. Lawyers – England – Fiction. 3. Lawyers' spouses –
  Fiction. 4. Murder – Investigation – Fiction. 5. Ely
  (England) – History – 19th century – Fiction. 6. Detective
  and mystery stories.
  I. Title
  823.9'2-dc22

ISBN-13: 978-0-7278-8103-8 (cased)
ISBN-13: 978-1-84751-403-5 (trade paper)

All Severn House titles are printed on acid-free paper.

Severn House Publishers support The Forest Stewardship Council [FSC],
the leading international forest certification organisation. All our titles that
are printed on Greenpeace-approved FSC-certified paper carry the FSC logo.

Typeset by Palimpsest Book Production Ltd.,
Falkirk, Stirlingshire, Scotland.
Printed and bound in Great Britain by
MPG Books Ltd., Bodmin, Cornwall.

Summer, 1645

*The morning was chill, with the grass and trees still wet from
the overnight rain. Yet the first streaks of pink were just visible to
the east. She could see them through the leaded window in the gable.
Her breath clouded on the little panes and she wiped them clean with
the sleeve of her nightshirt. The thick, uneven glass squeaked. She looked
back at the warmth of the bed which she'd just left. Her younger sister
slept on, unaware that something was wrong.*

*Anne, standing at the window and peering at the lightening sky, did
not know for certain that something was wrong. But she felt it. Had felt
it ever since the afternoon of the previous day when two men arrived at
the house on horseback. Anne saw them as she came back from examining
the progress of the strawberries in the kitchen garden, which she did
mostly by picking and tasting samples. The visitors had been riding fast
and their lathered horses were led away to be rubbed down in the stables
even as Mr Stilwell, Anne's father, welcomed the newcomers. There were
heavy clouds piling up on the horizon and she heard the rumble of distant
thunder. Perhaps the men were eager to reach shelter before the rain came.*

*From their clothing and demeanour, they were gentlemen. They gave
no sign of noticing the girl standing by the entrance to the kitchen garden.
From her father's distracted manner when he waved away one of the
household servants, and then his quick disappearance indoors with his
guests, Anne could tell that there was some urgent business in hand. She
did not think they were anxious because of the approaching weather.*

*The new arrivals were closeted together with Anne's mother and father
for much of the afternoon. That was odd. Anne could not think what
might concern her father and her mother equally. It was nothing to do
with her, of course. Any question, even had she dared to ask one, would
have been met with silence or a rebuke for her curiosity. But she was
curious, and, more than curious, she was troubled. She might have asked
James, but the old steward was nowhere to be seen.*

*Later Anne thought that the two men must have left. At any rate she
heard the sound of departing hooves and there was no guest at supper,
none that she was able to see from her partial viewpoint up in the gallery*

overlooking the hall. She was sent to bed – indeed, she should have been in bed even as she was standing in the gallery watching her parents dining with Mr Martin – but she could not sleep. Still the rain did not come, though the air was close and the thunder sounded like an encircling army. It was summer and the evening was endless, the thick light seeming to fade from the sky with reluctance. Her sister slumbered on beside her, but Anne could not help hearing strange noises in the house, unaccustomed footsteps and doors creaking; sounds that continued until after it had got dark, and long after the adults in the place usually went off to their beds.

Eventually, and as the rain at last started to batter at the house, she fell asleep. When she woke there was a grey glimmer at the little windows. She swung her legs over the side of the bed and padded towards the gable casement. She still felt something was wrong. She remembered the sound of footsteps and doors. There must have been other arrivals at the house last night. She rubbed again at the window panes, which fogged up almost as soon as she cleared them. She gazed at the line of trees which demarcated the land immediately adjacent to Stilwell Manor from the fenland which lay beyond. Anne saw a flicker of movement among the trees and caught her breath. After a few moments, a deer sprang into view and skittered across the open ground until it reached the safety of another copse of trees in the corner of the grounds.

Anne went back to bed, yet on this early summer's morning she could not drift back into sleep. She would definitely look for James today and ask him what was going on. The old steward was the one person in the household who always seemed to have time for her questions.

It was from him and not from her parents that she had learned something of the history of Stilwell Manor. He'd even told of the hiding places for priests, secret places behind panels, that had been constructed in the time of Queen Elizabeth. From James' description, they would be scarcely big enough to hold her and she wondered how a grown man could have survived inside one of them, not just for hours but days and weeks, as James said they did. Anne asked the steward if he had ever met the Queen and he laughed and told her she was a foolish child. The Queen would not have come to a remote fenland manor like Stilwell. Besides, she was an old lady when James had been not much more than a young lad and her royal days of gallivanting about her kingdom were over and done with by then.

Anne dreamed of those hiding places inside the house, and imagined desperate men subsisting in darkness on crumbs of food and drops of stale water, like mice and rats behind the wainscot, their terror made greater by the awareness that, in the world outside, men were hunting for them.

Anne found that sleep still eluded her. Once more she got out of bed and went to the casement window. The light was stronger now and the sun's low rays dazzled on the wet foliage and grass. Half attentive, she gazed at the line of poplars and willows from which the deer had appeared. And this time, she gasped and her heart began to thud beneath her nightshirt. A group of men was emerging from the trees, a ragged formation of perhaps a dozen armed men.

At the *Funereal Matters* Office

One fine morning in the spring of 1874 two men met in the London office of a periodical called *Funereal Matters*. It was a magazine devoted not just to the business of funerals but to their fashions and etiquette as well, and even to what might be called the 'philosophy of interment'. The office for *Funereal Matters*, or *F.M.* as it was familiarly referred to in the office and among knowledgeable outsiders, was situated in St Dunstan's Alley in the City, not far from the Monument to the Great Fire of 1666.

The two men were sitting on either side of a desk in a little side room off the principal room where the editor worked. The circulation of *Funereal Matters* was modest but as the editor, Alfred Jenkins, was fond of saying, he preferred it that way. Better to cast one's net not wide but deep. Among his subscribers were influential people like bishops and writers and thinkers, as well as the undertakers and the milliners and dressmakers who wanted to keep up with the latest styles. But a quality readership did not translate into a large income so Jenkins ran *F.M.* with a couple of assistants.

One of the men sitting in the cubbyhole on this fine morning was not a full-time member of staff but an occasional contributor and freelance. He wrote a column of gossip and news under the pseudonym of 'Mute'. He had come up with the name himself. When he suggested the name to Jenkins, the editor almost clapped his hands in delight. Mute was a first-rate pseudonym for a

contributor to the magazine since it not only described a paid
mourner at a funeral but also had a tinge of mystery to it.

The man styling himself Mute quickly proved his worth and
his column became essential reading for anyone interested in the
business of burial. Alfred Jenkins was well aware of this, which
was why the editor agreed to provide his columnist with a room,
almost a cubbyhole, at the Dunstan's Alley office, even though
Mute spent only a couple of days a week there. The two assistants
worked from an equally small room on the far side of the editor's
quarters but, unlike Mute, they had to pass through Jenkins'
room to get out of the building. Mute liked the fact that he was
able to come and go as he pleased, without having to explain
himself or consult anybody.

The other man in the cubbyhole was called Charles Tomlinson.
He and Mute had been at college together some fifteen years
earlier but had not seen each other during the intervening period.
Mute completed his degree while Tomlinson left before taking
his. In fact, he quit Cambridge early to avoid the humiliation of
being sent down for an offence which caused outrage among the
respectable majority but amusement for those few students who
considered themselves to be freethinkers.

Mute was one of those freethinkers who'd been amused by the
'incident' as they referred to it. Now, many years later, Charles
Tomlinson was amused to hear the pseudonym his old friend used
for the column in *Funereal Matters*.

'I think I prefer it to your real name. Henceforth you shall be
Mute to me,' said Tomlinson, glancing about the poky space. 'You
seem well established here.'

'Established?' said Mute, leaning forward to straighten a pen-
holder on the desk in front of him. 'I hope not. I see myself as
a gadfly, darting here and stinging there. The funeral trade is
frightfully stick-in-the-mud, you know. It needs a good poke
from time to time.'

'Which you provide.'

'I do indeed.'

'I met your editor on the way in. Jenkins. A pleasant fellow
but long in the tooth. Do you hope to step into his shoes one
day?'

'No,' said Mute. He did have plans but they did not include

the editorship of *Funereal Matters*. He changed the subject. 'Well, it is many years since we last met, Tomlinson. You've been travelling in the East, you say. Certainly you look . . .'

'Bronzed? Swarthy?'

'I was going to say burnished.'

'That sounds better, Mute. You always had a facility with words, despite the silent pseudonym which you have chosen.'

The funereal correspondent was not flattered by the compliment. Charles Tomlinson had been more glib and fluent than any of their college set. Now Mute said, 'So you've been travelling with a purpose, Tomlinson? To find your fortune perhaps?'

'I've travelled with no purpose at all apart from wanting to get away from this narrow, tight little island of ours called Britain. You can't get much further away in either miles or spirit than the Far East. I have seen the world or a good part of it – as well as some pretty bad parts of it. Now I'm ready to return.'

'What will you do?'

Mute did not ask the question out of mere curiosity. For all Tomlinson's 'burnished' complexion and his air of self-sufficiency, the man looked down at heel. He still had a strong gaze and a determined, clean-shaven jaw, which he frequently stroked. Yet the years had been rougher to him than they'd been to Mute, who retained something of his youthful appearance and who spent more than he could really afford on smartish clothes. By contrast, Tomlinson's clothes were worn and frayed. That wasn't the only sign of decline. Earlier in their conversation, Tomlinson had taken out a hip flask in a very open manner and swallowed a hefty gulp. He referred to this as 'just a nip on a sharp morning'. Mute raised his eyebrows but Tomlinson, used to a much hotter climate, said he found England cold and shivery even when the sun was out.

In addition to the frayed clothes and the hip flask, Mute noticed that Tomlinson had not given a direct answer to his remark about 'finding a fortune'. If Tomlinson had not prospered abroad – and his appearance suggested he hadn't, not at all – then perhaps he was returning to see what he might lay his hands on here. From the moment his old friend strolled into his office, the columnist for *Funereal Matters* was gripped by the anxiety that he might have come to ask him, Mute, for help in obtaining a post. There were no openings on this periodical, he was prepared to say, with regret.

'I'll make my way,' said Tomlinson. 'Don't you worry about *me*. I'll most likely be returning to Cambridge. I have family there, as you may remember.'

Mute nodded, quite relieved that Tomlinson was not planning to stay in London. And he did remember the man's links to Cambridge. It was one of the things which made Tomlinson's behaviour at college the more disgraceful, that he wasn't an outsider but came from a notable Cambridge family.

'Will you be . . .?' he began.

'Welcome? I believe so, Mute. In fact I know so. Quite a few years have passed since the incident. Letters have been exchanged, familial letters. On my side I have hinted that a black sheep may convert its fleece into a snowy white. On theirs, they have suggested that the prodigal could be greeted with open arms. Or at least not with closed ones. In particular, there is a cousin whom I remembered as a rather pretty young thing and who always had something of a partiality for me. She is married to some old fellow now and lives near Ely. I am glad to say that, on the basis of a single visit, she still has a partiality for me.'

'So you will be going there frequently?'

'There are other reasons for visiting beside the presence of my pretty cousin. I have come into possession of an intriguing document.'

'Yes?'

'A document containing information which may lead to the fortune you mentioned.'

'A metaphorical fortune?'

'Oh no,' said Tomlinson, glancing towards the door which separated the cubbyhole from the editor's room and speaking lower as if afraid of being overheard. 'I believe it is as tangible as . . . as that doorknob there.'

'We are talking money?'

'We are talking of an item which may easily be converted into money, and a great deal of it.'

Was Tomlinson teasing his old college friend, as he so often used to do? Mute did his best to appear uninterested. Then it occurred to him that this was not a very intelligent response.

Anybody would be interested in laying hands on a fortune, and to pretend otherwise was in itself suspicious. Certainly, he wouldn't object to a fortune himself. Mute's position as a columnist for *Funereal Matters* was secure but it did not pay a great deal, and although he had some resources he would, in the near future, require funds for an enterprise he was presently engaged on.

So, after a moment's thought, Mute made no attempt to hide the eagerness which he genuinely felt.

'Feel free to say more about that fortune of yours,' he said.

'I am free to say what I like, but what if I don't want to say anything?'

Suit yourself, thought Mute. I don't believe in your fortune now. But there was something in Tomlinson's look, an assurance, even a smugness, that caused the journalist to reconsider almost immediately.

It may be that Tomlinson sensed this for he continued, 'There is one thing though . . .'

'Yes?'

'I am looking for investors in this fortune-to-be. Would *you* like to be one of them, Mute? It would be to your undoubted advantage, but I also speak as a friend.'

The appeal touched Mute, not so much the mention of friendship but the idea that Tomlinson might be dependent on him. Was it possible his old friend really was on the track of a fortune? The man on the other side of the desk grasped his moment.

'Suppose you could see your way to investing, say, twenty pounds in my enterprise now, it would be returned a hundredfold – a thousandfold – when the time comes.'

'I can give you ten pounds,' said Mute promptly.

'You are *investing*, not giving. Twenty pounds would be better but ten is an improvement on nothing. I speak as a friend.'

So Mute passed over the ten pounds, a single five-pound note and five sovereigns. He could afford it, just about. But he handed it over in a lordly style as if to say, there's plenty more where that comes from. Tomlinson made the money disappear with the dexterity of a magician performing a sleight of hand. He didn't even glance at the cash, or thank Mute, but merely said, 'A wise decision, if I may say.'

Then he unbent his lanky frame from the small chair on the

other side of the desk. When he was standing he took out his hip flask once more and took another swallow.

'To fortify myself against the rigours of the English spring,' he said. 'Well, I have other business to attend to, my dear . . . Mute. It really has been a pleasure to see you again after these many years. I hope it will not be long before we meet again.'

'I hope not too,' said Mute, rising from his seat. 'Let me accompany you part of the way.'

Tomlinson picked up his top hat and brushed at some imaginary speck on his frockcoat. He had the bearing and manner of a gentleman, thought Mute, but his clothes did let him down. Using a door which issued directly on a passageway, the two left Mute's office and went down a narrow flight of stairs and so out into the close air of Dunstan's Alley. Together they strolled towards Eastcheap. Perhaps Mute wanted to see in which direction Tomlinson was heading. Or perhaps he hoped the other man would let slip something more about the mysterious document and the fortune it was supposed to signify. But he did not.

When they were near the Monument to the Great Fire, Tomlinson asked whether he'd ever been to the top of the column. Mute said he had, once, but had no intention of climbing those hundreds of steps again. So when Tomlinson suddenly announced that he was going to nip up the tower – in order to get the measure of London once more, he claimed – Mute was fairly sure it was a means of getting rid of him. His mild irritation was compounded when Tomlinson remarked that he ought to be getting back to his desk at *Funereal Matters*, back to his paper column while Tomlinson climbed a real column. Tomlinson laughed at his own joke, an irritating high-pitched laugh. So far, so witty, but then Tomlinson compared his old friend to a galley-slave who'd slipped his fetters for a moment. No doubt, the comment was (quite) humorously intended but Mute prided himself on his independent, freelancing spirit, and the words were unexpectedly hurtful. Particularly so when Mute thought of the ten pounds which he'd recently handed over. He'd lose face by asking for it back. Besides, he wasn't sure that Tomlinson would give it to him.

They shook hands but Mute looked daggers at Tomlinson's retreating back as he walked towards the base of the Monument.

The only thing that pleased him was the threadbare quality of Tomlinson's coat. As for the talk of intriguing documents and fortunes that could be converted into cash, he was more inclined now to think of it as flimflam. That's all. Wasn't it?

A Death at Scott, Lye & Mackenzie

M r Alexander Lye did not often visit the law firm which bore his name as one of the partners. When he did turn up at the office in Furnival Street near Holborn, it was usually to scrawl his signature at the bottom of some document, nothing else. The more junior and less charitable members of the firm wondered whether he knew what he was signing, since he seemed so old and doddery.

Tom Ansell, who'd been with the firm for not much more than a year, might have gone along with the prevailing opinion of Mr Lye had he not endured a brief bout of questioning from the old man. They met outside the aged partner's door one morning as Tom was returning from consulting Mr Ashley, the senior clerk, something he did quite frequently in his early days with the firm of Scott, Lye & Mackenzie. No sooner had Mr Lye emerged and closed his door behind him with a withered, claw-like hand than he was shaken by a violent fit of sneezing.

Tom stood there, clutching a wad of documents to his chest, and giving the old man time to recover. He had spoken to Alexander Lye on a single previous occasion, and despite having been introduced by the other senior partner in the firm, he was unsure whether Lye realized who he was at the time. Certainly he did not expect to be recognized again.

Now Mr Lye straightened himself and dabbed at his streaming eyes with a dirty-looking handkerchief. Judging the moment – enough to show concern but not enough to be detained – Tom said briskly, 'You're all right, I hope, sir.'

Lye raised his gaze. He had direct blue eyes, set in a nest of wrinkles. Despite the sneezing discomfort, there seemed to Tom to be some mischief in them. Lye's gaze narrowed slightly. He said, 'You know, Mr Ansell, I sometimes believe that our real business is dust.'

Tom was so taken aback to be recognized that he did no more than repeat, 'Dust, Mr Lye?'

'All these documents, wills and bills, what are they but magnets for dust?' said Lye, nodding towards the bundle which Tom was clutching. 'Then they turn to dust themselves. Which irritates the nostrils. But at least our documents outlast our clients, Mr Ansell. *They* turn to dust even sooner than their wills and stuff. The ultimate destination of paper and people and everything else – *dust.*'

Mr Lye spoke with relish. Tom nodded and made to go past him, thinking it was perhaps as well that the senior partner paid only occasional visits to the law office. But the old man continued to fix the younger one with his pale-blue stare and said, 'Helen is well, I trust? You are looking after her, Mr Ansell? She deserves to be looked after.'

Helen was Tom's wife. They were not long married. He smiled at the mention of her. Really, he could not object to the personal nature of old Lye's question. Helen was the daughter of the (now deceased) other partner in the firm, Alfred Scott.

'She's very well,' said Tom.

'No announcements to make?'

This was probably code for: Is she expecting a child? Tom was used to hearing – or rather overhearing – such roundabout comments, particularly from Helen's mother as well as his own. It was one thing to be quizzed by mothers about happy events or loss of appetite or a gain in weight, but it was quite another to be peremptorily questioned by an old lawyer. So Tom said, 'Announcements? Let me see. Helen has ambitions to be an author. She had a short story published in *Tinsley's Magazine* recently.'

'Did she? Well, she was always a bookish sort of girl.'

Alexander Lye's tone suggested slight disapproval of girls who were bookish, let alone women who were writers. But babies must have been hanging in the air, for he then seemed to make another oblique reference to the subject by saying, 'I hope your own affairs are in order, Mr Ansell, now that you are a family man. Your final dispositions and wills *et cetera.*'

'Oh yes, quite in order,' said Tom.

'You would be shocked at how many fellows, educated fellows at that, even educated fellows whose trade is the law . . .' Mr Lye paused and appeared to lose the thread of what he saying before picking it up again, but more feebly, '. . . you'd be shocked, I tell you.'

'Shocked by what?'

'At the fact that they do not take the time to put their affairs in order, of course. What do they go and do instead? They go off and die intestate. Highly irresponsible, you know. Consider the burden one is leaving for one's would-be heirs if one does not leave a will behind.'

'Yes, Mr Lye.'

'It doesn't matter how young you are. As soon as you have a bit of property, as soon as you have *extended* yourself into a family, look to your affairs. What do these young men think? That they are going to live for ever? Ha!'

The idea of living for ever caused Mr Lye genuine amusement. His face creased. He looked as though he was about to have another sneezing fit. Then he pulled himself together. 'Well, my dear sir, I bid you good morning. I have business to attend to even if the rest of the world has not.'

He moved away down the passage with an odd motion, alternating between a shuffle and a lope. Tom didn't know what to make of him. Some of the legal dust which Lye had been talking about seemed to have settled down in the old man's brain. But his blue stare had been shrewd enough, and the comments about attending to one's affairs were well meant in a dull, lawyerly sort of way.

Two or three weeks went by before Tom Ansell saw Alexander Lye again. It was a beautiful morning in early October, with the sun bathing the windows of Furnival Street in a golden light and showing up an infinite quantity of dust motes inside the chambers of Scott, Lye & Mackenzie. The specks hovering in the sunlight caused Tom to think of Mr Lye and his remark about dust, the ultimate destination of everything.

Then, passing the open door to Lye's office, he observed that this was one of those occasional days when the aged partner put in an appearance. He was sitting at his cluttered desk. Mr Ashley the senior clerk was standing beside Lye, bending forward slightly, his forefinger indicating some place on a document in front of them. Lye had a quill pen in his hand. Ashley glanced up at Tom, his brow even more furrowed than usual.

Tom walked on. He heard Lye sneezing, violently. Then there was a thump as if a heavy object had fallen from a shelf. He heard Ashley utter some words that sounded like 'Oh for heaven's sake.' Tom stopped. He looked round. Ashley stuck his head out of the door. He was gazing directly at Tom but seemed unaware of his presence.

'Is something wrong, Mr Ashley?'

'For heaven's sake.'

Tom walked back. By now Ashley had emerged into the passage, muttering the same phrase several times over in an irritated tone. No one else was in the passage. Tom peered round Lye's door. He saw the dust motes dancing in the shafts of sun, the smeared windows between their heavy drapes. He saw shelves with books arranged any old how and the desk covered with heavy legal volumes and beribboned sheaves of paper, with blotters and inkstands and pen-holders. In the centre of all this clutter, he saw the mottled dome of Alexander Lye. It was positioned on the desk like a ball. Mr Lye had fallen forward on his nose, fallen very neatly in the single clear space but on top of the document which he had doubtless been about to sign. His right hand grasped the quill pen. Tom thought that Lye must be the only person in Scott, Lye & Mackenzie still to be using a quill rather than a metal dip pen. He also thought that Lye would never again be using a pen of any sort.

Mr Ashley came back into the room. 'Oh for heaven's sake!' he said once more.

Helen Gets a Commission

'**H**e was shocked,' said Tom to Helen that evening. 'It's the first time I've ever seen old Ashley put out. He kept repeating himself as if he was irritated or angry that Lye had dropped dead in front of him. But I think it was his way of showing how distressed he was.'

'Mr Ashley has been with the firm longer than anyone now that Alexander Lye is gone,' said Helen. 'I find it hard to believe Mr Lye really is gone, though. He seemed ageless.'

The Ansells were sitting after supper in the small drawing room of their rented house in Kentish Town. The evening was dank and Helen was glad that she had asked Hetty, their maid-of-all-work, to light a fire before it got dark. On an otherwise unoccupied evening Tom and Helen would have been reading, Tom perhaps casting his eye over the newspaper or the *Cornhill Magazine* while Helen might have been working her way through the latest novel by Mrs Braddon. But this evening they were preoccupied by the death of Alexander Lye and, while there was not much to say about it, they nevertheless felt they ought to say something and then to go on saying it.

Helen had known the old lawyer ever since she had been a little girl. For his part Tom had hardly known Lye at all but, because he was the first on the scene apart from Mr Ashley, he had to repeat the story several times over to other people in the firm. He restricted himself to the bare facts: the sneezing, the sound of Lye's head as it struck the desktop, the utter suddenness of the event.

In the moments following the death Tom took charge because Ashley seemed incapable of doing anything. No one else had yet appeared. After another glance around, Tom shut the door to the dead man's room and ushered the senior clerk back to his own office. There he gently instructed him to sit down before going off to find David Mackenzie who was, as usual, wreathed in pipe smoke behind his own desk.

The firm's only surviving partner was grateful for Tom's calm manner and his discretion. Once Mr Mackenzie had arranged things – sending another junior lawyer, Will Evers, round to the undertaker's; seeing that Mr Ashley was fortified with a brandy and water while trying to get him to return home for the rest of the day (Ashley refused to go, respectfully); attempting to subdue the more excitable accounts of Lye's death which were already circulating round the chambers – once David Mackenzie had done all this he clapped Tom on the shoulder.

'Thank you.'

'I haven't done anything much, Mr Mackenzie.'

'Then thank you for what you didn't do. Didn't go telling the first person you saw but came to me, didn't go encouraging a gaggle of people to crowd round poor old Lye's door and stare and gawp. Instinctively you knew that decorum ought to be preserved.'

Then there was a pause before he said, 'I've known Alexander Lye for longer than I can recall.'

'His death must be a great shock to you.'

'No doubt I shall feel it in the course of time,' said Mackenzie in quite a cheerful tone while struggling to relight his pipe which, by Tom's reckoning, had remained unlit for almost an hour – a record. 'But at the moment I feel as Brutus felt about mourning for his old friend on the fields of Philippi: "I shall find time, Cassius, I shall find time." The Bard of Avon, you know.'

Now Tom said to Helen, 'And once he'd quoted Shakespeare, Mackenzie referred to Lye as a "wily old bird". An odd thing to say about your friend and partner just after he's dropped dead, don't you think?'

'I don't suppose it will be inscribed on his tombstone,' she said. 'It doesn't mean that Mr Mackenzie is unfeeling.'

'Well, I'm afraid I didn't feel very much,' said Tom. 'There was a definite excitement in the office, though, especially when Mr Lye's corpse was being carried out by the undertaker's men. Not much work was done for the rest of the day. I certainly didn't do much.'

'Poor Mr Lye,' said Helen, then, 'I had a letter today, Tom.'

It took Tom a moment to realize that his wife was deliberately changing the subject. He looked expectant and got up to stir the dying embers of the fire with the poker.

'It was a letter from Arthur Arnett. He is the editor of *The New Moon*.'

'*The New Moon*?'

'It's a periodical – a monthly periodical, as the title indicates.'

'I don't think I've seen it.'

'That is because the first issue has yet to come out. But plans are well advanced and I believe it is appearing imminently. Mr

Arnett has promised me an advance copy. *The New Moon* will be a magazine for town and country, Mr Arnett says, and it will be a publication for men and women equally.'

'Wide ranging then,' said Tom, rattling the poker so as to start a few feeble spurts of flame among the embers.

'He has asked me to contribute to it. He read my story in *Tinsley's Magazine* and obtained our address from Mr Tinsley himself. In his letter, Mr Arnett was kind enough to compliment me on my eye for detail, and my facility at description.'

'You're going to write another story for him?'

'No. He has asked me to compose a factual piece on any town or city I like, London aside. He stipulates only that it must be a place of inner beauty so I suppose that rules out an industrial town. He wants me to visit it and then to describe its buildings and byways, its corners and curiosities. I am to convey the quintessence of the place to the reader. Mr Arnett says that, by such means, we may introduce the inhabitants of these British Isles to one another. After all, we are sometimes more informed about the furthest outposts of the Empire than we are about our own backyards.'

Tom bent forward to kiss Helen, to plant a chaste kiss on her pale forehead. He did this partly to avoid having to comment directly on what she'd just said. The way she recited the editor's words – so many of them! – suggested she had read his letter several times over. Tom sometimes thought these literary types had a very convoluted way of expressing themselves, with their quintessences and inner beauties and their plans for introducing British citizens to each other. Even so he was glad for Helen. He had been proud, very proud, when she had a story entitled 'Treasure' published in *Tinsley's*. It pleased him to see the name of *Helen Ansell* set in italic type almost as much as it pleased her.

'Mrs Helen Ansell,' he said, 'intrepid reporter from our own backyards.'

'Be careful, Thomas.'

'Or should that be intrepid *reportress*? Seriously, though, may I accompany you on one of these visits?'

'That depends on your attitude.'

'Where are you going to choose? What place shall we visit?'

'I don't know yet where *I* shall go, Tom. I will have to think about it. Mr Arnett does not need the article for a while. He also said that he could not offer me much money. *The New Moon* is still very new, you see.'

Tom was not surprised to hear this but he did not say so. Instead he gave Helen another, longer kiss, and then, because the fire was losing its warmth and the night drawing on, they went upstairs to bed.

Mr Lye's Deed-Box

W hen Tom arrived at Furnival Street the next day, he was greeted in the lobby by Mr Ashley. The senior clerk had evidently been waiting for him to appear. It was unusual, almost unheard of, for Ashley to be found out of his office. If he wanted to see anyone, that person was expected to visit him. Yet here he was, waiting for Tom in the lobby. Graves, the ex-military man who was the doorman and general factotum for the offices of Scott, Lye & Mackenzie, looked on in surprise, especially when Ashley drew Tom to one side.

'Mr Mackenzie wishes to see you – urgently,' he said. '*He* was here before eight o'clock this morning despite the weather.'

This sounded like a comment on Tom's slightly late arrival in the office. It was a foggy morning, which somehow had the effect of retarding the traffic even though things seemed to bustle along as usual.

'Do you know what he wants to see me about?'

'Confidential, very confidential.'

An odd way of being confidential, thought Tom, to be intercepted by Ashley and then whispered at in a corner of the lobby where they might be seen by the doorman as well as anyone passing. It crossed his mind to ask Ashley if he had recovered from the events of the day before but he decided not to. Instead, he thanked the clerk and made his way to David Mackenzie's office.

He knocked. Rather than being told to enter, the door was

almost immediately opened. Mr Mackenzie stood there, a portly figure. Tom usually thought of him as monk-like on account of his shape and the benevolence of his countenance as well as his tonsure of white hair. On this occasion, Mackenzie looked drawn rather than benevolent and what little hair he had was sticking up in tufts instead of being arranged in a sleek ring. The only thing which was as normal was the cloud of pipe smoke that filled his room.

'Come in. Come in and sit down.'

Mackenzie retreated behind his desk, which was much more orderly than Lye's cluttered surface. Tom sat down on the other side. There was a silence. Tom's curiosity was piqued. What was so urgent that it called Mr Mackenzie to the office at eight o'clock? What was so troublesome that it had left him, by the look of things, deprived of a night's sleep?

'How well did you know Mr Lye, Tom?'

Mackenzie's use of his first name was a sign that whatever he wanted to discuss was likely to be more personal than business.

'Hardly at all, sir. I spoke to Mr Lye when I first joined the firm. It was you who introduced us. And the other day we exchanged a few words, outside his room.'

'What did he say? Anything of interest?'

What had Alexander Lye said? Something about documents and dust. Interesting in a vaguely philosophical way perhaps, but that surely wasn't what Mackenzie meant.

'He advised me to make sure my affairs were in good order,' said Tom. 'That I had made a will and so on.'

'Very sound advice,' said David Mackenzie, drawing deeply on his pipe. He was obscured by a cloud of smoke. The fug inside matched the thin brown fog nuzzling the window panes outside. It was a contrast to the previous sunny day, the day of Lye's death, and the room was dim despite the gas lighting. Mackenzie removed his pipe and seemed about to say something further but no words emerged. Tom filled the gap.

'I don't know anything of Mr Lye's domestic circumstances. He was married, wasn't he?'

'A widower. His wife died at least ten years ago.'

'Children?'

'No,' said Mackenzie. 'Or none that I am aware of. No legal issue, let us say.'

'Any other immediate family?'

'Immediate? Alexander lived with his sister near Regent's Park. A large house, for just the two of them. They did not get on, so perhaps it's as well they had plenty of space not to get on in.'

Tom sensed that there was more to come but that the senior partner was reluctant to say it. Even the information given so far seemed to have been imparted only half willingly. After a moment, Mackenzie said, 'Tom, I know I can rely on your discretion.'

Tom nodded. David Mackenzie pushed himself up from his chair and went to the far side of the room. From the floor he retrieved, not without effort, an oblong metal container, a deed-box. Holding it by the small handles at each end he brought it back to the desk before turning it round so that Tom could read the words ALEXANDER JAMES LYE stencilled in small yellow capitals along the side. There was a keyhole above the name. The box was little more than a foot in length and about half as high and deep.

'Fortunately the key for this was on Lye's key-chain,' said Mackenzie. 'I would not have cared to break it open although it wouldn't have taken much effort to do so. The box was inside the safe in his own office. The safe was easy to open too. Lye made no particular secret of the combination: seventeen-eighty-nine.'

'The French Revolution?'

'The year of Alexander Lye's birth.'

'It must contain something important,' said Tom, as he calculated Lye's age.

'I'm not going to say anything. I do not want you to, ah, have any preconceptions. Look for yourself. Go and hold it under the light over there. Have a good look.'

Tom carried the metal box across to the gaslight which was burning to one side of the fireplace, and opened the lid. He was surprised by what he saw. He examined the contents of the box for the best part of a minute before glancing up at David Mackenzie.

'Well?'

'I'm baffled.'

'Describe what you can see, Tom, if you would be so good.'

Tom rested the box on the back of an armchair near the fireplace and rummaged around among the contents. Some items he lifted up to the light.

'A small skull.'

'A weasel or stoat's probably,' said Mackenzie.

'A couple of feathers.'

'Goose feathers, I think.'

'A clutch of marbles and something that looks like a child's catapult or slingshot but with only the Y-shaped frame remaining. A lock of hair, fair hair. Several small lead soldiers – I had some very like these as a boy. And several keys, one of them much bigger and longer than the others, older, too, maybe. A ring, a wedding ring? A glass phial which probably held some potion or other—'

'Anything else?' said Mackenzie, growing tired of the itemizing which he'd asked for.

'Well, a few other things . . .'

'Never mind those. There is something missing, isn't there? Wouldn't you expect the private deed-box of a lawyer – a lawyer, mind you – to contain some pieces of paper, some printed or written material? Not just silly childhood mementoes or things with sentimental value like the lock of hair and the ring.'

Tom closed the box and took it back to the desk. He sat down once more. David Mackenzie had already resumed his seat and his pipe-fiddling.

'What I expected to find in that box, of course, was Alexander Lye's last will and testament.'

'Maybe the will was there but he removed it from the box and decided to put it somewhere else in his office.'

'Mr Ashley and I have searched his room thoroughly, so far without result.'

'You mentioned the house in Regent's Park, the one he shared with his sister. Is it there?'

'It might be,' said Mackenzie. 'I went round yesterday afternoon to see Miss Lye personally. To convey the sad news of her brother's death and also, I'll admit, to sound her out about Alexander's will. I planned to do it discreetly, of course.'

'What happened?'

'It may be that I have been misjudging Miss Edith Lye. I've said that she and her brother did not get on. The house was big enough for them to lead almost separate lives, and they do not have many servants. But she was certainly distraught enough at her brother's death, overcome by weeping. She would not have been capable of answering any questions and nor would I have wished to put any to her. I left Miss Lye in the care of her maid. But before I went I had a quick glance around Lye's quarters, his domestic office, as it were. I'm not sure I had been in that room before, or at any rate not for many years.'

Mackenzie paused, as if to gather his impressions.

'I do not think I've ever seen such a disordered space within four walls. Loose papers and documents, thousands of them higgledy-piggledy, together with law-lists and pocketbooks, all heaped in tottering piles, some so lofty that the uppermost articles had started to slide down like melting snow. In a hollow space somewhere in the centre of these mountains was an easy chair. I can imagine Alexander sitting there and contemplating this . . . this detritus . . . contemplating it with contentment.'

The single surviving partner in the firm sounded genuinely offended at Lye's piles of paper. The sight had driven him to poetic language, snow melting off mountains. David Mackenzie's own chamber was shipshape.

'It might be that the will is buried somewhere among those mounds at the Regent's Park house,' continued Mackenzie, 'but it will take weeks, months even, to go through them.'

'In the meantime . . .'

'Yes, in the meantime, Tom, we are faced with a problem. The possibility that my old friend and partner, Alexander James Lye, seasoned man of law that he was and wily old bird that I believe him to have been, has gone and died without leaving instructions as to the final disposition of his property.'

'That is the very subject which Mr Lye was talking to me about. The irresponsibility of those who die intestate. The burden they leave to their heirs. It's odd.'

At last David Mackenzie permitted himself a small smile. He leaned back in his chair. He drew on his pipe. 'Not odd at all. If there's one lesson that my law years have taught me, it is that there is no consistency in human beings, none at all.'

'Is it really such a problem, though? Mr Lye shared a house with his sister. You say his wife is long-dead and that there are no children. Surely his title in the house and the rest of his estate will simply pass to Miss Lye?'

'To Edith. Well, if only it were so straightforward. But before we come to that, imagine the damage to the reputation of Scott, Lye & Mackenzie when it emerges that one of the partners has been careless enough to die intestate. No one would say anything openly, not to me at least, but I can imagine the gossip and sniggers among the clerks in other law firms. It's a genuine instance of "Physician, heal thyself", isn't it? Such information is not going to endear us to our clients, either. Would you have confidence in a lawyer whose private affairs were such a . . . such a shambles?'

'Perhaps not,' said Tom. 'But Mr Lye has not done much in recent years as I understand it.'

'The good name of a law firm depends on the good name of all its partners. This has been troubling me ever since we found poor Lye, or rather ever since we *failed* to find his will. Of course it may turn up, probably when we have stopped searching for it. There was a mischievous streak to Alexander. He was a nonconformist, you know. But there is more than the riddle of this metal box and its miscellany. Alexander Lye had a wider family than himself and his Regent's Park sister. That is where the real problem may come . . .'

'The problem,' said Tom to Helen that evening at dinner, 'is that Alexander Lye did not have only the single sibling, the sister he shared his Regent's Park house with. There are others, a brother and a second sister, I think, who live in Ely. Or rather just outside Ely in a large old house.'

'All of whom might be entitled to a share of his estate?' said Helen.

'Yes,' said Tom, spearing the last piece of veal cutlet on his plate. 'I cannot believe that he did not make a will. I think it much more likely that he did make one and neglected to tell anyone where it is.'

'At least he had the power to make one.'

'What do you mean?'

'Not all of us have that power.'

'But you have made a will, Helen.'

'With *your* consent,' she said. 'It is absurd that a married woman has to obtain her husband's agreement before making a will.'

Such talk made Tom uncomfortable, as Helen did sometimes when she aired her advanced views. He changed the subject.

'So there is a possibility that Alexander Lye might have left a copy of his will in the Ely house. Mr Mackenzie has asked me to go and make some discreet enquiries there.'

'Why you, Tom? Why doesn't he go himself?'

'He made a remark about sharper eyes, quicker minds. Youth, you know.'

'What about the sister who lives in the house near Regent's Park – what's her name?'

'Edith.'

'Why not make enquiries, as you put it, of Edith instead of traipsing to Ely? Perhaps she knows the whereabouts of this missing document.'

'Mackenzie is going to attend to that himself in a day or so, when the lady has recovered from the first shock of her brother's death. But he still wants me to go to Ely. I shall have the chance to introduce myself to the brother and the other sister when they come to Lye's funeral. A visit will be arranged.'

'For discreet enquiries.'

'Helen, I was thinking of what you said the other day, how you had a commission from that magazine editor to write about any place you cared to write about.'

'Mr Arnett at *The New Moon*. That's right.'

'It occurred to me that we might travel together to the fen country. You could turn your eye on Ely or on Cambridge, perhaps.'

'While you are about your own business.'

'Well, yes.'

Tom was encouraged. Helen had been adopting a slightly mocking attitude about his 'enquiries' but now her expression changed.

'Why not?' she said. 'It would be a little expedition.'

'But before that,' said Tom, 'we have a funeral to attend.'

Summer, 1645

*A*nne witnessed the arrival of the men from her secluded position in the gallery overlooking the hall. The previous evening she had spied on her parents and Mr Martin while they dined. Now she watched as her father, still in his night attire, was summoned to speak to the leader of the armed band. He was accompanied by three of the men she had glimpsed at the edge of the grounds. The rest waited outside. The old steward of the house, James, stood by the front door, looking down at his feet. The men were soldiers, perhaps of an irregular sort. They wore dull-brown leather jerkins. Some were bareheaded with close-cropped hair. They carried pikes or staves but a couple had muskets. Unlike the others, the leader had lank pale hair and was wearing a cloak. He said that his name was Trafford. Then he was saying something about a fugitive. Even though his voice was subdued, it was possible to tell that he was angry.

By contrast, her father spoke calmly and briefly. Anne was unable to hear what he said but it seemed to be some kind of denial, accompanied by swift shakes of the head. Now her mother appeared on the scene but said nothing. The leader of the soldiers turned on his heel and, followed by the others, went outside once more. Trafford issued commands to his men, crisp sentences that penetrated the door which was still ajar. She could not catch every word but it was obvious that the men were being told to search the house.

Anne's mother and father turned and stared at each other. They looked so helpless that Anne became truly afraid. At that moment the steward gazed up and noticed her peering over the gallery railing. He gestured in her direction. Anne's mother looked up. She made frantic shooing motions with the back of her hand. Get away from there, go to your room.

Anne did as she was told. She returned to her chamber and perched on the edge of the bed, her hands grasping at the bedcovers and her feet curled tight on the floorboards. Her sister Mary was sleeping on and it irritated Anne that she was not awake to share in the fear and the excitement of what was happening. Very soon, there was the sound of heavy steps from all about the house, of doors being brusquely opened *and shut, the tramp of feet on stairs, the thud of fists banging on panelled walls without concern for any damage the blows might do. Once or twice Anne heard a female voice although it was so high and distorted that she could not tell whether it was her mother or one of the servants. By this time Mary had woken and, in her careful way, grown aware that something frightening was going on.*

Then the door to their room was flung open, without knock or notice. Anne was already sitting up facing the door, Mary was kneeling on the bed behind her. Two men stood on either side of the entrance. One of them was the leader called Trafford. His eyes were dark between pale curtains of hair. Anne was glad to see her mother behind the men but her mother's hand was clasped over her mouth as if to prevent herself from crying out.

Trafford took a couple of paces into the chamber. He had to stoop slightly to enter and the room was suddenly filled with a masculine odour and the overwhelming presence of a stranger. The other man remained on the threshold, with Anne's mother standing a little to the rear. She had taken her hand away from her mouth. She tried to smile at her daughters in reassurance but all she could manage was a grimace.

The man scarcely glanced at the sisters huddled on the bed. They might have been so much discarded linen. He edged his way to the window, stooping because of the pitch of the roof around the gable window, and squinted into the early sun which was streaming across the garden. Then he abruptly turned about, as if he hoped to catch Anne and Mary doing something they shouldn't have been doing. He ran his gauntlet hand over a little table that stood against the wall. He picked up the bible that lay there, sniffed at the binding, then replaced it on the table, delicately. Near the table was a small chest containing the sisters' few garments. Trafford kicked it, as if to compensate for his careful handling of the bible. Then he drew a knife from under his cloak.

Anne's mother gave a tiny shriek and her hand flew to her mouth once more. The other soldier, the one in the doorway, put his arm out as if to block any attempt to enter the room. Mary, still kneeling on the bed behind her sister, was clinging on to Anne's shoulders. Now her fingers dug in like claws. For Anne, everything seemed to be occurring at a distance. She was no part of it.

Trafford moved towards the girls where they cowered on the bed. In one smooth motion, he crouched, extended the hand holding the knife and jabbed the tip of it into the wall beside the bed. On this upper floor of the house, most of the walls were no more than lath and plain plaster

between the timber uprights. There was no elaborate panelling or decor-
ative plasterwork as on the lower floors. The knife went in easily and a
dribble of dust and plaster followed as the man withdrew the blade. He
chose another spot a couple of feet away and did the same thing, with
the same result. He stood up and grunted in satisfaction. He went
back to the door, nodded at Anne's mother and moved down the passage
to the next chamber, accompanied by the second soldier. Again, there was
the sound of a door being flung open and the tread of heavy feet
inside the neighbouring room. There was nothing there, Anne knew, or
rather there was no person there. It was a place only for storage.

Anne's mother remained on the threshold of the sisters' room for a
moment longer. Anne saw her throat working above the collar of her
nightgown as if she wanted to say something but no words came out.
Instead she reached inside and pulled the door shut. Mary was holding
on so tightly to Anne's shoulders that the older sister thought she would
have to prise her fingers away.

The smell of the man called Trafford still filled the room. It was not
that unpleasant but she would open the casement window when she was
capable of moving again. Anne looked at the ragged holes in the wall
made by the man's knife, and the little piles of plaster and stuff on the
floor beneath. She knew that there was no real thickness in the walls on
this level of the house. There were no hiding places for a man up here,
nothing like the nooks and chimney-corners down below. And the leader
of the soldiers must have been aware of that too. So why had he jabbed
with his knife at the lath and plaster?

The same thought had occurred to Mary who finally released her grip
on Anne and said, 'What was he looking for?'

'Nothing, he was looking for nothing,' said Anne.

'Why did he do it?'

'To show that he could. He did it to make us fearful.'

The Coffin-Bird

Cyrus Chase put down his pen, blotted the paper and read
over the words he had just written. He nodded to himself
in satisfaction and stood up. Holding the sheet of paper he walked

over towards the window. It was growing dark outside and the lights in the room were already lit. Mr Chase could see his reflection in the window panes. He preferred this partial, fragmented image to the less flattering portrait offered by a looking-glass.

Mr Chase struck a posture that was almost like a statue's, his left arm held forward slightly, his chest inflated. Once more he read through the words on the page, silently. Then he cleared his throat and read them out loud, his voice growing in confidence as he proceeded.

'The Chase security device is a godsend to an anxious populace. No more need anyone fear waking to a fate beyond human imagining. The day is at hand when the citizens of every civilized country on earth will be able truly to rest in peace, whether they are sojourning on this side amongst the living or whether they have joined the ranks of the departed on the farther shore of that bourn from which, in the words of Hamlet, Prince of Denmark, no traveller returns. The Chase security device is a most ingenious, inexpensive and reliable mechanism, one which supersedes all others presently on the market and which is guaranteed to provide mental quietude and bodily comfort to all purchasers.'

Mr Chase returned to his desk. He took up his pen again. He crossed out 'godsend' and put 'blessing'. He wondered whether the reference to the Prince of Denmark was, well, a little pretentious. Would enough people recognize it? And then he decided that the kind of clients to whom he wished to appeal would most certainly be familiar with Shakespeare. But there was something wrong with the final sentence. The mention of 'bodily comfort' lowered the tone of the piece. More work was required on that particular section.

He let his mind go wandering. He visualized himself as he had been standing a moment ago, one foot slightly in front of the other, the opposing arm extended, palm open, a posture that suggested he was offering assistance to all mankind. As indeed he was! Mr Cyrus Chase allowed his thoughts to drift further. To the possibility of official recognition for his inventiveness and hard work. The idea was not so far-fetched. After all, George Bateson had been awarded a medal by Queen Victoria for services not to the living but to the dead. If George Bateson, then why not Cyrus Chase of *Mon Repos* Villa, Prickwillow Road in the city of Ely?

Mr Chase permitted his imagination to stray wider still. To the statue that might be erected in his memory by a grateful nation. Did they erect statues to the living? He rather doubted it. Therefore he would have passed on by the time a statue was put up. So be it. At least he knew that he would be safely departed and comfortably dead, thanks to his own security device.

Cyrus Chase returned to the point in the room where he could see himself reflected in the window. He was about to run through his announcement again when he heard the distant sound of the doorbell. He went back to his desk and slipped the sheet of paper under the blotter. He did not want anyone to see or read what he had written yet. The maid knocked at the door, opened it without waiting for permission and announced the arrival of Mr Tomlinson.

'My dear Mr Chase,' said Tomlinson.

'Shall I draw the curtains, Mr Chase?' said the maid.

'No, Mattie,' said Chase, thrown off balance by Tomlinson's unexpected arrival, and then changing his mind, 'Yes, if you would.'

The two men waited while Mattie drew the curtains. Making conversation, Tomlinson said, 'It's going to be cold tonight. There is already a mist rising.'

It was true. Charles Tomlinson seemed to have brought some of the dankness in with him. He was a tall man, with a thin jaw, coal-black eyes and a weathered complexion. Chase had to look up to him when they were standing close. He was also conscious of his plumpness against the other man's slim lines and height. For this reason, and one or two others, he did not like to stand too close to Charles Tomlinson.

When Mattie left the room, Tomlinson said, 'I am sorry that I come a little earlier than promised. But I am eager to see the progress that you have made.'

'You are welcome at any time.'

'And you are always gracious, Mr Chase.'

'Would you like some tea?' said Chase, prompted by the other man's compliment. Anyway, he did not think the other would accept. Tomlinson claimed to have lost the English taste for tea on his travels.

'No, no. I would rather inspect what I have come to see and

then be on my way. But how very up to date and fashionable of you to suggest having tea in the late afternoon rather than after dinner.'

'It is my wife's preference,' said Chase.

'Then how very up to date and fashionable of *her*. How is the delightful Mrs Chase? How is Bella? Thriving, I hope.'

'She is well, thank you. Shall we go and see the . . . the apparatus . . . now?'

Cyrus Chase ushered Tomlinson from the room. He was uncomfortable whenever Charles Tomlinson turned to the subject of his wife, Bella, something which the other man did quite often. The two of them went towards the back of the house where Chase took a paraffin lamp from a cupboard. When he had lit it, he opened a door near the scullery and led the way into a small yard and from there out to the extensive garden that lay behind the house. There was a serpentine path leading off into the near-darkness. To the north and above the low-lying haze of mist Chase could just see the silhouettes of the willows fringing the rhyne or channel which marked the edge of his property. There was no noise apart from the hissing of the lamp.

It was cold, as Tomlinson had said, and Chase shivered. He should have taken a coat or muffler from the hallstand. He thought Tomlinson must be regretting having handed his overcoat to the maid on his arrival.

'These are the right conditions for the fen ague,' said Chase.

'I expect so,' said Tomlinson. 'English weather is a tribulation.'

The paraffin lamp which Cyrus Chase was carrying threw a fuzzy globe of light round the two men. They traced out the winding, flagged path until they reached an outbuilding half concealed by shrubbery. Chase put the lamp on the ground where it continued to hiss. He reached into a pocket and extracted a key which he inserted, after some fumbling, into the sturdy padlock securing the door to the workshop. The door opened with a creak. He picked up the paraffin lamp, went inside and deposited the lamp on the end of a long table which took up the central area of the workshop. Tomlinson followed him, his shadow swelling on the red brick of the interior. Once inside,

Tomlinson took out a pewter hip flask from his jacket pocket and gulped down a hefty swig. Chase wondered whether this was his way of protecting himself from the fen ague.

Inside were smells, of damp, of freshly cut wood, of something metallic. The shed was large, originally intended as a storage place for farm or garden implements – and indeed there were a few scythes, rakes and spades piled in a corner – but Cyrus Chase had taken over the outbuilding and adapted it for his own purposes. He alone possessed the key to the padlock. A window, with bars for security, looked out not towards the house but across the stream and trees bordering his garden. Even so, Cyrus kept the little curtain over the window shut tight most of the time. It could be chill in here too, but there was a furnace at the far end which Cyrus used for small-scale smelting, and when that was in operation the interior hummed with the heat.

On the long work-table were saws and chisels and hammers, but the principal item was an oblong box, coffin-sized and with a hinged lid. Anyone examining it would have concluded that it was a slightly odd coffin. At one end, the head end perhaps, were two metal constructions like miniature gantries. From the top of one hung a brass bell several inches high. The bell was surrounded by iron mesh. At the top of the other gantry was what appeared to be a little weather vane. Also emerging from the upper end of the coffin were a couple of tubes or hoses made out of pieces of leather stitched together. These presently hung down over the side of the work-table, like thick snakes. If it was a coffin, it wasn't what you might call a pretty coffin.

Cyrus Chase stood back, as far as the limited space would allow, and gestured for Charles Tomlinson to take a closer look at what the visitor had called 'the apparatus'. Slipping his hip flask back into his pocket, Tomlinson came forward. He peered first at the gantry that looked like a weather vane. It was indeed a metallic cockerel, about half life-size and painted a golden–yellow colour. It could be made to rotate by means of a system of cogs turned by a looping cord which ran through small holes in the coffin lid.

Tomlinson gazed inquiringly at Chase. The small man was beaming with pleasure.

'Do you see the symbolism, Tomlinson?'

'What I see is that the cockerel can be operated by the unfortunate person who is lying below.'

'Exactly. Its rapid circular motion, together with the bright gold that reflects the light, will catch the attention of anyone in the vicinity. To the bystander the sight of the spinning bird – especially on a windless day – indicates that there is life down below. Hence the symbolism of the bird. The cock crows or rather the cock spins. Signifying a new dawn – a new day – when one is sprung from the grave!'

'Ingenious,' said Tomlinson, stroking his smooth chin, 'and not only ingenious but almost poetic in its metaphorical aptness.'

He could not have said anything more pleasing to Cyrus Chase, who now urged him to examine the other construction on the coffin lid, the one containing the bell. A cord hung beneath the bell. Charles Tomlinson gave it an experimental tug. The bell tinged, a surprisingly sharp sound in the confines of the workshop. He clicked the fingernails of his right hand, fingernails which were rather dirty and ragged, against the iron mesh surrounding the bell. Again, he looked inquiringly at Chase. Why the mesh?

'Think of the different things which might set off the bell accidentally,' said Chase. 'A bird – a real bird – alighting on it, a gust of wind. The whole purpose of the thing would be defeated if it could be sounded by accident. The mesh protects against that.'

'Isn't this like Bateson's Belfry?' said Tomlinson.

'There are important differences between his bell and mine,' said Cyrus. He was touchy on the subject. It was George Bateson who had been honoured by Queen Victoria. Cyrus, who had been working along the same lines, considered that he had been beaten to the finishing post.

Tomlinson pulled the little bell rope again, harder this time. Then several times more, quickly. The repeated sound was so much like an impatient summons to a servant that he could not resist looking at Chase and raising his eyebrows.

'You rang, sir?'

He giggled. Cyrus Chase was taken aback. The high laugh came incongruously from a man like Tomlinson. Chase did not like such levity anyway, not when it concerned his own creations. Nor did he like it when Charles Tomlinson tinged the bell yet again and continued in the same tone. 'Would sir like to emerge now? Would he care to re-enter the world? Yes? But sir may have to wait a while until I have fetched a digging implement.'

He made a pretend move towards one of the spades piled in the corner of the shed. He stopped when he saw the look on Cyrus Chase's face. At once, he was all contrition.

'I am sorry, my dear Chase. A thousand pardons. You are quite right to disapprove. You don't have to say a word, I can tell from your expression. Your novelty coffin is not a topic for lightness or careless joking. Forgive me.'

'Of course,' said Chase, not sure of the phrase 'novelty coffin'. He preferred to think of the coffin as a work of art.

'Tell me the function of these,' said Tomlinson, picking up one of the snake-like leather pipes.

'To breathe through, of course.'

'Wouldn't a straight, metal tube be simpler? It could be run up beside the bell and use the same support.'

'What about rainwater?' said Chase, wondering that such an obvious point had not occurred to Tomlinson. 'Imagine rainwater pouring down the pipe. The unfortunate occupant might drown.'

'Or suffer the torment of constant drips on his face,' said Tomlinson. 'I had not thought of that. I believe they employed such a system during the Spanish Inquisition. Drops of cold water falling on to the forehead. Drives one mad eventually, they say.'

'There is also a fine gauze set inside those tubes,' continued Chase. 'To prevent insects climbing inside or flying down and annoying the occupant.'

'You think of everything, sir.'

'I do my best. The tubes and the bell are hardly new, I admit, but I am proud to say that the little bird on top of the coffin is entirely my own device. I believe it will be the deciding factor in making my coffin the choice of the discerning.'

'They might even name it after you,' said Tomlinson. 'The Chase cockerel, that sort of thing.'

'And then there will be something else. An addition that will truly differentiate my invention from anything else on the market. Something that will make the Chase security device unique.'

'Do tell,' said Tomlinson.

Cyrus Chase seemed about to explain but then he caught sight of Tomlinson's shadow as it was thrown on the wall of the shed by the paraffin lamp. Something about that black shape swelling against the chipped red brickwork caused him to hesitate. Not only that but the light was shining upwards on Tomlinson's face, giving it a strange, almost sinister cast. Chase had made a little progress on the final feature of his security coffin, the thing that would make it as unique as he claimed, but he was suddenly reluctant to give the details to Charles Tomlinson.

'I would prefer to say nothing further, not until it is more certain.'

'Very well, Mr Chase,' said Tomlinson. 'You're in charge, after all.'

'Yes, I am, aren't I.'

Tomlinson clapped him on the shoulder.

'A while ago you mentioned tea. What about a drop of something a bit stronger when we return to your abode? It is a cold evening. Fen ague and all that.'

'I am afraid that I have a prior engagement, an early evening engagement,' said Chase, improvising.

'Oh, a pity. And Mrs Chase, Bella, she is accompanying you to this engagement?'

'Yes of course.'

After a final look round, they left the workshop. Chase asked Tomlinson to hold the lamp while he fastened the padlock and then they retraced their steps along the winding garden path. At one point Tomlinson stooped to pick up something from the ground and handed it to Chase. It was the key to the padlock of the workshop. Cyrus was unaware he had dropped it and thanked Tomlinson.

Once inside his house, Chase hoped to get his visitor to the front door and on his way before anyone else in the place was aware of his presence. The maid Mattie appeared but Chase waved her away. Then, as bad luck would have it, his wife Bella began to descend the stairs while Tomlinson was putting on his overcoat.

She halted halfway down, peering uncertainly at the two men. She was short-sighted and the lighting in the hallway was not good.

'My dear Mrs Chase,' said Tomlinson.

'Mr Tomlinson, is it?'

'The vèry same.'

'Cyrus, why didn't you tell me we had a visitor?'

'Mr Tomlinson is on his way,' said Chase, helping Tomlinson on with his coat with one hand and reaching for the front door with the other.

'In a moment,' said Tomlinson. He turned to face Bella who was walking towards them. Cyrus Chase thought he could detect an extra sway in her movements as she approached. Tomlinson cradled her hand in both of his and lifted it to his lips.

'Je suis enchanté, madame, comme toujours.'

He held her hand a fraction longer than necessary and Bella made no attempt to draw it away. Instead, she reddened slightly and said, 'Such a shame you are leaving us, Mr Tomlinson.'

'But I understand you are already engaged, Mrs Chase.'

'Yes, we are,' said Chase, opening the front door so that the autumn mist and chill entered the hall. He wanted to prevent Tomlinson inquiring about that fictitious engagement. Charles Tomlinson took the open-door hint. He also took his hat, which Chase pressed into his hand. Although it had once been a fine top hat, Chase was pleased to note that it was old and battered, the silk covering frayed. Like his overcoat, like the man himself perhaps, it had seen better days.

'You will visit us again soon, I hope, Mr Tomlinson?'

'Wild horses could not keep me away, Mrs Chase.'

He made a little bow and wafted his hand in her direction. He said, *'Arrivederci, Bella.'*

When their visitor was launched into the gathering darkness and the front door safely closed, Cyrus Chase almost sighed in relief. He glanced at Bella. She was a small, delicate creature, quite a lot younger than her husband. She had a round face, a bit like a doll's and like a doll's there was a spot of red on each cheek. The result of the cold night air or the effect of seeing Mr Charles Tomlinson?

'What did Mr Tomlinson want, dear?'

'Oh, nothing much. To see the . . . you know.'

Chase gestured vaguely in the direction of the back of the house and the garden beyond. Fortunately Bella was not very interested in what she called his 'shed activities'. She rather felt that they were morbid. It suited both husband and wife to keep them at a distance from the house. Bella went off to talk to the cook about dinner. Chase delayed in the hall. He was thinking of the unwelcome spark of warmth between Tomlinson and his wife.

Later that evening, over supper with Bella and in between their sporadic conversation, Chase reviewed his relationship with Charles Tomlinson. At one stage he might have called it a budding friendship, but not now. In fact, he was beginning to wish that he had never encountered Tomlinson. That meeting had occurred a few months earlier in the bar of the Lion Hotel, the old Ely coaching inn which sits in the shadow of the great cathedral. The two got chatting – or, more accurately, Tomlinson got chatting to Chase – and the man with the lantern jaw had shown a most flattering interest in Chase's research and his creations. 'You will be a benefactor of mankind,' said Tomlinson, which put into words an idea that Chase did not quite have the nerve or assurance to express for himself. It also struck him, whether by accident or design on Tomlinson's part, on a vulnerable spot.

Cyrus Chase lived in the shadow of his late father, rather as the Lion Hotel lives in the shadow of Ely Cathedral. In the 1840s Howard Chase patented a system of hooks, chains and pins for joining railway carriages that came to be known as the Chase Coupler. To his son, he claimed that such a device – functional, potentially ubiquitous – was as elegant as a work of art. Although the Chase Coupler and other patents, mostly to do with the railways, did not achieve worldwide success they were taken up by enough companies to ensure that Cyrus would never be required to work for a living. Rather, he was free. Free, as it turned out, to emulate his father, by creating and patenting devices.

Cyrus looked not to the railways or the other great iron-and-steel constructions of the age, but to something more elemental. He turned back to the earth, and to interment in the earth, and to the most basic human fear of being buried alive, a fear which had haunted him ever since a terrifying dream in childhood. Cyrus was aware his father had done things that were both profitable and useful. He too hoped to bring a benefit to humanity by easing the fear of death. He believed one could only sleep

easily in this life if one was confident of sleeping easily after
death. It was one of the reasons why he named his villa *Mon
Repos*.

The flattering words from Charles Tomlinson about being a
benefactor led to a first visit to the Chase home and a trip to the
bottom of the garden to inspect his workplace. On this first visit,
Tomlinson had also been introduced to Bella, who fluttered and
flustered and whose cheeks went red at the gentleman's gallantry.
Chase didn't mind initially – it gave him a glow to show off his
wife in almost the same way as it did to show off his security coffin
– but when Bella repeatedly made comments and asked questions
about Tomlinson and when she reacted with even more flutter to
a second visit and then a third, he grew uneasy. It wasn't only Bella's
interest; it was the slightly unnerving look of the man, the narrow
jaw that gave Tomlinson a predatory appearance, the dark eyes.

Another cause for unease was that he could not discover what
Tomlinson did. The man was an occasional visitor to Ely where
he always stayed at the Lion. But why he came to the town,
Chase could not discover, since the other batted away any attempt
to find out. This riled Cyrus, especially because he had been so
open about his own hopes and plans and creations. He resolved
to be more guarded in future. Guarded about his creations, guarded
about his Bella.

The Interment of Mr Lye

David Mackenzie had mentioned that Alexander Lye was a
nonconformist so this was perhaps the reason for the choice
of Abney Park Cemetery for the funeral. The cemetery, which
was half burial-ground, half parkland, was in Stoke Newington,
itself half in London and half out of it, and was the preferred
resting-place of many nonconformists.

On a bright morning in October, less than a week after Mr Lye's
death and with weather to match the day when he died, Helen
and Tom Ansell stood waiting near the ornamental gates of Abney
Park. A few representatives of Scott, Lye & Mackenzie were there

too, talking in subdued tones or brushing flecks from their outfits or inspecting the pavement or the sky. There was a cluster of Stoke Newington locals, too, with nothing better to do, drawn by the prospect of a funeral or perhaps just a turn in the sunshine. The air was clearer and fresher here than in the heart of the city.

Helen was the only woman present in the official party, although others were due to arrive in the funeral carriages, including her mother, Mrs Scott. Helen looked especially fetching dressed in black, Tom thought. Her delicate complexion glowed through the veil she wore. He suppressed the desire to reach out and touch her. He reminded himself that he was here not only to pay his respects to an esteemed member of his firm but also to be introduced to Lye's brother and sister, the two siblings who lived somewhere near Ely. There was to be a wake afterwards at the Regent's Park house.

Helen glanced at the gates to the cemetery. The columnar gate-posts were designed after a curious Egyptian style. There were hieroglyphic inscriptions above the single-storey lodges on each side. Tom said, 'It gives a very un-English feel to the thing, doesn't it?'

'That is probably the purpose of it,' said Helen, squinting at the inscriptions in the sun. 'I wonder what they mean.'

'I can enlighten you, madam.'

They turned to look at a man who was standing behind them. He was short with a face as wrinkled as a walnut. He too was in funeral garb but professionally so. He made a small bow.

'I am with Willow & Son, undertakers of Camden Town. We are in charge of the exequies today for Mr Lye. I am the advance guard, so to speak. Eric Fort at your service. I have a supply of mourning cards with me. One for you, sir, and for you, madam?'

The black-lined cards announced the date of Alexander Lye's death and his age (85) as well as the place and time of his inter-ment at Abney Park. There was a discreet but embossed image of an inverted torch to one side and a willow tree to the other. The weeping willow was an appropriate symbol but it also reminded the recipient of the name of the undertaker's. Tom thought that a handful of these cards had already been sent to Furnival Street but he took one anyway, as did Helen.

'You were wondering what that queer writing says?' said the man, indicating the hieroglyphs above the lodges. 'It says, "The Gates of the Abode of the Mortal Part of Man". It's Egyptian.'

'Very un-English,' said Helen, with a glance at her husband. 'The idea makes one think of the great pyramids at Giza. I should like to see them one day.'

'Those are funerary monuments too,' said Eric Fort. He smiled, showing large discoloured teeth, like old tombstones. 'Just as well the architects did not decide to put down a great pyramid here, eh? It would have obliterated Abney Park.'

He might have said more but at that moment a hearse rounded the corner, drawn by four horses, followed by several other carriages. The hearse was accompanied by the mutes, walking at a stately pace, with their black sashes and practised doleful faces. The quantity of black velvet on the carriages soaked up the autumn sunlight like a blotter. Everyone waiting by the Egyptian gates became suddenly alert. Their postures stiffened. They stood back to allow the cortège to roll through the entrance.

As well as the official mourners, paid and unpaid, the gaggle of locals trailed after the procession and along the winding paths towards the chapel. They passed by pines and cedar trees and in between the monuments. Eric Fort, who seemed to have attached himself to Tom and Helen, made occasional comments in a subdued voice. He pointed out a beehive sculpture on one of the tombs.

'It stands for wisdom while the sculpted veil draped over the domed hive represents the dimming of wisdom.'

'Very interesting, Mr Fort,' said Helen.

They reached the chapel with its tall, spike-like steeple. Set among trees, and reached by those winding paths, it resembled something out of a fairy story, half enchanted, half sinister. Here the coffin was unloaded from the hearse and taken in by the bearers. The mourners clambered down from their carriages and waited until all had been made ready inside the chapel. Helen greeted her mother. Tom said hello to Mr and Mrs David Mackenzie. Mr Ashley, the senior clerk, was with them. The other men from Scott, Lye & Mackenzie stuck together, as if by instinct. Some of the Stoke Newington locals examined the carriages and funeral trappings with experienced eyes.

The Ansells took their places inside the chapel. A dour-faced clergyman was officiating. As the service proceeded, Tom's attention wandered as he tried to identify the other members of Alexander Lye's family. There were two ladies who could have been the senior partner's sisters, but they were so heavily swathed and veiled it was difficult to be sure. A gentleman who was keeping them company might well have been Lye's brother. He had a touch of the old lawyer's look.

Tom thought of another burial, one which he had not attended and which, at the time, he was ignorant of. His father's death occurred when he was still a small boy, and not on land but at sea. Tom retained almost no memory of his father except for the image of a tall man in a blue uniform. Captain Thomas Ansell had been on his way to take part in the Russian War in the Crimea. He died on board of a fever before he could arrive and he was buried near the Dardanelles. Tom supposed that a military, shipboard burial must be an altogether brisker affair than a land-locked civilian one. A few prayers were intoned, a volley of shots was fired, the body was dropped over the side, the ship sailed on.

Tom learned of these details from a comrade of his father whom he had met recently. His mother Marian did not talk much about his father, hardly mentioned him at all in fact, although it had of course been many years since the Captain's death. His most tangible legacy to Tom apart from height and dark hair had perhaps been the form of his given name, since his mother called him Tom from his earliest years to distinguish him from Captain Thomas. After a longish interval Mrs Ansell got married again, to an attorney who behaved towards Tom with distant affection. It was on account of Mark Holford that Tom had decided to make a career in law. His stepfather was dead as well now.

These musings carried Tom most of the way through the service for Mr Lye. When it was over the congregation followed the coffin outside, where the other carriages were waiting. The coffin was returned to the hearse to be transported to its allotted place in Abney Park. While the chapel bell was tolling, the women left in a separate party since they would not be present for the actual interment, but at the wake later that day.

The men went on foot after the hearse. Tom was introduced by David Mackenzie to the gentleman who he had assumed, correctly, was Alexander Lye's brother. Ernest Lye was closer to middle age than old age. He was fairly slight. He had the same penetrating blue gaze as Alexander. The likeness was enhanced when he sneezed and drew out a black-bordered handkerchief.

Tom had forgotten until that instant that a sneeze was the final earthly sound he had heard from Ernest's brother.

Tom was introduced as a trusted member of the firm. David Mackenzie said to Ernest Lye, 'He will be visiting you soon on that business we discussed.'

'I'll be pleased to see you, Mr Ansell,' said Ernest.

They spoke in low tones, not merely because they were following a hearse but because the missing will was a delicate topic. They reached the burial place and clustered round the open grave as the bearers brought the coffin out once more. Tom was near the back and found Mr Eric Fort standing next to him. The little undertaker's man said in a professionally subdued voice, 'I have to say that I prefer Abney Park to Norwood or Highgate. It is quite my favourite among the London burial grounds. What do you think, sir?'

'I expect you're right. I have not as much experience as you,' said Tom in an offhand way which he hoped would finish the conversation. While the dour-faced clergyman was running through his lines on the edge of the grave, Mr Fort sometimes nodded in vigorous agreement and muttered, 'Very true, very true'. Tom found Mr Fort's presence unsettling. Perhaps it was the other man's relish for the whole business. Maybe it was his teeth, which every time that Tom glanced at him seemed more and more to resemble old gravestones, uneven and stained and chipped.

He was glad to escape the company of the toothy individual from Willow & Son when the interment was over. He travelled back with David Mackenzie, Mr Ashley and another junior member of the firm, a pleasant chap called William Evers, with whom Tom was friendly. The journey in one of the funeral carriages towards the smoky air and clogged streets of north London took some time. There was a general sense of release and relaxation. The mourners were looking forward to the food and drink waiting for them at the Regent's Park house that belonged to Alexander Lye and his sister Edith. Tom said nothing of his mission to Ely, since Mr Mackenzie had stressed how confidential it all was. But he did make some comment about how Ernest Lye seemed much less, well, old than his brother.

'I can enlighten you there,' said Mr Mackenzie. 'I have only just discovered that Mr Lye's father was twice married. Mr Ernest Lye was the child of his second wife, Mr Alexander of his first, as is Miss Edith. Alexander Lye is a child of the eighteenth century, Ernest is a product of the nineteenth like the rest of us. Therefore the Lyes are stepbrothers.'

'If you'll allow me, sir,' said William Evers, 'I believe that "half-brothers" is the appropriate term for issue who share a parent. Those who do not share a parent are step-siblings.'

Mr Ashley, who was a stickler for accuracy, nodded in approval. Mackenzie seemed not too put out by the correction. He added, 'There is more though. Something else I have recently discovered. The lady with Mr Ernest Lye is not his sister but his wife. The Lye brothers have only the one sister, Edith, who we are on our way to visit now. And before you can put me right, Mr Evers, I should of course have said *whom* we are on our way to visit . . .'

Tom was sitting next to Evers and he could almost feel the heat of his companion's blush in the confines of the carriage. Mackenzie, pleased at his little victory, patted his black-clad stomach and ruminated on human behaviour.

'There was no obligation on my late, lamented partner to be clear about his family circumstances, of course, and I do not believe that the brothers – or half-brothers, Mr Evers – were close but it is strange how one may have only the sketchiest notion of people one has spent half a lifetime with.'

As he said this, he glanced at Tom who was sitting in the opposite seat. Tom had no doubt he was thinking of the missing will.

The Wake

The wake at the Regent's Park house was a quite jolly affair, even jollier than most wakes. Tom wondered whether it was because there was no one there who truly regretted the passing of Alexander Lye. As David Mackenzie said, the half-brothers had not been close. His sister Edith, who had apparently been distraught to hear of his death, now behaved like a puppet. She was guided to a chair by her half-brother Ernest and a glass of port put in her frail grasp. Tom didn't hear her speak a word or see her take a sip. As far as she was visible, she looked at least as old as Alexander had been – which tended to confirm they were real brother and sister, with no halves or steps involved – but she remained heavily veiled. She possessed a lot of white hair, which came shooting out from under her hat. Her maid fussed about her, despite being nearly as old as her mistress. Age seemed a qualification for the other servants and, like the house itself, they had a faded, worn-out air.

As for the general mourners, they were either those with a professional connection from Scott, Lye & Mackenzie and a couple of other law firms – although the days when Lye had been a familiar figure in the legal world were long gone – or they were neighbours, who pulled the appropriate faces and uttered the right words but then got on with the business of eating, drinking and chatting.

There was plenty of port and sherry, as well as tea. Hams, pies, cheeses and cakes were piled high in the dining room and guests wandered between there and the morning room. The women were already at the house, Helen and her mother Mrs Scott and Mrs Mackenzie and others, and pretty soon the rooms were full of noise and even the odd burst of laughter, quickly checked. The cemetery at Abney Park with its burial rites was a distant memory. William Evers cornered Tom by one of the high windows that looked out over the Park. He seemed anxious.

'I say, do you think I really upset the guv'nor by putting him right about step-brothers and so on? Should've kept my mouth shut, I suppose.'

'I think he enjoyed putting you down, Will. In a good-natured way.'

'Then I suppose I'm glad to have been a source of pleasure for him.'

Tom put a hand on Evers' despondent shoulder and the junior brightened at once. He took another swig of sherry.

'I hear you are going on confidential business to Ely,' he said.

'Not confidential enough, it seems.'

'Oh dear, another mistake.'

'No, no,' said Tom. Yet he was surprised at how quickly things got round an office.

'You are lucky to be in Mr Mackenzie's confidence.'

Tom shrugged. To change the subject, he said, 'Have you seen Mrs Ernest Lye?'

'I have indeed,' said Evers, looking towards an attractive woman on the other side of the morning room. As Ernest Lye was a lot younger than his brother Alexander, then Mrs Lye was in turn appreciably younger than her husband. Will Evers sighed and Tom thought he knew what the matter was.

'How is Miss Rosamond?' he said.

'Thriving and . . . and as beautiful as ever,' said his friend. 'I must speak to her father next week. I *will* speak to him.'

Miss Rosamond Hartley was the daughter of a doctor. Will Evers had been her admirer for some time now. He thought – he hoped – that his feelings were returned. All that remained was for him to approach Dr Hartley, man to man, and ask permission. Tom had lost count of the number of occasions on which the junior lawyer had stated that he intended to speak to the doctor next week. That 'next week' never seemed to arrive.

'I have sounded her out and think my prospects are good, but I do not know for sure. If only I could have a glimpse of her diary,' said Will, draining his sherry and then examining the empty glass as though he expected more drink to materialize by magic. 'Women confide their secret thoughts to their diaries, don't they? If I saw what she was writing, it would give me some clue as to her real feelings. Then I could call on her father, armed with some ammunition, so to speak.'

'You must be bold, Will,' said Tom, thinking that Will might find a message he didn't like in Miss Rosamond's diaries. 'Speak to her father. Really do so next week.'

'I suppose you're right. You are a lucky man, Thomas Ansell, to have such a wife as you have.'

Automatically, Tom looked round for Helen. He noticed that she was talking to Mrs Lye, the wife of Ernest. They were having an animated conversation.

'I met an author the other day,' said Will. Tom struggled to catch the connection, then realized that Helen's reputation as a writer was spreading round the firm, like other things. Will Evers continued,

'I suppose he wasn't an author exactly, but a journalist. It was at Willow & Son. Mr Mackenzie had sent me there on business to do with today's funeral. A fellow who called himself Mute.'

'Mute?'

'Not his real name but a pseudonym of course. He writes a column in a periodical called *Funereal Matters*, I think.'

'Not part of my regular reading.'

'Nor mine. But there are plenty of people interested in the subject of death and funerals and the like.'

'There are,' said Tom, thinking of Eric Fort.

'Oh look, here comes the guv'nor. Expect he wants to talk to you,' said Will, disappearing in the quest for fresh alcohol.

David Mackenzie took Tom to one side, saying that he wanted to show him something. They skirted the knots of mourners and the islands of old chairs and occasional tables which littered the large room. They climbed the stairs and walked down a dark passage towards the rear of the house. It was here, Mackenzie explained, that Alexander Lye kept the room which served as his private office or den. He produced a key.

'I am holding this key with Miss Edith's permission. As you've probably seen, Tom, she is not capable of very much.'

He unlocked the door. A window gave on to a garden where the sun shone on autumn leaves and an untidy lawn. There was enough illumination to glimpse the interior of the room, which was as Mackenzie had described it to Tom a few days before. Even if things had been neatly arranged, it would have been a packed chamber with all the documents, law books, boxes, almanacs, records, files and folios. But, as it was, it seemed as though a miniature whirlwind had bored into the centre and thrown everything everywhere.

In a kind of hollow in the middle, again as Mackenzie described it, was a comfortable armchair. A tasselled, red smoking-cap sat on the seat. The velvet cap was a reminder of Alexander Lye, and for some reason Tom became more aware of his death at that moment than at any time during the last week. The two men stood just inside the door of the room, gazing at the mess. Attempting to advance any further might have added to the confusion, so precarious were the mounds of paper. A smell of mould and disuse emanated from the den.

'Mr Ashley and I are going to spend time here, attempting to bring this collection to order,' said Mackenzie. 'It is not just a question of the missing will. There could be other items in this room which are, let us say, pertinent to the good name of Scott, Lye & Mackenzie and which should not find their way on to the King's Cross dust-heap.'

'Rather you than me,' said Tom without thinking.

'If by that you mean that I am better placed to judge what matters to the firm, then you are right,' said Mackenzie. Then, in a milder tone, 'But your mission is important too, Tom. You must do your best to discover whether Alexander left any kind of testament or will in the house at Ely. I think it unlikely. I gather he was an infrequent visitor. But it is possible that you will find *something* and we should leave no stone unturned. You are a dab hand at investigating.'

Tom wondered whether Mackenzie was mocking him with this last remark but he seemed to be serious. He continued, 'Mr and Mrs Lye are apprised of the situation, and willing to give you every assistance. Mr Lye doesn't believe you'll find anything but he did say that there were some family papers deposited by Alexander at the Ely house, papers which he has never examined properly.'

'And if we find nothing . . .?'

'Then we shall have to apply to the Court of Probate and they will follow the law, of course, which states that in cases of intestacy . . .?'

Luckily, Tom had been reading up on this and so was able to answer. The situation was more complicated than usual because Lye had left neither widow nor children, who would have been the automatic beneficiaries. In such instances as this the law was that the estate should be divided among the heirs of the intestate's father. In other words, it would go to Alexander's sister, Miss Edith, and to his half-brother, Mr Ernest.

'Which is most likely what his will says or would say, if it exists,' said Mackenzie. 'What we want to avoid is going to the Court of Probate, and having the intestacy business being broadcast everywhere.'

He was thinking of the firm's reputation. Tom nodded in agreement.

'We haven't a great deal of time, either.'

'I'll do my best, Mr Mackenzie.'

But, privately, he didn't believe there was much chance of success.

Dinner in Ely

On the evening of the day of Alexander Lye's funeral to the north of London, there was a smallish dinner party at the house of Mr and Mrs Cyrus Chase some seventy miles away in Ely. Apart from the host and hostess, in attendance were the Reverend and Mrs Gordon Coffer, Mr and Mrs Frank Hardwick, Mr Charles Tomlinson and Miss Dora Selwyn. The reverend's parish was in the city of Cambridge, so he and his wife were required to make the short journey by train to Ely, while the Hardwicks had to do no more than walk from the neighbouring street where they lived in order to spend the evening with the Chases. Frank Hardwick was a local brewer. Miss Selwyn was an ageing cousin of Mr Chase's, useful to call on to make up numbers round the table. She, too, lived close by. And Mr Tomlinson? Well, Chase still wasn't sure exactly where he lived or precisely what he did or where he came from, or sure of anything about him, really.

The dinner party was being held mostly at the urging of Chase's wife, Bella. She'd been in earnest about her wish to see Tomlinson again and soon, after his last visit to inspect Cyrus' 'apparatus'. She badgered her husband to invite him, so Cyrus, who was afraid of displeasing his wife for too long, thought up the plan of inviting Tomlinson along with several other guests who might somehow muffle the Tomlinson effect. The Tomlinson effect on his wife, that was. Also, he now found the prospect of seeing Charles to be alarming rather than enjoyable, so he considered it would be better to have company. As usual, when he wanted to communicate with Mr Tomlinson, he left a note at the Lion Hotel and received a reply within twenty-four hours.

As for the other guests, Chase invited the Reverend Coffer

and his wife because they were church people, and so might have a restraining influence on Tomlinson, and because Gordon Coffer was well disposed towards his researches into security coffins. The Hardwicks were old acquaintances and neighbours, while his cousin Miss Dora could always be summoned at the last moment.

Cyrus Chase hoped that he had set things up to go as smoothly as possible at the dinner table. But the first surprise, a very disconcerting one, was that the Reverend Coffer and his wife already knew Charles Tomlinson. Not only did they know him, but they were distantly related, second cousins or something like that. In addition, Tomlinson had recently renewed his acquaintance with the daughter of the Coffers, who lived near Ely. Well, this was a bit of a facer for old Cyrus, but he put a good front on things.

The Coffers and Tomlinson greeted each other warmly. Although Mrs Coffer was getting on in years, Tomlinson showed towards her − second cousin or whatever she was − almost the same degree of insinuating gallantry he showed towards Bella. Even Coffer, who tended to be rather grim-faced, was pleased to see Tomlinson. The gentleman was nearly as attentive to the mousy Mrs Hardwick. Only against cousin Dora did his charms seem useless. She peered at him quizzically and simply said 'I expect so' to the two or three remarks he addressed to her, whether her response made sense or not.

Then things went wrong with the placement or seating. Cyrus thought he had arranged it so that Tomlinson was near him and instead the fellow ended up next to Bella in the seat where Coffer ought to have been. Cyrus spent much of the meal with his eyes darting towards the other end of the table for signs of over-familiarity. For example, Tomlinson's mouth being a little too close to Bella's curled hair as he whispered some aside in her ear or the sight of her hand momentarily resting on his arm as she responded.

The food was the only part that, to Cyrus, was a definite success. Artichoke soup and salmon fillets, then boiled turkey and leg of lamb, followed by cabinet pudding and a cheese fondue, served with all the trimmings and washed down with plenty of sweet white wine. Cyrus reminded himself to compliment the cook.

The conversation never really took flight or, if it did, went winging off in alarming directions. Mr Hardwick spent some time outlining his ambition to become the biggest brewer in Ely, to knock Legge's and Eagle's and the others off their perch and into the River Ouse. From time to time he looked at his wife who nodded in frantic agreement. Cyrus, as a good host, tried to shift the discussion to a topic which he considered both inoffensive and interesting: the recent decision of the General Post Office to paint their boxes and pillars red rather than bronze-green. But no one seemed very concerned and some reference to taste and orthodoxy caused the Reverend Coffer to go down a totally different path and launch an attack on an individual called Sir Henry Thompson and his dangerous views.

Extending a bony forefinger and with his brow furrowed, Mr Coffer said, 'To think that they saw fit to give him a knighthood, whatever he may have done for the King of Belgium and his kidney stones.'

'I am not sure everyone round this table is familiar with Sir Henry,' said Charles Tomlinson.

'He is a surgeon,' said Coffer, 'and I wish he had restricted himself to meddling with people while they are still alive, whether they are kings or commoners. But Thompson is the moving spirit behind this new Cremation Society. I cannot believe that such a heretical idea will catch on with us but it never does to under-estimate people's gullibility and their willingness to try the latest fad.'

Cyrus had heard of Sir Henry Thompson, of course, since he was attentive to any news concerning death and disposal. But he did not care for the way Tomlinson now looked in his direction with a cocked eyebrow as if to say, It would not do much for your security-coffin business if cremation came into fashion, would it?

Tomlinson did not say any of this out loud. Instead, after a glance at Bella, who was seated on his right, he inclined his head towards Coffer and said, 'With all due respect to you, sir, both as a man of the cloth and as someone who is kin to me, I wonder whether this conversation is really a suitable one when the ladies are present. Cremation isn't quite the thing over the dinner table. After all, we are not on the banks of the Ganges gazing at the burning ghats . . . which are quite a sight, I can assure you . . .'

The remark, as it was probably intended to, made all the ladies sit up. Bella put her hand on Tomlinson's sleeve – again! – and said, 'You have been to India, Mr Tomlinson? You have seen the way they burn bodies in public?'

'That, and many other strange things, dear lady.'

'Is there not a terrible rite in India which they call *suttee*?' said Mrs Coffer.

'There is, indeed,' said Tomlinson with enthusiasm, and appearing to forget the remark he'd just made about unsuitable topics. 'The wife throws herself on the funeral pyre of her husband out of sheer grief and the desire to join him.'

'Barbaric,' said Reverend Coffer.

'Dreadful,' said Mr Hardwick.

'Other lands, other customs. If we put our very natural prejudices to one side for a moment, one can only imagine the fidelity and the – the passion – which would cause a widow to do that.'

The idea, and perhaps the word 'passion', caused a temporary silence round the table. Cousin Dora now made her first intervention of the meal. And Cyrus was proud of her. She said, 'I do not believe that all those wives act out of choice. Some are forced to it.'

'Well, that may be so,' said Tomlinson smoothly. 'Anyway, *suttee* is a practice which has been outlawed in India these many years.'

'I expect so,' said Dora Selwyn, but something in her voice suggested she didn't quite believe Tomlinson.

After that the conversation, even over the puddings, seemed incapable of rising above somewhat morbid subjects, such as the practice in the German states of building elaborate mortuaries at public expense. Naturally, it turned out that Charles Tomlinson was familiar with Germany; was there anywhere that the man had not visited, anywhere that he could not comment on? Once the ladies had withdrawn, there was some enjoyable if desultory chat over the port, and Cyrus relaxed. He even began to think that, after all, there was some value to knowing a man of the world like Tomlinson.

But the worst moment of the evening for Cyrus Chase was still to come. Their guests were departing. The housemaid Mattie was in attendance to hand out hats and coats and umbrellas. The

Hardwicks had already left, and were accompanying Cousin Dora back to her house before returning to their own. The Coffers were about to go. Coffer insisted on jabbering all the way to the garden gate, telling Chase that he would send him a copy of a recent pamphlet that laid out the arguments against cremation, laid them out irrefutably. And what did Mr Cyrus Chase think of the idea of starting an Anti-Cremation Society, eh? With Mrs Coffer tugging at her husband's sleeve and telling him that they must hurry to catch the last train to Cambridge, Cyrus turned back towards his own front door.

He could not be absolutely certain of what he saw there. The front door of *Mon Repos* was almost closed and the light from the hall was dim. His wife Bella and Charles Tomlinson were standing together on the porch. It appeared that the pair had just moved apart, as though from an embrace. Their arms were extended slightly and their heads were very close together. Were they merely exchanging compliments or something more intimate? Cyrus coughed as he walked back up the path and Tomlinson emerged from the shadow of the porch, giving a casual waft of his hand in Bella's direction.

'Goodnight, Chase,' he said as he passed. 'A pleasant evening, most pleasant.'

By the time he reached the porch, Bella was inside again. Cyrus secured the front door and turned round to face his wife, who was standing by the entrance to the morning room as though she was about to speak to him. Or expected him to say something to her. But Cyrus could think of nothing to say. He might have commented on her flushed cheeks – but then it was a cold night.

Summer, 1645

*E*verything in Stilwell Manor was suspended that morning. No smell of baking bread or roasting meat emanated from the kitchen quarters, no servants bustled or slouched from one task to the next, no laundry was hung out on the frames to dry in the midsummer sun, no one came to consult the steward or Anne's father and mother about household business or the estate. Instead, it was as if the soldiers owned the place, they moved about so arrogantly and surely, while the proper occupants of the house seemed to shrink into the wainscoting and avert their eyes while the men went by. The men took no personal interest in anybody in the household – which was a relief – apart from Mr Martin. He was shut up in one of the offices with Trafford for a long time. When he emerged he looked more white-faced than usual.

The searchers discovered one of the priest-holes. Later, Anne saw the wooden panelling which had been splintered and smashed by boots and fists and sword hilts. She smelled the damp earthy odour of the tiny chamber that lay revealed behind a passage off the main hall. Even to the soldiers it must have been apparent that no one could have been using the hole in the recent past. There was a tapestry of cobwebs across the 'entrance' and a timber in the low ceiling had fallen, cramping the space even further to the extent that a child would have had difficulty accommodating himself there.

The soldiers departed soon after midday. They had spent more than six hours in Stilwell Manor. They searched the outbuildings and scoured the grounds but with less zeal and energy than formerly. Before they went, Anne's father offered them a small beer and cheese and stale bread. They accepted the food and drink, and there was even some laughter among them while they stood around chewing and slurping under the sun in the courtyard. Then they left at a pace that was more of a walk than a march. The leader acknowledged Anne's father with a nod of his head as he turned to go.

Anne wondered that they were on foot but James told her that they must have left their horses tethered at a distance so as to creep up on the house in the early morning light without raising the alarm. It was to the steward that Anne turned for explanation rather than to her parents. In fact, her parents left the house after the soldiers' departure, travelling by carriage to Peterborough for reasons that she did not know.

James was reluctant to say much, whether because he was shaken by the events of the morning or because he felt bound by some instinct of secrecy. But he did tell Anne that there had been a great battle a couple of days before, in which the Parliamentary side had been victorious. The battle had been fought not so very many miles from Stilwell. A number of individuals, important individuals, had escaped capture on the battle-field. James did not say that these people were the King's men, he did not have to. He simply added that the soldiers must have been looking for these important fugitives. They had found no one.

Anne thought of the hurried arrival of the two well-dressed gentlemen at the house the previous afternoon. She thought of the unusual noises later in the night. She said nothing of this. Instead she asked why Mr Martin had been shut up for so long with the leader of the soldiers.

'Mr Martin has the air of a – a scholar – of a priest,' said James. 'Perhaps that is why Captain Trafford wanted to talk to him.'

Mr Martin was not a priest, as far as Anne knew, but he did occa-sionally act as tutor to Anne and her sister, giving lessons which neither girl enjoyed. They did not like Mr Martin's pale-faced sourness any more than he appeared to enjoy their company. Anne had never quite worked out his position at Stilwell although he seemed to be some kind of advisor to her father and mother, a man to whom they regularly turned for counsel and wisdom. Like Anne, James did not care for Mr Martin but the steward was too loyal to let any explicit critical word escape from him.

Slowly, after the soldiers' departure, the house resumed its normal pattern for the day. Anne was left to her own devices, as usual. Mary had shut herself away with a book, which was her way of retreating. Anne felt on edge, apprehensive but also oddly excited. The afternoon was warm and fine, with high slow-moving clouds. She set off, intending to wander through the gardens and the outlying grounds. She stopped on hearing the familiar, unwelcome voice of Mr Martin behind her.

'What are you doing, Anne?'

'Nothing. Walking, that's all.'

'It may not be safe.'

This seemed an odd thing to say and she could not think of a reply. She was old enough to ignore Mr Martin if she chose, so she turned her *back on him and paced towards the point where she had watched the men emerge from the trees that morning.*

The land was mostly low-lying marsh hereabouts, and Stilwell was protected from regular flooding only because it lay a few dozen feet above the rest of the neighbourhood. There were channels through the marshes known to the eel-catchers and the fowlers, and sometimes on her wanderings Anne would glimpse a boat in the reeds. If you crouched down, the water disappeared from sight altogether and you might think that the vessel was voyaging through tall grass and rushes.

Beyond the line of trees the ground slanted away until it became darker and more bog-like. Even in summer the earth here was never completely dry. The soldiers must have approached from the south where a narrow track was delineated by scattered willows. On the other, northerly side was a curious low bump or dome that, at first sight, looked almost natural. Only when you drew closer did it become apparent that the dome – like a large, upturned coracle – was some kind of hut, constructed out of pleated willow branches but constructed so long ago that it had become obscured by matted creepers and grass and mosses. On the east side, the one facing the marshes, was a crude door also made from willow and attached to the frame by fraying cords.

Anne did not know what the hut or shelter had been used for, or who had used it. She guessed it was where some hunter or fowler waited for his prey or stored it after capture. Or even where he lived for a time. Inside the tiny circular space, the ground had been beaten flat in a rudimentary way and in the centre was a ring of stones blackened and cracked by fire. She and Mary occasionally used the place for hiding in, but Mary was frightened by the damp and darkness of the interior, even on the sunniest days. From the inside, one could peer out through the interstices of the willow branches and the overhanging creepers and get a fairly clear view of the surrounding countryside and of the east side of Stilwell Manor.

Anne looked behind her. She feared Mr Martin was still watching her but could not see him. Yet when she approached the hide, she was conscious of being watched from inside by someone else. She sensed eyes squinting through the minute gaps in the meshed branches. She thought of the black gaze of the man, Trafford, who had searched her bedroom that morning. Her heart began to thud and her mouth was dry. For a moment she was tempted to turn back, to run off to the safety of her home, only a few hundred yards distant. But she did not run. Instead she took several more deliberate paces towards the willow hide before halting and saying in as steady a voice as she could produce, 'You can come out now. They've gone.'

Incident at Liverpool Street Station

Two days after Alexander Lye's funeral, Tom and Helen Ansell set off for Cambridge and Ely. They went with different objectives and Helen's seemed more feasible and enjoyable than Tom's probably futile hunt for a missing will. Helen had obtained from Arthur Arnett, the editor of *The New Moon* magazine, a commission to write a piece about the old university city and perhaps Ely as well.

In his letter commissioning the article, Arnett expressed his approval of her choice, saying that Cambridgeshire was a county he knew well, and that he would be interested, most interested, to read her views on the region. Helen showed Tom the letter and, although he was pleased for her, he thought privately that the letter was a bit overblown, a bit fulsome. But then, he supposed, that was what these literary types were like, never quite knowing when to stop talking or rein things in. Several times Helen told her husband that the fee for the article would be modest but that the commission might lead to bigger and better things. Tom didn't mind about the fee and was glad to have her company.

In Cambridge, they were to stay at the Devereux Hotel overlooking an open area known as Parker's Piece. Mr Ashley had arranged their stay and described the location of the hotel. During the day Helen planned to wander round Cambridge and capture the 'very quintessence of the place', as Mr Arnett phrased it, while Tom made the short railway journey to Ely and Phoenix House as the Lyes' place was called. Helen had also been invited to visit by Mrs Lye, whose acquaintance she'd made at the funeral party.

Tom was curious to hear his wife's impressions of Mrs Lye. He had not talked to her himself. They were in a cab on their way to Liverpool Street Station. The journey was slow because the autumn weather, which that year alternated between clear skies and fog as regularly as a metronome, was today in its foggy phase. Through the glassed front of the cab, they saw the copper disc of the sun above the outline of the city's roofs.

'She is a handsome woman,' said Helen, in answer to Tom's question about Mrs Lye.

'Is she? I didn't notice.'

'Yes you did.'

'Well, I could not see much beneath all the apparatus of mourning.'

'Men are quick to detect attraction even beneath a veil.'

'The veil suited *you*, I must say.'

'You're changing the subject, Tom.'

'I only wanted to know what you made of Mrs Lye. Her background and character, not her looks.'

'I am not sure what I made of her but I did glean a few things about her history. She is the daughter of a cleric in Cambridge. She considered the service for Mr Lye to be somewhat "plain and low" – those were her words – so from that I deduce that her father and his church must be high.'

'Incense and bells and so on,' said Tom.

'Yes. She has been married to Ernest for a few years now, I'm not sure how many. He is like the squire of the village where they live, a few miles outside Ely. It's called Upper Fen. I had the impression she found life there rather . . . rather confining. She was pleased to be in London even if it was to attend her brother-in-law's funeral. That is all I found out, I think.'

'You found a lot.'

'And her name is Lydia.'

'Lydia Lye has a certain ring to it.'

At Liverpool Street Station they had to leave the cab at a slight distance from the entrance because the terminus was so new that the approaches were not quite finished. They stepped out of the hansom. After the enclosed cab, the air smelled dank and brassy. The driver handed down their cases. Tom paid him off and the generous tip caused him to touch his hand to his cap in an appreciative salute.

A couple of loungers came forward, offering to carry the cases inside the station but Tom waved them away. He preferred to keep his own eyes or hands on the bags until they might be entrusted to a porter. In between stowing his money securely – any railway terminus was fertile ground for pickpockets – and glances at the luggage where it sat on the pavement a few feet away, he failed to notice what was happening on the other side of him.

Helen was standing closer to the kerb. She was lifting the hem of her skirts clear of the dirt and debris on the pavement, and she was looking downwards, not out or around. It was the cab driver who saved her. He was about to urge his horse out to rejoin the stream of carriages and carts and omnibuses that flowed sluggishly along Bishopsgate. Looking over his shoulder into the murk, he shouted, 'Miss! Look out, Miss!'

Both Tom and Helen turned round simultaneously. A horse and carriage had lurchingly mounted the pavement and were bearing down on her. Tom saw the flare of the horse's nostrils, the muffled face of the driver and his raised hand bearing a whip. Without conscious thought, he reached out, seized Helen about the waist and tugged her towards him. They half stepped, half stumbled out of the path of the horse and carriage. Tom's legs struck against one of the bags and he fell on his back, Helen on top of him.

The carriage rumbled past, the horse's hooves and the ironclad wheels thudding and grinding on the pavement. With a crash, it settled back on to the roadway and jostled its way past Tom and Helen's hansom and into the slow flow of vehicles. During the few seconds that had passed, the driver showed no awareness of having almost struck down a couple of foot-passengers.

Both Tom and Helen were too winded and shaken to react straightaway.

The loungers, whose offers of help Tom was rejecting a few moments earlier, now assisted them to their feet and were public-spirited enough not to attempt to make off with their bags. Perhaps this had something to do with the policeman who wandered over while the couple were brushing the dust and smuts off their coats with small, almost involuntary gestures. Tom began to explain what had occurred, and several bystanders threw in their accounts too. Tom's mouth was dry. Helen was white in the face. He feared she might faint but she shook her head when

he asked if she wanted to sit down. Instead she gripped his arm
hard.

The policeman, realizing he was dealing with a lady and a
gent, was all attention and concern but in truth there was nothing
to be done. The murky air was swallowing up the traffic within
a hundred yards in either direction along Bishopsgate, obscuring
all traces of the runaway carriage. Tom had seen nothing of the
driver apart from a slice of face between his muffler and his cap.
The interior of the carriage was occupied, though. As he was
dragging Helen out of the way, Tom was aware of a face
momentarily pressed against the window. Like the driver, the
passenger apparently did not care enough to give the order to
halt or even to slow down.

Tom cut short anything more he might have said to the
policeman. He wanted to get Helen inside the station, into
the comfort and shelter of the buffet where they might recover,
and fortify themselves with something warm and liquid before
boarding the train. He nodded at the policeman's comments about
carriage drivers who should know better and the danger of
untrained horses, and indicated to a couple of the station loungers
that they might, after all, carry the luggage inside. The Ansells
entered the new concourse of Liverpool Street, Helen still holding
tight to his arm and Tom suddenly conscious that he had injured
his shoulder when he fell to the ground. Still, that was so little
compared to what might have happened!

A little more than an hour later, and calmer and more at ease
after a pot of tea (Helen) and a measure of brandy (Tom) in the
station buffet, they boarded the Great Eastern train for Cambridge.
Tom had already suggested they might abandon their journey for
the day and go back home but Helen wouldn't hear of it. Instead
she insisted they purchase their tickets. In the buffet, Tom tried
again.

'Nonsense, Tom. It was an unfortunate accident – or nearly
an accident. If it hadn't been for you . . .'

Her voice trailed off and Tom put a reassuring hand on her
arm. She gave a little smile and said, 'Anyway, I am quite recovered
now.'

Her bloodless complexion and the way she concentrated on

her movements as she lifted the teacup to her lips told a slightly different story. But Tom did not want to contradict her. Also he thought that a train journey might distract her.

He said nothing to his wife but he was not so certain that their near-miss was an accident. The carriage driver's face had been well wrapped up, because of the foggy cold or perhaps because he wanted to conceal himself. The driver made no attempt to restrain his horse – indeed, the raised whip seemed to show he was urging the animal on – nor did he slow to see if any harm was done. There seemed something deliberate, something very non-accidental, about the way in which the horse and carriage mounted the pavement as if aiming at the very place where Helen and he were standing.

They walked to the platform where their train was waiting. The upper reaches of the glass canopy were obscured by fog and smoke. Down below a train, hissing and clanking, was pulling into a neighbouring platform. Through the gloom, its lights showed a dirty yellow and white. Tom thought of the face he'd seen pressed against the window of the carriage that almost ran them down. The face was familiar. He had only a half-second's glimpse but something about its wrinkled curiosity, its toothy mouth, reminded him of the man from the Abney Park undertakers Willow & Son. Reminded him of Mr Eric Fort.

The Spy

Tom said nothing to Helen about his suspicion that the face at the carriage window belonged to the undertaker's man, Eric Fort. During the hour-long railway journey to Cambridge he tried to put the pale apparition out of his mind and concentrated instead on distracting Helen who, from her rather stiff gestures and silence, was still recovering from the shock. But there was little to distract her. Not much to look at in the flattish countryside that unfurled outside the window, nor any fellow passengers who looked interesting enough to speculate about.

They took a cab from Cambridge railway station to the Devereux Hotel, where they were staying. The hotel was on the edge of the older part of town and overlooked a large grassy area which seemed to have been caught up in the spread of new housing. While the outside porter was bringing in their bags, Helen and Tom gazed round the spacious lobby. Several individuals were lounging there, either hiding behind newspapers or staring with interest at any new arrivals. One of these loungers, a rotund little man, lifted himself out of an armchair and bowled himself in their direction. He came to a stop in front of them. He was shorter than both Tom and Helen.

'Mr and Mrs Ansell,' he said. It was more of a statement than a question. Tom nodded.

'I thought so! I am a friend of Jack.'

'A friend of Jack?'

'Jack Ashley, the senior clerk of Scott, Lye & Mackenzie. It is a pleasure to make your acquaintance.'

He stuck out his hand, to Tom then to Helen. As they shook hands, Tom was thinking, here is a tiny mystery solved, the mystery of Mr Ashley's first name. But who is this fellow?

'Forgive me for getting things the wrong way round and not introducing myself straightaway. My name is John Jubb, and I am the senior clerk at the firm of Teague and Bennett, one of the oldest legal practices in the city of Cambridge.'

'We are pleased to meet you,' said Helen.

'But you are wondering why I am here?'

'We are, rather.'

'Jack Ashley and I have known each other ever since we were small. We were born on the same street in the same London borough in the same year which was – oh quite a long time ago now – and we played together very amicably, unlike most small boys. We shared first names too and Jack became Jack so as to distinguish him from me, John, when any grown-up wanted to call us indoors or to scold us, which was often enough. Anyway, both Jack and John went into the same profession, the legal one, and they have risen to the height of a senior clerkship in their respective establishments, and have kept in touch over these many years, and – to cut a long story short, Mr and Mrs Ansell, since you must be tired after your journey – Jack communicated the fact to me that you were arriving in Cambridge today and he asked me, well, asked me to look out for you.'

Finally running out of breath, John Jubb looked from one to the other as if for approval. Tom was a bit taken aback. Did they need looking out for? But Helen said, 'How thoughtful of Mr Ashley. Thank you, Mr Jubb.'

Jubb was pleased. He said, 'I must not detain you any longer but if I can be of any service, for example by informing you as to the sights of our fair city, whether town or gown . . . though I say it myself, I am a veritable mine of information. Did you know, for example, that Parker's Piece by this very hotel is so named because a college cook named Parker acquired the right to farm it once?'

Tom hoped that Jubb's other nuggets of information might be slightly more interesting than this. But the little round man showed no sign of leaving until Helen stepped in again.

'That might be very helpful, Mr Jubb,' she said. 'You see, I am commissioned to gather impressions of Cambridge.'

'Are you?'

'To write a magazine piece.'

'My dear Mrs Ansell, I did not know that you were a writer. In that case, if you'll forgive me, I must insist − I must almost insist − on showing you and your husband around. Tomorrow morning, say. It is a Saturday and I am for once at leisure in the morning.'

'I'm afraid I have to go to Ely on business for my firm tomorrow,' said Tom.

'Of course,' said Mr Jubb, tapping the side of his nose as if he understood all about business. 'Mr Ashley hinted that your work was to take you to Ely. But it would be my privilege to escort your fair lady about the town.'

So it was agreed that John Jubb would give Helen a tour the next day. 'That was one way of getting rid of him, I suppose,' said Tom to his wife when the law clerk had finally quit the hotel lobby and they had been shown up to their rooms, a bedroom and a sitting room, each of which had a view across the expanse of Parker's Piece.

'Do not be mean, Tom,' said Helen. 'I quite took to Mr Jubb. He was so eager to please that I did not want to disappoint.

Besides, it will be useful to have someone to show me the town. Useful for the article which I shall be writing.'

Tom thought, as he often did, that Helen not only had a nicer nature than his but good practical sense too. They ate a late luncheon in the hotel and then went on a preliminary walk about the town, admiring the fine old facades of the colleges and the glimpses down narrow high-walled lanes. It was a grey afternoon and lights were burning in some of the college rooms. Tom imagined scholars bent over dusty volumes while mist rose from the fens and the gargoyles crouched overhead.

They were walking towards King's Parade and he was on the point of describing the picture in his mind to Helen – it was the kind of thing she might put in her magazine piece, wasn't it? – when he became aware that she had stopped and was staring at something or someone on the other side of the street. Tom looked but could see nothing out of the ordinary, only cabs and carriages passing, and people on foot going in both directions.

'What is it?'

Helen shook her head, as much to herself as to him.

'It's nothing,' she said. 'I think I must still be a little on edge from that business this morning. Shall we go back now?'

Tom took her arm and they returned to the Devereux. He thought it just as well that Mr John Jubb had offered to escort Helen on the next day since he did not like the idea of leaving her by herself in this unfamiliar town. Back at the hotel Tom was handed a letter by the clerk in the lobby. He glanced at his name on the envelope without recognizing the handwriting and tucked it in his pocket.

It was only later when Helen was lying down in the bedroom and Tom was in the sitting room, idly leafing through the newspaper he'd bought at Liverpool Street, that he remembered the letter. He retrieved it from his coat pocket and took it to the window. The gasolier in the room was not yet lit and the afternoon light was fading fast. Tom looked again at the envelope. It was not surprising he hadn't recognized the writing since, now he looked more closely, the name and address appeared to have been written by a child. The letters of THOMAS ANSELL ESQ and DEVEREUX HOTEL were awkwardly formed and of slightly different sizes. Whatever was inside did not have the thickness of a letter.

Tom took a paper knife from the writing desk near the window. He slit open the envelope and his first thought was that it was empty. A slip of ragged paper fluttered down to the carpet. He picked up the fragment, which had obviously been torn from a book. He held it up to the light from the window, and read it. The words made sense but they did not mean anything to him. He read the scrap several times over without becoming any the wiser. He looked out the window. A large group of young men was playing football on Parker's Piece, in a raucous, good-natured way. Tom estimated there were at least forty players. He presumed they were students, gownsmen.

'What are you doing?'

Helen was standing in the door of the bedroom.

'I don't know. This was in the envelope that was given to me downstairs. It's a piece of poetry, I suppose. The funny thing is that I know it, half know it.'

'Let me see.'

Helen scrutinized the bit of paper. She too looked puzzled until she said 'Oh yes' under her breath.

'Oh yes what?'

'"*There's no art to find the mind's construction on the face. He was a gentleman on whom I built an absolute trust*",' she recited. Then, 'You still don't recognize it, Tom?'

'I don't.'

'These are the words of King Duncan in the play of *Macbeth*, after he has been told of the treachery of the Thane of Cawdor, the first Thane of Cawdor to whose title Macbeth succeeds. We saw the play not long ago, don't you remember?'

Tom felt slightly foolish. It was true, they had recently gone to a performance of *Macbeth* at the Lyceum Theatre with Henry Irving and Ellen Terry. Tom recalled Miss Terry, with her long, red tresses and her green gown embroidered with gold, presenting a less ferocious version of Lady Macbeth than he expected.

'These lines have been torn from a book of Shakespeare's works,' said Helen. 'Duncan is identified as the speaker but nothing else has been included. What does it mean?'

'Here is the envelope it came in. My name looks as though it was written by a child.'

'Who delivered it?'

Tom went downstairs and spoke to the hotel clerk who passed him on to the outside porter who, after a lapse of memory that required a small coin to make good, was able to say only that some lad had approached and given him the envelope. 'Some lad' was just a lad, normal height, not fat, not thin, with darkish hair under a cap, and so on. Tom almost asked for his money back but instead he returned to Helen who was sitting at the writing desk studying the envelope and the *Macbeth* fragment. While he was gone, she had drawn the curtains and lit the gas chandelier so that the room was more cosy but also shut-in.

'The envelope was delivered by a child, a boy,' said Tom. 'The porter couldn't tell me anything useful, but I suppose the same child might have written my name on the envelope.'

'I don't think this is a child's writing,' said Helen. 'It's more like an attempt on the part of the writer to disguise his or her own hand, by using the left instead of the right. The lettering is clumsy but it can still be read, while your name is spelled correctly and the hotel too. Devereux is quite a difficult word. I think an adult wrote this.'

'An adult who likes playing childish games,' said Tom in irritation. 'What does it mean, cutting a few lines out of Shakespeare and sticking them inside a clumsily addressed envelope?'

'Think of what the words mean first.'

'They're a warning against putting your trust in someone.'

'Not quite,' said Helen. 'They are more like a – I don't know – a declaration that you can never tell what someone is thinking or what they're really like inside from the way they look.'

'Anyone who's been working in the law for more than a few weeks could tell you that. It's nothing new. We're still in the dark.'

'Not quite,' said Helen again. 'We do know one or two things. Whoever sent this is aware that you – that we – are staying in Cambridge at the Devereux. Since Mr Mackenzie said you were to be discreet about our trip here, there can surely be only a handful of people who have that knowledge and so could have sent this strange missive.'

'A few in Scott, Lye & Mackenzie,' said Tom, thinking that William Evers knew, for one. 'And of course Mr and Mrs Lye at Ely. Though I can't imagine why any of them would want to send such . . . such a warning. But if the sender took the trouble to disguise his handwriting then that must mean he feared I would recognize it.'

'Or would recognize it in future,' said Helen. 'It might come from someone you've yet to meet.'

Tom's head whirled with the possibilities. Perhaps it was no more than a silly joke, he told himself, a prank. He went over to the window, parted the curtains and peered out. The football players had finished and it was nearly dark. Lights were springing up in the houses around the edge of Parker's Piece. A lamplighter was working his way down a row of lamps along the street stretching beyond the hotel. Where they were overhung by trees, the blooms of gas showed leaves fluttering down as the evening breeze strengthened. For no reason, Tom shivered slightly.

A few hundred yards away the man stood in Regent Street looking up at the facade of the Devereux Hotel. He did not know which floor or room was occupied by Mr and Mrs Thomas Ansell but it would be easy enough to find out, if that became necessary. He turned up the collar of his coat against the colder air. He envied the young couple the warmth and comfort of their hotel rooms and the undoubtedly pleasant supper they'd enjoy in the hotel dining room this evening. He envied Mr Tom Ansell his wife, the pretty Helen. No, not the pretty but the beautiful Helen.

For a moment there, during the afternoon, he thought Mrs Ansell might have spotted him in the street. She had stopped in her tracks and stared quite hard at the general area where he was walking, trying not to look too hard in *their* direction. But the man did not think that he had been identified. He wore his hat low and his chin huddled into his coat. Besides, he had the knack of passing unnoticed, of being unobtrusive.

Like the lamplighter, now he came to think of it. The man watched as the lighter, who was moving off further down the street, set his ladder against the crosspiece of the next lamp standard, then clambered up three or four rungs, turned the gas-cock and held his own light to the mantle until it flared up. All this was achieved with a couple of practised motions. Perhaps the lamplighter was so accustomed to his trade that he could perform it automatically. The people in the houses along the street would scarcely be aware of his presence. Any more than they were aware of the unobtrusive, watching man who now shrugged himself further into his coat and set off towards the darkness of Parker's Piece.

The watcher walked towards the suburbs on the edge of the city, the terraced houses occupied by clerks, skilled workers and the like. He stopped about halfway along an ill-lit street off a long main road and knocked on the front door. It was opened within moments. There was a light burning in the hall but it was turned so low that the caller could see nothing beyond a silhouette. 'Ah, it is you,' said the man inside.

He ushered the other in and gestured him towards the front room. There was a light in here as well but once again turned down so far that it seemed to emphasize the gloom rather than dispel it. The man indicated a chair to his visitor. He sat opposite and, by chance or design, in such a way that his face was mostly in shadow.

'How was your spying?' he said.

The visitor did not quite know what to make of this blunt approach. Was he a spy? He supposed he was.

'I was in the Devereux when they arrived, Mr and Mrs Ansell, that is.'

'Not seen by them, I hope.'

'I was situated behind a newspaper . . .'

'Good.'

'But close enough to overhear them.'

'Even better.'

'There was another person waiting for them. Some sort of legal fellow, a clerk, I believe. He introduced himself as a friend. Quite forward he was. Person by the name of Jubb.'

'Go on.'

'The main thing is this,' said the spy. 'I overheard their plans for tomorrow.'

'You have done well.'

'Mrs Ansell is to be escorted round the town by this Mr Jubb. She's to see the sights. While Mr Ansell, he said that he had to go to Ely on his firm's business.'

'Ah yes. So husband and wife will be separated for a time?'

'It appears so.'

'You have done remarkably well. And you left them . . . ?'

'Tucked up snug in the Devereux. I don't suppose they'll stir again on a chill evening like this. I would not stir. Not if I was married to a woman like Mrs Ansell.'

'You think she is attractive?'

'Most attractive. And refined too. Can I ask you one thing?'

'You can ask.'

'You don't mean them any harm, do you? Mr and Mrs Ansell?'

'No harm at all. Yes, it is chilly,' said the other man, changing the subject. 'I am forgetting my duties as a host. Would you like a nip of something to ward off the cold and damp of the fens?'

'Very well.'

'Let us have something together then. To toast your success as a spy.'

The Man in the Moon

As they'd arranged, Mr John Jubb called on Helen Ansell at the Devereux on the Saturday morning shortly after Tom departed for Ely. The lawyers' clerk was full of good humour and information. He enjoyed being in Helen's company, and she had quite taken to him and was prepared to be shown around the town, although she had to slow her usual walking style to fit with his pace. The sun sparkled on stone facades and brick walls which had been dull and blockish in yesterday's gloom. With pride, Mr Jubb pointed out Peterhouse as the oldest of the colleges, and the Great Gate of Trinity with its alcoved statue of Henry the Eighth, and the covered bridge over the river Cam which had been much admired by the present Queen – who called it pretty and picturesque – and which was modelled on that one in Venice whose name for a moment escaped him . . .

'I believe it's called the Bridge of Sighs,' said Helen.

'That's it, Mrs Ansell. It was on the tip of my tongue.'

And by the time these and a few other sights had been admired, Mr Jubb was running out of energy and puff and suggested they stop at a coffee house. He took Helen to a place which was most suitable for ladies, he said, neither flyblown nor frequented by the lower type of person. Above all, it sold a refreshing mocha, untainted by chicory or horsebeans. The inside of Morris's was almost as neat and bright as its gold-lettered and freshly painted exterior. The attendants greeted Mr Jubb like an old friend as well as a good customer and showed him and Helen to a stall near the back from where they had a clear view of the room. Judging by the number of people there, this was a popular place to chat or to read newspapers and periodicals.

Once they had been served their coffee, Mr Jubb relaxed and tucked his small legs beneath the seat while Helen took out her notebook and pencil to scribble down a couple of points.

'For your article, Miss Ansell?'

'I find that I forget things if I don't note them down. But two or three words are usually enough to bring it back.'

'Like a painter's sketches, I believe. I am full of admiration that you are so professional. Quite the modern lady.'

It had occurred to Helen that anyone seeing them together might wonder at their connection. Father and daughter? The difference in years was about right. Oddly, Helen didn't object to the idea, perhaps because her actual father had been a very distinct figure from John Jubb. Where the clerk was rotund, chatty and cheerful, Alfred Scott had been tall, silent and dour. And it turned out, as Mr Jubb chattered on, that the clerk was a widower but did indeed have a married daughter of about Helen's age. She lived all the way up in Yorkshire so Mr Jubb did not see her or his son-in-law or his grandchildren very often.

While Helen was half listening to all of this and enjoying her coffee and attempting to marshal her early impressions of Cambridge, her eye was caught by a well-dressed individual slouching in a chair close by. He was a pale-faced young man wearing spectacles whose lenses were tinged a light violet. He had long, lank hair which he tugged abstractedly with the fingers of one hand. With the other he was turning the pages of a magazine, reading it with furrowed attention. Parts of it he evidently didn't like, because from time to time he tutted or shook his head slightly.

Whenever Helen saw anyone reading a book or a periodical in public, she was curious to know what it was. In this case, it was easy to find out since the man was balancing the magazine on his cocked knee so that the cover was clearly visible. It featured a simple line drawing – slightly oriental in style – of a bare-branched tree with a sliver of moon rising beyond it. And the title *The New Moon*, also rendered with a faint Eastern flourish, appeared in large capitals to one side of the tree.

For a moment Helen was undecided what to do, then she startled Mr Jubb by suddenly getting up from the table and approaching the young man. Jubb overheard and saw the following.

'If you'll excuse me for interrupting you . . .'

The young man stopped tugging at his hair and looked up, peering through his violet spectacles.

'Of course.'

Helen hesitated before saying, 'I couldn't help noticing the title of the magazine that you are reading. *The New Moon*, isn't it? I wondered where I might obtain a copy.'

'I fear any such quest will be fruitless, madam. This is a printer's proof. You are welcome to have a look at it, but I suspect that you will find the contents are somewhat repetitive in style.'

He rose to his feet and held out the magazine. Helen took it and examined the moon-and-tree cover before leafing through a few pages, enough to glimpse a mixture of prose and poetry. She gave it back to the bespectacled man. By now, he had taken Helen in, taken in her attractiveness, her inexplicable interest in *The New Moon*. She didn't have to ask anything further, he was only too happy to explain.

'As I say, this is a proof of the magazine. Probably not as it will actually appear when it is offered in the booksellers and the station stalls but a simulacrum of how it might look. The thing is done only to give a general impression to the sponsors and subscribers.'

'And called *The New Moon* because it is to be a monthly?'

'Yes. Not too obvious a title, I hope. I do abhor the obvious.'

'Obvious or not, I like the name,' said Helen.

'I ought to add that the items within these covers are similar because most of them were written by the same person.'

'But you did not altogether approve of what you were reading? I saw you shaking your head occasionally.'

'It is one of my maxims that the truly creative man is his own best critic.'

'And I am looking at such a creator-critic?' said Helen.

'Arthur Arnett at your service,' said the man, extending his hand. 'A creator, a critic of the self as one should be – and editor of *The New Moon*. I'm the man in the moon, you might say.'

Helen had already realized who he was. Even so, she was a little flustered by Arnett's announcement although she managed to conceal it, more or less, by laughing at his witticism. She glanced back at John Jubb who was gazing at them both with a puzzled expression.

'We are already in correspondence, Mr Arnett. We've exchanged letters. I am Mrs Ansell, Helen Ansell. I had the advantage of you once I saw the name of your magazine. You have been kind enough to commission a piece of writing from me.'

'Yes, yes. A portrait of Cambridge and Ely. Mrs Ansell! Of course! Well, this is a most extraordinary thing, such a coincidence, such a coincidence. And now, Mrs Ansell, you are come here in search of your material together with this gentleman . . . with your husband perhaps?'

'That's right. I am in search of material. But no, this is not my husband. He is a . . . a friend of my husband's. Mr Jubb lives in Cambridge. He is sacrificing his free time to show me the city.'

'I am sure he regards it as a pleasure and no sacrifice.'

By this time John Jubb had joined them. Arthur Arnett put out his hand once more and introduced himself before saying, 'You are fortunate to be a denizen of this beautiful city, sir, and to be in the company of a lady whom even the most envious could only regard as its match in fairness.'

'I think so,' said the clerk after a slight hesitation.

'We should always strive to surround ourselves with beautiful things. Only in the contemplation of the beautiful is the soul fed and the spirit nourished.'

'No doubt,' said John Jubb.

'I shall not detain you any longer,' said Arthur Arnett. 'For all of us *tempus fugit* – time flies, you know – although for some it flutters on vanes of gold while for others it sinks down with wings that are shot through with lead. Enjoy your tour of the town. And, Mrs Ansell, I am looking forward, greatly looking forward, to receiving your piece for *The New Moon*.'

They watched as he retrieved his hat and stick and made his way to the door of the coffee house. John Jubb turned to Helen. For once Mr Jubb did not say anything though his eyebrows rose a fraction in query. Helen did not know what to make of Mr Arthur Arnett either. The gentleman's flowery style was appropriate for someone who styled himself a creator, critic and editor, she supposed. At the same time there was something a little ridiculous about his talk of the fluttering wings of time and the rest of it. Only later did it occur to her to wonder what he was doing in Cambridge.

When Helen was setting off to look round the sights of Cambridge, Tom Ansell was taking the train to Ely to make his visit to Ernest Lye at Phoenix House, in quest of the missing will. He wondered whether Mackenzie and Ashley had yet started their search of Alexander's den in the Regent's Park house. Tom had no expectation he'd find the missing testament. In fact he doubted that the senior partner had ever drawn one up. He remembered the flash of mischief in old Lye's blue eyes. Also, there was something satisfyingly perverse – as well as almost inevitable – about a legal man who advised others to keep their affairs in order while neglecting his own.

The railway journey from Cambridge to Ely did not take long. Tom looked out of the smeared compartment window at the sun glittering on the black earth and on pools and channels of water. He still felt a little uneasy after the events of yesterday, the near-accident at Liverpool Street Station and then the strange note delivered to the hotel and bearing a torn-out quotation from *Macbeth*.

Even though it was a Saturday morning the platforms at Ely were busy since the station was a junction for destinations to the north and south as well as for travellers on their way from Manchester and Birmingham to the east-coast packet-boats. Tom squeezed his way through the crowded ticket-hall and, as instructed, went to wait under the colonnaded entrance. Ernest Lye had said he would be met and now a two-wheeled dog cart drew up. A lad with wide-set eyes beneath a cap said, 'Mr Ansell, is it?'

Tom clambered aboard and sat with his back to the driver,

who swung the carriage out of the area in front of the station. They trotted through some streets of well set-up houses, then more slowly up a gently slanting road to reach the older part of Ely. They went by a church with a short spire and after that the cathedral itself. The young driver said something and gestured with his whip. Tom assumed he was pointing out the facade and the great west tower. But, no, he was indicating an object on the green which fronted the cathedral. As they passed, Tom glimpsed a cannon mounted on the grass and pointing in their direction.

'That's from the Rooshian War,' said the lad over his shoulder. 'From the Crimea. It's an enemy gun. We won it from the Rooshians, and the Queen, she gave it to us.'

Tom paid more attention. His father had died on the way to the Crimea. He craned his head forward but by now his view of the cannon was obscured by houses. The cathedral could not be obscured, however. The only way to ignore it would be to look in another direction altogether. Otherwise, whether seen out of the corner of the eye or full-face, the great west tower and the central many-sided tower were dominant, an effect emphasized by the level landscape that began to unroll as they left the outskirts of the town.

They were riding along a slightly elevated way between fields, some of peaty, broken earth, some with a dark-leafed crop that Tom couldn't identify. The town of Ely slowly shrunk to his backward-facing gaze until only the bulk of the cathedral remained. Lines of willows and poplars fringed the fields, interrupted by the occasional hut or meagre dwelling. There was the sense of water everywhere, either dazzlingly visible in the pools and channels beneath the slanting sun, or lying very close underground, or waiting just beyond a horizon that lay straight as a ruler.

Tom had never seen anywhere so open and clear. Turning forward, he could see no sign of their destination, yet Phoenix House was supposed to be only a couple of miles from Ely. He wondered what it would be like to live in the remotest places in these fenlands, with the sky for company. It was exposed on top of the dog cart and he was glad to be swathed in coat, muffler and hat. By contrast, the lad who was driving wore no more than a shirt and tattered waistcoat and breeches. The driver muttered some words that Tom didn't catch. He asked him to repeat what he said.

'I seen him the other night.'

'Seen who?'

Tom had to raise his voice above the rumble of the cart and the thump of the horse's hooves. The driver shook his head. 'Don't ask me. But I seen him in all his pomp and finery.'

Tom might have dismissed the words as meaningless or, rather, as having meaning for the boy but of no significance to him. Then the boy took his gaze off the track and looked round so that his face was screwed in towards his passenger's. He grasped Tom's arm where it lay on the top of the seat. There was a strange, fixed look in his eyes, which were very dark brown, almost the colour of the peaty soil that lay all about. His mouth was set in a grimace.

'I did see him,' he repeated. 'In all his pomp and finery. In the graveyard. And the others too.'

Whether the cause was the fixity of the lad's expression or the mention of a graveyard, or whether it was merely the cold draught that blew across the exposed fields, Tom felt a sudden chill. The hairs on the back of his neck stood up. Then he noticed that the horse was beginning to veer on the already narrow road and indicated with a nod of the head that the boy should see to his job. The driver faced forward again and steadied the horse, leaving Tom to wonder what he had been talking about.

The dog cart changed direction and set off along a new route. Tom was aware of a slight uphill slant in their progress. He looked round and was surprised to see that they were approaching a village. Or at least a place large enough to boast a church with a small tower, a neighbouring house that was most likely the parsonage, several scatters of cottages, a few clumps of trees, and a house that was larger than a dozen of the other dwellings put together. This must be Upper Fen. The sudden appearance of the hamlet out of nowhere was like a conjuring trick on the part of the landscape.

'That's Phoenix,' said the driver, pointing to the big house.

Tom had guessed already that it was where the Lyes lived and, just possibly, the place where Alexander's missing testament might be found.

On the edge of the village, they passed a single-storey cottage with a shed clinging to one end. The door to the shed was open and a man was kneeling in a patch of sunlight and chipping away at a block that looked like a headstone. He was using a mallet and graver. He looked up as the dog cart rolled by and exchanged a nod with the boy in the carriage.

A couple of hundred yards further on the boy had to slow and swerve to avoid a man walking towards them. At first, Tom thought it might be Ernest Lye since the walker was dressed like a gentleman, wearing a hat and carrying a stick. But closer to, Tom realized that he was bigger than Alexander's brother, and most likely younger too. He could not see the man's face because it was obscured by his top hat and because, after an initial glance at the dog cart from a distance, the walker kept his head down, trusting in the driver to keep out of his path. Tom wondered where he was going. There didn't appear to be anything between here and Ely, and it was quite a long walk to Ely.

The Vision

The man kneeling in the doorway of the shed by the cottage was Gabriel Parr. He was the sexton for the church. But he was also a mason and, among other skilled tasks in the village, he carved any headstones that were required in the churchyard. That was what he was doing as Tom Ansell passed him in the dog cart, putting the finishing touches to the headstone commemorating a woman called Ada Baxter who'd died and been buried earlier in the autumn. At present, her grave was marked with a wooden cross but that would be replaced on the following day, a Sunday, with Parr's handiwork.

Gabriel Parr was a careful worker, as one has to be when using the graver and mallet to inscribe words on a piece of sandstone. He took pride in getting the details of the deceased absolutely right, consulting the parson and sometimes Mr Lye at the big house if the surviving members of a family had a difference of opinion about, say, the age of the departed or the exact spelling of the surname – assuming they had a notion of how to spell it in the first place.

When Gabriel had the agreed version, he wrote it all down and kept the paper beside him as he carried out the work. Any verse or other inscription on the stone had to be approved by the parson, Mr Eames, and was usually written down by him as well. In addition to words, Gabriel Parr also carved images, such as laurels or the heads of cherubs, at the top of the headstone. Now he was completing work on the fluke of an anchor, chipping out a tiny triangle of stone, when a shadow fell across him. He looked up in annoyance.

A man was standing just beyond the doorway. Because he was between Gabriel and the sun, the stonemason could not see the other clearly. Besides, he was wearing a tall top hat which cast his face into shadow. From his clothes and the stick he carried, the mason knew the man was not a vagrant or labourer but, even so, he said, 'You're in my light. I'd be obliged if you shifted yourself.'

The man moved a foot or so, enough to show a willingness to comply but not enough to allow Parr to finish his work. Anyway, the mason's concentration was broken. He sighed, put down his tools, clasped his hands on his dusty knees and waited for the other to explain himself.

The standing man sensed his irritation for he moved slightly further to the side and said, 'I hope a man is allowed to admire the work of an artist.'

Gabriel was not won over. He was a solid individual, with a broad, seamed forehead above bushy eyebrows, and if he knew anything it was that he was not an artist. He said nothing in reply.

'What does the anchor stand for?' said the man, bending forward to peer at the image in relief at the top of the headstone and tilting the end of his stick towards it. Gabriel had a glimpse of a narrow jaw.

'It stands for hope and steadfastness,' said the mason.

'These are the qualities we need to see us through the storms and rough seas of this life,' said the man.

'Amen to that.'

'And who was Ada Baxter?'

'One of the souls who live hereabouts and now lives here no more.'

'You have lived and worked here a long time yourself?'

'Before I answer that — if I answer that — perhaps you would like to tell me your business,' said the mason. 'Do you wish me to carve you a headstone?'

'Heavens, no. Not for a long time, I hope! My business is purely amateur. You see, I am an occasional representative for the Society for the Protection of Rural Treasures, and my particular interest is in churches. I am sorry for wasting your time.'

The stranger turned as if to walk away and Gabriel suddenly felt that he had been too abrupt, not so much because the gentleman was a representative of some learned society but because he was being 'civil enough and so deserved a reply. Where was the harm in answering?

'I was born here,' he said, 'I've lived here all my life and I shall die here. And when I go, I'll not be going far for I shall be laid to rest over there. I am sexton to the church.'

He gestured with his mallet in the direction of the tower of St Ethelwine's.

'That must be a comfort, to know your end,' said the man. 'It's poor ground though, isn't it?'

'What do you mean?'

'Only that it is so confoundedly waterlogged in these parts that an interment must be like a burial at sea.'

'Depends where you are,' said Gabriel, warming to the subject. 'In this place we are on a kind of island, and it is higher still where the church and parsonage and Phoenix House are. It's true the ground is inclined to damp but there are dry spots if you know where to look.'

'Inclined to damp, I like that,' said the man and then he said, more as if giving information than asking questions, 'It is an old church, St Ethelwine's, with some traces of the Saxon in its construction, I believe. And possessing a crypt.'

'Not used these many years,' said Gabriel. 'We prefer to be buried under the sky in the churchyard.'

'I notice the churchyard is on the north side,' said the man. 'That's unusual, isn't it? Felons and bad characters are buried on the north side.'

'It's on account of the nature of the ground. Not on account of bad characters. We don't have many of those around here.'

'So there is plenty of room in your northerly churchyard, I hope?'

Gabriel couldn't tell if the man was being humorous. In fact, there was a space set aside for him in the churchyard, where he would be laid in a brick-lined grave next to his wife when the time came. But he did not say any of this, since it was nothing at all to do with the man. The mason picked up his graving tool as a signal that he wished to carry on, and the stranger took the hint. With a 'Good day to you then', he turned about and walked back up the road towards the village. Gabriel watched him for a moment, wondering what his business really was. He did not believe the remark about idle curiosity.

He resumed his work, putting the finishing stroke to the fluke of the anchor. When it was done, he stood up and stretched and examined the headstone in memory of Ada Baxter. Everything was as it should be, the rows of words properly aligned, the lettering clear and crisp, the impression of the anchor simple and straightforward.

For the second time in half an hour, a shadow fell across the headstone. Gabriel looked up and smiled slightly to see who was standing in the doorway. It was the boy who had been driving Tom in the dog cart. He was called Davey and he was Gabriel's son. The stonemason told him that he had returned at the right moment since he wanted help with transporting the newly carved headstone to the church. First, Gabriel wrapped it in some sacking and then he rolled a small, two-wheeled handcart from the rear of the shed. Together, father and son hoisted the stone on to the bed of the cart and, with Gabriel steadying it and Davey pushing, they steered their way towards the stubby tower of the church that stood near Phoenix House.

'Who was that with you in the dog cart?' said Gabriel.

'Gent called Ansell.'

'Going to the big house?'

Davey grunted. A reply was hardly necessary since, apart from the parsonage, there was nowhere else that a visitor to the village was likely to go, or at least not the kind of visitor who was picked up in a dog cart at Ely Station. Gabriel did not ask whether Davey had glimpsed the top-hatted individual who had recently interrupted his work. Even if Davey had, it was unlikely the lad would have been able to tell him anything beyond the little which he had realized for himself. Father and son did not talk much. There was not much to say. Davey was anyway a rather quiet, dreamy individual, who seemed to prefer silence and his own company to anyone else's. He helped his father and did occasional jobs or errands for the big house, like collecting Tom today in the dog cart.

They reached the churchyard of St Ethelwine's, which was surrounded by a low drystone wall. The parsonage lay on slightly higher ground to the north of the church and behind a high beech hedge. Beyond the churchyard to the east was visible the top of Phoenix House, surrounded by trees.

Father and son wheeled the cart through the lychgate. They stopped to get their breath back. Gabriel indicated that Davey should remain with the cart. He walked across the tussocky, uneven ground, skirting mounds and gravestones. He noted the spot where Ada Baxter's headstone would be set on the following day. What Gabriel was going to look at was not Mrs Baxter's final resting place but his own. The conversation with the stranger had reminded him that it was several weeks since he had looked at the grave belonging to his wife, Martha. Now he halted before her headstone. It gave him a jolt to see that there had been a recent visitor. A jam jar nestled at the foot of the stone, crammed with a few wilted ox-eye daisies. Only one person would have left this simple tribute. Gabriel glanced back towards the lychgate where his son waited with the handcart. But the boy had his back to him, perhaps deliberately.

The mason noticed too that some weeds growing at the base of the headstone had been uprooted and placed in a neat pile a few feet away. Again, it could only have been Davey. Gabriel read the inscription, which he himself had carved. His own name was there too, with his date of birth and a space for the date of his death. That would have to be carved on the spot. Carved by Davey, he supposed. So far the lad had not shown any great aptitude with the mallet and graver but he should be capable of incising a few figures. Gabriel's realization that his son had been visiting the grave was somehow encouraging in this respect.

He turned back towards the lychgate. He said nothing to Davey about what he had seen by Martha's grave, and the boy averted his gaze from his father. They trundled the handcart up to the church itself. Gabriel stopped by the porch and, with his son's help, deposited the headstone, still wrapped in cloth, against the porch wall. He opened the inner door and walked inside. The interior was simple to the point of bareness. Large windows, mostly plain, let in quantities of light and sky, as well as rain in places. There was some panelling in the chancel but otherwise the walls of the church were unadorned plaster, streaked with green. It was damp and the cold rose up from the flagged floor.

Gabriel reminded himself to light the brazier for tomorrow's service. It would be placed in the aisle near the back and the villagers would, as if by chance, choose the nearest pews. Parson Eames did not altogether approve of the brazier, believing that a brisk coldness encouraged more attention to his sermons. But Gabriel told him that its use had been permitted, even encouraged, by his predecessor, and that it helped to keep at bay rheumatic aches and the fen ague. Eames was not a local man so he was not qualified to judge the accuracy of what the sexton told him.

Davey waited in the shelter of the north porch. He was used to waiting, and did not mind being left to himself. He glanced at Ada Baxter's headstone, swaddled in sacking, leaning against the wall. This made him think of his mother's grave and the visit he had paid to her a few days earlier.

It was not the first time that Davey had left some small tribute at his mother's burial place. His memories of his mother – she had died three years before – varied. Sometimes they were as sharp as if she had just finished speaking to him; at others he struggled to recall the features of her face. Until now, his offerings had an accidental air, as it were. A little mound of pebbles or a swag of blossom left at the foot of the stone, or a trail of ivy draped over the top of it, things which might have fetched up there by chance. But the jam jar with its ox-eye daisies was a more deliberate gesture. Davey didn't know what had prompted him to do it, any more than he knew the meaning of what had occurred just after he placed the flowers next to the headstone and while he was standing there in contemplation.

It was almost dark. The weather had been fine and the sky to the west still glimmered with some streaks of day. In the distance an owl hooted and, with the evening breeze strengthening, the weathervane cockerel on a corner of the tower creaked as it shifted round. Davey had picked this unoccupied moment to visit the graveyard, expecting not to see or to be seen by anyone. He ran his fingers over his mother's name, MARTHA PARR, and her dates, 1825-71. It was his mother who had taught him to read and write and how to do his sums. He had grown used to seeing his father's name alongside hers, and the oddity of it – that his father was still alive – did not trouble him.

He stood up. A flickering movement at the corner of his eye caught his attention. He turned towards it. Directly in front of him to the east was the drystone wall which marked the end of the graveyard. Beyond it lay the grounds of Phoenix House, whose boundary was delineated by trees and shrubs. In the fading light these were no more than blocks and irregular shapes.

Over the wall there came a scrambling figure, the outline of a short man. As he topped the wall, he dislodged several fragments of stone. Ignoring whatever damage he'd done, he tumbled on to the grass, started to his feet and set off in Davey's direction, clasping one hand to his hat to keep it in place. Yet, while Davey watched, too astounded to move himself, he detected something odd about the man's motion. It was more of a glide than a run. At several points where there were obstacles in his way – gravestones, low earthen mounds, simple crosses – the moving man did not appear to weave his way around them or to stumble but simply to ignore them.

The fear that had seized the boy slackened for long enough to make him aware of his exposed position. He ducked down behind his mother's headstone. And at that instant the man drew level with him, paused in his flight and looked back as if he expected to see pursuers. In the uncertain light, Davey had the impression of a bearded fellow, dressed in clothes and a hat, which were quite unfamiliar in their style. Not only unfamiliar clothes but grand ones, rich garments. The very 'finery' which he'd mention to Tom Ansell several days later. The fleeing man's mouth was open and he was breathing hard, yet Davey, huddled in the shadow of his mother's headstone, could hear not a sound.

The man looked to one side and down at the point where Davey was. He stared at the boy for several seconds, apparently without being aware of him. Perhaps his eyes were not yet accustomed to the gloom. Then he swung out his arm as if about to use Martha Parr's gravestone for support. Davey huddled even further into himself. He sensed, rather than saw, the man's hand move rapidly above him, move through the area occupied by the headstone. He noticed that the man's hand was bandaged. There was no sound of a hand striking stone, no cry of pain. Nothing.

Davey looked up. The man was looking intently in the direction from which he had just come. The boy peered round the edge of the grave. Now a whole pack of men was tumbling over the wall, knocking down more stones and as heedless and excited as dogs in a hunt. The spectacle was frightening, but almost more frightening was the absence of noise from the pursuit. It was as if he had suddenly been struck with absolute deafness.

Yet Davey was not deaf. He heard again the cry of the owl in the distance, not once but twice. It was as if he were able to hear some sounds but not others. By now, the man was moving away from Davey's hiding place and heading towards the lychgate and the path which led from the churchyard. He never reached it. Two or three other shapes suddenly appeared on that side, so that his escape route was blocked. In the indistinct light Davey saw a scuffle – saw, not heard – before the runaway broke from the milling group and turned back in Davey's direction. His hat had been knocked off. By this stage the other band, the ones who'd scrambled over the wall, had rushed silently past the headstone so that they too arrived to form a ragged circle around the man.

One of the pursuers, more hot-headed or violent than the others, was carrying some kind of stave and he struck at the runaway behind the knees. The man buckled and fell forward, and the other first thrashed him with the stave, then treated it like a spear, making repeated jabbing motions at the figure on the ground. There must have been noises to accompany this: the thud of the blows, the cries and gasps of breath. But no sound was audible to Davey.

The man who'd been stabbing at the other on the ground moved back as if to admire his handiwork. Davey had a clear sight of his profile, of long straight hair beneath his hat. The

other pursuers started to close in, but the fugitive was not so
badly injured that he did not make one final effort to get away.
Like huntsmen watching a fatally wounded stag, the ring of men
allowed him to stumble to his feet and stagger towards the church,
where he seemed to become absorbed by the shadows of the
porch. Then, Davey supposed, the man entered the church itself.
The pursuers stood for a while, undecided what to do next,
before the one with the stave made a sweeping motion with his
free arm. They all clustered towards the porch and then shoved
their way inside.

Davey looked back towards the wall between the churchyard
and the big house. He saw two more figures standing there, not
men, not women either, he thought. They looked almost like
children. They stared, unmoving as statues, at the scene which
had just unfolded. Perhaps they shared Davey's horror. He turned
his attention back towards the church. If the wounded man
believed that holy ground would provide sanctuary then he was
wrong. For many minutes Davey stood watching the church porch
and waiting for someone to emerge, for something to happen.
He listened for blows, for cries and screams from within, but no
sounds came apart from the creaking of the cockerel on top of
the church tower and the sighing of the wind.

Curiously, Davey was not so afraid now, or not so very afraid.
He thought he knew what was happening even if he could not
begin to understand it. Then he heard the sound of the church
door opening. A figure walked out from the shelter of the porch.
It was holding a lantern. Davey's heart beat faster and his mouth
was dry. The figure traced a path across the churchyard towards
the beech hedge which screened it from the parsonage. A circle
of light flowed over the straggling grass and the stone monuments.
Davey heard the sound of a man humming fragments of a hymn
tune. He recognized the source of the humming. It was Parson
Eames. He was making his way home. There was the sound of
another gate opening and closing, the one set in the hedge which
gave on to the parson's garden.

Davey stood and thought. The parson must have been inside
the church all the while that he was gazing at his mother's headstone. He must have been inside the church even while the injured
man took sanctuary and his pursuers burst in and did whatever

it was they did in that sanctified place. Yet Mr Eames showed no sign of having witnessed anything terrible. The parson's humming was good-humoured – especially good-humoured considering it was Mr Eames – and he was not running in fear. He had seen nothing because nothing had happened while he was inside the church.

Everything that Davey Parr saw of the pursuit had occurred not as darkness fell during an October evening in 1874. It had taken place here in the graveyard of St Ethelwine's and inside the church during another time, another century, and it involved people that Davey did not know and performing actions whose purpose he could only guess at. Who was the fleeing man? Who were his pursuers? Did they want him, or did they want to take something from him?

Similar things to this had happened to Davey before. Once he had seen a troop of men moving in line and on foot towards the village, all wearing fighting gear and carrying old swords and spears like those in an illustration to a children's history book which his mother used in his reading lessons. The men moved with the same queer gait that Davey observed in the fleeing individual in the churchyard, and they moved in complete silence. On that occasion, too, Davey's fear had swiftly been replaced by a confused curiosity. He was not in danger, his village was not in danger. Indeed the armed men passed by the cottages as if they didn't exist.

He realized that whatever he was witnessing was not happening now, in the present, but happening in the past, happening then. Though when the *then* was he had no idea. The strangely fluid motion of the armed men was explained by tiny alterations in the level of the land. They were walking on the ground as it had been many years earlier, slightly lower, slightly higher. In the same way, the fleeing man had been running through the grave-yard when it wasn't so full of graves and memorials and so his path was clearer.

At this moment, while Davey waited in the church porch for his father to come out, he puzzled again over the running man with the hat and over his pursuers. He had not mentioned the vision in the churchyard to his father. He had not mentioned it to anyone apart from the gentleman he had been instructed to collect from Ely Station. He did not know why he'd told Mr Ansell. Perhaps it was because he had never seen him before and did not expect to see him again.

He was startled by the creak of the church door. It was his father. Gabriel Parr noticed the way Davey's head jerked round, he observed the alarmed expression on his white face.

'Are you all right, Davey? You look as though you've . . .'

He'd been about to say 'seen a ghost', but the thought of how the lad had been secretly visiting his mother's grave made him pause and his voice tailed off.

They left the churchyard, Davey pushing the cart. Gabriel wondered at his son's startled and distracted manner. Perhaps the boy really was seeing ghosts.

The Perpetual Curate

From the upper floor of the parsonage, the Reverend George Eames watched the Parrs, the son wheeling the handcart through the churchyard and out of the lychgate. He was not in a good mood. There were two immediate reasons why he was not in a good mood, both of them to do with the parsonage and its occupants. And there was another deeper reason why he was out of sorts, but he pushed that to the back of his mind and concentrated on domestic discontents.

His housekeeper had insisted that he inspect some water damage to two of the upstairs rooms, damage caused by a leaking roof. His inclination might have been to shut up the dank, mouldy chambers and leave them to their own devices, since they were never used, but Mrs Walters was insistent not only that Mr Eames should examine them for himself but that something must be done. This request – no, this peremptory demand – from the housekeeper had come straight after an unpleasant scene involving Hannah, the maid-of-all-work and the only other servant employed in the parsonage.

Earlier that morning, Eames had entered his study to see the ignorant girl standing near the fire, which she had just lit, and, idly and carelessly, feeding sheets of paper on to the tiny flames. It took him an instant to realize that the sheets were his sermon notes. In a moment of laxness the previous evening he had taken the notes from his desk across to the armchair near the fire so that he might ponder the outline of what he was going to say on Sunday, ponder it in slightly more comfort. He had neglected to return the notes to the desktop, placing them on the floor instead, and now here was Hannah distributing them to the flames.

'What are you doing, girl!'

He spoke loudly and the girl froze, in fear or confusion. A single further sheet fluttered from her grasp and settled into the back of the fireplace as if that was its inevitable destination. Eames strode across the room and snatched the remaining pieces of paper from her grasp.

'What do you think you are doing?' he said, though less fiercely this time.

'I . . . I'm sorry, sir. I saw these papers on the floor and I thought . . . thought . . .'

'Thought what?'

'That you didn't need them no more, sir. From the way they was left, all scattered and scrawled . . .'

George Eames looked at the topmost sheet in his hand. It was true; it did have an unfinished look, with words crossed out and others inserted as afterthoughts. But that did not excuse the girl. How was she capable of judging what he had written? Who was she to judge it, scrawlings or no? She could scarcely read at all. Her signature was as rudimentary as a child's.

Hannah realized what she had done wrong. She made a dart at the fire and tried to retrieve the sheet which was lodged, blackening but still intact, at the back of the grate. Even as her fingers closed about it, the paper burst into flame and the maid let go and jumped back with a shriek. She held up her hand, which was all smutted with smoky dust.

'Leave it,' said George Eames. 'It's too late.'

'I . . . I am . . .'

Hannah was not an attractive girl. She was quite small and her face had a red and raw look to it, emphasized by her black eyebrows. Now, with her smudged hand held up like an admission of guilt, she seemed close to tears. But Eames observed – couldn't help observing – the momentary curve of her back and the swell of her hips as she bent to get the bit of paper from the fireplace. There was a grace to the movement which he was unable to deny. He had often noted these and other aspects of her figure even though they were masked by the drab, shapeless maid's outfit she wore. And now, as she stood facing him with her head down, a curl of black hair protruded from beneath her cap. Something about the insolent way the hair curled in on itself as well as its sheer blackness caused him to feel uncomfortable and to look away. This did not matter since she was not looking at him either.

Mrs Walters came into the room. Perhaps she was alerted by Eames' shout. Without waiting to find out exactly what was wrong, she shoo-ed Hannah out of the study, tutting and fussing. Then, as if to distract the parson from the foolish behaviour of the maid by bringing up another problem, she started speaking about the rooms on the upper floor, the dilapidated roof, the water which was ruining parts of the house. To quieten her, Eames promised that he'd come up and look. In a moment. First he had things to attend to.

When Mrs Walters had shut the door, he sank into the armchair by the fire which, by now, was burning cheerfully. He flicked through the sheets of paper that he had saved from the flames. He sighed and replaced the notes on the floor. He struggled to hold back a wave of gloom that threatened to overwhelm him.

George Eames laboured over his sermons, organizing his material so that he proceeded from points of lesser significance to those of greater importance, but constantly keeping before the minds of the congregation the text about which he was preaching. He strove always to find the right phrase, the exact word, which would strengthen his – or rather, God's – argument. He wished to be both forceful and fluent, and believed that he sometimes came close to achieving that end. But Eames could not deceive himself that his congregation of tenant-farmers and field-labourers attended to his sermons with a tenth, or even a twentieth, of the care and devotion which he gave to composing them. When he looked down from the pulpit, it was often to see dull, uncomprehending expressions or sidelong glances. The only people who showed a real understanding and appreciation were, as one would expect, Mr and Mrs Lye from Phoenix House.

Now, as he stood up from the armchair, gathered the sermon notes and deposited them on his desk, he reflected that Hannah's indifference and ignorance were only too typical of the people of this place. The image of Hannah standing in front of him, dejected, the stray curl escaping from her cap, led him to the thought that was never far from his mind. What he needed to help him in his daily work was not a more capable maid or a less peremptory housekeeper. What he needed was a wife, a helpmeet.

He needed someone who would attend to the dozen little tasks that had to be attended to around the parsonage. Someone in whose presence he could rehearse his sermons, someone whose love and care for him would ease his pilgrimage through this troubled world. Someone – although he did not dwell for too long on this thought – to lie beside him at night and bring him comfort, spiritual, mental, and physical. Even someone who might bear his children.

Yes, a wife was definitely needed, as a wife was needed for every man who was well embarked on his fourth decade. But what sort of woman would be attracted to such a place as this? What did it have to offer? What did he, George Eames, the perpetual curate of St Ethelwine's in Upper Fen, have to give? Eames was not the son of a wealthy father. He did not come from a particularly prosperous family. He might, in time, obtain a better parish, true, but who knew when that time would come?

He walked upstairs, to check on the damp rooms which so exercised Mrs Walters. He heard her out. He nodded, in weary agreement that something had to be done. On the way downstairs he watched the Parrs leaving the churchyard. Eames decided to speak to Gabriel Parr about the leaking roof.

But this was not the only thought in the head of the Reverend George Eames. Nor was he solely occupied with ideas of a wife. There were other things on his mind. There was murder, for example.

Summer, 1645

'You can come out now. They've gone.'

There was no response and for a moment Anne thought she must be mistaken. Yet she was convinced that there was someone lurking inside the little willow shelter, someone whose presence was connected to the soldiers and their searching.

'They have gone,' she said in a firmer voice. 'The soldiers have gone.'

A man emerged from the hide. He stood blinking in the sunlight. He was short, with a broad forehead, curled auburn hair and a pointed beard. There was a long diagonal gash on his cheek and blood on the cloak he wore. His right hand was wrapped about with a makeshift bandage. There was blood on that too.

'How did you know I was here?' he said.

'It is where I would come.'

'You are a daughter of the house?'

Anne nodded.

'Did they do much damage?'

'They broke down part of a wall, they uncovered a place where a priest might have hidden once.'

'It's not priests they're looking for.'

'They . . . spoke roughly,' said Anne. She did not mention her fear when Trafford was in her and Mary's room.

'You were lucky.'

'I know,' said Anne.

'What's your name?'

'Anne. What's yours?'

The man seemed taken aback by the question. Or at least he did not answer it straightaway.

'Loyer,' he said. Anne must have looked puzzled at this unusual name for he spelled it out. 'L-O-Y-E-R. Mister – no, Monsieur Loyer if you require a title.'

Anne repeated the name and the man said, 'Yes. You are a quick-witted girl and I expect you can work it out for yourself.'

'You are French?' said Anne, not understanding what he meant.

This time the man did not answer the question but gazed at the path which snaked away among the willows. Anne didn't think that he sounded French but then she had no clear idea of what a French person might sound like.

'I do not think you should stay here, Anne. You're bringing danger on yourself. The soldiers have gone, you say, but they may return and do more than break down a wall or indulge in some rough speaking. If they found you here in my company . . .'

'You are wounded.'

'It's nothing. Less than nothing, believe me.'

'Wounded in the battle?'

'How would you know about the battle . . .? I suppose you must have been told. No, young lady, these wounds, as you call them, were not sustained in battle. I was in the battle but I escaped unscathed from it. I got this little hurt from jumping out of a window in Market Harborough. The ground was further and harder than I expected.'

'Now you are a fugitive,' said Anne, recalling the steward James' choice of word.

'If you mean by that that I have run away in fear for my life, no, I have not. I am a fugitive on purpose. I am like the fox who shows himself every now and then to encourage the hounds.'

Again, Anne did not quite understand his meaning. Surely a fugitive, or a fox for that matter, would want to go undetected? For some reason, she felt apprehensive for this man. Beneath his cloak she had a glimpse of rich, brightly coloured fabrics. But there was a woebegone look to him. She thought of the hard-faced individuals whose boots had thudded through the manor that morning.

'What are you going to do?'

'I shall stay one more night, not in the house but here. Then I intend to make my way east, to the coast. To Lowestoft perhaps.'

'That is a distance to travel, on foot, without company,' said Anne, who had never visited the coast. *Was this Monsieur Loyer intending to return to France?*

'I have helpers.'

'Like my mother and father?'

'Do not ask. The less you know, the better for all of them. Forget everything except that I am on my way to – to Lowestoft – tomorrow. You may repeat that, if you please. But go now.'

'I can bring food and drink from the house.'

'No, no. Go now. In French if you prefer, va t'en!'

Anne walked up the slope away from the willow cabin. She was hardly conscious of her surroundings, the rustling trees, the high clouds, the house that had been invaded that morning. Instead she was thinking of the stranger and his manner. She was thinking of the name which he had supplied at her request, Loyer, Monsieur Loyer. It wasn't his real name, she was sure. Just as she was sure he was no Frenchman. She had an idea of who the mysterious, injured stranger might be, but the idea was so overwhelming, so disturbing that she tried to push it from her mind.

Mrs Lye

O nce he'd got down from the dog cart and the lad had driven it round to the stable area, Tom stood in the drive and gazed at the front of Phoenix House. It was well proportioned but the stonework, even on a bright day, was dull and solid. The central section was set back slightly between two wings. There was a handsome, pillared portico over the front door but the whole place had a dilapidated feel. The double gates through which they had just driven were rusted open.

The front door under the portico opened. Ernest Lye emerged. Something about his way of walking reminded Tom of his brother, Alexander, but, oddly, he did not seem as energetic as the older man. They shook hands.

'I saw you arrive from my library,' said Ernest, indicating a window in one of the wings. 'Did you talk to the boy on the way over?'

'He didn't seem willing to say much, one or two things only.'

'He is a good enough lad but he lives in his own head.'

'Thank you for inviting me to visit,' said Tom.

'You are very welcome at Phoenix House.'

'It's an odd name.'

'Not odd at all if you know your ancient lore, Mr Ansell. That's L-O-R-E, not your sort of law.'

'The phoenix was the only one of its kind, wasn't it? A

legendary Arabian bird that burned itself up, only to rise from its own ashes.'

'Just so. And with this house too. Parts of it were destroyed by fire. When it was rebuilt, it seemed natural to christen it Phoenix. The facade is early eighteenth century but the back quarters are much older.'

Ernest Lye ushered Tom through the door. A maid appeared and took Tom's coat and hat. They went across the large hall, which was crowded with paintings, and then to the right. Ernest showed Tom into a book-lined room, which smelled faintly of cigars. A fire was burning. There were sconces for candles as well as oil lamps about the room, but the light from outside was sufficiently strong for them to remain unlit. Tom, who was used to the gas-lit conveniences of town life, was suddenly reminded of the drawbacks of living in the country. He and Ernest Lye sat in armchairs on either side of the fire.

'Mrs Lye was wondering whether your wife would be accompanying you,' said Ernest. 'They were talking after my brother's funeral, and she was much taken with your lady. She invited Mrs Ansell to visit Phoenix.'

'I'm afraid Helen has a previous engagement in Cambridge.'

'Well, you must both of you come to Ely tomorrow,' said Ernest. 'To be our guests at the Lion Hotel. I hope you are free for that?'

'Thank you.'

'In the meantime, I will leave you to get on with your search for my brother's will. Your needle in the haystack, your wild goose chase.'

'You seem certain that I'll find nothing, Mr Lye.'

'I told David Mackenzie that some years ago my brother sent a cache of family papers up here. They have remained undisturbed since, but I took a cursory look when I knew you were coming, and have not so far turned up anything resembling a will or testament. Perhaps you'll have better luck.'

'Wouldn't Phoenix House be a natural place for your brother to store such a document, though? The family home?'

'Not at all, Mr Ansell. You see, this place was not a family home for Alexander. Phoenix House came to my father through his second wife, my mother. She was a Stilwell, an old family in these parts. And from my father and mother the house came into my hands.'

'I see,' said Tom, wondering why he hadn't known this before. And then wondering who could have told him anyway.

'I am aware that Alexander's own papers were kept – or not kept – in a somewhat disordered state,' said Ernest, revealing that he must have had at least a glimpse of the Regent's Park study. 'But every so often my brother was overcome by a fit of *organization*, as you might call it, and it was during one of those that he sent on this material to Phoenix House, since it related mostly to our father. There is not likely to be anything confidential there, however, and you are welcome to go through it.'

'I am grateful for that,' said Tom. 'We can't afford to leave any stone unturned.'

'Exactly what David Mackenzie said. I understand how embarrassing it is that poor Alexander seems to have died intestate. And all of us have a duty to the dead to do our best for them.'

Ernest explained that the papers were stored in one of the upper rooms of the house. He and Tom left the library. In the hall they met Mrs Lye. She was accompanied by a tall gentleman with a prominent jaw. Introductions were made, although of course she had already encountered Tom at her brother-in-law's funeral. The gentleman with her in the hall was Mr Charles Tomlinson, her cousin. Tom rather thought Tomlinson might have been the man he'd seen walking down the road earlier.

It was Tom's first opportunity to take a close look at Lydia. She was quite tall – she had an inch or more on her husband – and striking, with a full mouth and a decided gaze. Her voice was low but still feminine. There was a slight physical similarity between the cousins, Mrs Lye and Mr Tomlinson.

'How is your wife, Mr Ansell?' said Mrs Lye.

'She is well, thank you.'

'But she is not with you?'

'No, she's in Cambridge, she has business there,' said Tom for the second time that morning.

'Mr and Mrs Ansell have accepted an invitation to come to dinner tomorrow at the Lion,' said Ernest.

'I am glad of it,' said Lydia. 'I am most eager to renew my acquaintance with her.'

Tomlinson looked sharply at Lydia. As if to cover the moment, he said, 'I have just been on a stroll through your fascinating village, Ernest. I met a fellow down the other end, a craftsman, who was busy carving a headstone. Also the sexton in this place.'

'Gabriel Parr,' said Lydia.

'I was curious to learn something of the burial conditions around here, the soil and so on. You know it is an interest of mine.'

This remark was directed at Ernest, who nodded. He did not seem inclined to have much talk with Tomlinson.

'If you'll forgive us, my dear,' said Lydia to her husband after a pause. 'We have things to catch up on, you know.'

The cousins went off towards the morning room. Tom was wondering what sort of 'catching up' was required but Ernest told him, as they made their way up the stairs, that Tomlinson had very recently reappeared in his wife's life after many years of absence. He'd been voyaging in the Far East and other exotic places. No doubt they had family memories to share while Charles had traveller's tales to impart.

'Tomlinson is a capital fellow, full of . . . instructive and amusing anecdotes,' said Ernest Lye, pausing for breath as they reached the upper floor after climbing a narrower and steeper set of stairs. 'Yes, a capital fellow,' Ernest repeated. Something in the man's tone seemed to cast doubt on his own words.

They went down one passageway, then another at right angles. Tom peered down what was almost a tunnel, interrupted by a few doors, for which the only illumination was a gleam from a small window at the far end.

'These are the older parts of the house,' said Ernest. 'In those days it was on an east-west axis, now the front faces south.'

They stopped outside a door. Working more by touch than sight, Ernest produced a key, unlocked and opened the door.

'There.'

'There' was a lumber room. The light was brighter inside since, though the window was small, it gave directly on to the wide Cambridgeshire skies. Tom glimpsed a rocking horse and a doll's house, as well as some broken kitchen chairs, an armchair which was oozing stuffing, and other items of furniture. There were trunks and cases, and in the corners lay bundles of paper secured with string or ribbon. The fireplace was occupied with another pile of paper. The objects in the room were dusty and neglected but the space did not have the almost wilful disorder of Alexander's study.

'My mother's playthings,' said Ernest, gesturing towards the doll's house and the rocking horse. 'She grew up in this house.'

Ernest threaded his way between the items on the bare boards until he came to a studded leather trunk that sat on the floor near the window. He reached down and threw back the lid so that it clattered against the wall. Tom saw more piles of paper in the trunk.

'I suppose you might find what you're looking for in here, Mr Ansell. It contains the documents that brother Alexander sent on to me – oh, some eight or nine years ago now – material which is mostly to do with our father. His name was Roderick Lye. As I said, Alexander occasionally suffered from fits of organization and he obviously thought the contents of this trunk were more appropriately stored here than in his own house. It is not beyond the bounds of possibility, I imagine, that he included among these items a copy of his own will.'

Standing in the light from the window, Ernest Lye opened his palms in a gesture that expressed the futility of the idea.

'Thank you, Mr Lye. I know it seems unlikely but . . .'

'No stone unturned, eh? The light is good enough in here? I can have a lamp or two brought up.'

'I'll manage,' said Tom.

'Very well then.'

Ernest closed the door behind him. Tom ran a hand through his hair. He walked across the creaking floor to the window. The view was to the east and so looking across the open fenlands, the land stretching flat and level until it met the sky. Down below, the lawn of Phoenix House was interrupted by clumps of shrubs and orna- mental beds, all somewhat bedraggled.

It was chill in the room. Tom decided it would be best to get on with his task. Soonest started, soonest finished. He dragged the leaking armchair closer to the window, raising little clouds of dust. He settled himself into the lopsided seat and took the topmost sheaf from the pile of papers belonging to Mr Alexander Lye. The rocking horse was close by and the single glass eye that was visible seemed

to Tom to be looking at him with amusement. The first half-dozen
sheets he glanced at were brittle and yellowed with age. They were
invoices for items of furniture. One, for a mahogany bookcase, was
dated 13th November, 1763. The bookcase cost three guineas. Tom
sighed. He looked the rocking-horse in the glass eye. He replaced
the invoices and reached for the next handful of papers.

Ernest Lye came to himself with a start. He was standing at the
bottom of the stairs on the ground floor of Phoenix House, but
he could not remember arriving there. He could remember what
he had been thinking beforehand, the gist of which was: I don't
believe that Mr Thomas Ansell is going to find anything at all. I
don't believe my brother ever made a will in the first place. But
Ernest Lye did not recall descending from the top of the house
to the bottom. A small matter perhaps, but these little bouts of
forgetfulness were happening with increasing frequency. He would
suddenly become aware that he was not quite where he had been
when last conscious of his surroundings. In a different part of the
house or its grounds. Even sometimes on a different street in Ely
or Cambridge. Habit had carried him along, while his mind was
otherwise engaged. It occurred to him that perhaps he was suffering
from some disorder in the brain, but it was more comfortable to
think of it as a relatively harmless symptom of encroaching age.

However, now Ernest Lye was at the bottom of the stairs he
paused in the hallway, and paused with a purpose. In front of
him was the door to the morning room. It was shut. On the
other side of the door were his wife and her cousin. Ernest
hesitated. He looked about to confirm that he was unobserved
and then moved rapidly towards the closed door. He pretended
to have dropped something and, in stooping to examine the floor,
brought his ear nearer to the door.

He was able to hear voices inside but not what they were saying.
The two were talking in low tones. He heard Lydia's throaty laugh.
She had not laughed at anything he had said for . . . a long time.
Well, he told himself, Charles Tomlinson did have the advantage of
novelty, and he was full of those amusing stories, and they were
cousins after all. Not only was Charles spending quite a bit of time
at Phoenix House, but he and Lydia sometimes went on expeditions
to Ely or Cambridge. They went to the shops, they called on family

members like Lydia's mother and father, who was also a cousin to Tomlinson. Lydia and Charles were all very cousinly, Ernest told himself. Nothing to object to. He straightened up and walked in the other direction towards his library.

Inside the morning room Lydia Lye was complaining to Tomlinson. Her laughter, which was not really happy but rueful, had been caused by a remark of his to the effect that she was stuck away in this place. It was as if she were buried in Phoenix House in the village of Upper Fen. He said this with genuine concern, as if he wanted to be the one to rescue her. The remark about burial might have been prompted by the conversation he'd just had with the sexton.

This wasn't a very cheerful topic, but Lydia didn't object. She enjoyed almost everything that cousin Charles had to say. She relished his accounts of strange and barbaric foreign customs, many of which he had witnessed at first hand. She enjoyed his tales of savage courtship rituals and pagan funeral rites. As a citizen of the world, it was only natural that he should take an interest in local burial conditions, whether in Upper Fen or the islands of the South Seas. And she had to acknowledge the harsh truth that her life here was a bit like being buried.

'I know, I know,' she said, to forestall any further comment from cousin Charles. 'It is a fate I have chosen for myself. To be married and to come and live here.'

'Could you not persuade Ernest to purchase or rent a place in town, somewhere in Cambridge or even London?'

Lydia knew that there were not even the funds for some very necessary repairs to Phoenix House, let alone anywhere else, but she said, 'He likes it here too much. It was his mother's family's house.'

'Even so . . . I should think that you could twist Ernest round your little finger if you wished to.'

Lydia did not answer directly. Instead she went to gaze out of the window.

'I prefer to think of being here as being like a perpetual Sunday, a Sunday afternoon of eternity.'

'You have a gift for metaphor, Mrs Lye,' said Tomlinson. 'A Sunday afternoon of eternity. How poetic.'

'The only saving grace is that there is only *one* church and *one* set of bells in this place and not the cacophony of ringing which you are forced to listen to in a town.'

Tomlinson came to stand at the window near her. He said, 'I sometimes forget how very used you must be to the sound of bells.'

'They are music to my father's ears.'

'It seems to me that your mother and father – especially him, especially the Reverend Coffer – are somewhat less severe than I remember them, less inclined to judge one to one's disadvantage.'

'Are they?' said Lydia. 'That is probably because you are accustomed to real despots and tyrants among the tribes you have seen.'

'It's true I have seen some strange things.'

'Let us talk no more of death and burial, Charles. Tell me again about that ceremonial dance which you witnessed in . . . somewhere in the South Seas.'

'The dance in which the maidens of the village parade themselves in front of the young men, in order to be chosen as brides?'

Lydia suddenly found something of great interest to look at from the window of the morning room. Even so, she nodded slightly and said 'Yes' under her breath. Tomlinson was watching her closely.

'Well,' he said, 'the day before the ceremony the young men are not supposed to eat any food at all and to drink nothing apart from a few sips of water. They must sequester themselves in the jungle that surrounds their village on every side. The girls, meanwhile, undergo rituals of purification while the older women prepare the garb they are to don on the morrow. Perhaps "garb" hardly describes what they wear – or rather what they do not wear . . .'

Two of Charles Tomlinson's Enemies

While Charles Tomlinson was turning away from the subject of death and burial in favour of premarital rites, his sometime friend Cyrus Chase was settling down to his favourite reading matter in his house in Prickwillow Road, Ely. This was a quarterly periodical called *Funereal Matters* and it contained a wealth of news, information and even gossip on everything pertaining to the business of interment. Cyrus kept all the old copies, arranged by date.

Cyrus was aware that Bella did not care for the magazine. If his wife caught sight of the title, she pulled a face or instinctively looked away. For her, it was a reminder of his morbid interests. Accordingly, Cyrus usually hid his copy away when it arrived and waited for some private hour when he might devote himself properly to *Funereal Matters*. He resented having to do this. Really, he thought, Bella was most unreasonable. To judge from his wife's attitude it was as if he were proposing to look through the kind of salacious material – books, postcards, photographs – which a gentleman could obtain from certain emporia in Holywell Street off the Strand. Or so he had heard. Yet *Funereal Matters* could not be a greater contrast. What was more respectable and necessary than to meditate not on the world or the flesh or the devil, but on last things?

Now, since Bella was out of the house, having taken the train to Cambridge to do some shopping, Cyrus had more than a spare hour. Time enough to read the magazine from cover to cover. Cyrus took up his paper knife and slit the uncut pages. He replaced the knife on the small table next to his chair. It was his habit to flick through the pages of the magazine to give himself a taste of the treats to come. With approval he read an editorial that deplored the growing taste for simplicity in funerals and the move away from what ignorant critics called 'ostentation'. He glanced at a feature about making the cast of a hand after death and another about the propriety of taking photographs of the deceased in his coffin. Yes, this promised to be a good issue.

Then Cyrus arrived at a particular favourite of his: the column of notes, observations and chat which was signed simply 'Mute'. Each item occupied one or two paragraphs and was introduced with a sub-heading that was frequently punning or humorous. Cyrus could permit himself a smile at Mute's dry wit. Whoever penned the column was a knowledgeable fellow – probably a Londoner since he made frequent references to the capital's undertakers – and conversant with the latest trends and fashions whether above or below the ground. Cyrus enjoyed the aptness of an anonymous writer styling himself 'Mute' as well as the fact that the term described a paid funeral attendant. He began to read Mute's latest offerings.

Moments later, the housemaid Mattie, passing the door of the room, was startled to hear the thud of an object striking the floor. Then some incoherent words and a loaded silence, followed by another meaningless babble. Mattie hesitated before tapping on the door. After a muffled 'Yes?' she turned the handle.

'Is everything all right, sir?'

'Yes.'

Cyrus Chase's face was suffused with red. He was staring down in bewilderment at the floor where an occasional table lay on its side next to his chair. He must have knocked it over as he stood up. As far as she could see, no damage had been done.

'Do you want me to pick that up, Mr Chase?'

'No, no. I'll do it,' he said, waving her away with a distracted hand. Mattie withdrew, quietly closing the door. The appearance of the maid had partly restored Cyrus Chase to himself. He had no idea what words he'd uttered or what gestures he'd made during the last few minutes. He righted the overturned table and groped his way back to the armchair. He picked up *Funereal Matters* from where it had dropped to the floor out of his nerveless grasp. He fumbled through the pages until he came once more to the column by Mute. He blinked several times, as if to remove a bit of grit from his eye, and read again two particular paragraphs. Then he read them several times more.

There was a sub-heading: *A Little Bird Tells Us . . .*

Below was this item: *We are reliably informed of a fresh advance in the field of security coffins. Warning devices such as bells and tubes are already familiar to our readers, although there is always room for the improvement and refinement that are an inseparable aspect of progress. But a certain gentleman has approached a well-known firm of London undertakers, which happens to trade under the name of a most appropriate tree, with a view to developing something quite novel.*

Without giving away too many secrets, this gentleman's device involves a familiar farmyard fowl, brightly painted so as to draw the attention of bystanders and capable of being rotated rapidly from underground. The installation of such avian devices in substantial numbers would not only add to the gaiety of the graveyard — if we may be permitted a paradoxical phrase — but also greatly enhance the likelihood of rescue for any poor unfortunate who is buried prematurely and awakes to find himself still alive beneath the sod.

Cyrus Chase did not know where to begin. Here in cold print was a picture, accurate in every detail, of the coffin-cockerel which was his creation, and which he'd unwisely shown to Charles Tomlinson. The references in Mute's article to a 'familiar farmyard fowl', to its bright colour, to the way it could be rapidly spun from underground, left Cyrus in no doubt that he had been betrayed by Tomlinson.

He was certain that Tomlinson must be the unnamed gentleman for the simple reason that the inventor had shown the cockerel to no one else. Had he been able to pick up all the detail he needed on that single visit? Or had he somehow got inside Cyrus' workshop for a second and closer look? It was precisely the kind of ungrateful and deceitful behaviour to be expected of a 'gentleman' like Tomlinson. Cyrus was even able to identify the London firm approached by that treacherous individual. It could only be Willow & Son, described as the 'well-known undertakers, which happens to trade under the name of a most appropriate tree'.

The fellow was a rogue and a blackguard.

He was a thief and a traitor, pretending an interest in Cyrus' work only in order to steal it.

The problem for Cyrus was that he had no legal recourse. The Chase coffin-cockerel was not yet patented. Indeed, there were a couple of refinements to it that he was considering before he applied to the Patent Office. He could write in protest to Willow & Son, he could even call at their London offices in person, and he vowed to do both those things. But he could not prove beyond dispute that the spinning bird was his own creation. If Tomlinson carried the affair off with enough impudence – and he would, he would – then *he* would get the fame and glory for all the ingenuity and labour of Cyrus Chase!

Cyrus became aware of a shooting pain in his hands. He looked down. He was clutching the copy of *Funereal Matters* so hard that he had almost reduced several pages to pulp. It required an effort to unclench his hands. He allowed the ruined periodical to drop to the floor and, breathing deeply and evenly, placed his hands on the arms of the chair.

The Chase cockerel wasn't the only thing, of course. There was

Bella to be considered as well. Cyrus hoped to win back his wife's regard and affection through his invention of the coffin-bird. No longer would she be able to talk about his morbid occupation when she saw him respectfully referred to in the quality press or when manufacturers applied for the right to produce the Chase cockerel in quantity. The two might recapture the warmth that existed in the early days of their marriage when Bella would ruffle his hair as he was sitting down. Sometimes she would even sit on his lap and ruffle his hair.

Now the thought occurred to Cyrus that perhaps Bella had colluded with Charles Tomlinson in this whole business. The idea was a knife in his brain. He struggled to keep calm. Bella could not have shown Tomlinson the coffin device again since Cyrus kept the only key to the garden workshop on the chain in his pocket. Unless she had somehow managed to take a hasty impression of the key while he was off guard, while he was sleeping. It could be done. Even if she had not resorted to such duplicity, she might have encouraged Mr Tomlinson with words . . . and she might have done more than encourage him with words . . .

Cyrus recalled that moment after the dinner party the other night when he'd caught sight of the pair standing under the porch. Their heads close together in an intimate encounter. Exchanging compliments? Or plotting? Or talking about him, Cyrus? Laughing at him?

Did Bella know that Tomlinson had visited Willow & Son in London?

Was she in on his plans? He did not really believe his wife would be so unfaithful, so treacherous, and yet . . . Once doubt and suspicion appeared at the door, they didn't just tap gently, they beat it down. Where was Bella now, for example? She'd said she was going to Cambridge to do some shopping. Perhaps that was true. She liked Cambridge, she liked shopping. But was she by herself? If not, in whose company was she?

Cyrus got up from his chair and retrieved the paper knife which he had used to slit the pages of the funeral magazine and which was lying on the carpet where it had tumbled from the table. He put a tentative forefinger to the tip. He rested the cushion of his thumb on the side of the blade. The knife was a short little thing but it was stout and it was sharp. Not much use having a blunt paper knife if one wanted to cut the pages of a book or a periodical, cut them cleanly and neatly.

Would the knife pierce someone's body, Cyrus wondered? Would it pierce Mr Charles Tomlinson's body, for example? If that black-guard wandered into the room at this instant and if he, Cyrus, rushed at him brandishing the paper knife and struck him at the right spot – say, here (Cyrus felt for the gap in the ribs that overlay his heart); or somewhere here (Cyrus prodded his belly) – would he manage to inflict a fatal wound or would he merely do some damage? On balance, Cyrus thought that aiming for the guts would be better than trying further up. There seemed to be too much bony armour around the heart. A knifepoint might easily be deflected in that area. The belly was a bigger, softer target. In either case, there would be blood. Blood over the carpet. Bella would not like that. No, it would be best not to carry out such an attack in the drawing room of one's house. Or anywhere in one's own house, come to that. Best to do it elsewhere.

Best not to do it all, a little voice whispered in his ear. You, Cyrus Chase, are not a killer; you are an inventor and a creator. But another voice was speaking more loudly in the other ear. It was saying, this Tomlinson man has cheated you, he has stolen from you the fruits of your labour and – perhaps – deprived you of your wife and helpmeet. The same voice said, murder is no more than he deserves.

Murder was also on the mind of the Reverend George Eames as he worked on his sermon for the next day. He was using the notes which he had prevented the foolish Hannah from consigning to the flames. After his earlier outburst of anger, he was surprised to find himself quite calm and level-headed. He sat at his desk, alternately writing a handful of sentences and then glancing up at the beech hedge at the end of the garden, across the graveyard and beyond that to the squat tower of the church.

George Eames was reflecting on a text from Ephesians: *Be ye angry and sin not* (Chapter 4, verse 26). This was not the text for the coming Sunday but he intended to allude to Ephesians anyway. It suited one of his purposes, which was to distinguish between two types of anger, the righteous and the ungodly. Thoughts of anger led George Eames to thoughts of violence, of death and murder.

Not by coincidence, ever since he had caught a glimpse of a certain visitor to the parish of Upper Fen, images of violence and death were never far from his mind.

Now laying down his pen and gazing unseeingly out at the church, Eames mused on some of the more dramatic deaths in holy scripture. A killing such as that of Abel by Cain was beyond question a wicked crime. But there were other killings which could be called righteous. Jael, the wife of Heber, drove a tent-peg through the sleeping head of Sisera, enemy to the Israelites, and was applauded for the deed. Another fearless woman, Judith, beheaded the drunken Babylonian general, Holofernes, using his own sword and she was praised for her daring.

These images of decapitation floated through the mind of George Eames. He had no idea what Sisera or Holofernes looked like, although he visualized swarthy and bearded visages scarred by battle. But there was another head which, were Eames to permit himself such a bloodthirsty wish, he would have been glad to see similarly separated from its body. This was a clean-shaven head, possessing gaunt features and a prominent jaw. The individual to whom it belonged had once been a friend of George Eames. They had met when both were studying at the same Cambridge college.

They possessed different views of the world, Eames and his friend. One held that God created the world as the tale was told in Genesis, the other maintained that new theories were sweeping away that old story. The two argued fiercely, but Eames believed that such intellectual debate was proof of the elevated, disinterested quality of their friendship. There was nothing personal to it. He even derived a thrill from knowing someone with such unorthodox, dangerous opinions.

But then things got out of hand. Reasoned debate turned to impassioned argument before descending into slurs and insults. Not on Eames' side, or not so much. But the other man began to pursue him in a spirit that combined malevolence with mischief. He spread stories about Eames, formed a cabal against him. George Eames felt persecuted and, although he told himself that persecution was the fate of all true Christians, this was not much comfort for him.

The climax came when Eames' opponent did a terrible thing, performing an action that was both wounding and absurd. The college authorities had found out and been swift to send the culprit down. But by then the fellow had decided to quit Cambridge anyway – or so he claimed – and he avoided being formally rusticated. He was tired of the narrowness of the place, he said, he was weary of its provincialism. He wanted broader horizons. Eames had no clear idea what happened to him after that, although he heard that his one-time friend had not merely left the city but the country. He pretended that he did not care. He attempted to put the whole affair out of his mind, particularly that afternoon when he returned to his college rooms to discover . . .

Even now he did not want to recall it. And he had thought little of it in the intervening years. So it had come as an almighty surprise when he recently caught a glimpse of a man looking remarkably like Charles Tomlinson emerging from the front door of Phoenix House. Tomlinson looked older, inevitably, and more drawn in the face, but the years had not done much damage to him. Luckily, Eames himself had not been seen by Tomlinson, who was busy taking leave of Mrs Lye. The parson was on his way to call at the house but had time to take shelter behind some convenient shrubbery. He felt a fool for hiding like a child but his heart was beating fast and his face was hot with anger and embarrassment, suddenly rekindled after all these years.

A discreet question or two established that, yes, the stranger was indeed Mr Charles Tomlinson, lately returned from a period of extensive travelling in the Far East. A distant cousin to Mrs Lye, he was renewing his connection with her as well as meeting her husband for the first time. He'd made a number of visits to Phoenix House. It was Ernest himself who told all this to Eames. Something in Lye's tone of voice suggested that Tomlinson's reappearance wasn't altogether welcome, although Ernest referred to him as an 'excellent fellow', one with a fund of exotic stories at his disposal. Of course, George Eames said nothing of his old friendship with Tomlinson nor of the shameful way in which it had terminated. He wasn't surprised that Charles was related to the Lyes, or at least to Lydia. The man had a knack for useful connections.

As far as he knew, Tomlinson was unaware that he, George Eames, ministered to the parish of Upper Fen. And that was how Eames preferred it. He might have deceived himself that he had risen above his anger at his old friend but the brief glimpse of Tomlinson outside Phoenix House showed he had not. He feared coming face to face with Tomlinson again. He feared too that Tomlinson would find out that his progress so far in life had taken him no further than a perpetual curacy in the obscure parish of Upper Fen. At least there was no risk of his attending a service in the church!

George Eames turned again to his sermon for the next day. He contemplated the different species of anger. He thought of God's wrath and how it should be visited on the unrighteous. He thought of Charles Tomlinson.

A Former Admirer of Charles Tomlinson

The Reverend George Eames and Ernest Lye and Cyrus Chase were not the only ones with reasons to hate or fear Charles Tomlinson or, more simply, to be wary of him. There were others. Among them was Chase's wife. At this moment, while Cyrus was flinging down his copy of *Funereal Matters* and doubting Bella and even suspecting that his wife might have invented a story about going shopping in Cambridge, Bella Chase was actually doing what she said she would be doing. That is, she was walking the streets of Cambridge and looking in shop windows, even though she was not in the mood for buying.

Nevertheless, her husband's suspicions about her and Tomlinson were partly true. She had not revealed any of his trade secrets to Tomlinson. Nor had she taken a hasty impression of the padlock key which Cyrus kept on his chain. Tomlinson had actually managed to take an impression of the key on that earlier visit to Cyrus' workshop, returning the inventor's key after pretending he'd found it on the ground.

No, Bella would not have betrayed Cyrus by passing on his pitiful and morbid attempts at invention. The question was whether she would have betrayed him in other ways. From the moment of first meeting Mr Charles Tomlinson in the summer of this year – how long ago that seemed! – she had been very taken by this mysterious gentleman. It was as if a glowing new planet had appeared in the wide skies over Ely. She understood that Cyrus had encountered Mr Tomlinson in the Lion Hotel in the town where the two swiftly struck up an acquaintance which was partly based on Tomlinson's curiosity about burial customs. Bella didn't object to that aspect of Tomlinson. Instead, it was evidence of the breadth of his interests, his *worldliness*. The stranger's interest in death was exotic; her husband's was little more than gloomy.

Charles Tomlinson was the opposite of Cyrus Chase in almost every respect. He was tall and well built where Cyrus was scarcely taller than Bella herself and certainly much stouter. He had travelled while her husband was a stay-at-home. He spoke foreign languages, or at least sufficient to greet Bella in French (*Je suis enchanté, madame, comme toujours*) and to say goodbye in Italian and to tell her that her name meant 'beautiful' in the same language (which she already knew but which she was very ready to hear again, particularly from a man like Tomlinson).

He was gallant and attentive. He leaned close and listened to her with absolute concentration, as if the two of them were the only people in the world.

She was *enchantée* herself even if she was often reduced almost to tongue-tied silence in his presence. To silence or else to giggles, like a young girl. He whispered in her ear and his warm breath and the words he said gave her a most delicious, and rather naughty, feeling.

For example, he learned at some point that Cyrus' father had invented a useful piece of railway equipment which was called the Chase Coupler. For some reason, the name of this device never failed to cause Tomlinson a good deal of amusement. He often referred to the 'Chase Coupler' in his asides to Bella and, if they weren't being observed, he would hook and twine a finger of his right hand with a finger of hers in a manner that, she supposed, was imitative of a railway coupling. But which also hinted at something else that she was not quite willing to drag into the full light of day . . .

Bella was not a fool, however. She knew where all this was headed or might have been headed, had she permitted it. Now, during this time on a Saturday while she walked the streets of Cambridge or stopped to gaze at the milliners' and dressmakers' windows without really seeing anything that was on display, she was grateful that she had not allowed Mr Charles Tomlinson to overstep the bounds of propriety. Well, perhaps, he had overstepped them just a fraction. But at least he had not taken any liberties, real liberties.

True, they had whispered and laughed together and intertwined fingers while he made his comments about the Chase Coupler. Then there was that moment after the dinner party the other evening when, standing close to her in the porch of the house and bending forward to say his goodbyes, he had brushed his lips against hers. More than brushed. Pressed. This was far from accidental. Bella quickly drew back, not affronted, not at all, but reacting rather as if she'd received a tiny electric shock. She might have responded but her husband was coughing his way back up the garden path after seeing off the other guests, and it was Charles Tomlinson who turned away.

The next day he sent her a note of thanks. In among the compliments about the food and her charms as a hostess was a remark about 'the warmth of the heart which beat in her bosom' (the whole phrase underlined) and a reference to 'Mr Leigh Hunt's well-known line of verse about stolen kisses being the sweetest'. He signed it 'your devoted servant'. This note had a much greater effect on Bella Chase than the encounter in the porch. She withdrew to her room and read it a dozen times. She folded it and pressed it to the bosom that Tomlinson had emphasized with his underlining. She smoothed the note out again and read it a dozen times more before tucking it away in a drawer and then, afraid that her maid might come across it, she removed it from the drawer and locked it away in one of her jewel boxes.

For a while Bella Chase allowed herself to believe that this was a love letter – which it wasn't, not exactly – and from there she made the leap into fantasy. She imagined herself leaving her tubby Cyrus, leaving behind his coffin-bells and his carefully preserved copies of *Funereal Matters*, and sailing off into the blue with Mr Charles Tomlinson, that mysterious stranger and man of the world. They would have to sail off into the blue, of course, since remaining in England was out of the question. How would they live? What would they live on? She didn't know, since she had no idea of the extent of Mr Tomlinson's wealth, but she didn't doubt that he had means. The idea of running away with a man of the world made her feel quite young again.

The fantasy had dimmed slightly by the time evening came, although she returned to it at intervals during the largely silent supper she shared with Cyrus, such a contrast to the sparkle and diversion of the dinner party the previous night.

But the fantasy was to be killed off altogether the next day when she witnessed Charles Tomlinson in Ely High Street, in the company of another woman. Bella saw the two but they didn't see her. Bella was walking under the wall which forms the northern boundary of the cathedral precinct. Tomlinson and the woman emerged from a glove shop on the other side and started walking in her direction. Instinctively, Bella turned her head aside to avoid being seen but the pair were more interested in each other than the world around them.

Bella glimpsed Tomlinson leaning down slightly to catch what his companion was saying and then smiling before making some remark in return. His words caused the woman to laugh in a lady-like fashion. The laughter was delicate but genuine. The sound of it seemed to reach across the High Street, rising like a bell above the passing pedestrians and the traffic but piercing Bella's ears like a knife.

Straightaway Bella realized that this woman was more of a lady than she was or ever would be. It was not just the quality of her clothes but the way she held herself. Her carriage. She was taller than Bella, which meant that Tomlinson did not have to lean down so far to listen to her soft voice or to whisper some words of a private nature. The two of them went together, as it were, much more plausibly than Bella Chase and Charles Tomlinson could ever go together. Why, they even looked slightly alike!

If it hadn't been a very unladylike thing to do, Bella would have stopped and stared after the couple as they proceeded along the High Street in the direction of Fore Hill. In quick glances over her shoulder she saw the pair moving at the same leisurely pace, not quite touching but far too close for comfort. Before she could stop herself she had slipped across the street and gone into the shop from which Tomlinson and the unknown woman so recently emerged.

Bella knew Mrs Johnson, the petite proprietress of the glove shop. She produced a small leather-bound book, like a diary, from her purse.

'Mrs Johnson, I wonder if you can help me. A lady left here a few moments ago and dropped this on the pavement outside. I picked it up but, when I looked round for her, she was nowhere to be seen. I wonder if you know who she is. There's no name inside, you see.'

Bella held the diary in her gloved hands and flicked through a few pages while taking care that Mrs Johnson should not have a close sight of it. This was because it was actually her – that is, Bella's – diary. Mrs Johnson did not appear to suspect anything.

'Was the lady accompanied by a tall gentleman?' she said.

'Yes, I rather think there was a gentleman with her.'

'I do know her. Like you, Mrs Chase, she is a customer of mine, a valued customer.'

Bella put on an expectant face. Was Mrs Johnson going to reveal this valued customer's name?

'Mrs Ernest Lye of Phoenix House. Lydia Lye, such a musical name.'

Bella had heard of the Lyes, of course, and she knew that Phoenix House was in the village of Upper Fen, a couple of miles to the north of Ely. She might even have glimpsed Mrs Lye before, in the town or elsewhere, but she had had no reason to pay any attention to the elegant woman. Not until she saw her in the company of Mr Charles Tomlinson.

'That was her husband with her, I expect?'

Bella wasn't sure what prompted her to ask this, since she already knew that Mr Tomlinson could not be married to Mrs Ernest Lye. Perhaps she was just curious to see how the glove-shop proprietor responded.

'Oh no, not her husband,' said Mrs Johnson quickly, before adding with more caution, 'At least I do not believe so. I cannot be sure of course.'

Bella felt anger bubbling up, anger at Charles Tomlinson. Meanwhile, Mrs Johnson was saying something.

'I said, would you like me to take the diary, Mrs Chase? To relieve you of any anxiety. I can keep it here in case Mrs Lye discovers her loss and comes back. Or, better still, I shall arrange for it to be returned to Mrs Lye. It would be my pleasure.'

This stumped Bella. Even while spinning her story to Mrs Johnson, she had been congratulating herself on her quick wit and her acting skills. But now she didn't know what to do. If she handed over the diary, Mrs Johnson would soon realize that it was not hers – that is, Mrs Lye's – but Bella's, for the simple reason that Bella had written her name inside the cover. She thought quickly, possibly more quickly than ever in her life.

'Why, how foolish I've been!' she said to Mrs Johnson, opening the diary again and peering at it. 'I see that there *is* a name written down here after all. It belongs to . . . the writing is not so easy to read . . . to Mrs Amy Hunt . . .'

'I thought you said that it was dropped by Mrs Lye,' said Mrs Johnson.

'Then I was mistaken,' said Bella. 'There is quite a press of people out there, you know, coming and going. No, this clearly says Mrs Hunt, now that I can read it properly.'

Mrs Johnson looked confused, then disappointed that her chance of doing a small service for Mrs Lye had been frustrated. She says, 'Mrs Hunt? I don't think I know any Mrs Hunt. She is not one of my customers, at any rate. What are you going to do with it?'

'Oh well,' said Bella. 'By good fortune, there also happens to be an address written below Mrs Hunt's name. I see she lives in Cambridge. Don't worry, Mrs Johnson. I shall personally ensure that this is returned to its owner. I have taken up enough of your time. You have been too good.'

Bella's exit from Mrs Johnson's glove shop was covered by the entrance of another customer. Once back in the High Street, Bella turned right and walked in the direction of Palace Green. Her behaviour during the last ten minutes made her feel very odd, as if she had boarded a boat and stepped off in a foreign country where everything was done differently. She was so absorbed in her thoughts that she almost walked into a pack of loungers outside the Greyhound Inn. Then she was out on the open grassy space before the west front of the cathedral.

She continued to be surprised at the quickness of her wits, at what she was capable of. Her ability to think up an imaginary name – although not altogether imaginary, since Amy was actually Bella's middle name while Hunt was her maiden one – and then her pretence that 'Mrs Hunt' lived in Cambridge, had enabled her to get out of a tricky situation unscathed. She had not even deceived Mrs Johnson, not really, since the diary did belong to 'Mrs Amy

Hunt' (under another name) and has already been returned to its rightful owner (that is, it never left Bella's possession). Bella felt pleased with her ingenuity. Her success. Above all, pleased that she had discovered the identity of the woman with Charles Tomlinson.

What to do next? Slowly, she traced a large oval around Palace Green, keeping to the paths on the perimeter. In the centre of the lawn a group of boys were clustered round the Crimean cannon, either sitting astride it or peering into its mouth. Bella did not feel angry at Mrs Lye (*Lydia Lye, such a musical name*). No, Bella felt angry with Mr Tomlinson. He had misled her, he had caused her to think that she had a special place in his heart, tricked her into fantasies that she might sail away with him into the blue. She felt she'd been made a fool of.

Her anger did not diminish during the day but, if anything, grew stronger. She was too distracted to exchange more than a few words with Cyrus during supper. In private, she took Tomlinson's letter out of her jewel box and reread it several times. Bella considered tearing it to pieces — she'd like to do the same to that man, tear him to pieces — but she replaced the letter in the box where it sat, no longer a token of love, but evidence against him.

The next day Bella took the train to Cambridge and did no more than she told Cyrus she was going to do: look in shop windows. He was pleased enough that his wife was out of the house and had no notion of the rage bubbling inside her. It gave him the chance to spend time with *Funereal Matters*, although he was driven into his own rage by the information in Mute's column and dreamed of plunging the paper knife into Tomlinson's treacherous heart.

By coincidence, and at that same instant, Bella Chase found she had wandered away from the more prosperous parts of central Cambridge and was staring, unseeing, at a dingy shop door in a narrow side street. In faded gold on the door was the legend 'Bartle & Co.' and beneath that 'Money advanced on plate, jewels, wearing apparel, and every description of property'. Bella read the words several times over without taking them in. When she did understand that she was standing in front of a pawnbroker's she shifted to look through the window, which was streaked and dusty. There were no plate or jewels on display in the window, only a jumble of cups and coral necklaces and prayer books, of boots and handkerchiefs.

In pride of place was a carpenter's set, the planes and saws neatly arrayed as if the pawnbroker were boasting that here, at last, was an item worth buying.

Bella looked at the teeth on the saws and the bevelled edges of the chisels. She wondered what extremity drove the carpenter, or someone in his family, to pawn the tools of his trade. Then she forgot to think of the carpenter because her eye had been caught by a carving knife which was positioned near the carpenter's set. Nothing to do with the chisels, etc., but perhaps placed alongside other sharp, cutting implements by association. Indeed, the carving knife, with the dull gleam of its blade and its solid, graspable ivory handle, looked ready for use. It was almost inviting her to go in and redeem it. This would have been absurd since the canteen case in Bella's Ely home already contained a perfectly adequate carving knife. But the sight of the knife in the pawnbroker's put the idea in her head.

Bella imagined herself wielding the carving knife against Charles Tomlinson. Just as her husband was imagining himself wielding a knife against the same individual. Although, in his case, it was a smaller weapon, designed for slicing paper not meat.

Annals of a Fenland Village

While all of this was going on – Mr and Mrs Chase pursuing their separate courses, the Reverend Eames contemplating his righteous anger at Charles Tomlinson – Tom Ansell was still at Phoenix House. He discovered nothing in the top-floor room, or at least nothing in the form of Alexander Lye's absent will or testament. Under the cold glass eye of the rocking horse, he rummaged through the contents of the leather trunk, uncovering deeds and indentures that were stiff with age, as well as more bills and invoices. There were bundles of correspondence, much of which dated from the previous century. The name Roderick, father to Alexander and Ernest, came up often enough, but there were other Lyes who must have been earlier family members. Some of the letters were personal, others were to do with business or land and property, or the shipment of goods. But there was no will.

Ernest Lye sent up one of the maids with a mug of mild porter. The girl asked Tom if he required any food. Perhaps unwisely, Tom said no. By three o'clock the soporific effect of the porter, the tedium of his task, the coldness of the room and the increasingly poor light were making him impatient to finish for the afternoon. Telling himself that, if necessary, he could return to Upper Fen on another day for a final look round, Tom blundered his way along the dark upstairs passages and went downstairs. He found Ernest in his study, settled in an armchair by the fire, smoking a cigar and reading.

'No luck?'

'Not so far. To be frank, Mr Lye, I do not believe that your brother left any kind of will or testament here.'

Ernest Lye nodded and said, 'Well, now you can report to David Mackenzie with a clear conscience. On a different subject, Mr Ansell, did I hear that your wife Helen is a writer? I rather think that Lydia said something of the sort.'

'Yes, she is,' said Tom. 'That is, she has had a story published in *Tinsley's* – which is a magazine – and she is presently at work on a novel.'

'I'm something of an author myself,' said Ernest, indicating the book in his lap.

'You are?'

'I have written the history of Phoenix House and of the little community which surrounds us here. I have called it *Annals of a Fenland Village*. I composed this for my own pleasure and, I hope, the edification of others. It is privately published. What I am wondering, Mr Ansell . . .?'

Ernest hesitated and Tom waited. He had an idea of what was coming next. Ernest stood up.

'. . . is would you be so good as to take a copy and ask your wife to cast an eye over it? Not to read it from cover to cover, of course, but to glance through a few pages. I would value the opinion of a professional.'

'I'm sure she'd be happy to do that.'

'Perhaps she would be in a position to oblige me with her views as soon as tomorrow?'

Tom took the book which Ernest Lye was holding out. It occurred to him that perhaps this was the reason for the supper invitation on the following day. Ernest was eager for Helen's opinion of his work, which naturally meant her good opinion.

Tom left Phoenix House without seeing Lydia Lye or Charles Tomlinson again, although he noticed an extra top hat on the stand and assumed Mrs Lye's cousin was still in the house. The same lad who'd driven him over drove him back to Ely railway station in the dog cart. Tom established that his name was Davey but could get nothing more out of him. The boy did not mention again the mysterious 'him' in the churchyard.

While he was waiting on the platform for the Cambridge train, Tom leafed through Ernest Lye's history of the house and the village. Lye was so modest or tentative about his authorship that he was merely identified as 'E.L.' on the title-page. Tom was surprised to realize how deeply *Annals of a Fenland Village* delved into the past. There were allusions to the Germanic tribes and the Scandinavian marauders who settled the region in the Dark Ages, as well as references to Hereward the Wake and the 'Norman interlopers' against whom Hereward led a heroic resistance. There was quite a bit about the manor house called Stilwell Manor, parts of which had been swallowed up by Phoenix House. Tom was no judge of prose style – he left that sort of thing to Helen – but it seemed to him that Ernest Lye's approach was brisk and straightforward.

As he gazed unseeing out of the window of the train carriage, Tom looked back on a day that hadn't produced much. Not produced anything, really. He felt tired and hungry. He hoped Helen had enjoyed a better time in the company of Mr John Jubb.

Back at the Devereux, he found Helen in good spirits. Not only had she been taken on a thorough tour of some of the Cambridge sights, but in a coffee-house she had met – 'And this really was the most extraordinary coincidence, Tom!' – had met Mr Arthur Arnett, the editor of *The New Moon*, the magazine to which she was contributing.

'What was he like?' said Tom.

'You might find him a little . . . precious,' said Helen.

'Oh,' said Tom, understanding that it was actually Helen who'd found Mr Arnett a bit precious. He told her a bit about his day and the fruitless search for the missing will, the meeting with Mrs Lye and her warm enquiries after Helen, and the invitation to Ely for the following day. He mentioned the memorable gentleman who was a guest at the house, Mr Tomlinson. Then he said, 'Oh, I almost forgot. I have a book for you.'

He passed over Ernest Lye's *Annals of a Fenland Village*, explaining that the author was eager for Helen's opinion on his work when they met on the Sunday. To Tom's surprise, Helen seemed pleased to be asked for her views. She flicked through the pages. Her attention was caught by a page here, a paragraph there.

Tom went towards the window of their room. As yesterday, there was a large band of young men playing football in the fading light on Parker's Piece. Tom remembered something else.

'No more mysterious notes?' he said to Helen.

She looked up from Mr Lye's book. 'Oh, you mean like the *Macbeth* lines. I had forgotten them, almost.'

'I expect it was a joke,' said Tom, although privately he did not believe this.

St Ethelwine's

L ater that same evening, two men were making their way round the north side of St Ethelwine's Church in Upper Fen. One of them was Eric Fort, the occasional representative of the Camden Town undertakers, Willow & Son. The other was Charles Tomlinson, cousin to Mrs Lye and friend to Mr and Mrs Chase. Tomlinson was carrying a shuttered lantern while Fort was toting a bag.

A cold wind was rising, sending leaves skittering through the air. They could not risk showing any light, or no more than a sliver of it, so the two men felt rather than saw their way down the worn and slippery flight of steps that led to the door to the crypt. Once at the bottom they crouched in the recessed entrance. Tomlinson reached into his pocket and extracted a key. He fumbled it into the lock and, after a bit of experimental twisting, turned it.

'How the blazes . . . how did you . . .?' said Fort.

'Wait until we're inside,' said Tomlinson, turning the handle and pushing at the door. It opened with a slight creak, nothing more. He and Fort ducked inside. Tomlinson pushed the door to after them, and then slid back the shutter of the lantern. A yellow light spilled across mildewed stonework and on to a floor that was composed of earth and shards of stone. The roof was so low that Tomlinson had to remove his top hat. He placed it carefully by the entrance to the crypt. For once, Eric Fort was glad of his lack of height. It meant that he could keep his hat on and so protect his head from the strands of nameless material – animal? vegetable? – that hung, dripping, from the roof.

Charles Tomlinson fumbled in his coat and produced the pewter hip flask which Fort had grown quite used to seeing. He tilted his head back and seemed to gulp down most of the contents of the flask. Then he sighed happily and the little space was suddenly filled with the reek of alcohol. Fort thought it would have been companionable of Tomlinson to offer him a nip as well. Not that he would have accepted, since he drank sparingly, but the gesture would have been appreciated. Tomlinson, however, was oblivious to such things.

'Now then, what was your question, Mr Fort?' he said.

'It doesn't matter,' said the little man, noting the way their voices resonated in this underground chamber.

'You are wondering how I got hold of the key to the crypt?'

Fort was aware that Tomlinson had connections in this place, that he was related to the lady in the big house. But it didn't seem likely that she would have a key to the church crypt. In any case, Fort had learned that Charles Tomlinson liked to keep his secrets and so didn't expect to be given an answer. Yet he said, 'You must know the parson here?'

'The incumbent of Upper Fen? As a matter of fact I do know George Eames,' said Tomlinson thoughtfully, rubbing his prominent chin. 'Or let us say instead, that I did know George many years ago. We attended the same Cambridge college. Then we had a . . . falling-out over something and have never spoken or seen each other since. But I did approach a certain person who has access to the keys to this place. That person was easily persuaded to lend them to me for a time, and I made a copy of them.'

Eric Fort wasn't surprised. Tomlinson was good at persuading people to do what he wanted. He guessed that the 'certain person', if it wasn't the parson, must nevertheless be someone up at the parsonage, a woman probably. Most likely, a girl. Yes, Tomlinson was a good persuader.

Fort himself had been moulded into an easily persuadable state by Charles Tomlinson ever since their first meeting in London. And now look where he found himself: in the middle of a cold, damp October evening, standing underground in a crypt in a church in a remote fenland in search of . . . God knows what.

This was the culmination of a short acquaintance which began when Tomlinson first made himself known at the undertakers, Willow & Son. Eric Fort was not a full-time employee of the firm but he was a sometimes-useful presence in their office and he grabbed hold of any little commission that came his way. As an aficionado of English funeral practices and the London cemeteries, Fort was entranced by Tomlinson's talk of how differently foreigners did things in lands which were thousands of miles away, things ranging from the horrid (the practice of suttee) to the charming (the placing of ceramics alongside the body in the ground).

Recently, Tomlinson had sparked some enthusiasm at Willow & Son with his invention of a so-called coffin-bird, a mechanical device intended to be set atop a burial mound while being operated from below by the unfortunate victim of a premature burial. But they were down here in the St Ethelwine's crypt not in pursuit of any coffin-bird. Rather, Tomlinson was engaged on a quest about which he'd been even more cagey than usual. When Fort asked, Tomlinson simply said, 'We're going fossicking, that's what we're doing.'

It was a mark of his hold over Eric Fort that the little man had been 'persuaded' to come out to Upper Fen as evening was drawing in, clutching his bag of implements. Fort took a train to Ely shortly after Tom Ansell arrived back in Cambridge. The two did not see each other. Once in Ely, Mr Fort hired a carriage to take him to the outskirts of the village, as per Tomlinson's instructions. If the driver saw anything odd about the request to drop his passenger on the edge of Upper Fen, he didn't show it.

While he was being driven the couple of miles to the village, Eric Fort huddled up against the cold and thought of the odd twists and turns which his life was taking. As well as his occasional work for Willow & Son, he was presently serving two masters. There was not only Charles Tomlinson but the other gentleman for whom he was keeping watch on the Ansells, keeping watch or spying. Precisely why he was required to do this he did not know. But he was being paid for it, and Fort welcomed both the money and the employment. His wife had recently died and he did his best to distract himself with activity.

As Tom suspected, it was the undertakers' man who had been inside the hansom cab that almost knocked down Helen on the approach to Liverpool Street Station. Fort was horrified when he realized what might have happened: death or serious injuries inflicted on an innocent young lady. He ordered the driver to halt but by this time they had run a couple of hundred yards into the fog along Bishopsgate. The driver seemed confused and scarcely aware of the near-accident – Fort thought the man had been drinking – and after he'd tossed a coin and a warning in his direction, he hurried back through the murk.

To his relief, he saw that Mrs Ansell was all right. She and Mr Ansell were both on their feet and brushing distractedly at their garments. There was a policeman in attendance. Fort hung back among the bystanders. Still keeping a discreet distance he observed the Ansells enter the station, then, after purchasing tickets, go into the buffet. Fort would have welcomed a drink himself to steady his nerves but he decided to take advantage of the delay. He caught an earlier train to Cambridge and, knowing their destination, was settled in the lobby of the Devereux Hotel by the time the Ansells arrived. There he overheard their encounter with the solicitors' clerk, Mr John Jubb.

Afterwards, it was Fort whom Helen glimpsed on the streets of the town. And as it grew dark over Parker's Piece, it was Fort who sought out the anonymous terraced house in the anonymous road where his other employer was waiting. There, in the parlour, he gave his report, as you have heard. He was in earnest when he asked the man whether any harm was intended towards the Ansells and he was reassured, or partly reassured, by the other's reply. It wasn't Tom Ansell that Eric Fort cared about, although the solicitor seemed a good enough fellow. No, it was Mrs Ansell. He had been taken with her from the moment he glimpsed her, veiled as she was, by the Egyptian gate at Abney Park cemetery. For Fort, no woman looked more handsome than when she was garbed in mourning clothes.

Mrs Ansell expressed a wish to visit the great pyramids at Giza. Fort, too, would give his eye-teeth to see those supreme examples of exotic funerary monuments. For a few seconds, he dreamed of visiting Egypt with Mrs Ansell, of touring Giza in her company. Absurd, of course. The dream evaporated. But he would not, for anything, wish Mrs Ansell to come to harm.

At the outskirts of Upper Fen he got out of the carriage and paid off the driver. Carrying his bag, he made his way through a straggle of dwelling-places towards the church and the big house. Charles Tomlinson was waiting for Eric Fort in the shadows of the south side of the church. They waited until it was completely dark before making their way to the north side and the entrance to the crypt.

Now, here they were, underground, about to go fossicking.

Holding up the lantern, Tomlinson led the way along the short passage. They emerged into a large room-like space with a slightly higher ceiling. There were wide stone shelves along the walls and coffins on the shelves, some made of wood but most of lead. It was damp and draughty and cold, so cold that Fort clamped his teeth to stop them chattering. Through some trick of ventilation, the sound of the wind from outside was transformed into a sequence of cries and moans. Yet the whole scene – the crypt, the stacked coffins, the ghostly noises – did not disturb Eric Fort. Despite his chattering teeth, it was rather to his taste.

Tomlinson passed the lantern light over the coffins. The lead ones had no markings and the brass plates on some of the wooden coffins were too tarnished to be legible. They must have been centuries old.

'We're not breaking into one of these?' said Fort, as the tall man drummed his fingers on the top of a wooden coffin.

'No, no,' said Tomlinson. 'I'm just getting the lay of the land.'

Fort was almost disappointed. Inside the bag that lay at his feet were, among other implements, a chisel, a jemmy and crowbar, and several hammers. Tomlinson moved to the end of the underground chamber. Here there were no shelves or coffins. Just an expanse of wall, crudely plastered. Tomlinson took off his gloves and felt the surface. He pressed it with his fingertips.

'Here, I think,' he said. 'We need to get behind here.'

Summer, 1645

*A*nne had to tell someone. It was a secret, of course, but she could not keep it absolutely to herself. It was like a burden too heavy to be carried by one person. She contemplated talking about it with James, the old steward, but in the end it was her sister Mary that she turned to. She described the man who had escaped from a battle and was sheltering in the willow cabin; she mentioned his fine clothes beneath the cloak, his injured hand, his plan to make his way towards the coast.

Mary thought for a time, then asked Anne to spell out the name that the man had given himself. Loyer.

She found a piece of paper and wrote down the stranger's name in large capital letters. The supposedly French name that he had, rather too deliberately, spelled out for Anne's benefit. L-O-Y-E-R. Mary gazed at the letters, and Anne watched her sister as she puzzled over them. Mary enjoyed words, liked to find different ways of saying the same thing. After a short time, Mary nodded to herself, satisfied. Satisfied but also, to judge by her expression, alarmed.

'The letters, rearranged, spell out Le Roy,' she said.

Anne shook her head. She was fearful of what might come next.

'It is French. You remember those French terms which Mr Martin has taught us?'

'Some of them.'

'It means "the king".'

'The king,' repeated Anne.

'Yes. The . . . the person you say is hiding out on the edge of our land − the person the soldiers were hunting for − it is our king.'

'King Charles?'

'Yes. Does he look like the king?'

'I do not know what the king looks like. Why would he be by himself?'

Anne, who had half identified the fugitive, now wanted to find reasons why she was wrong. Mary, who hadn't yet seen the man, was sure her sister was right.

'He might be alone − if he's escaping,' said Mary.

'Come and see,' said Anne.

The sisters made their way back to the willow shelter. After a moment the man emerged again. This time he was wearing a wide-brimmed hat that kept his features half hidden.

'I told you not to return,' he said.

'This is my sister,' said Anne.

Mary made a clumsy curtsey. Then she said, 'How do I know you are who we believe you are?'

The man looked thoughtful for a moment. Then he fumbled beneath the lacy collar at his neck and drew out a locket on a silver chain. The locket was the size of a crown-piece but three times as thick, too large for a picture or a strand of hair. Using his bandaged hand, the man picked awkwardly at the clasp on the locket. He undid it, to reveal a fragment of glass nestling inside. But it was no glass. He held it up to the sun, so that it caught the light and at once flashed with a rainbow of colours.

Mary opened her mouth to speak. But she got no further. There was a sudden flurry of movement from the area of ground above the willow hut and nearer to the house. The sisters saw a group of men striding down the slope. The man had his back to them but he saw the expression on the girls' faces. He just had time to shut up the precious stone in the locket and to slip it back inside his shirt.

Then Mr Martin appeared, with Trafford and three of the leather-jerkined soldiers who were at the house that morning.

The man in the cloak said to the sisters, 'You have betrayed me!'

He started to run towards the open, fenny stretch in front but he was too slow for the others, who were primed for pursuit. They'd dragged him down in seconds and, holding Loyer by the upper arms, two of them brought him back. Anne and Mary stood, terrified. And at the back of Anne's mind was the thought: he believes we are traitors.

The Crimean Cannon

On the Sunday afternoon, Tom and Helen caught the train to Ely. They would arrive a little too early for the supper with the Lyes at the Lion Hotel, but Helen said she wanted to have a look at the cathedral. She'd spent part of the day dipping into Ernest Lye's history of Phoenix House and the surrounding village. 'Very interesting,' was her verdict. Once arrived in Ely, they took a cab from the railway station and got down near Palace Green. The day, which had started fine, was turning damp and autumnal. The top of the west tower of the cathedral was already obscured by mist.

Once inside the doors of the west porch, the Ansells stood admiring the vista down the nave, whose flanking columns and arches framed the distant east window. It was not yet time for Evensong and there were only a handful of people and occasional points of light to be glimpsed in the cavernous interior. Near Tom and Helen were two men, both quite elderly and one in clerical garb. The latter was pointing at the tiled floor and talking about some detail to do with the pattern. Tom looked down and saw no more than an arrangement of grey and white tiles. He was about to walk further into the nave when Helen shook her head and moved closer so as to eavesdrop on what the cleric was saying.

The clergyman noticed her and, rather than moving away or lowering his voice, he beamed at Helen. He said, 'I was pointing out a new feature of our ancient foundation to this gentleman here.'

'Who is himself something of an ancient foundation,' said the other man, wheezing at his own joke.

'However ancient, we may all be renewed, and if not here then in a better place,' said the cleric. By this time Tom had come across to join them and their guide looked delighted at the addition to his audience. He explained that the tiling on the floor was only a few years old and represented a labyrinth.

'A labyrinth and not a maze, please note.'

Helen nodded and said, 'A labyrinth has only a single winding path, hasn't it? But a maze sets out to confuse you. It has false turns and dead ends.'

The cleric looked even more pleased at this. He clapped his hands.

'You are quite correct, madam. If you trace out the path among the tiles on the floor here you will, sooner or later but infallibly, arrive at the centre. You cannot go wrong provided you do not stray from the path. And another thing: the distance from the entrance of the labyrinth to the centre is exactly the same as the distance from the floor to the roof above our heads.'

Instinctively, they all looked up to where the higher reaches of the tower disappeared into the shadows. Meanwhile the cleric was saying something else. Had the lady and the two gentlemen by chance observed the new stone and fresh ironwork in the Galilee Porch on their way in? Like much of the cathedral restoration, it was the work of that distinguished architect Mr George Gilbert Scott – *Sir* George, he should say, very recently knighted. The Galilee Porch was paid for by Mrs Waddington – a most generous benefactor – widow of Canon Waddington. Had they noticed the work on their way in? No? Well, they ought to take a careful look on their way out.

Somehow, Helen and Tom found themselves taken on a tour of the cathedral by the enthusiastic cleric. Somewhere on the way, names were exchanged. His was Herbert though whether it was his first or last, they couldn't be sure. Perhaps wisely, the other old gent slipped away early so it was left to the Ansells to learn about the newly painted roof panels over the nave, the new stained-glass windows, the long-delayed restoration of the Lady Chapel after the depredations of the anti-papists and the Puritans, and so forth. After about half an hour they came to a halt under the Octagon. Herbert was explaining how a great medieval tragedy (the collapse of the old Norman tower) was followed by a great medieval triumph (the construction of the Octagon), when he suddenly interrupted himself.

'Heavens! I have allowed myself to be carried away, so great has been the pleasure of our conversation. The night cometh, when no man can work. Or to adapt the scriptures, Evensong cometh, and I have work to do. Please excuse me, Mr and Mrs Ansell. It has been a delight showing you around our ancient foundation. Do please excuse me . . .'

Herbert scurried off towards the north transept, leaving Tom and Helen half sorry, half relieved to see him go. They'd hardly said a word during the whole half-hour. They made their way back down the great concourse of the nave and towards the west entrance. As they walked across the patterned tiles Tom was about to say something to Helen about the distinction between mazes and labyrinths (how had she known *that*?) when he was distracted by the abrupt appearance of two men through the wicket-gate which was cut into one of the larger doors. The gate was narrow and, for an instant, both men struggled to pass through it at the same time. They were wearing vestments of some kind. Priests? Vergers? Whoever they were, their mission must have been urgent for, with robes flapping and without a sideways glance, they ran past the Ansells and into the body of the church.

Wondering what was going on, Helen and Tom walked out into the dank, foggy air. It was not so very late in the afternoon but the gloom was thick enough and already some of the street lights were lit. Directly in front of them on the Palace Green were a couple of bobbing lantern-lights and a ragged circle of people, visible only as shadows. There was some landmark situated on the Green, Tom thought, and then he recalled his drive in the dog cart on the previous day and the boy whose name was Davey mentioning the cannon from the Crimea. '*We won it from the Rooshians and the Queen, she gave it to us.*'

Someone cried out, a woman's voice, almost a scream. Out of the murk emerged other figures, in ones and twos and from every direction but all converging on the same place.

'Something is wrong,' said Helen. The magnetic draw of seeing the aftermath of an accident or disaster meant that she and Tom were already pacing across the soggy grass towards the spot.

The growing crowd was assembling on the far side of the cannon, which pointed away from the west front of the cathedral. Apart from that single scream, there was an ominous silence from the onlookers. Tom started to move faster, though he couldn't have said why. He reached the fringe of the group of men, women and even a few children. The light from the lanterns cast a fuzzy glow into the moist air. Had everyone decided to come together to gaze into the cannon's mouth? Then he looked down and saw a body arranged between the wheels, its head and shoulders resting on the crosspiece. Or rather he saw the legs sticking straight out in alignment with the gun, and he half saw, half guessed at the rest. But even in the uncertain light, it was impossible to ignore the dark pools of blood glinting on the ground.

Tom sensed Helen's arrival beside him. Seeing what he'd seen, she gave a sharp intake of breath and grasped him by the upper arm. For an absurd moment, Tom wondered whether the cannon had somehow discharged itself and here was its latest victim lying underneath.

'Who is it?' said Helen.

'I don't know,' said Tom.

'That was a foolish question,' said Helen. She gave a nervous laugh. Tom was aware of how tightly she was gripping his upper arm.

One of the bystanders who was carrying a light now placed it on the ground. Tom noticed that it wasn't a lantern but a domestic oil lamp. It must have been brought from one of the nearby houses. More curious or more ghoulish than the rest, the man squatted down on his haunches and inched closer to the body until his knees were almost touching the dead man's upturned feet. Tom's attention was caught by the sight of a top hat, which was resting on its brim and close to where he was standing. He knew the abandoned hat was the dead man's.

There was a shift in the circle of watchers as a burly figure thrust its way through them. From his position under the cannon's mouth, the man on his haunches looked over his shoulder at the new arrival. Now he inched back, stood up and gestured towards the corpse. Is this what you've come for? the gesture seemed to say.

'All right, all right,' said the newcomer to no one in particular. 'That'll do.'

It was a police constable. There were sighs of relief at the uniform, perhaps of actual recognition of the man wearing the uniform. Ely wasn't a big place.

'Give me that light, will you, sir?' said the constable to the man who'd approached the body. 'It's Mr Grace, isn't it?'

'It is,' said the man, stooping to retrieve the lamp. He handed it to the constable who now ducked beneath the cannon and angled the beams so that they shone full on the upper part of the body. Instinctively, several of the men and women who were gathered nearest to the cannon crouched down in sympathy with the policeman. Also to see whatever they could see.

There was blood on the man's coat, bright in the light. He had evidently sustained wounds to the chest or throat. His head was tilted forward so that it was scarcely possible to make out anything of his features. Nevertheless a child's excited cry, a boy's voice, said, 'There 'e is!'

Tom experienced a thrill of recognition. Again, he glanced at the hat on the ground. He had seen that hat before, he was certain of it, although he could not have pointed to any distinguishing features of what was nothing more than a rather battered piece of headgear. But he'd glimpsed it yesterday, dangling on the hatstand of Phoenix House, home to Mr Ernest Lye. Almost without thinking, he bent down to pick it up. The attention of everyone else on the scene was fixed on the body and the policeman under the cannon.

Tom turned the hat so that he could see the lining. He twisted the interior this way and that until it caught a gleam of light from the lamp. There was a name written in ink in the lining, the capital letters faded but still just about distinguishable. Or at least the first three letters of the name were. Perhaps Tom recognized them so quickly because they were familiar to him. They were the same as his own. T–O–M. He looked back at the policeman and the lamplit corpse and, despite the unhelpful tilt of the dead man's face, he now observed the prominent jaw. The thrill of recognition turned into a sickening certainty. Very carefully, much more carefully than he'd picked it up, he replaced the top hat on the ground.

'I do know him,' Tom said to Helen. 'It is Charles Tomlinson. The man I met yesterday at Phoenix House. I told you about him, remember. He is Mrs Lye's cousin.'

'Oh this is terrible. Do they know?'

How can they know? thought Tom.

'Of course they do not,' said Helen, completing his thought. 'How could they know? They'd be here otherwise.'

'We are due to meet the Lyes. Someone must tell them.'

'Yes,' said Helen. 'Whose hat is that down there?'

'His hat.'

Their whole conversation was conducted in whispered asides. Neither of the Ansells moved. They watched while the constable came out from beneath the black shaft of the cannon and stood up. He returned the light to its owner. With both hands free, he made shooing gestures at the crowd, now several people thick and with those at the back craning their necks and standing on tiptoe to get a better view. Then he fumbled beneath his cape. Tom guessed he was reaching for his rattle in order to summon help. It wasn't necessary for another figure emerged from the onlookers, who promptly parted to let him through.

'Parr,' he said softly. He was not wearing a uniform but his manner and the way in which the constable came to attention showed that he must be a superior officer, perhaps an Inspector.

'Sir!'

'There 'e is!' said the same little boy, who could have been referring either to the dead man or to the new policeman. This time a woman shushed the boy. The Inspector said nothing but looked in the lad's direction. He waited a moment before turning to the constable.

'Tell these people to move back, Parr.'

But no further command was needed. The onlookers recognized this individual as well, or at least they responded to his tone of quiet authority, and shuffled back so as to form a looser semicircle. The procedure with the household lamp was repeated, with the newcomer borrowing it and ducking beneath the Russian gun. He scrutinized the dead man who, Tom was convinced by now, had to be Charles Tomlinson. The three letters in the lining of the top hat, the prominent jaw. He debated with himself whether it was his business to inform the senior policeman of the corpse's identity.

The man who owned the lamp waited until the second officer completed his own scrutiny. Then he came forward and, gesturing towards one of the houses that edged the north side of the Green, said, 'I have information to give, Inspector. I saw what happened. I live over there.'

He spoke firmly and clearly, aware of his audience, as if staking a claim to the event.

'Of course, Mr Grace,' said the policeman. 'I recognize you. I know where you live. I am Inspector Francis.'

'I am a witness to this crime,' the other said.

There was an outbreak of murmuring and then absolute silence among the people standing around as they hung on for the information. Inspector Francis clapped his hands together, softly but as if he'd come to a decision.

'Then let's move over there, shall we? Parr, keep an eye on

things. People will soon be arriving for Evensong in the cathedral. Do not allow anyone to approach the body or to touch anything in the area.'

'Sir.'

Tom felt a twinge of guilt on hearing the Inspector's order that nothing was to be touched. The constable stayed near the cannon's mouth, his attention swivelling between the body and the crowd. A few people were already drifting away since they'd already seen all there was to see and were no longer to be permitted to hear anything of interest, but others, including some soberly dressed citizens arriving for the cathedral service, couldn't resist coming across to see what was going on. Meanwhile the Inspector and Mr Grace walked to the rear of the gun, and, half obscured by the growing gloom, started to converse in low tones.

Tom was relieved. Neither he nor Helen had been witnesses to anything except the other bystanders. So there was nothing more they could do or should do here. He decided it was not his job to reveal he'd met the dead man and knew his name. Not his job or his duty. The police were in command now. They'd soon find the top hat and decipher the name.

Helen and he walked away from the Crimean cannon and the body of Mr Charles Tomlinson and the remnant of the crowd. With Helen holding tight to her husband's arm, they crossed Palace Green at a diagonal towards the west front of the cathedral and the High Street. On a road just beyond lay the Lion Hotel, where they were due to meet Mr and Mrs Ernest Lye.

Neither Tom nor Helen said a word to each other. Helen thought of Lydia Lye and the terrible surprise she was about to receive on hearing of her cousin's death. As for Tom, he was struggling to compose his thoughts. He did have a duty to perform now, a most unpleasant one, and his mind was split between that and the image of the dead man. A body laid out beneath the gun barrel, head tilted forward and front all bloody. The top hat with T-O-M inked in the lining.

Assuming the Lyes were already at the Lion – and they should be since the arrangement was that they were meeting the Ansells there at about this time – then it fell to him to report that Mrs Lye's cousin had died. As a result of a violent attack. Therefore, had been murdered. At least that was what it looked like.

Maybe if they walked slowly enough, someone else would get to the hotel first and break the bad news. But who else knew of the Lyes' plans and whereabouts for the evening, except possibly the dead man? Tom foresaw the course of the next hour or two: breaking the news, then the shock and the condolences, followed by no supper, then a visit to the police house, his and Helen's return to Cambridge. He rehearsed imaginary conversations in his head. Decided to say as little as possible to the Lyes of the details of Charles Tomlinson's death. It would be easier that way. Then he rebuked himself for considering matters so calmly while a man was lying dead beneath a Russian gun. Rebuked himself even for having an appetite for supper. Yet, strange as it might be, he was hungry. Helen interrupted his thoughts.

'Tom, I do hope this is not the beginning of another . . . drama.'

'I'm not sure what . . .?'

'You know, a *drama*, as in Durham.'

Now he understood. The Ansells had recently been caught up in a murder and its aftermath in Durham. Helen had even spent a few hours in a prison cell because she had been apprehended close to the corpse of a murdered man and her guilt assumed. Before their marriage, too, they had been involved in something similar in Salisbury. Tom was quick to reassure her that, this time, it was different. They weren't involved. Innocent bystanders only.

'But you knew Mr Tomlinson,' said Helen.

'Knew him? I met him yesterday for a few minutes. This nasty business is nothing to do with us.'

'Whether it is or not, it is strange to think it all happened while we were inside the cathedral being shown around.'

By now they had reached the Lion. The hotel was an old coaching inn that had not only survived the coming of the railway but was prospering because of its proximity to the cathedral and the High Street. Two porters were standing to one side of the hotel entrance. They barely acknowledged Tom and Helen but continued talking, their heads close together and eyes casting sidelong glances in the direction from which the Ansells had just come. Evidently, the news of the murder – or at least of some violent incident occurring only a few hundred yards away – was already spreading like a stain.

Inside the lobby there was an air of suppressed excitement. Staff and a handful of guests stood in two distinct clusters. There was a low buzz of conversation. Every face turned towards Tom and Helen when the couple entered the lobby. When it became obvious that the newcomers had nothing to say, either because they couldn't or they wouldn't, the faces turned in again and the buzzing resumed.

A middle-aged man hovering between the two groups, staff and guests, came towards them. To judge by his clothes and manner he was the manager or perhaps the proprietor of the Lion Hotel. His expectant expression said, How may I be of assistance? or perhaps, Have you really got no information for us? Tom explained they were at the hotel to meet Mr and Mrs Lye.

'Oh a pity, you have just missed them. They went out a little while ago. For a walk, I believe. An evening stroll.'

The man paused. He rubbed his palms down a rather greasy-looking waistcoat. He leaned forward as if to say something confidential.

'Have you heard anything?'

'I don't understand,' said Helen. 'What is there to hear?'

'Never mind,' said the manager or proprietor, put off by Helen's cool tone. 'If you would please to wait for Mr and Mrs Lye in there. I'm sure they'll be back soon.'

After asking their names, he ushered them into a snug off the dining room. There was no one else in the little room. A fire was blazing and, though it was too hot as well as airless, Tom was glad to be away from the curious glances in the lobby. What he had to report was for the ears of Ernest and Lydia Lye alone. Although the rumour of some shocking event on Palace Green had reached the hotel, he guessed that the people inside were prevented from seeing for themselves either by fear or a sense of propriety or because, as staff, they could not wander off the premises.

'Perhaps Mr and Mrs Lye already know what has occurred,' said Tom.

'Not if they went for a walk, as we were told,' said Helen. 'You do not go for a walk if you know it will lead you to a body.'

Helen and Tom might have sat in one of the several armchairs crowding an already small space but they were too tense, too distracted. They busied themselves keeping out of reach of the fire and examining the pictures – hunting scenes or views of the town in which the Lion Hotel generally figured somewhere – that hung on the walls.

There was patterned glass in the upper part of the door separating the snug from the hotel lobby. The glass darkened and a man walked into the room. It was Ernest Lye. Immediately behind him came Mrs Lye.

'Mr and Mrs Ansell,' she said. 'We were told you were in here. What a pleasure it is to see you once more.'

Tom and Helen realized in an instant that the Lyes knew nothing, had discovered nothing. Wherever they had wandered in their early evening stroll, their route couldn't have taken them anywhere close to the west front of the cathedral or Palace Green. Otherwise they would surely have . . .?

'Has something happened?' said Lydia Lye. She glanced over her shoulder. 'What are all those people waiting for out there?'

Helen looked at Tom. He said, 'I have some bad news, I'm afraid.'

Now Lydia looked towards her husband. Ernest had said not a word since coming into the snug, had not even uttered a perfunctory greeting. He stood there, his gaze switching anxiously between the Ansells. He did not return his wife's glance. He was pale, strained. Does *he* already know? Tom thought.

Tom was about to tell them that Mr Charles Tomlinson was dead, when another shape darkened the glass panel to the snug. A man opened the door and peered round. It was Inspector Francis, the policeman from Palace Green. By the better light indoors, Tom saw a short man with a slightly upturned nose which might have been created for sniffing the air. The police officer looked briefly at the two couples, before coming right inside the snug. He closed the door behind him and stood against it. There was nothing exactly threatening about his actions but, as if by instinct, the four people already inside moved back. The Inspector nodded at Tom and Helen before turning to the Lyes.

'Mr Lye, Mr Ernest Lye?'

'Yes.'

'I am Inspector Francis of the Ely police force. May I speak to you, sir?'

'Yes.'

'I mean in private.'

'Speak to me about what?'

Ernest's voice was subdued, not much above a whisper. Perhaps he was merely responding to the Inspector's manner. The policeman was as calm and authoritative as he had been by the body on the cathedral green. Ernest Lye looked more drawn, older. Tom's mouth was dry. He was conscious of a wave of heat emanating from the fire.

'If you don't mind, sir, I would rather not say in front of . . .'

Tom shifted slightly to get away from the fire, but Ernest Lye must have thought he was going to leave for he raised his hand and said, 'No, Mr Ansell. Do not go.'

The policeman looked surprised. To Tom, he said, 'Are you a friend of Mr Lye?'

'I'm a lawyer. Thomas Ansell. This is my wife.'

'Not with a local firm?'

'A firm in London.'

'You have just arrived in Ely?'

'We have been here a couple of days,' said Tom, wondering where this was leading. 'We are staying in Cambridge.'

'Well, a London lawyer is already in attendance,' said the Inspector, half to himself. 'But, just to clarify things, you *are* Mr Lye's lawyer.'

'In a manner of speaking,' said Tom.

'Why are you here, Inspector?' said Lydia Lye. It was her first comment since the policeman's entrance. Her face was as drawn and pale as her husband's. Inspector Francis ducked his head very slightly in acknowledgement of the question but he did not answer it. Instead he brought his hands together in a decisive gesture.

'I must really request you to come with me, Mr Lye, request you for the second time.'

He allowed a few seconds to pass and when it was plain that Ernest Lye, for whatever reason, was not going to comply, said, 'Then, despite the present company, I must say what it is my duty to say. Ernest Lye, you are under arrest.'

Lydia Lye grasped her husband's arm. Helen gasped. Tom felt trickles of sweat running down his face. Of all of them, Ernest Lye seemed the least affected. He sighed and said, 'Arrested on what charge, Inspector?'

'On suspicion of murder. The murder of Mr Charles Tomlinson.'

'Very well. Look to my wife, will you, Mr and Mrs Ansell?'

He moved towards the Inspector, who still stood by the door. The officer opened it and ushered Lye past him. Moments later, there was a groan, and Lydia Lye crumpled to the floor. Helen at once moved to attend to her, indicating to Tom that he should call the others back. Tom went to the door of the snug. At first he thought the lobby was empty but, in fact, everyone was crowded into the hotel entrance, looking at the retreating figures of Inspector Francis and Ernest Lye.

He turned back to see Helen sitting on the floor, cradling Lydia Lye's head in her lap and wielding her vial of sal volatile. Tom's wife carried smelling salts in her bag. Not for herself, she'd once told her husband, since she was not the sort of lady who felt an obligation to swoon or faint. No, she carried them for others who might need reviving. That covered men as well as women, she insisted, since even representatives of the male species had been known to faint from time to time. Now she uncapped the vial and held it under Mrs Lye's nose.

Lydia inhaled deeply and a shudder ran down her body. Her eyes opened. It took her a while to focus, to see Helen above her with Tom standing at a little distance.

'What happened?' she said.

The Witness

What happened was straightforward or seemed straightforward. Mr Grace, the witness from one of the houses overlooking Palace Green, informed Inspector Francis that he had not only seen the murderous attack which occurred by the Crimean cannon but that he knew the identity of the murderer. He told his story to the policeman while they stood together by the same Russian cannon. George Grace was a witness to be taken seriously, or at any rate he was one who took himself seriously.

From his father Mr Grace inherited a leather-tanning factory on the edge of the city and, like many inheritors of manufactories, he was keen to put a little distance between himself and the source of his prosperity. He was a justice of the peace and a benefactor of the cathedral (in the company of his family he had already attended this Sunday's Matins). George Grace was young, or at least not so far into middle age, and he considered that his senses were sharp. On this late Sunday afternoon he was sitting in his drawing room, reading the paper. He had positioned himself near the window in order to catch the fading light from outside, and also because he liked to look out at the view from time to time. Not that there was much to see on a dull autumn afternoon with the mist coming down.

When it grew too dim for him to continue reading in comfort, George Grace got up to light the lamp. Pausing by the window, he glimpsed through the railings which formed the boundary between his property and the Green a figure that he recognized. It was, as he explained to Inspector Francis, a gentleman called Charles Tomlinson, whose acquaintance he'd recently made. (He didn't add that he had first met Tomlinson in the Lion Hotel and had been struck by the other's exotic tales.)

Tomlinson was not out walking by himself. There was a figure on his far side. The two were pacing almost in step, so that the identity and even the outline of the second individual was obscured from George Grace. Nevertheless, as they passed his window, he heard Tomlinson clearly address the other man as Lye. The afternoon was still and Tomlinson had a resonant voice. Yes, he had definitely referred to his companion as Mr Lye. George Grace already knew of Ernest Lye since he was familiar with the names of any notable families who lived in the area. And he also recalled from his conversations with Charles Tomlinson that that interesting gentleman was related to Mrs Lye. It was one reason for his presence in Ely.

Thinking no more about it, Mr Grace returned to his chair and his newspaper. But soon afterwards he heard a cry from the Green, a masculine cry of distress or pain. He returned to the window. It was, as he admitted to the Inspector, difficult to see clearly, but there were two individuals facing each other near the mouth of the cannon. One was tall, and unmistakably Charles Tomlinson. He was weaving about as if inebriated. The other figure, a shorter one, stood at a distance, not giving any assistance.

George Grace observed Tomlinson sit on the ground and then seem to push himself backward into the shelter of the cannon. The second individual hesitated a moment, bent down and then walked rapidly away, soon to be lost in the gloom. Mr Grace waited for Tomlinson to emerge from beneath the great gun but he did not.

Feeling increasingly uneasy, George Grace took up the light and emerged from his front door. As he stepped through the gate in the railings fronting his house, he was aware of other people converging on the same spot on the Green. The next few minutes were all confusion. Heads swivelling in every direction, hands gesticulating or pointing at random through the mist. Scarcely coherent comments. Then tentative approaches to the body, a full view of which was obscured by the way it was lodged under the cannon. What had happened? Was the person still alive? Could anything be done?

No one was willing to approach the corpse. Individuals were despatched – or despatched themselves – to the police-house. From what he overheard, Mr Grace didn't think that anyone had witnessed the actual moment of the attack. Like him, they were alerted by a man crying out. Two or three had also glimpsed a second person disappearing in the gloom, in the direction of the High Street. No one seemed to have thought of taking off in pursuit. No one seemed to know who it was. But George Grace knew. It was Mr Ernest Lye. He had witnessed Tomlinson and Lye passing his window moments before the assault, he'd heard Tomlinson call Lye by name.

Mr Grace hung on to this important piece of information, actually two important pieces. The probable identity of the dead man and the probable identity of his murderer. He envisaged giving testimony in court, testimony treated with respect on account of his standing as a citizen of Ely, testimony which could deliver a man to the gallows. Then he decided to examine the body for himself, in case he might see something to add to his testimony. He heard the judge complimenting him on his sharp senses, his cool head, his quick wits.

Mr Grace squatted down, with some difficulty, and inched

closer to the body. Almost immediately he regretted his bravado. He felt his gorge rise when, with the aid of his lamp, he saw the damage inflicted on Tomlinson. Or at least he saw the dreadful, contorted expression on the man's face, which was soaked in blood. There was more on his chest. George Grace observed a particularly severe wound to his forehead. That it was Charles Tomlinson, however, there could be no doubt. Somehow this also confirmed for Grace that Tomlinson's companion, and murderer, had been Ernest Lye. Fortunately, Mr Grace was prevented from having to do or see anything more by the arrival of the constable, and then of Inspector Francis.

The Inspector listened attentively to what Mr Grace had to say. It was his habit to listen attentively. And to observe carefully. It seemed that quite a bit of his work as a policeman had already been done. Grace's identification of the body was quickly confirmed by the discovery of Tomlinson's top hat. In addition, Francis himself was familiar with Tomlinson's features. The probable murderer was also named. Now there remained only the small matter of apprehending him.

In normal circumstances, insofar as a murder can ever be normal, he would have followed up George Grace's account by interviewing Ernest Lye, establishing his whereabouts during the afternoon, probing his links with the dead man, and so on, before making any further move. Inspector Stephen Francis was a cautious man.

But it happened that Inspector Francis' wife was the sister to Mr Salter, the manager of the Lion Hotel, the man with the greasy waistcoat. Inspector Francis' wife often passed on titbits of information, or even mere chit-chat, which she picked up from her brother, to whom she was close. Salter was a good hotel manager but he was a busybody and a gossip. His sister Mrs Francis was a helpless chatterer, and her husband was her involuntary listener. Stephen Francis listened to her (most of the time) as attentively as he listened to everyone else. The policeman did not disdain any information, even that provided by his wife.

He was already familiar with Charles Tomlinson, or at any rate had glimpsed him going about the town. A queer-looking cove, he thought, one not entirely to be trusted. He knew that Tomlinson frequented the Lion Hotel. He was aware, too, of the friendship between Mrs Lye and Tomlinson, or at least aware that they'd been seen together on occasion. Nothing remarkable about their keeping company since they were cousins, weren't they? But a comment which had been passed on to Francis by his wife, perhaps originating with Salter, to the effect that they made 'a handsome couple', stuck in the Inspector's mind. Do cousins make a couple? Some do. So if one were to go looking for a reason for antagonism between Ernest Lye and Charles Tomlinson . . .

By itself, this would have been sufficiently interesting for Inspector Francis to interview Ernest Lye. Interest would have turned to suspicion with the discovery that the two men had been seen together by a reliable witness only moments before the death of one of them. But even that would not have been enough to lead to Lye's immediate arrest. There was another reason for the arrest, a detail that Francis had noticed in the snug of the Lion Hotel.

Not that Inspector Francis had gone to the Lion in pursuit of Ernest Lye. No, he went to pick up extra information about Tomlinson. He knew that the man was in the habit of staying there. He wanted to speak to his brother-in-law and his staff, to find out whether anyone had seen Tomlinson in the company of any individual, and not only Ernest Lye, at any period during the afternoon.

So, choosing a single constable by the name of Collis to accompany him and leaving the rest to handle the aftermath of the scene on the Green, Inspector Francis strode the few hundred yards to the Lion. An extra reason for walking this way was that he'd heard from George Grace and others about the second person fleeing in this direction. It was possible that someone might have spotted something. Yet not likely. To the mist was added the gathering dark.

When Francis and Collis arrived at the Lion they entered a lobby which was unusually crowded with staff and guests. The Inspector's brother-in-law, Salter, greeted him warmly. The manager did not expect to prise any details out of the policeman, who was like a clam compared to his wife, but it was always gratifying to show off one's connections in the upper reaches of the Isle of Ely constabulary. Without giving anything away, Inspector Francis

established, within a few moments, that not only was Mr Charles
Tomlinson presently a guest of the Hotel but that his cousin Mrs
Lye, together with her husband, was also here. In fact, said Salter
pointing to the snug, they are all in *there* now. All? said Francis.
There are four of them, said Salter. Mr and Mrs Lye and two
friends of theirs, I suppose.

Telling Collis to remain outside, Inspector Francis entered the
snug and saw four individuals, two of whom he recognized. He
was a little thrown by the realization that there was a lawyer
already on the spot. Up to that point he had politely asked Ernest
Lye if he could speak to him. It was only when Lye put out his
hand as if to detain Thomas Ansell from leaving that Francis
changed tack. For Inspector Francis observed that the cuff of Mr
Lye's shirt was stained with something that looked very like blood.
The man himself seemed unaware of it. The others hadn't noticed
either. Their attention was fixed on the Inspector.

To give himself time to think, the Inspector turned to the
lawyer fellow, Thomas Ansell, and asked him a few questions
without really wanting to know any of the answers. He didn't
mind whether the Ansells came from London or Timbuktu,
whether they'd arrived yesterday or last year. What was going
through Francis' mind was as follows: the evidence against this
man standing in front of me is mounting up by the minute. Ernest
Lye has been observed near the scene of the crime. Ernest Lye
may have very good reasons to resent or hate Charles Tomlinson
on account of the latter's connection with his wife (who is indeed
a handsome woman, the Inspector noted again). And Lye has
blood on his shirt cuff. That was the clincher.

In addition, Inspector Francis was struck by Ernest Lye's
manner. It was not exactly shifty, but it was somehow vague and
evasive. There was a distant look in Ernest Lye's blue eyes. Francis'
experience told him that men of Lye's class were generally happy
to assist the police, even if they sometimes did so in a manner
that suggested they were dealing with servants. So he made one
final request that Lye should accompany him and, when that got
no response, he had no choice but to announce the gentleman's
arrest.

Inspector Francis and Ernest Lye exited the hotel lobby under
the eyes of everyone. No one said a word. Once outside, Francis

indicated that Constable Collis should walk on the far side of their man. He didn't think Lye would be so foolish as to run for it but you never knew of course . . .

'So Ernest Lye did go for a walk by himself,' said Tom.

'Yes,' said Helen. 'He and his wife arrived in Ely sometime in the middle of the afternoon. He claimed that he wanted to stretch his legs while she preferred to stay behind in the hotel and rest. According to what Mrs Lye told me, he was gone for about an hour or so. When he came back, she said she'd grown tired of resting and would also like some exercise. So Mr Lye went out for a second time, to accompany his wife. This time they were out for only a short time. They returned to find us in the snug.'

'And the Inspector turned up a few minutes later.'

'Could Mr Lye have done this thing?' said Helen.

'It is hard to believe,' said Tom. 'He's a mild-mannered sort of chap. And what would be his motive?'

'There seems to have been . . . a closeness . . . between Mrs Lye and this Mr Tomlinson.'

The same idea had occurred to Tom, ever since seeing the two cousins together at Phoenix House, but he was reluctant to say it out loud. Maybe it was the cautious lawyer in him. Besides, it was quite a stretch to take 'closeness' as a plausible reason for murder, at least for a mild-mannered chap. Though you never knew of course . . .

'I'm sorry,' said Tom. He was lost in his speculations while Helen was saying something.

'I said, did you observe the cuff of Mr Lye's shirt?'

'I don't think so. Why?'

'There were stains on it. Blood perhaps. I noticed the Inspector noticing.'

Tom hadn't seen this. Helen was so sharp-eyed! The detail put a new complexion on the matter. Blood on the husband's cuff. The 'closeness' of the cousins. Ernest Lye's absence for an hour when he was apparently walking about in Ely. His strangely resigned manner when he was arrested. Was it so hard after all to believe that Lye had done the deed?

Helen and Tom were finally back at the Devereux Hotel in Cambridge. It was late on the Sunday night of the murder.

Returning by train from Ely, they arrived cold, exhausted and supperless. Tom might have been hungry before but his appetite was gone now. Helen said she couldn't eat. The Ansells had remained in Ely for some time after the murder of Tomlinson. Mrs Lye wanted Helen to keep her company for a while. Fortunately, a room was already reserved at the Lion. Realizing that the evening weather would be unpleasant, the Lyes had booked a hotel chamber rather than intending a return to Upper Fen.

Meanwhile Tom tried to find out what he could about the circumstances leading up to the death of Charles Tomlinson. He felt an obligation towards the Lyes and towards Ernest in particular, as the brother of the late senior partner of his firm.

Tom's enquiries did not take him very far or very long. Leaving Helen and Lydia Lye at the Lion, he returned to Palace Green. There was only the original constable — Parr? — left on duty, armed with a lantern and keeping a few dawdlers at bay. The body of Charles Tomlinson had been removed. Tom got into conversation with Parr on the pretext that he'd been on the scene earlier and noticed a top hat, discarded. Evidence perhaps? As a law-abiding citizen — as a lawyer, in fact — it was remiss of him not to have mentioned the hat to the policeman in charge. Constable Parr assured him that the top hat had been recovered and furthermore that the lining supplied the dead gent's name: Tomlinson.

The constable seemed happy to chat. Tom expressed surprise that the body was gone so soon.

'Normally a body might be left in sit-oo, sir, but we had to remove this one, given where it was. Almost sacred ground.'

The constable gestured towards the invisible cathedral.

'This is a terrible business,' said Tom.

'We do not enjoy much murdering on the Isle of Ely.'

'How did Mr Tomlinson die?'

'It was what we call a frenzied attack, sir. A knifing, we believe. Perhaps a knifing.'

Tom glanced around. The beams from the policeman's lantern were soon blotted up by the dark and the mist. On the periphery of the light stood three forlorn dawdlers, with nowhere better to go to on this damp Sunday night. Nearby was the dripping cannon and its black mouth. For all the houses close to, and the great western facade of the cathedral, the little group might have been hundreds of miles from anywhere. Tom shivered. It wasn't altogether feigned.

'Aren't you afraid, Constable . . . afraid that the person who did this might still be out there?'

'Afraid, sir? No, I have my trusty rattle to summon help. And besides we have already apprehended the individual who did it. Who perhaps did it. There was a witness, see. He says—'

The dawdlers, poised on the edge of the light and straining to hear, moved closer like dogs ready to pick up any scrap. Parr stopped what he was about to say and cleared his throat. Evidently thinking he'd given too much away, he said, 'If you don't mind, sir, I am not at liberty to say more.'

'Of course not, Constable.'

Tom contemplated going on to the police-house to try to see Ernest Lye, but he did not want go any further without getting instructions from David Mackenzie. There might be more information on the murder but, on balance, it seemed unlikely so early on. The only fresh piece of knowledge he'd picked up on the Green was that the cause of Charles Tomlinson's death was a knife attack. Perhaps.

He went back to the Lion Hotel. Mrs Lye was resting in her room. She seemed quite composed after her bout of fainting, considering that her husband had just been arrested on suspicion of murdering her cousin. Composed enough, in fact, to have given some account of Ernest's movements to Helen. Yet, if her story was meant to exonerate him, it actually provided another suspicious circumstance since Ernest was out of her sight during the time of the murder.

'Her calmness is the shock, I suppose,' said Helen to Tom later in their rooms in the Devereux. 'She will feel it later.'

'A sort of calm before the storm.'

'Yes. What are you going to do, Tom? I mean, do about Mr Lye.'

'I cannot do much for him directly. If he didn't commit the . . . this crime . . . then I am sure he will shortly be released. If he did, then I think that the Inspector will surely find it out for certain . . .'

'The Inspector seemed to me the sort of person to get at the truth.'

'. . . and if he did do it, then Mr Lye will require an altogether different type of lawyer from me.'

'Anyway, this nasty business is nothing to do with us.'

'Did I say that?'

'You did. Before we arrived at the Lion.'

'Well, I'll know better next time. Helen, do you want to go to bed?'

'After everything that's happened this evening?'

'I mean that I am going to have to stay up for a while. I must write an account for David Mackenzie. I'll send a cable tomorrow but he will require all the facts in a letter.'

'In that case I shall go to bed now,' said Helen, sounding slightly disappointed. 'Join me soon, it has not been an agreeable evening.'

They kissed, chastely. Tom settled down at the desk in the sitting room and, using the headed notepaper of the Devereux Hotel, he set about writing to David Mackenzie. It was too late for the Sunday post but, burning with news, he intended to get it off first thing the next morning. Tom confined himself to an outline but it still took three pages. A sketch of the connections between the Lyes and Tomlinson, an account of how he and Helen had by chance been present soon after the discovery of Tomlinson's body, a description of the subsequent arrest of Ernest Lye in the hotel. Tom didn't give any opinion on Lye's guilt or innocence or go into details about the reasons for the arrest. Instead he wrote only that the Inspector was 'acting on what he perceived to be the facts.'

After he finished, Tom read the letter through several times. Even though he was writing to his employer as well as to someone he considered an almost-friend, the language was stiff and constrained. Burning news it may have been, but it read more like a police report than a newspaper one. Perhaps Tom was trying to avoid saying that he believed Ernest Lye to be responsible for the murder of Charles Tomlinson. Setting the business down on paper somehow made Lye's guilt more likely. Perhaps Tom was, between the lines of the letter, asking for help. Obviously the search for Alexander Lye's missing will should be called off. But what was his, Tom's, responsibility now? If Lye went before the magistrate, as he surely would, and was then committed to trial, the heavy guns would have to brought in to defend him.

Tom sealed the letter, turned off the gas lights and sat in darkness for a while. Eventually, he joined Helen in the next-door bedroom. She was asleep but he did not find it easy to drop off himself. Details from the past few hours kept flashing through his mind: the letters T-O-M in the lining of the dead man's hat, the arrest of Ernest Lye in the overheated snug, the police constable saying, 'We do not enjoy much murdering on the Isle of Ely.'

Inspector Francis Investigates

I nspector Stephen Francis was not satisfied with his arrest. The circumstantial evidence pointed at Ernest Lye but he wondered whether it was strong enough to gain a conviction. All that would change, of course, following some sort of confession from Lye. But that confession the gentleman was refusing to provide.

Francis spent a couple of hours talking with him at the police-house in Lynn Road, first on the Sunday evening and again on the Monday morning. The policeman was aware that Lye would have to be charged or released, and sooner rather than later. This was not some labourer or laundrywoman ignorant of the law. This was a gentleman, someone to be handled circumspectly. When Lye expressed a wish for a cigar, Francis sent out for some at his own expense and the two men sat in a pleasant fug, which made the talk go easier. As it happened, talks were more Francis' style than interrogations. He made better progress with malefactors that way.

But he made no progress with Ernest Lye, despite the cigars. The gentleman conceded that he did not greatly care for his wife's cousin, Charles Tomlinson. Had not cared for him ever since the fellow hove into a view after an absence of many years in foreign climes. Why not? asked Francis. I simply didn't care for the fellow, said Lye, I thought he was, well, a bit of a fraud. Further prompted by Francis, Lye owned up to a touch of 'resentment' towards Tomlinson. At least he did not demur at the

Inspector's choice of word. But resentment was a long way from murderous rage.

Mr Lye willingly agreed that he had been by himself, walking about Ely for an hour or so during the late afternoon while his wife was resting at the Lion Hotel. He could not now remember the route he had taken, although it would almost certainly have included the cathedral precincts. He thought he might have walked around the Dean's Meadow on the south side of the cathedral. Had he met anyone else while he was out walking? said the Inspector. No, he did not believe so. What was he doing then? Walking and thinking. An Englishman has the right to walk and think, Inspector.

Then Lye returned to the hotel, only to find his wife impatient for a breath of foggy autumnal air. The two of them went out, briefly, and came back to find their supper guests, Mr and Mrs Ansell, and, shortly afterwards, the Inspector himself appeared. Next Francis brought up the account of George Grace – though he did not name the witness – who had seen Ernest Lye with Tomlinson late on the afternoon in question, the two men walking together on Palace Green. At this Lye looked genuinely puzzled and surprised. He maintained he had met no one, and definitely not Tomlinson. The Inspector made a mental note to visit Mr Grace and check his story. He remembered that Grace did not actually claim to have seen Lye, only to have heard his name uttered aloud.

Finally, Francis brought out his trump card. What was that stain on Mr Lye's shirt cuff? It looked remarkably like blood. Ernest Lye examined his cuff, as if he had not noticed it before. Yes, it was blood. Whose? Mine, he said, and went on to explain how while he'd been out walking in the Dean's Meadow – or perhaps it was elsewhere, he couldn't recall now – he scraped his wrist against a raggedy piece of iron as he passed through a kissing-gate. The wound was slight, not much more than a scratch, and he staunched it with a handkerchief. By the time he returned to the Lion Hotel he had forgotten the scratch, didn't even mention it to his wife.

As proof, Ernest Lye now produced a bloodstained handkerchief which he proffered to the Inspector, who waved it away. Lye showed him the jagged red line on his wrist which, to the

Inspector's eyes, looked to be a bit more than a 'scratch'. However, there was no way of absolutely disproving Lye's story.

So much had Stephen Francis learned from Ernest Lye on the Sunday evening after his arrest. The man appeared quite calm, and gratefully accepted soup and cheese (all that the police-house could provide) in lieu of the proper supper. Francis saw him accommodated as comfortably as possible in his cell, and promised he would be back early on the Monday morning. He did return early, and had what was essentially the same conversation with Mr Lye, whose story hadn't changed.

Finally Lye said, 'When am I to be released, Inspector?'

'I cannot say, sir. My investigations are not yet concluded.'

'Well, you know best, I suppose.'

Inspector Francis left the police-house, hoping to find George Grace still at his home on Palace Green. He wanted to hear from Mr Grace once more his account of seeing Tomlinson and Lye together. As he walked towards the cathedral area he noticed Mrs Lye. No doubt she was on her way to visit her husband. She was on the other side of the street from Francis, and she looked preoccupied. He would have liked to talk to her too, to discover whether she had observed anything out of the ordinary in her husband's manner when he returned from his 'walk' on the previous afternoon. But, of course, there would be little point in such a conversation since any evidence in her husband's favour was not admissible in court.

Really, Inspector Francis was baffled. Baffled not only by the murder of Charles Tomlinson but baffled by the manner of the man who, he was increasingly sure, was not the guilty party after all. Stephen Francis was used to nailing a felon almost straight-away, since in a small place like Ely it was hard to run or hide. Once caught, the felons tended to cough. On the rare occasions when someone held out against him during one of their 'talks', the person did it with a mixture of bluster and sullenness which was as good as an admission. Less often, the guilty party was subdued or even cowed, not so much by the presence of the police as by the realization of what he'd done. This was the case with one of the only two murders to have hitherto come Francis' way, a farm labourer who beat his wife to death.

But the case of Ernest Lye was quite different. Lye was not

cowed. Nor was he sullen or blustering. Francis had never before encountered a suspect who told him, 'Well, you know best, I suppose.' The man was not protesting his innocence in loud terms but he definitely expected to be released. Certainly Lye could not remain in the police-house or even be kept in Ely, which had no gaol. Prisoners were transferred to the County Gaol in Cambridge. Was that where Ernest Lye was headed? Unless another witness came forward, the sole testimony against Mr Lye would be Mr Grace's. Which was the reason the Inspector was on his way to see him now.

After the Inspector left the police-house, Ernest Lye gazed at the wall of his cell. He was sitting on the hard bed and not seeing the plain stone or any of the few features of the sparsely furnished room. Instead he was contemplating the events of the previous day and his part in them. He had given a truthful account to the Inspector of his actions, as far as he knew them. He thought he remembered going for a stroll in the Dean's Meadow. He believed he had scraped his hand on the rough metal of a kissing-gate. And he did not recall any meeting with Charles Tomlinson. But he could not be absolutely sure of a single one of these items. Ernest Lye had been suffering more and more often from those lapses of memory, those blank spots of time, which resulted in his being uncertain of his activities or at least of his movements.

Of course, he did not really imagine he had carried out a murder unawares, even if he'd read of such extreme crimes being committed by a sleepwalker or a person under hypnosis. But a small voice inside him, the merest whisper, told him that he could not really regret the death of Tomlinson, that he was almost glad someone else had done it. He'd admitted to Inspector Francis that he did not care for the dead man, even resented him. The source of the resentment was, yes, his sense that there was something fraudulent about Tomlinson. But, if Ernest was honest, he could have put up with the fraudulence. What he did not at all approve of was Lydia's partiality for Tomlinson. Why, if the two had not been cousins, he might have gone so far as to suspect . . .

Ernest Lye glanced down at his hands. They were clenched

tight in his lap. He noticed the zigzag weal on his wrist. How had that got there? Then he remembered the injury from the kissing-gate. The story he told to the policeman. Inspector Francis appeared to be a capable man, one who could be relied on to establish the truth. The truth that the murderer of Charles Tomlinson was . . . not him, not Ernest Lye.

So now as Ernest sat staring unseeingly at the blank wall, he could acknowledge to himself that what he felt towards Tomlinson was more than resentment. It was jealousy, hatred. It was quite safe to own up to that now. The man was dead, and he had not done the deed.

Had he?

Inspector Francis sat in the drawing room of George Grace's house on Palace Green. Mr Grace told him that he was fortunate to find him at home, rather than engaged on business (or good works, the manufacturer almost added). But, Francis thought, judging by the well-creased newspaper on the nearby table and the familiar way he was nesting in his armchair, George Grace must be quite often at home in the morning. Sounds could be heard, distantly and intermittently, from other parts of the house. A baby crying somewhere near the top, doors opening and closing at the back.

The view through the sash window was of the cathedral green. There were a few sightseers, gawpers, in the area of the Crimean cannon. But no constable now. On his way here, Francis went to examine the spot once more. The ground round the cannon was churned up, the grass worn away and gouged, with footprints overlaying each other. Such blood as was shed by Tomlinson had soaked away. Any evidence was obliterated. It occurred to the Inspector that this could scarcely be the first time that a body had been found in the region of the cannon, at least in other lands.

Now, sitting in George Grace's drawing room, Inspector Francis took the witness through what he'd seen and heard the day before. He consulted a notebook. In one hand he was holding a pencil. He found his notebook useful, a kind of professional prop. Sometimes it reassured those he was questioning, sometimes it discomfited them, especially if he looked at it for a long time or if he wrote down what seemed to be a trivial detail. In fact, Francis had written only two words on the page in front of him. He'd come to those two words in a moment.

'So yesterday afternoon you were sitting there, Mr Grace, reading the paper? Just where you are sitting now. And, when it got too dark for you to continue reading, you got up to light the lamp. And then through the window, you observed – what did you observe?'

'I observed Mr Tomlinson and Mr Lye walking past. Is it true that Mr Lye is in custody, Inspector?'

'We will come to that in due course, sir. First I want to pin down exactly what you saw.'

'I saw exactly what I said I saw, Inspector.'

'You identified Mr Tomlinson by his appearance and his voice. But the other individual, the one walking on the far side of him . . . what can you say about that person?'

George Grace shifted slightly in his armchair. 'I did not see a great deal of him.'

'Any impression of what he was wearing?'

'No.'

'Was he tall or short? Fat or thin?'

'He was short and thin,' said Mr Grace finally.

'You must have had a fair sight of him to see that much, sir.'

'I am *deducing* it, Inspector. Isn't that what you fellows do? Deduce, deduce?'

Francis said nothing. The tetchy tone of the other man was revealing. The Inspector pretended to write in his notebook. He glanced through the window. He had already noticed that the strip of garden which separated the front of Grace's house from the railings was well planted with shrubs. In addition, the iron railings were entwined with some sort of creeper whose leaves were turning a tawny autumnal orange. He wondered how clearly Mr Grace had been able to see through these impediments. He thought of the late afternoon light, the gathering mist.

After a pause, during which Mr Grace did some more shifting about in his chair, he said, 'If I am to be completely frank, I did not actually see the fellow who was with Tomlinson. He must have been short and thin because Tomlinson was quite a large man – or a tall one at any rate – and therefore anyone walking alongside him would be largely obscured when seen from the angle provided by my window here. And another thing. Tomlinson was walking with his head tilted slightly to one side, from which I also deduce that he was listening to a slightly shorter companion. There you have my reasoning, unfolded for you stage by stage.'

George Grace sat back with arms folded as though he had scored a decisive point.

'Very good, sir. You would make a fine detective.'

'One tries one's best to help the forces of law and order.'

'You say Mr Tomlinson's companion must have been small, and I concur with your reasoning. Is it possible this companion was a woman?'

'No, you're quite in the wrong there. Remember I heard Tomlinson call him 'Lye'. No mistake there.'

'Yesterday, I believe you stated –' and here Francis earnestly studied his notebook – 'yes, you stated that Mr Tomlinson said, "Mr Lye". Which was it? "Lye" or "Mr Lye"?'

'Does it make a difference?'

'Please try to remember, Mr Grace.'

'Tomlinson said – well, now that I come to think of it – he said simply "Lye". No "Mr" was involved.'

'And you heard no other bits and pieces, not a single fragment of conversation, from either individual?'

'Only the word "Lye".'

'Because it was uttered with some force?'

'Yes.'

Francis glanced down at the two words pencilled in his pad. They were LYE? and LIE? He closed the book with a snap and tucked his pencil away. He got up.

'I must not take up any more of your time or detain you from your business, Mr Grace.'

George Grace also rose to his feet. He looked so dissatisfied that Francis threw him a titbit.

'You have been very helpful.'

'Mr Lye is safe in custody?'

'He is safe,' said Francis, adding to himself, but he will not be in custody for much longer.

As he walked across Palace Green and past the site of the murder, Inspector Francis summarized what he had learned from

the interview with George Grace. Or, rather, what he had
unlearned.

He did not doubt that the tannery owner had glimpsed Charles
Tomlinson passing his window late on the previous afternoon,
nor that Tomlinson was in the company of someone else. The fact
of the murder a few minutes later indicated as much. The policeman
was even prepared to accept that Tomlinson's companion was
someone relatively slight and short. The probability was that it
was a man, given the nature of the attack. But a woman could
not be ruled out altogether. Of the two murder cases which
Stephen Francis had hitherto investigated during his time in Ely,
one concerned the farm labourer who'd killed his wife while
the other involved a female servant who knifed her employer
when he broke a promise to marry her after his wife's death. The
ferocity of that attack shocked even the hardened members of the
constabulary. Francis was shocked too but it told him nothing
new. Women were as capable of violence as men, even if they did
not resort to it so often.

As for the LYE question . . . Inspector Francis was as sure as
he could be that the word which George Grace heard through
his drawing-room window was actually LIE. Charles Tomlinson
had been arguing with his companion and rebuking him – or
her – for lying, which was why he was speaking loudly. It was
an argument or a rebuke which would shortly lead to his murder.

Monkey Business

From Cambridge early on the Monday morning, Tom Ansell
posted his account of the Ely events to David Mackenzie
in London. Since a letter seemed almost too leisurely, even
though it would arrive the same day, Tom also sent a telegram
to the senior partner. Knowing how many hands a cable passed
through, he wanted to avoid spelling things out in black and
white but he also wanted to alert Mackenzie to the trouble that
was coming. Keeping within the twenty-word limit that was
covered by a single shilling, Tom dictated the following to the

clerk in the telegraph office: E.L. DETAINED IN ELY AFTER VERY GRAVE PROBLEMS UNRELATED TO MY MISSION. LETTER FOLLOWS WITH FULL DETAILS. PLEASE ADVISE. T.A.

Tom expected the postal letter to arrive at the office in Furnival Street that afternoon, which meant that he would not hear back from Mackenzie before the next day. He was surprised therefore to receive a cable at the Devereux Hotel during the late morning. It was in answer to his telegram. HAVE ALREADY GLEANED SITUATION FROM REFERENCES IN PRESS. STAY THERE. HELP AND INVESTIGATE. D.M.

'There must have been some newspaper stories,' said Helen. 'Murder in Ely, local man detained, that kind of thing, but without naming names.'

'Yes,' said Tom. 'Mackenzie tells us to stay but we couldn't leave anyway. Not at this juncture.'

'Who are we meant to help?' said Helen.

'The Lyes, surely, not the police?'

'The police are the ones doing the investigating.'

'I think he means me to do it too,' said Tom, recalling Mackenzie's reference to his dab hand at investigating.

'Means us, perhaps.'

'Yes, us.'

'This is turning into another drama, Tom.'

'I know.'

Yet Tom and Helen were able to continue their investigation into the murder of Charles Tomlinson without leaving their hotel, without making much effort at all in fact. The cheerful and rotund John Jubb, senior clerk at the firm of Teague and Bennett in Cambridge and boyhood friend of Jack Ashley back in Furnival Street, suddenly turned up outside their rooms. They invited him in, pleased enough to see someone without homicidal connections. But, before they even sat down, Jubb explained that he was visiting the Ansells with what might be significant information about the murder in Ely. Although it was an ordinary working day, he had taken time off to do so.

'When you have been with a firm as long as I have, Mr and Mrs Ansell, you acquire a little latitude in setting your own hours.'

Tom noticed that while he addressed both of them he kept his eyes on Helen, in a puppyish sort of way. Mr Jubb had obviously fallen a little under her spell.

'So you already know about the Ely murder?' said Tom.

'Oh yes, I have been alerted by my old friend Ashley. Telegrams have been flying to and fro. Also the matter is reported in the Cambridge papers this morning and no doubt in the London ones as well. Not much is said in the papers, apart from the names of the deceased and the detecting officer, and the location of the crime. If we give the press time, though, they'll begin to work up their theories and point their fingers.'

'Otherwise known as making things up and starting rumours,' said Helen.

'Dear me, yes,' said Jubb. 'You have got the measure of the fourth estate, Mrs Ansell. Though it's not surprising, I suppose, since you have one foot in the trade. Ha, I nearly said, one foot in the grave. That wouldn't have done, not at all. Have you met that interesting gentleman again, by the way? Mr Arnett, wasn't it? The editor who has a way with language.'

'I haven't seen him,' said Helen. 'To tell you the truth, I've almost forgotten my commission for *The New Moon*. There have been other things on my mind.'

'Mr Jubb,' said Tom, 'you have something to tell us about the murder?'

'Not exactly about the murder. But about the murderee, if that is a legitimate word, Mrs Ansell.'

'It is now, Mr Jubb.'

'I am able to provide you with a story about Charles Tomlinson. It may tell you what kind of person he is – or was. You see, he was once involved in a scandalous event here in the city, in the university itself, which resulted in his having to leave his college before his time.'

'He was sent down?' said Tom.

'I believe he left of his own accord before that could happen. Went abroad. He had turned into a bit of a black sheep among his family.'

Tom and Helen exchanged looks. What had some long-forgotten student scandal to do with a murder the day before?

'It was about fifteen or more years ago. You may remember

– no, of course, you probably do not remember, you are too young – but anyway there was much debate in learned circles about whether mankind was descended from the apes.'

'There is still debate,' said Tom.

'I thought it was settled,' said Helen. 'We are all the children of monkeys, at several removes of course.'

She said it to tease, thought Tom, but he was slightly taken aback by her directness. So was John Jubb, who said, 'Well, it may be so. Cleverer people than I have said it is so. Yet clever men, and even clever women, are not always right. Myself, I hold no particular view.'

'What has this to with Charles Tomlinson?' said Tom.

'These arguments were at their height when Mr Tomlinson was a student at Cambridge. He was part of a circle of young men who thought of themselves as being very much in the forefront of opinion, especially if that opinion was likely to be shocking or upsetting to tradition. Among his friends was an individual at the same college who was planning to take holy orders. I believe that the debates, the arguments, between Tomlinson and this friend were especially keen and lively. Tomlinson held that mankind was descended from the apes and he ridiculed the church for preaching otherwise, while this person held out against him. Then, for some reason, their friendship went sour. As a consequence, Tomlinson did something which . . . well, if one was being charitable, one could describe what he did as a joke, a practical joke played on the intending cleric.'

Mr Jubb paused. Tom and Helen gazed at him expectantly.

'From somewhere Mr Tomlinson obtained a stuffed monkey. He waited until his friend was out one day and then he placed the monkey in that gentleman's room with a mocking sign hanging around the creature's neck. I believe that the sign read, "It is a wise child that knows its own father".'

Tom's instinct was to laugh but he managed to control it. Helen's hand flew to her mouth, but he could not tell whether it was a gesture of shock or stifled amusement. John Jubb shook his head.

'After all these years, I know it sounds like a malicious prank, no more. But at the time it provoked outrage. The victim of Tomlinson's joke was very badly affected. The college authorities

were horrified. Charles Tomlinson's reputation was already dubious
as far as they were concerned, and this monkey business set the
seal on their determination to have done with him. As I say, if
he hadn't left of his own accord, he would have been sent down.
In fact, he was only permitted to stay at the university for as long
as he did because of his connections. He comes from a family of
local clerics.'

'That could explain his animosity towards the church.'

'I suppose it might, Mrs Ansell. The idea hadn't occurred to me.'

'Can I ask how you know all these things?' said Tom. 'After
all, the business with the monkey happened a long time ago, and
it doesn't sound like the kind of affair that anyone would want
spread about.'

'It was not. But the Reverend Gordon Coffer, who has one
of the Cambridge parishes, is also one of our oldest clients at
Teague and Bennett. He is a cousin to Tomlinson and the father
of Mrs Lye. I remember the original scandal. Like the rest of the
family, the Reverend Coffer was angry and displeased but at
the same time I always thought he had a bit of a soft spot for
his reprobate cousin. He talked about the business in our office,
he consulted one of our partners. I remember it still. You see,
the whole story is stored inside here.'

The solicitors' clerk tapped his forehead. Tom was reminded
of their own clerk, Jack Ashley, who was able to recall every
client and case, it seemed, for the last forty years.

'There is more to say,' said John Jubb. 'You're familiar with
Crockford's Clerical Directory, I hope? It is an invaluable work
of reference.'

'I know it,' said Tom, who supposed that there could not be
a legal firm in the land which did not have a couple of Crockford's
on its shelves. For Helen's benefit, he said, 'Crockford's lists all
the English benefices and the names of the incumbents.'

'And the Welsh and Irish ones,' added Jubb. 'As I said, the
fellow student made fun of by Charles Tomlinson was deeply
hurt by his behaviour, humiliated too. Nevertheless, he persisted
in his intention of entering the church. His name is George
Eames. I have tracked him down with the aid of Crockford's. It
turns out that he has not moved far since he has a living just
outside Ely.'

Tom guessed what was coming next but kept quiet. Mr Jubb was so evidently enjoying his story and his detective work.

'It is in the village of Upper Fen.'

'Isn't that where the Lyes live, where Phoenix House is?' said Helen.

'And where I met Mr Tomlinson,' said Tom.

'The question is, Mr Ansell, whether George Eames and Charles Tomlinson met there again after all those years . . .'

'. . . and what happened if they did,' said Helen.

Some Other Suspects

Whatever Helen's speculations, George Eames and Charles Tomlinson had never actually met in the village of Upper Fen. On one occasion the cleric glimpsed Tomlinson while he was walking towards Phoenix House and hid in the shrubbery to avoid an encounter with his old friend and nemesis. But the perpetual curate knew of Tomlinson's status with the Lyes, and was fearful that at some point they must inevitably meet.

On the Sunday morning of the day on which Tomlinson was murdered in Ely, George Eames officiated at the morning service at St Ethelwine's. The church was one place where he thought himself safe from the risk of seeing Tomlinson, unless the man had undergone some sort of Damascene conversion. Eames delivered the sermon which he had saved from the flames of the fire and, as planned, he alluded to the subject of righteous anger, taking his cue from the Ephesians verse: *Be ye angry and sin not.* He was glad to see his housemaid Hannah looking contrite. This almost compensated for the fact that Gabriel Parr had lit a brazier at the back of the church to keep the worst of the chill out of the air. Eames did not altogether approve of braziers in churches. Or rather, he valued the bracing effect of discomfort.

Mr and Mrs Lye and their few servants were in the congregation, as were the more respectable or devout members of the community. Sitting in a pew near the brazier at the back was an individual whom Eames did not recognize. Sometimes there were unfamiliar faces at Sunday services but they were usually visiting relations at one of the Upper Fen households and were sitting in company. This man was by himself. At several points in his sermon, Eames noticed the man nodding in agreement.

Once the service was over, Eames more or less forgot about the stranger. He attended to the placing of the new tombstone over the grave of Ada Baxter, the tombstone for which Gabriel Parr had been carving the final flourishes on the previous day. Mrs Baxter's husband and her sons and her aunt and other kin, as well as some casual bystanders, looked on while the sexton and his son, Davey, removed the simple wooden cross marking the woman's grave and lugged the stone into position. The lettering and the sculptural detail of the anchor were admired.

Once the tombstone was firmly planted in the soil, and some fresh flowers placed at its foot, the Reverend Eames cleared his throat as a signal for a respectful silence and uttered a prayer. He might have said more but, although Mr Baxter dabbed at his eyes with a handkerchief and one of her sons sniffed very audibly, the rest of the little crowd seemed eager to leave. The entertainment for the day, which consisted of watching the Parrs manhandle a gravestone into place, was over.

Eames was about to walk back to the parsonage, when Gabriel Parr approached him.

'Begging your pardon, Reverend, but there is a man who's been waiting to speak to you.'

The sexton gestured towards the lych-gate. Eames turned and saw, lurking in the shadow of the gate, the individual who'd been sitting by himself at the back of the church. He sighed. He said something about the meal that was waiting for him.

'He said it was urgent,' said Parr, before shrugging and turning away himself. It was up to the parson what to do next.

Eames recalled the way the man nodded in agreement during his sermon. His style of dress had not suggested that he was a mere labourer wearing Sunday clothes. For these reasons, and out of simple curiosity, the clergyman went towards the lych-gate. As soon as he got closer, he regretted it. The man's clothes might have been decent enough but they were stained and streaked with some chalky substance. Also, he had an unprepossessing look, wrinkle-faced and with large teeth.

Yet, within a couple of minutes of this individual beginning to speak, George Eames was all attention. A few more minutes and he reached a state of amazement and outrage.

It was more than an hour before he returned to the parsonage. The food that was waiting for him was burnt and dried-up but it did not matter because the cleric had lost his appetite. There followed an uncomfortable period while Eames berated Hannah the maid for lending a key to a stranger. The girl's incomprehension, then her tears and repeated denials finally convinced Eames that she genuinely didn't know what he was talking about. Then he summoned Mrs Walters for questioning – or rather asked if he could have a word with her – and that normally stolid housekeeper grew flustered. In other circumstances, Eames might have been glad to see this reaction since much of the time he felt under Mrs Walters' thumb. But now he only wanted to establish what had happened.

'He seemed a very honest gentleman,' said Mrs Walters, stressing the last word. 'Very smooth and—'

'Glib, I expect is the word you want, Mrs Walters.'

It wasn't the word she wanted but Mrs Walters did not contradict her employer as she would usually have done. Instead she said, 'He knows Mrs Lye in the big house. A distant family member, I think.'

Eames said nothing so Mrs Walters ploughed on, 'He represents a Society called . . . let me see . . . it is called, yes, the Society for the Protection of Rural Treasures. I remember it now because the first letters of some of the words spell out another word, which is SPORT. The gentleman pointed that out himself, made a little joke out of it. Yes, Society for the Protection of Rural Treasures. SPORT for short.'

Eames still said nothing. His earlier outrage had been replaced by cold fury, directed not at his housekeeper but at the man who'd had the impudence to come up with that name. Deliberate and brazen, a gesture almost as insulting as the sign whose wording he could not forget ('It is a wise child that knows its own father').

Mrs Walters must have taken his continued silence for agreement for she continued, 'He said that he was the secretary of the Society. He said they were particularly concerned about old country churches. He described them as our real rural treasures. I ask you, Mr Eames, what could be more respectable than that?'

'I doubt that such a society exists, Mrs Walters. And if it does, that gentleman, as you call him, is most certainly not the secretary of it.'

'I wasn't to know. He came one day when you were out and so you weren't here to be referred to for advice, Mr Eames. He only wanted to borrow the keys for a short time.'

'Including the key to the crypt.'

'I don't know. He took a bunch of keys for the church. He returned them later. No harm done.'

There was no point in prolonging the session. Eames dismissed Mrs Walters with an angry wave of the hand. For some time he strode from side to side in his study, at each turn envisaging the cunning of Tomlinson's actions. Taking care to visit the parsonage when the incumbent was out, using his 'smooth' style to get Mrs Walters to hand over the bunch of keys, having a free run at the church and in particular at the crypt, making a copy of the key (Reverend Eames wasn't sure how this was done but he rather thought a wax tablet was involved) before handing the bunch back to Mrs Walters, all the while pretending to be the secretary of the Society for the Protection of Rural Treasures. SPORT for short. Yes, Charles Tomlinson was still sporting with him, George Eames, after all these years.

Before returning to the parsonage to confront the female servants, Eames had gone down to the crypt with Eric Fort, the man who'd been waiting for him after the morning service. The door was not locked, which tended to confirm the other's story. On the ground was a bag containing a chisel and crowbar and assorted implements, another confirmation. The two men did not go very far inside since, without a light, not much would be visible. But Fort was able to describe the inner chamber and the coffins in enough detail to convince Eames that he'd indeed been in there with Tomlinson as he claimed. As for the rest of the story, about breaking down a section of an internal wall to gain access to *another* chamber (of which Eames was unaware), about Tomlinson's scrambling through by himself in quest of whatever lay on the far side, well, all that might have seemed far-fetched, but by now Eames was inclined to believe his old friend was capable of anything, however implausible or apparently purposeless.

Eric Fort spoke as if he had taken part in the enterprise under some sort of duress. Now he was acting like a repentant sinner. He wished he'd never got involved with Charles Tomlinson. He said that he hadn't been himself since the recent death of his wife. That late event had knocked him over, had turned him upside down. He was acting in ways that he wouldn't have acted, perhaps, if she'd still been alive.

The realization had come to him most forcibly when he was left in the dark and among the coffins on one side of the broken-down wall while Mr Tomlinson was fossicking about – that was the man's word, fossicking – on the other. Fort understood then that, whatever they were doing, it was wrong. No, he had no idea what Tomlinson was searching for underground. Had he found anything? Eames asked. Did he emerge from the inner crypt with an item? Nothing, said Fort, except a lot of dust and foul language.

Presumably frustrated in his search, Tomlinson left the crypt and left Eric Fort too. Fort didn't know where he'd gone, and didn't care either. Unfamiliar with the road back to Ely and not willing to risk it in the dark, he spent the night underground. It was a wretched night, but not on account of the dead lying around. The presence of the dead did not frighten him, not in the least. But he vowed to have nothing more to do with Charles Tomlinson. Why, if he saw that 'gentleman' again, there was no telling what he would say . . . even what he might do . . .

Then on the Sunday he attended the morning service at St Ethelwine's, despite his ragged state and his dirty, crumpled clothing. He listened intently to Reverend Eames' words and he thought of his life, and decided to do a little better in future. It was a modest ambition. Listening to this, George Eames experienced a touch of pity for Eric Fort, even of fellow feeling. Here was another victim of the wiles of Charles Tomlinson. Although Fort participated in a criminal act by breaking into the church, he had not gained anything by it. Indeed, he seemed properly remorseful. Eames left him to his conscience and returned to the parsonage, where he confronted Hannah and then Mrs Walters. It did not occur to the vicar of St Ethelwine's to go 'fossicking' about in the crypt himself. He was not much interested in what Tomlinson was looking for down there. Anyway, whatever it was, the would-be thief had not found it. Eames decided the time had come to confront his old friend and enemy. That man was guilty of a crime for which he could be exposed and hauled up in front of the magistrates. It would be some small revenge for the event of many years before, the humiliation of which had come back to Eames in its full force ever since he glimpsed Tomlinson outside Phoenix House, busy taking his leave of Mrs Lye.

Eames knew from Eric Fort that Tomlinson was staying in Ely. In a small place, it would not take long to track him down and confront him. As he rode towards the city, he felt within him that righteous anger which had formed one of the themes of his sermon that morning. Charles Tomlinson was about to encounter the wrath of George Eames . . .

There were at least two other people who had reasons to hate Charles Tomlinson and who would not have objected to seeing him dead. As it happened, they were married to each other. On the Sunday afternoon of Tomlinson's death, they were not together and so were not able to provide mutual alibis. Each was engaged on his or her own activity.

Cyrus Chase was locked away in the workshop at the bottom of the garden of his house in Prickwillow Road. He remembered the time he had been in here with Tomlinson and the keen interest which Tomlinson took in his coffin, the novelty coffin as his visitor termed it. For Chase, the coffin remained a work of art. Not because of its appearance which was, frankly, unappealing on account of the leather tubes that protruded from it like giant worms and the metal gantries at the head. No, it was a work of art because it was *useful*, rather as his father's Chase Coupler had been useful.

Alone in his workshop, Chase tinged the bell, recalling Tomlinson's facetious gesture and comment ('You rang, sir?'). He spun the Chase cockerel, unable to forget Tomlinson's brazen theft of his idea, a theft which he discovered from reading Mute's notes in *Funereal Matters* ('*this gentleman's device involves a familiar farmyard fowl*'). He had already written an indignant letter to Willow & Son, but writing indignant letters did not do much to soothe his anger. Beyond all the coffin business, Cyrus thought of Bella's partiality for Tomlinson, and of his wife's interest in that man. Were there ever so many reasons to hate an individual as he hated Charles Tomlinson?

In normal circumstances Cyrus Chase might have passed a pleasant few hours in his workshop, tinkering with his devices and dreaming of the fame that surely awaited him. But he had no appetite for any of that. Instead he paced about the workshop, which he did not leave in the course of the afternoon. Or so he would later tell Inspector Stephen Francis.

On the same Sunday afternoon, Bella Chase was out and about in Ely, attending Evensong in the cathedral, or so she said. Naturally, the service proceeded despite the discovery of Tomlinson's body on Palace Green. Most of the worshippers were unaware of the drama taking place outside. Perhaps Bella attended the service – if she did attend it – in order to try to suppress the jealous feelings that bubbled up inside her whenever she thought of Tomlinson together with Mrs Lye. And she thought of them often. The almost murderous impulse she'd felt when gazing at the carving knife in the pawnshop window in Cambridge had not gone away.

According to her own account, the one that she gave to Inspector Francis, Bella left the cathedral after Evensong and returned home still unaware of all the activity on the Green. She did not see anyone she knew at the service. No one noticed her presence either. Bella did not meet her husband until supper. It was an almost silent meal. From some comment he made, she gathered he had spent much of the day in his workshop. He understood that she had been to the cathedral service. Charles Tomlinson was not mentioned. Certainly, neither husband nor wife gave the slightest indication of knowing that their one-time friend was dead.

A Visit to the Doctor

The names of Cyrus and Bella Chase came to Inspector Francis' notice because he was by now almost convinced that Ernest Lye had nothing to do with the murder, and so was starting to cast round in other directions for a potential killer. From talking to Mr Salter, his brother-in-law and the manager at the Lion Hotel, he learned something of the methodical way Tomlinson had made acquaintances there. It was almost as if he was setting out to cultivate the more important or useful citizens of Ely.

He also learned that Tomlinson's position in the hotel was slightly irregular, not so much from anything that Salter said but from reading between the lines. Tomlinson was being provided with accommodation on special terms because, it seemed, the housekeeper had an understanding with him and, in turn, Salter had an understanding with the housekeeper. The 'understanding' was not explicitly stated but it was hinted at in response to Francis' question about how a man with few apparent means could afford his frequent stays at the Lion. At this point Mr Salter became evasive. Francis had the impression of an invisible thread linking Tomlinson to the housekeeper to his brother-in-law, a thread none of them had wanted to break. He didn't mention any of this to his wife. She believed her brother was something of a paragon.

Among Tomlinson's connections in the city, Cyrus Chase's name was mentioned. Francis had also heard from the owner of a High Street glove shop, Mrs Johnson, that Chase's wife, Bella, had recently made urgent enquries in her shop concerning Tomlinson and Mrs Lye. Mrs Johnson knew more than she let on to Bella but she instinctively preferred to keep her customers' affairs private. Her suspicions had been roused by something odd in Bella Chase's manner – that story about the diary hadn't convinced her, not for a moment. Normally she would have kept her suspicions and speculations to herself. But everything changed when it came to murder. This was why Mrs Johnson had been among Inspector Francis' visitors on the day following Tomlinson's demise.

So the circle of those who might want to do away with Charles Tomlinson widened. Francis began to write notes on them, on Mr and Mrs Lye, on Mr and Mrs Chase. Nothing amounted to very much yet, apart from the circumstantial evidence against Lye. But even this started to look shaky when the Inspector received a note from the local doctor who, at Francis' request, examined the body. The note which he sent by way of a brief report surprised the Inspector. Like everyone else, Francis had assumed from a superficial look over the corpse that Tomlinson died of what Constable Parr termed 'a frenzied attack', probably carried out with a knife. That is, there were wounds to the face and a quantity of blood on the clothes on the upper part of his body suggesting severe wounds in that region as well. But Dr Wallace's note indicated otherwise.

The Inspector went to see Wallace in his consulting room in Fore Hill. The doctor was a young man, not yet married and settled down with wife and children. Perhaps because of his age, he did not have a large number of patients. Yet Francis occasionally asked for his professional opinion precisely because he was young and less stuck in his ways. He doubted the doctor would stay in the city for long. Wallace was pleased to see the Inspector and asked him to sit down.

'If I understand you correctly, Doctor, Mr Tomlinson did not die of his visible wounds,' Francis began. Wallace's note was absolutely clear on this point but Francis wanted verbal confirmation. He learned much more from seeing and hearing people than reading statements or reports.

'In my opinion he did not. There was a severe laceration across his forehead here –' Dr Wallace traced a long diagonal line from his hairline to his right eyebrow – 'and this produced much of the blood that the witnesses saw. There are plenty of blood vessels near the surface of the body in this region, and to the non-medical eye even quite slight damage can take on the appearance of a major wound. In addition, there were a couple of minor lacerations on his left cheek. There was nothing more in the area of the head.'

'But elsewhere . . .?'

'He suffered a bad gash, quite a deep one, across the palm of his right hand,' said Doctor Wallace, holding up the same hand in illustration. 'It is very likely that, with this wounded hand, he instinctively touched his face and the upper part of his clothing. All this would have added to the general sanguinary impression.'

'These wounds to Mr Tomlinson's head and hand, they could have been produced by a knife?'

'Almost certainly they were caused by a knife or some sharp implement. And they were inflicted while he was still alive, hence the freely flowing blood.'

'It is not difficult to see what happened.'

'No,' said Dr Wallace. 'Mr Tomlinson was assailed by an individual with a knife. He saw him coming—'

'Or saw her,' interrupted the Inspector.

'Or her, yes. It may seem unlikely it was a woman but they are as capable of wielding a knife as a man would be.'

Francis was glad the doctor agreed with him. Somehow it showed the unprejudiced way he thought. He urged the other man to go on with his reconstruction of the attack.

'Tomlinson instinctively put up his arm to ward off the assault, palm outwards. His assailant slashed at the open hand, causing the first gash. Then, while Tomlinson was reeling from that initial wound, the attacker moved in closer and delivered another stroke across Tomlinson's brows, as well as a couple of lesser ones down his left cheek. There would be blood pouring down from the head wound by now, which made it hard for him to see and increased his confusion and helplessness.'

'According to a witness, it seems he tumbled to the ground and then tried to take shelter under the cannon on the Green. After which the perpetrator, man or woman, ran off.'

'Running off is what Tomlinson should have done in the first place, when he realized that his attacker was coming for him with a knife.'

'Perhaps he was taken by surprise,' said Inspector Francis.

'Or perhaps he could not run, for some reason.'

'Anyway, Doctor, you say the wounds were not sufficient to kill him?'

'I cannot definitely say that they did *not* kill him, Inspéctor. But I would be surprised, even amazed, if they were the cause of Mr Tomlinson's death in themselves. The fact is that these various lacerations, although productive of a fair amount of blood, could have been staunched without great difficulty once the assailant left the scene. Provided he did not panic he might even have managed it for himself, at least until help arrived. You say that help was not long in coming?'

'People began to arrive within a couple of minutes of the attack. But by then it was too late.'

'Well, what I can say is that this gentleman did not bleed to death.'

'How did he die then, if not from his wounds?'

'I have one or two ideas – speculations – but I don't know.'

'You could speculate,' said Francis.

'Anyone can speculate, Inspector.'

When the policeman still said nothing, Doctor Wallace continued, 'It is possible, of course, that the shock of such an attack was enough to provoke some kind of seizure. Just as it is possible that Mr Tomlinson had a weak heart, though I could not know that without a much more radical examination . . .'

Wallace meant a dissection of the body, a proper autopsy. That would take at least an additional physician if evidence was to be prepared for any trial.

'. . . but I feel that too is unlikely. He seemed to me in reasonable physical condition for a man of his age. On a preliminary examination, you understand.'

Inspector Francis shrugged. He said, 'So we are not any closer to finding the cause of death?'

'One way or the other it must be murder,' said Wallace. 'But how exactly it was accomplished, I cannot tell you – yet.'

And, thought the Inspector, I cannot tell you who did it – yet.

Summer, 1645

*T*he gentleman called Loyer was under guard in a small room off the main hall of the Manor. Nearby was the jagged, excavated space where the panelling had been broken down to reveal the disused priest-hole. Anne took in a salver bearing some ale and cheese for the prisoner and Trafford and three other guards. They were standing at a distance from the captive and, Anne noticed, they kept their eyes down as though reluctant to meet Loyer's glances.

'I want to thank you,' said Trafford to Anne. 'You led us to this gentleman here.'

Trafford spoke slowly, with deliberation, as if he wanted to lay the blame for the capture elsewhere. Loyer was sitting on a bench against the wall. He was still wearing his wide-brimmed hat and he was wrapped in his cloak, although it was not cold. She tried to signal to him with her eyes. No, I did not betray you. I did not mean to lead these men to your hiding-place. But she did not think the message had got through. When she returned to collect the salver, however, he gave her an almost infinitesimal nod. Her heart a little less heavy, she left the room.

It was James who explained things to Anne. The man they had seized by the willow cabin was not the King but a member of Charles' entourage. He was a most brave impostor, deliberately fleeing eastwards and intending to be seen in flight. To make the pursuers think he was the King, so as to allow the real monarch a chance to escape. This was the plan that had been hatched by the two visitors of the previous day with Anne's mother and father, or rather it was the plan that had been put to them. If all had gone well, the man would have made his circuitous getaway towards the coast, perhaps even taking a boat to the continent.

At some point, it would be known that the real King Charles had fled in the opposite direction. Perhaps it was already known. That did not matter. The man, Monsieur Loyer, as he styled himself, had given the necessary breathing space to the King. At considerable risk to himself. Even perhaps the risk of death.

'Do they know who he is?' said Anne. She was referring to the soldiers in the house. *The fear of the morning had returned, doubled and then redoubled. Only now Mr and Mrs Stilwell had gone to Peterborough, perhaps thinking the danger was over, and there was no one left to deal with Trafford and his men.*

'They are not sure,' said James. 'I believe they are in awe of their captive. They think they may have their hands on our monarch and it frightens them a little. But Mr Martin has ridden to Ely. There are people there who can identify the King for certain.'

'It is Mr Martin who has betrayed him.'

'He has betrayed us all. That is why he was talking to Trafford earlier. He has seen which way the wind is blowing. It's fortunate he was in the dark about this imposture. He is not certain whether the gentleman is the King either.'

'When they discover that their prisoner is not . . . what they think . . . what will they do?'

'They will be angry and vengeful.'

'If we could help Mr Loyer to escape again . . .'

'Do not be foolish.'

Anne tried to talk to Mary. But her sister was sitting still and silent and miserable in their room. She was not even reading, her usual recourse when she was unhappy (as well as happy). If Anne was going to do anything it would be done alone.

With no parents present to send her to bed, and the servants including James huddled away waiting for the inevitable return of Mr Martin and the others from Ely, she went outside and looked towards the town. It was starting to grow dark. The cathedral alone was visible. Anne detected a flurry of movement on the track leading to Upper Fen. On this still midsummer's evening she could hear the thud of hooves. As soon as they reached Stilwell, the prisoner would be revealed as an impostor and not the King. They might kill him there and then in their frustration and fury.

Anne was desperate. It was her fault. She was guilty for having led the treacherous Martin to the willow hide. She paced up and down the gallery until she heard the horses arrive in the yard and the clumping steps of men entering the hall. Among them was Mr Martin, together with the rest of the leather-jerkined retinue from the morning. And two strangers, from Ely no doubt, capable of identifying the King. She watched, heart in mouth, as they tramped towards the little chamber beyond the priest-hole. A few moments more and the truth would be out.

Anne snatched up a candle and darted downstairs. Moving through the shadows, she found a tinderbox in the kitchen quarters of the house. With candle and tinderbox, she crept towards the priest-hole. Once inside the musty nook, it took her a few moments to start a flame and light the candle and heap it around with rubbish and fragments off wood. Soon the flames were licking at the dry timber and the lathe and plaster.

She rushed out.

'Fire!' she shouted. 'Fire!'

Meetings in Cambridge

O n the afternoon of the same day as Inspector Francis was busy investigating – that is, on the Monday following the Ely murder – Tom and Helen Ansell had two encounters in Cambridge. One of them was pleasant enough, the other disturbing. The Ansells had already been called on by John Jubb with his story about George Eames, the stuffed monkey and Charles Tomlinson. All this would have been so much dead wood, were it not that Eames' church in Upper Fen was close to Phoenix House and so there was the possibility that the cleric and his one-time friend might have met again, with unknown consequences.

Tom and Helen were wondering whether they should take Jubb's account to Inspector Francis. It didn't exactly exonerate Ernest Lye but it showed that there were other individuals who had a grudge against Tomlinson. Mr Jubb did not suggest he should carry the information himself. It was Tom who had the connection with the Lyes.

Tom and Helen were walking down King's Parade. They had just decided to catch the train to Ely and visit the Ely police-house later that day when they were hailed by a man emerging from a college on the other side.

'Mrs Ansell! Mrs Ansell!'

It took Helen a moment to recognize the boyish features of Arthur Arnett, the editor of *The New Moon*. He came to a halt opposite them and tipped his hat. He was plainly pleased to see them, or at least to see Helen. She made the introductions.

'It is a pleasure to meet you, Mr Ansell. You are a toiler in the snares of the law, I believe?'

'That's right.'

'And Mrs Ansell, you are surely pursuing your commission for my magazine, promenading around Cambridge, absorbing its sights and sounds for the delectation of our future readers?'

'I confess I have not done much recently, Mr Arnett, having other things on my mind.'

'Nothing too weighty, I hope?'

Helen might have replied that murder was weighty enough but, rather than get into a subject which was nothing to do with the editor, she answered with a question of her own.

'What are you doing in Cambridge, Mr Arnett?'

'Doing?' said Arnett, as though the concept of activity were foreign to him. 'I am wandering through the groves of academe in quest of writers and readers both. I wish *The New Moon* to have tone, you see, and nothing confers tone like subscribers in our older universities.'

'You're drumming up business,' said Tom.

For an instant Arthur Arnett looked as though he was going to object to Tom's description. Then he smiled and said, 'Of course I am, Mr Ansell. Pithily put. I wonder . . . since the delightful Mrs Ansell is already writing for *The New Moon* . . . I wonder whether I might interest you too in penning a piece on . . . the byways of the law, on its curious corners and the like.'

Tom's instinct was to laugh and reject the offer straightaway. There was something absurd in Arnett's flowery style. But the editor was eager and Tom was just the tiniest bit flattered by the suggestion.

'Yes, why don't you, Tom?' said Helen.

'I can't write. I leave that kind of thing to you.'

'Oh, folderol and flapdoodle, Mr Ansell. One does not give credence to a lawyer who claims he cannot write. At least think about my suggestion.'

Tom agreed that he would, and they parted from Mr Arnett, all smiles and nice words.

'I told you he was a little precious,' said Helen.

'Oh, folderol and flapdoodle, to coin a phrase,' said Tom.

'Admit you are tempted by the notion of writing something for publication.'

'Perhaps I am.'

As they were talking, the couple had wandered away from the main thoroughfares and into a rather dingy side street. For no reason they paused outside a pawnbroker's with the name 'Bartle & Co.' in grimy gold lettering on the door. Helen indicated a set of carpenter's tools in the window.

'I wonder what misfortune caused the owner to bring those here.'

A man emerged from the pawnbroker's. He peered at the Ansells from under his hat brim. He was short and Tom could not see him full face but he recognized this individual by his large and uneven teeth. Also, it was evident that the man recognized Tom and Helen for he gasped, allowing a glimpse of those teeth.

'It's Mr Fort,' said Tom.

'Why, it is . . . Mr and Mrs Ansell.'

The undertaker's man did his best to act as if this were no more than an unexpected social encounter but he looked pale and shaken. He met Tom's gaze only for a moment. He would not look at Helen at all.

Tom remembered that it was Eric Fort who was (probably) inside the hansom that almost ran them down outside Liverpool Street Station. He was working out some way of referring to this, without a direct accusation of attempted murder, when Helen said, 'Mr Fort, it was you I saw the other afternoon, here in Cambridge. I thought you worked in London.'

Fort's small frame shrank even further.

'I work where I can get work. To tell the truth, things are not going very well for me at present. I have been in that place to – my wedding ring – never mind . . .'

His voice faltered and he nodded towards the pawnbroker's window. He made to move away but suddenly halted. For the first time, he looked straight at Tom and Helen and seemed to come to a decision.

'Mr and Mrs Ansell,' he began, in a stronger tone. 'There is something I would very much like to say to both of you. I have a . . . a confession to make . . . if you can spare the time to listen to it. I can even purchase some refreshment for you, now that I have a little change.'

Once again, he glanced towards the pawnbroker's. There was an abject quality to him but at the same time a sort of determination.

'Of course, Mr Fort,' said Helen.

'Thank you,' said the undertaker's man. 'Oh, thank you.'

The three went to Morris's, the coffee house which Helen had visited with Mr Jubb. When they were established in a quiet corner, and had been served, Eric Fort started to speak. It was as if a dam had been breached.

Fort explained that he had no full-time employment but picked up work when and where he could get it. His interest in the funeral trade meant that he felt most at home when running errands for Willow & Son in London. But his impecunious state also meant that he sometimes had to stoop to other, less honourable types of work. That was what he had been doing lately in Cambridge and in Ely.

'Ely?' said Tom.

'Outside Ely, to be precise, Mr Ansell.'

'Have you been involved with a man called Charles Tomlinson?'

'Yes,' said Fort, half relieved, half disappointed. 'How did you know?'

'Mr Tomlinson is dead,' said Helen.

'He was murdered in Ely,' said Tom.

'When?'

'Yesterday. We are on our way there with information for the police.'

If this was an attempt on Tom's part to intimidate Fort, it did not work. Nor did he show any visible surprise or much concern at the news of Tomlinson's murder.

'It may be uncharitable in me to say it, but it is no more than he deserved. The gentleman was a bad lot. He drew me into enterprises that were wrong. I have seen the error of my ways now. I want to make a clean breast of things.'

'Did Tomlinson instruct you to try to run us down in London, outside Liverpool Street.'

'That was an accident,' said Helen, more to her husband than the undertaker's man.

'I will swear on my wife's grave that it was an accident,' said Fort. 'The driver lost control of his horse. I believe he had been drinking. As soon as I realized what happened, I ordered him to stop and I got down and ran back to the station. Thank God, I saw that you were not harmed, Mrs Ansell.'

'Was it you, Mr Fort, who sent that message to us at the Devereux Hotel, the lines from *Macbeth*?' said Helen.

'"*There's no art to find the mind's construction on the face.*" Yes, I sent that.'

'Why?'

'As a warning.'

'A warning of what?' said Tom, his temper beginning to slip. 'Let me warn *you*, Mr Fort, that I find your behaviour bizarre or worse than bizarre. The cab you are in nearly runs us over in London, you send us baffling communications, you seem to be trailing my wife and me around the place. Is there any reason why we shouldn't report you to the police?'

Looking miserable, Eric Fort huddled into himself. Speaking more to Helen than Tom, he said, 'I sent those lines of Shakespeare in good faith. I did not want to put my name to anything. But I wanted to . . . to warn you not to put your trust in appearances, not of anyone that you might meet. I did not want to name any names, though. I thought a roundabout approach might be more effective with cultured people such as your good selves.'

'Why did Tomlinson require you to follow us? What was the point of it?'

Eric Fort was about to say something, then changed his mind. He looked down at the table top.

'Later,' he said. 'I will tell you later on, not in here. You say you are going to Ely. I also need to go there. Perhaps we could travel in company. There is an individual in that city to whom you should speak, since you are so interested in Mr Tomlinson, the late Mr Tomlinson, I ought to say. I have a commission from Willow & Son, from whom I have just received a letter. Here is the letter. When I have carried out this task, they will pay me and then I can go back to the pawnbroker's and . . . and redeem my wedding ring . . .'

'Never mind all that,' said Tom. 'Tell us why you are going to Ely.'

'Willow & Son are in receipt of a written complaint from Mr Cyrus Chase who lives there. He is an inventor. He says that his father was an inventor too, of a mechanism for linking together railway carriages. He says that an invention of his own, a refinement to a security coffin, was stolen from him and offered to Willow & Son. You may guess at the identity of the thief, the supposed thief, who is actually named by Mr Chase. It was Mr Charles Tomlinson. Willow & Son have requested that I look into the matter. I don't suppose that his death makes any difference to that.'

With their different reasons for going to Ely, it was decided that the Ansells and Eric Fort should take the train together. The undertaker's man was eager for their company. Tom tolerated Fort's presence, although he still felt irritated at the man's actions as well as being baffled by them. For her part, Helen was curious and in the mood to learn. She asked about security coffins and her questions prompted a description from Eric Fort of the various ways in which human ingenuity was striving to avoid the dreadful fate of premature burial.

Fort had been dejected and defensive in the Cambridge coffee-house, but once the three of them were on the train and traversing the flat landscape towards Ely he became more animated and even cheerful. As the train was reaching their destination, Fort was expounding on an old and elaborate scheme – 'German in origin, Mrs Ansell' – whereby hollow tubes sticking up from the coffins of the recently interred were to be sniffed at by the vicar on his morning round of the graveyard and withdrawn only when the smell of putrefaction was undeniably advanced.

'If there was no smell of decay, then the parson would immediately be on the alert. If that state of affairs continued, then he would command that the coffin and its occupant be exhumed.'

'Let us hope it will not be too late by then,' said Helen.

'It will be too late for us if we don't get down now,' said Tom. 'We've arrived at Ely.'

From the station Tom and Helen planned to take a cab to the police-house. Eric Fort gave them directions for Mr Chase's house and said that he would see them there when they had finished their own business. In the police-house the Ansells were informed that Inspector Francis was out and that Ernest Lye had been released earlier that day. This was a relief to Tom. But the sergeant on duty either could not or would not say any more. So Tom didn't know on what terms the brother of Alexander Lye had been let out, or whether he was still under suspicion for Charles Tomlinson's murder.

From the sergeant they obtained directions to Prickwillow Road where the Chases lived. It was a short walk from the police-house. The autumn afternoon was closing in as Tom and Helen waited outside the door of a solid, recently built villa in a street containing a few similar houses and then a scatter of smaller dwellings. A housemaid answered. Was Mr Chase expecting them? No, but they were here to meet both Mr Chase and Mr Fort.

The maid looked uncertain but nevertheless went ahead to announce their arrival before showing the couple into a drawing room, where a man was reading a magazine called *Funereal Matters*.

'Mr and Mrs Ansell, is it? You wished to see me?'

Cyrus Chase was short and quite chubby. He did not fit Tom's notion of an inventor, even if he could not have said quite what that notion was. The man was polite enough but did not seem pleased to have visitors. Once again, Tom explained they were expecting to meet Eric Fort. Chase looked as uncertain as the housemaid.

'Mr Fort has been sent by Willow & Son in London,' said Tom.

A change came over Cyrus Chase, although it was hard to say whether he was gratified by the news.

'Willow & Son? They are responding to my letter?'

'I believe they are. Mr Chase, you are familiar with a Mr Charles Tomlinson?'

This time there was no doubt about the expression on Chase's face: it was a mixture of anger and apprehension.

'Yes, I was acquainted with him, to my regret. And I know that he died yesterday – or was murdered, apparently. Inspector Francis from the Isle of Ely constabulary has already talked to me about Mr Tomlinson, and he has talked to my wife as well.'

Tom glanced at Helen. Chase made no bones about his hostility to Tomlinson. Another suspect to add to the list? Presumably this was the reason for the Inspector's visit.

'Mr Fort said that Tomlinson, ah, stole an idea from you . . .'

'A device for a security coffin,' added Helen.

'He did steal it,' said Chase. Then, more cautiously, 'Or at least I have good reason to think that he intended to steal it. I don't suppose it matters so much now that he has been . . . now that he is dead.'

There was a pause. Then Chase continued, 'I am afraid I am not familiar with any person by the name of Fort. You say he is on his way to see me?'

'We left him at the railway station about an hour ago.'

'Perhaps he has got lost.'

There was another silence, as if they were all waiting for the imminent arrival of Eric Fort. It was broken by Helen.

'Mr Chase, we were hearing from Mr Fort about the latest developments in security coffins. I would be interested to have a look at your invention.'

'Well,' said Cyrus Chase, brushing at his waistcoat. 'It is not often that the ladies express interest in such things. My wife in particular thinks . . . well, never mind what she thinks. Yes, it would be a great pleasure to show you *my* creation.'

He led them through the house and out into the garden. A winding path ended in a good-sized brick outbuilding. Cyrus explained that the building pre-dated his house, which was relatively new. It was a suitable place, he said, for him to get on with his work alone and undisturbed. Undisturbed by his wife, Tom guessed.

He unlocked the door and ushered them in. He pulled back a curtain covering a barred window which gave a view on to open country. The light in the interior was still poor so Cyrus Chase lit an oil lamp. There was an odd, faintly disagreeable odour in the room. On a large table in the centre of the room was a coffin. An unusual coffin, a security coffin, since it was surmounted with a couple of constructions like miniature towers at the top end. Also, several tubes protruded from various points along the sides of the coffin.

Lifting up the lamp so that it shed a better light, Cyrus Chase gestured with his free hand towards his creation. As if giving a public address, he outlined its salient points, the tubes, the bell-tower, the little bird that could be rotated from underground. He invited them to step closer, to see for themselves. Helen went forward while Tom hung back. He was not especially interested in the subject of burial. He thought of his father being dropped clean over the side of a ship.

'Mr Chase,' said Helen. Her voice was strained.

'What's wrong?' said Chase.

By now the inventor was standing next to Helen. Tom was facing them across the coffin. He saw that the lid was not fitted properly but overhung slightly on his side. Helen was staring down, her eyes wide, a gloved hand to her mouth. Cyrus Chase was bending forward, angling the light so that it shone more directly into the gap between the coffin lid and the interior.

'Good heavens, there is someone inside here,' said Chase. He looked across at Tom, who felt the hairs rising on the nape of his neck. 'There shouldn't be anyone inside.'

Tom pulled at the lid so that, with much clattering caused by all the metalwork that was fixed on the top, it moved clear of the coffin. Helen gasped and stepped back. Chase remained bent forward, the arm bearing the oil lamp as stiff as a statue. By its light, Tom saw a body laid out in the coffin. He recognized it. He had last seen the owner of the body alive and well at Ely Station a little more than an hour ago.

The Second Murder

Two murders on the Isle of Ely in two days was as many murders as Inspector Stephen Francis had dealt with in the space of twenty years of police work. Those killings, of a labourer's wife and of a servant's master, had been straightforward in execution, easy to solve. The guilty parties, one male, one female, had been apprehended straightaway. But the deaths of Charles Tomlinson and Eric Fort were genuine mysteries. In the morning and afternoon he was investigating the first murder, by the evening he was looking into the second. He wondered whether any British policeman had ever had so much on his plate. Nevertheless, Francis proceeded in his usual calm fashion.

The deaths of Tomlinson and Fort were connected mysteries, surely? For one thing, the two events had various characters in common. There were Mr and Mrs Chase, who each had some involvement with Charles Tomlinson even if both husband and wife had been wary and evasive when he spoke to them earlier on the Monday. And now the body of this Fort fellow had been discovered in an outbuilding in the Chases' garden.

Mr Chase claimed never to have heard of Fort before, let alone seen him. As for Bella Chase, she was so overcome by the discovery of a dead body on her husband's property that she retreated to her room. From there she conveyed the information, via her maid, that she could not possibly converse with the Inspector, not at present. He reflected that he had already talked with her about one murder today. The latest killing could wait until tomorrow.

It was fortunate – but it was somehow suspicious as well – that the other couple, the Ansells, who had some connection with Tomlinson or at least with Ernest Lye, were not only on the spot when Fort was discovered in the security coffin but had actually travelled to Ely with him.

The Ansells were able to identify the dead man and give his occupation. They explained that Fort was intending to visit Cyrus Chase on some business to do with a London undertaker. They helped to fix the time of his death too. The three of them arrived together at the railway station at four o'clock and Fort had been found in his coffin not long after five o'clock. Like an efficient train company, the murderer was working to a very tight timetable.

Francis might have considered the Ansells under the heading of suspects were it not that they had the most convincing alibi. The couple took a cab from the station to the police-house, where they asked to see him, Francis, as well as making enquiries from the sergeant about Ernest Lye. They obtained directions to Prickwillow Road, walked to the Chases' house, were shown in by the maid to talk with Cyrus, taken out to the garden shed, and the rest of it. There was no possible interval of time during which Mr and Mrs Ansell could have carried out a murder, either singly or together. He wondered why the Ansells wanted to see him but since, whatever the matter was, it could have no bearing on the death of Eric Fort, Inspector Francis decided to leave the question for the time being. One murder a day was sufficient.

As for Ernest Lye, he had been released earlier on the afternoon of Fort's murder. One of the reasons for letting Lye go was that Francis had returned to the Lion Hotel to talk not with his brother-in-law, Salter, but with an ostler who worked in the stables behind the Lion. What the ostler said threw even more doubt on the case against Ernest Lye.

Yet although Inspector Francis did not believe Lye to be guilty of Tomlinson's murder, or at least not on the basis of George Grace's account, he was not convinced of his innocence either. And now the death of Eric Fort made things more complicated. Ernest Lye had apparently returned to Upper Fen with his wife. Francis wasn't aware of any link between Lye and Fort, but then he knew almost nothing about Fort. It would be only prudent to establish Lye's whereabouts during the late afternoon. If the gentleman claimed once more to have been wandering about Ely, well . . .

The connection between Tomlinson and Fort might also be found in the way they'd died. Fort was lying in the coffin, which contained a fair quantity of blood. Once again, this seemed to have come from wounds in the area of the head or neck. But until Doctor Wallace had a look, Inspector Francis decided to form no opinion at all. There were other matters he could investigate.

One of them was how the body had been conveyed to the outbuilding. Or rather how Eric Fort was enticed into the building and then persuaded or compelled to lie down, still living, inside the security coffin. There was no trace of blood or any kind of struggle in the workshop itself, so Fort must have been alive when he lay down to die, or to be killed.

Once the body was removed, Francis examined Chase's workshop with the help of several lamps. Then, with Constable Collis, he came back the next day and went over the scene again. After that he questioned Cyrus Chase about the access to the outbuilding. Chase said that there was only one key for the padlock, which he kept in his possession, but that he had reason to believe that lately someone might have made a copy. He rather thought one or two items had been disturbed inside the building. Why hadn't he changed the lock? asked the Inspector. He'd been intending to, was Cyrus' simple answer.

The possibility that Cyrus or Bella (or both) murdered Fort was one of the first that Francis considered. He talked to the servants in the Prickwillow Road house but nothing much came of it. The staff who tended on Mr and Mrs Chase were as affected by the murder as their mistress, and were busy either having the vapours or attending to those who were having them.

From Mattie, Inspector Francis learned that she had not seen Mr Chase during the afternoon until the Ansells arrived at around five o'clock. Cyrus was sitting in the drawing room and reading a periodical. Mattie said that she rather thought her employer might have been dozing when she knocked to announce the visitors. If this was the behaviour of a murderer, then it was astonishingly cool and calm behaviour. And Cyrus didn't strike Francis as especially cool and calm. Having discovered what Cyrus Chase did, he thought of the inventor merely as being a bit odd. Premature burial did not rank highly on the Inspector's list of worries. From Mrs Chase's personal maid, Francis discovered that Bella spent the afternoon in her room. She had gone there after he'd talked with her about the *first* murder, that of Charles Tomlinson, in order to establish her whereabouts on the Sunday afternoon (at Evensong etc.).

If the murderer of Eric Fort was not someone from within the Chase household then it must have been an outsider. No one had been seen, no suspicious figures lurking outside the house, no interlopers in the garden. Yet it had been a gloomy afternoon, with dusk beginning to come down. Though the trees were not thick with leaves any more they would still provide some cover for anyone determined to sneak on to the Chase property.

By the light of the following day, Francis, accompanied by Constable Collis, walked very carefully around the house and the garden. There were quite substantial gaps between the villa and the adjoining houses on both sides. One of them was fenced with a gate, though the gate was latched rather than locked. The other side was open but planted up with shrubbery. It was easy to gain access to the garden and to Chase's workshop by either route, without disturbing anyone inside. In fact a trespasser would only be seen by someone looking out of the window at the moment he happened to pass, and as there were only a few small windows to the sides, the chances of going undetected were high.

The whole thing was baffling. Francis was happy to admit to Collis that he was baffled. He had no false pride. He was even in the dark about why Eric Fort was planning to call on Cyrus Chase. The inventor of the security coffin informed him that he believed it was to do with a device which he was developing to reduce the risk of premature burial. Fort represented an important London firm interested in the device as a commercial prospect. Chase claimed not to know any more. In any case, Fort never got to him but was intercepted before arrival. Francis made a mental note to ask the Ansells whether they were aware of any more details concerning Fort's trip, since they had shared the train journey to Ely.

Otherwise, he was in the dark. Then he received another visitor. This one wished to talk not about the Fort murder but the Tomlinson one. He was a clergyman from St Ethelwine's in the village of Upper Fen. His name was George Eames. His first words, once the introductions were made and the niceties exchanged, were, 'I have a confession to make, Inspector.'

Sleuth hounds

T om and Helen Ansell returned to Cambridge on the evening following the discovery of the body of Eric Fort. It was the second time they had gone back to the Devereux Hotel and discussed a murder to whose aftermath they were witnesses. Another murder occurring in the same town and at around the same time of day and being investigated by the same Inspector. If it were not so grim, the situation might have been almost comic in its coincidences.

The Ansells had given some preliminary details to Inspector Francis – about their visit to the police-house, about finding Fort's body in the company of Cyrus Chase, and the likely timing of the murder – but had so far said nothing concerning John Jubb's tale of George Eames and the stuffed monkey. There had not been the opportunity, since the policeman was otherwise occupied.

Tom thought he ought to write again to David Mackenzie with the news that they would be detained in Cambridge for a while longer. Although Ernest Lye was free, he and Helen were likely to be required as material witnesses to this second killing. How should he phrase it? Mr Mackenzie might start to wonder why this stretch of the fen country was suddenly becoming so murderous. And why the Ansells, apparently by chance, were to be found on the scene of every serious crime. Tom and Helen were certainly wondering.

'You've recovered?' Tom said to his wife.

They had managed to eat a little supper – appetites better than they were yesterday after Charles Tomlinson's death – and were now fortifying themselves with brandy. Helen said brandy was more effectual than smelling salts as a restorative. They were comfortably ensconced in armchairs on either side of a slumbering fire in the sitting room of their hotel suite.

'Almost recovered. It's not the first time we've stumbled across a body, Tom. Not even the first time this week. I wouldn't say I am getting used to it but . . .'

'If you wrote it in a story, it would scarcely be believed.'

'Do not be so sure,' said Helen. 'You can get away with a great deal of implausibility between hard covers.'

'Anyway, we must go back to Ely tomorrow—'

'Back again . . .'

'Back again, to see that Inspector Francis, and this time tell him everything.'

'You're making it sound as though we set out to conceal things.'

'We haven't deliberately been concealing anything,' said Tom. 'It's just that this business has grown so tangled. It's like . . . like the maze in Ely Cathedral.'

'That is a labyrinth rather than a maze,' said Helen. 'And the cathedral labyrinth was not tangled. The path may be tortuous but it is clear. You will reach the end if you do not deviate from the right course.'

'Very well,' said Tom, who had been pleased with his maze

analogy and was less pleased to be put right. 'In that case, perhaps you'd like to conduct us to the end, Mrs Ansell.'

'In the manner of an investigator?'

'Do you think Mr Pinkerton in the United States employs female agents?'

'If he doesn't, he should do,' said Helen. 'They call them sleuth hounds over there.'

Both of them took more brandy. They felt light-headed, either because of the drink or what they had been through, or both.

'Poor Fort,' said Helen. 'I feel sorry for him.'

'Why? He was following us around and making a nuisance of himself, sending silly cryptic messages.'

'Nevertheless justice should be done. A solution ought to be found to both these murders.'

'Then lead us to the solution then, Mrs Pinkerton.'

'Taking Mr Tomlinson first,' said Helen, putting down her glass and tapping her elegant forefingers together. 'By late this morning we already knew that there were at least two individuals who might have been his enemies. There is Mr Lye, whose wife had a – what did we call it? – a closeness with Mr Tomlinson.'

'Yes. And suspicious circumstances meant that he was arrested on the evening of the murder. Even though he's been released, he is not necessarily out of the woods yet. And the second individual?'

'Number two is someone we have not yet met,' said Helen. 'The cleric from Upper Fen, George Eames, who was humiliated by Tomlinson all those years ago – the affair of the stuffed monkey, remember? – and who may have encountered Charles Tomlinson again and who, if he did encounter him, might have been driven to take a delayed revenge . . .'

'May and might and if,' said Tom. 'I don't think those little words would stand up in court. Not without evidence.'

'Evidence like blood on a cuff?'

'That and a bit more. Go on.'

'By this afternoon we'd learned of two more people in the – what shall we call it? – the anti-Tomlinson party.'

'Eric Fort was fearful of him, didn't like him.'

'To put it mildly. When he heard of the murder, he said it was no more than Tomlinson deserved.'

'He didn't seem surprised to hear the news either.'

'As if he already knew about it – or had done it.'

'Fort was on his way to see Cyrus Chase in Ely,' pursued Tom. 'Mr Chase may have had an excuse to dislike Tomlinson if he'd stolen some idea of his connected to that security coffin.'

'I thought we weren't allowing little words like "may" and "if", Tom.'

'I make an exception for myself.'

Helen ignored him and ticked off their suspects (Ernest Lye, George Eames, Eric Fort, Cyrus Chase) on her fingers before saying, 'Of course, there are probably other individuals we don't know about with a reason to hate or fear Mr Tomlinson.'

'I should think so. He seemed a person easy to dislike or be afraid of. Now you've disposed of Tomlinson and come up with a quartet of individuals with a motive for murder, and allowed for plenty of others we are ignorant of, what about Eric Fort? Who killed him?'

'The cast of characters is more limited here, very limited indeed, since we only know of Mr Chase, who did not have the appearance of a murderer but was sitting somnolently in his drawing room and reading a magazine called *Funereal Matters.*'

'Nor did he look much like an inventor, even an inventor of security coffins.'

'We can be certain of one thing, Tom.'

'Yes?'

'It wasn't Charles Tomlinson who murdered Mr Fort.'

'And vice-versa. Or probably vice-versa. Doesn't Fort's death exonerate him from any role in Tomlinson's death?'

'Unless he was not the main actor but an accomplice in the business.'

Tom had not thought of this possibility.

'Mr Fort didn't answer your question, did he?' said Helen. 'You asked why Tomlinson paid him to follow us. He was going to tell us later. Why not tell us there and then, in the coffee-house?'

'I don't know. Maybe he was frightened. He was about to say something and then he stopped himself.'

'Why should he be frightened of revealing the truth? Tomlinson was already dead. There's another thing, Tom. If Mr Fort was really being paid to follow us around and the rest of it, then why would it have been Mr Tomlinson who set him on to do it? I never met the gentleman at all while he was alive and you saw him for, what, a few minutes at Phoenix House.'

'He might have learned about us from Mrs Lye,' said Tom. 'But I agree, there does not seem to be any good reason why Tomlinson should have bothered us or been bothered by us.'

'Which means . . .'

Helen paused. Tom glanced at her where she sat opposite him, the dying fire casting a faint glow on her cheek. She was looking away. He thought he knew what she was about to say, but did not want to interrupt. Then she gazed straight at him.

'What it means is that there's someone else. Someone else who has been after us all this time.'

George Eames' Confession

'I have a confession to make, Inspector.'
With these words, George Eames announced the reason for his visit to the Ely police-house.

'You have, sir?'

Stephen Francis stared hard at the cleric sitting on the far side of his desk. Eames was a slight man, with features that were firm, almost rigid. Francis received the impression of one who was closed off against the world, shut up inside a shell.

'I am aware that an individual by the name of Charles Tomlinson was murdered here in Ely on Sunday afternoon. Furthermore, I know that a second person by the name of Fort suffered a similar fate yesterday.'

'You were acquainted with Tomlinson and Fort, Mr Eames?'

'I was. Tomlinson I knew many years ago. The other one – Fort – I met only recently.'

Francis waited. Whatever Eames wanted to say was costing him an effort. The Inspector just stopped himself from drumming his fingers on the ordered surface of his desk. He looked out of the small barred window at the sunlit rooftops on the other side of Lynn Road. Was the gentleman opposite him about to confess to a murder? Or even to a couple of murders? Francis doubted it.

'I – I . . . this is difficult for me to say, Inspector, but I had cause to dislike and distrust Charles Tomlinson.'

'So did others, it seems.'

'My reasons for hating him were particularly strong.'

An odd rippling movement travelled across George Eames' features, as though in register of some deep internal struggle. Francis drew his notebook towards him, as much to give Eames a chance to collect himself as anything else. He'd noticed how the clergyman's professed dislike of the murdered man had rapidly changed to hatred. And he wondered why the cleric should want to claim some sort of first place among Tomlinson's enemies.

'Tell me about those reasons if you would, sir,' he said, at the same time spreading his hands as if to say, we have the time, we have all day. He didn't really. The Inspector was due to see Dr Wallace, who was at this moment casting a professional eye over the corpse of Eric Fort. But Francis felt that Eames was the sort of person who could only be teased out of his shell, rather than bullied.

'I said that I knew Charles Tomlinson many years ago. We were fellow students at Cambridge University. Fellow students and also friends. Our backgrounds were different. Charles came from a distinguished local family of scholars, churchmen, and the like. I come from – let us say, I come from a more humble background. Yet we were friends even though we disagreed about many things and held conflicting opinions about almost everything of importance. I enjoyed our debates. They were vigorous discussions, serious and manly ones. For my part, I am not ashamed to say that I was glad of Charles' companionship, his friendship. He was like a—'

George Eames paused. Inspector Francis glanced up from the notebook which he was pretending to study in order to give the other man some breathing space.

'Like a kingfisher,' said Eames finally. 'Yes, a kingfisher. He was bright but rarely seen and fleeting. Then it grieves me to say that we fell out, and our debates became quarrels, our friendship turned to antipathy.'

'Something happened?'

'It did. I do not wish to go into details. The memory is painful even now. But Charles played a joke on me – that is, he did something which he might have regarded as a joke. But it was more of an outrage, an affront to all decency and, I may say, to civilized values.'

Naturally, Inspector Francis was curious to know about the outrage. But Eames was not prepared to say a word more on the subject. His hands were clenched in his lap. A dull flush was visible on his pale cheeks. Francis revised his opinion of a moment before. This was a man who might be capable of murder after all. Outwardly, he was in control of himself but, beneath the surface, he was burning.

'After what he did, Charles Tomlinson left the university of his own accord and before he could be sent down. He left the country too, for many years.'

'Why did he come back?'

'Who knows? I was not in confidence. I was not in communication with him. Perhaps he was tired of wandering about the globe. As I said, he has family in Cambridge. Perhaps he hoped to be reconciled with them. Even when Charles was at the university, and despite his sometimes wayward behaviour, he generally managed to retain the affections of his family and of others besides.'

'When did you become aware that Charles Tomlinson had returned to this country, Mr Eames?'

'Quite recently. He has a cousin who lives out at Upper Fen—'

'Mrs Lye?'

'Yes. I believe he was in the habit of visiting her at Phoenix House.'

'She welcomed his visits?'

'I expect so. Most people seemed to welcome Charles Tomlinson, at first anyway.'

'You saw Mr Tomlinson in Upper Fen?'

Eames hesitated before answering. 'I saw him but I did not speak to him. In fact, I went out of my way not to speak to him.'

'Mr Eames, you came in here saying you had a confession to make . . .?'

'I rode over to Ely on Sunday afternoon with murder in my heart.'

'Many people have murder in their hearts.'

'It was Charles Tomlinson I was looking for.'

'Because of an incident – an outrage – which occurred many years ago? Because of the hurt which he caused you at the university?'

'No, no, Inspector. You have disturbed the train of my narrative.'

'I apologize. Please go on.'

'On the Sunday morning a person remained behind after Matins who wished to speak to me. It was Eric Fort. He too had become involved with Charles Tomlinson, as some sort of paid agent for the man. But Fort had undergone a change of heart after spending a night in the crypt of St Ethelwine's—'

'In the crypt of your church, Mr Eames?'

The story was taking such a peculiar turn that the usually impassive Stephen Francis could not resist breaking in. He wanted to confirm what his ears were telling him.

'Yes, the crypt. Tomlinson had got the idea into his head that there was some item of value down there, and together with Eric Fort he determined to break into the place and ransack it.'

'Did they break in? That's a criminal offence, you know.'

'Tomlinson obtained the keys without my knowledge. He got them from my housekeeper so I suppose that, from a legal point of view, he did not break into the crypt.'

'And what did he take?'

'Nothing at all according to Fort. He departed angrily, setting off into the night and leaving Fort to consider the error of his ways. That gentleman attended the morning service and then came to me to confess all.'

'And now he is dead as well.'

'Yes. Poor fellow.'

'Mr Eames, this business is becoming more complicated by the minute. Are you saying that it is a complete coincidence that your one-time friend Charles Tomlinson should gain access to the crypt of *your* church in search of, well, in search of something? Was he playing another joke on you? Was he looking to commit a further outrage?'

'I do not think so,' said Eames. 'No doubt Charles enjoyed the knowledge that I am the incumbent of St Ethelwine's. Perhaps it satisfied him to know that I had not made as much of my life as I once believed that I would, but was isolated in a remote fenland parish . . .'

Eames' voice tailed off before he rallied and said more firmly, 'No, I believe he came to Upper Fen on account of his connection to Mrs Lye and nothing else. Then he stumbled over some information which decided him to go poking around in the church crypt. Poking around without result. When I found out from Mr Fort that Charles was behind this, I grew very angry indeed. By another coincidence, the theme of my sermon that morning was righteous anger.'

'So you rode to Ely with murder in your heart?'

'I freely confess it, Inspector.'

'What happened? You encountered Mr Tomlinson here?'

'I left my horse at the stables in the Lion Hotel and walked about the town. It was a miserable afternoon and the weather was closing in. I expected to see Charles at any moment. I thought the very force of my feelings might conjure him up before me, like a genie. It was as if my steps were being guided not by a higher power but by a lower one.'

George Eames paused again.

Was this it? wondered Francis. The climax of the confession?

'I was wrong. I was being guided, thank God. But guided by my better angel and to a place of safety. The operations of grace led me to a church.'

'To the cathedral?'

'No, I was not in spirits for a cathedral, if you catch my meaning, Inspector. I entered St Mary's and knelt down in an obscure corner and I prayed that all sinful thoughts and impulses should be expelled from my heart and mind. By the time I departed it was dark.'

'Did you notice anything unusual when you left St Mary's?' said Francis. St Mary's was close to Palace Green.

'No. I was scarcely aware of my surroundings. I did not reclaim my horse from the Lion stables since it was too late by then to ride back to Upper Fen. Instead I sought out a lodging house in one of the lower areas of the town, near the railway station.'

'Why? I mean, why there and not at the Lion?'

'I wanted to avoid the light and clamour of the town.'

This was an odd way of describing Ely on a Sunday evening although, Francis supposed, it was an accurate enough statement after the murder of Tomlinson. He suspected that Eames was somehow atoning for his sinful heart and mind by seeking out the kind of lodging-place he'd never consider in normal circumstances. That is, if the cleric was speaking the truth.

'You remember the landlady at the lodging house?'

'Not her name. I did not find out her name. She had – she may have reddish hair.'

'You remember the street?'

'Potter's Lane, perhaps, or it might be Station Road or . . . I am not really sure, Inspector.'

'What happened the next morning? Yesterday morning?'

'I returned to the Lion Hotel and paid for the stabling of my horse and rode back to Upper Fen.'

'Without hearing the news of Charles Tomlinson's death?'

'I heard the news. It was the talk of all the ostlers at the Lion, especially as Charles regularly stayed at the place. I was very surprised when I realized the identity of the murdered man. It was as if my wishes were being translated into reality. I have spent much of the last day reflecting and praying for guidance. Then I heard of the death of Mr Fort.'

'How?'

'From St Ethelwine's sexton, Gabriel Parr. He and his son were in Ely this morning on some errand. He has a brother in the Constabulary.'

'Yes, he does,' said Francis, thinking of Parr, who had been first on the scene at the murder of Tomlinson and who, though a good man, was inclined to loose talk. 'So you got the story from your sexton who in turn got it from his brother in the force. And then you rode over here again . . .?'

'I have come to you, Inspector, because two men have died in a short space of time, both of whom I knew and one of whom I had every reason to wish ill to.'

'This is your confession, Mr Eames?'

'It is.'

'So – let me get this clear – you are not confessing to an actual crime?'

'Only in my heart.'

'Not yet an organ that can be indicted under English law.'

'There are higher authorities than English law.'

'Thank you for coming to see me, Mr Eames. The information you have provided about Tomlinson and Fort is most interesting.'

And with that, Francis signalled that his talk with Eames was at an end.

Once the St Ethelwine's cleric had departed, the policeman spent some time reflecting (though not praying). He'd had some rum conversations with people in the more than twenty years that he'd served with the Isle of Ely force but this one with Eames took the biscuit.

What was Francis supposed to do? Arrest the clergyman for crimes of the heart? Of course not. Not even a head-in-the-clouds man of the cloth could be so foolish as to suppose that he might be found guilty for his thoughts. What Eames was looking for, in the opinion of Stephen Francis, was forgiveness, some sort of absolution. That was what he intended by coming in with his 'confession'. Well, the only absolution which Francis was capable of offering was that provided by the due process of the law, followed by the prison cell and even the scaffold.

There was the remote possibility that George Eames was playing an extremely clever game. According to his own 'confession', he'd spent the afternoon of Charles Tomlinson's death here in Ely, and been close to the site of the murder. He had strong reason to hate Tomlinson. Whatever the story behind the outrage in Cambridge all those years ago, it still weighed very heavily on Eames. Francis thought of his clenched hands, the dull glow in his cheeks. Yes, he hated Tomlinson all right.

Suppose that he was pre-empting suspicion by coming to the police-house to admit to these things? Suppose that, with all the stuff about crimes of the heart, he was deliberately presenting himself as a naive and unworldly figure incapable of actual bloodshed? Which was the light in which Francis saw him. And there was Eames' link to Eric Fort as well. There was the odd story of the search in the St Ethelwine's crypt. Perhaps, thought Francis, he should go and take a look at this mysterious crypt for himself.

The Inspector sighed. He added George Eames to that list of

individuals who might have been out and about in Ely at the time of Tomlinson's murder. They were Ernest Lye and Cyrus Chase and Bella Chase, each of them buzzing around like angry flies. Or hornets, given that Tomlinson had been stung, stabbed.

The thought reminded Francis that, as Eames arrived, he was on his way to see Wallace, to discover whether the doctor had gleaned anything from his examination of Eric Fort's body. Putting on his hat and coat – the day was cold but bright – Francis walked to Fore Hill and Wallace's consulting room. He did not learn much that was new from the doctor. Eric Fort's death was similar to Tomlinson's. That is, there was some wounding in the region of his head and neck which resulted in the spill of blood inside the security coffin, but in Wallace's view the injuries were once again insufficient to cause death. He raised the possibility of poison, which was suggested by some discharge and frothing from the corpses' mouths as well as their expressions. But this was still speculation, he insisted. There was no question now that autopsies would have to be carried out on both bodies, whatever the delay and the expense. This would require doctors to come from Cambridge, something which Wallace said he would arrange.

Inspector Francis walked away from Fore Hill, dissatisfied. This wasn't Doctor Wallace's fault. It seemed evident that the same person killed both Fort and Tomlinson. While there were a number of individuals, from Ernest Lye to George Eames, who might have wanted to do away with Tomlinson, none of them had much of a motive for wanting to kill the undertaker's man.

So Stephen Francis was forced to the same conclusion as the Ansells were arriving at: there was someone else involved in all this.

The Murderer's Story, Part One

There *was* someone else. He went by the name of Mute, or at least that was the pseudonym he employed when penning his column for *Funereal Matters*. During the course of the six months from spring to autumn, Mute had progressed from being a humble journalist to being a double murderer. Looking back, he would not have predicted such a course for himself. The odd thing was that he was pleased to find that he had it in him to do such things.

After Charles Tomlinson visited him in the spring of that year at the magazine office in St Dunstan's Alley, Mute found himself increasingly preoccupied with his old friend. Despite his irritation with the man, he couldn't stop thinking of Tomlinson. Thinking of the charm, the whiff of excitement and the danger which that gentleman wanderer brought with him like some exotic spices from the east.

They encountered each other for a second time, apparently by chance, in an Eastcheap chop-house. Here Tomlinson unfolded a little more of his scheme for acquiring wealth. It transpired that he had come into possession of a handwritten document that told a story and, almost as an aside, indicated the whereabouts of an item of great value. A piece of treasure. Here was a tale from the English Civil War, a tale about the occupants of an isolated house in a fenland village, a noble fugitive from a terrible battle, the aid provided by daughters of the household, the priceless trophy carried by the fugitive, his violent death, and so on.

Previously, Mute considered Tomlinson's talk to be so much flimflam even though he'd given him money on the strength of it. But now he saw that behind the other man's banter Tomlinson was quite in earnest. Tomlinson actually believed in what he was saying. So Mute began to believe in it too. That second encounter in the chop-house was followed by other meetings, more relaxed ones. There was eating and drinking, then there was more drinking than eating. Mute not only found himself paying for their refreshment but also making further 'investments' in Tomlinson's schemes. It was hard to resist Tomlinson when you were in his company.

Occasionally Charles Tomlinson dropped round at the St Dunstan's Alley office. Mute introduced Tomlinson to Jenkins, his editor. Tomlinson promised Jenkins an article on funerary habits of the Southern Seas. Mute did not think that the article had been written. It would never be written now.

Whether he was in liquor or not (and he was generally in liquor, his hip flask often in his hand), Tomlinson was an easy talker. In addition to the story of the treasure, Tomlinson fed Mute with his Eastern tales. Appetizing or revolting accounts of foreign customs and tribal rites, of native women and savage men. Mute adopted a man-of-the-world attitude but really he lapped this stuff up. All of it, but especially the details of the lost treasure.

Gradually, from the details that Tomlinson let drop, Mute started to build up a picture, piece by piece. The treasure was a portable item of great value – an almost priceless object – in the possession of the noble runaway. He was betrayed, pursued and struck down in the churchyard. His death was a shameful, bloody business. He was interred in the vault of the very church where he met his end. With his body was buried the treasure.

The treasure was still there, said Tomlinson. Still down there.

Mute asked how his friend could be so sure, at the same time noting from Tomlinson's comment that the treasure must be buried underground. He already knew that it was connected to Tomlinson's visits to Ely and the cousin who lived near the city.

'How am I sure it's there? Because, my dear Mute, I am certain that not a soul has seen this document for at least two hundred years, and because the document describes the whereabouts of the treasure.'

'Document?'

'It is more of a journal, I suppose. A female diary. Put away and forgotten about for more than two centuries. I think of it as . . . as the Ely testament.'

'A testament uncovered by you, Tomlinson?'

'Yes. Aren't I the lucky one!'

'Suppose that someone else has come along in the meantime and, by chance or otherwise, stumbled across this item of treasure? What is it, by the way?'

'You won't get that information from me. I have no intention of telling you what "it" is. As for your other question, there is no one who could have stumbled across the thing. It is tucked away tight, all walled up.'

'If you know where it is, why haven't you laid hands on it already?'

'Patience, Mute. "Softly, softly, catchee monkey", as the wise natives say under hotter skies than these. I need time, I need assistance.'

Mute stayed silent. Was Tomlinson about to request that he,

Mute, should help? Mute couldn't resist a thrill of pleasure at the idea.

This last conversation between Mute and Tomlinson was taking place, not in the office of *Funereal Matters* or in a cheap eating-place or a pub but on the viewing platform of the Monument to the Great Fire. When Tomlinson suggested for a second time that Mute might like to accompany him to the top, so as to get 'the measure of the city', Mute did not refuse. By now he was on better terms with his old friend. They were almost intimates again, as in their student days.

He and Charles Tomlinson climbed the tight spiral stairs inside the fluted column and, breathless, emerged on to the viewing platform. The platform was like an animal cage in London Zoo, with iron bars all round and a mesh overhead to prevent people from tumbling over or throwing themselves off. A handful of other sightseers were already up there. Mute and Tomlinson snugged themselves into a corner. While they recovered their breath, they gazed at the curve of the river and the dark path of the Monument's own shadow across the rooftops of the houses. It was smoky down below but fine up above.

Tomlinson took out his hip flask and downed a swig. He said, 'I can see from the look in your eyes, my dear Mute, that you would like to join me in this quest for treasure. But no, I am afraid not. I owe you an explanation, though. There is a very useful suffix in Hindi. It is *wallah*, which may be translated simply as "man". One attaches to it all sorts of words to describe a fellow's occupation. As in a kitchen-wallah or a punkah-wallah – that's the servant who operates the great hanging sheets which serve as fans in India. Well, Mute, when I think of you it is – without disrespect – as a word-wallah. Someone who makes his living by juggling with words. Quite safe, really, words are. They cannot cut or bruise you as you juggle them. You are better off in the realm of words. You are not equipped for, ah, dubious enterprises.'

'What about my money, Tomlinson? The money I've been giving you over the last couple of months.'

'Those are investments. Haven't I made that plain? Anyway, you've already had your return, Mute.'

'What return? What are you talking about?'

'You've had my company and my conversation. That is what you've really been paying for, isn't it? Haven't I given good value? Cheap at the price I would have thought.'

Had there been no bars or mesh around the platform where they were standing, Mute would have pushed Charles Tomlinson to his death hundreds of feet below. If he'd possessed the strength of ten he would have torn aside the mesh with his bare hands in order to create a large enough gap to propel his old friend out into the smoky air of London.

'No, you are not cut out for adventure,' mused Tomlinson. 'I was rather thinking I might approach that Fort man. The one I met in your office lately.'

Once again Charles Tomlinson was toying with Mute. Leading him on, seducing him, only in order to enjoy the look of rebuff on his face when he was rejected. Not for the first time Mute recalled the joke that Tomlinson had played on George Eames, their Cambridge friend destined for holy orders. Previously he'd seen only the funny side of the joke. Now he experienced a stab of sympathy for Eames, though it came years too late.

Mute felt rejected and insulted. To be referred to as a word-wallah and, earlier, as a galley-slave! To be told that he had been purchasing the other's company and conversation, as though he were buying a friend! Throughout their talk Mute had been smiling in a game sort of way, but these last remarks caused the tight smile to vanish.

There and then, standing on top of the Monument to the Great Fire, he swore to himself that he would take revenge on Tomlinson. If his old college friend thought of him, Mute, as an effete, desk-bound fellow while he, Tomlinson, was a romantic wanderer about the globe, well, so be it. He'd show the other man the kind of action of which he was capable.

When they parted company at the base of the column, they shook hands and even talked of meeting again for a chat and a drink or two. Tomlinson really seemed oblivious of the mortal snub he'd just delivered to Mute. As for the funereal columnist, he decided it was best to maintain the appearance of 'friendship' while he plotted his revenge. As his eyes bored into Charles' retreating back – still conscious of that threadbare coat, which it was a pleasure to see his friend could not afford to replace – Mute determined to scupper Tomlinson's ridiculous treasure hunt or, better still, to lay hands on the precious item himself.

For some reason he did not doubt the truthfulness of Tomlinson's story. As Mute saw it, there really must be an article of genuine value tucked away in some fenland village, and Tomlinson had the key to finding it. Why shouldn't he lay hands on it before Tomlinson? Or take it from Tomlinson once the other obtained it? Getting the 'treasure' would not only be a satisfactory revenge on his old friend but also a very useful source of funds for a scheme which Mute was presently engaged on and which was not so far from being realized.

It happened that Mute was on good terms with Eric Fort, who did occasional jobs for Willow & Son. Mute was welcomed at Willow & Son as someone whose favourable comments were good for business. Like Mute, Eric Fort had a deep knowledge of the burial trade. In Fort's case it amounted almost to a love of the profession and all its appurtenances. The man had recently lost his wife, but his funereal obsession long pre-dated her death. Sometimes he brought to the *F.M.* office a juicy titbit to do with interment, partly for the pleasure of doing so and partly for the small change Mute slipped him if the story was juicy enough for his column. A typical item was the information about the coffin-bird, invented by Cyrus Chase but lately presented to Willow & Son by Tomlinson as his own idea, although neither Mute nor Fort were aware of these details. Fort was glad of any monetary reward from his tips. He seemed constantly on the edge of impoverishment.

Charles Tomlinson and Eric Fort had coincided on one such visit to Mute's room at *Funereal Matters*, and the talk among the three became so animated that editor Jenkins poked his nose round the door to see what all the good-humoured noise was about. And now it appeared that Charles was going to get Fort to help him in his dirty business.

Fort was already eager to please Mute, and he willingly agreed to keep the journalist informed of what Tomlinson was up to. He did this partly out of friendship and partly because, Mute suspected, he was a little frightened of Tomlinson. If that was the case, he wasn't alone.

From Eric Fort, Mute gleaned a few more details. He learned

that the village where the 'treasure' was to be found was called Upper Fen and that it lay a couple of miles outside Ely. In the village was sited Phoenix House, the home of Mr and Mrs Lye. It was Mrs Lye who was Tomlinson's cousin. Her presence in Upper Fen provided the pretext for Tomlinson's visits there. The church which had been the scene of a killing during the Civil War and whose crypt was the burial place of the murdered royalist was called St Ethelwine's.

The one thing that Fort was unable to discover was the nature of the supposed treasure. But, like Mute, the little undertaker's man was convinced that it existed. Not only did Charles Tomlinson talk about it in terms of absolute certainty but he really did possess a document that he called the 'Ely testament'. This was a battered, leather-bound little volume filled with handwriting which (from the brief glimpse that Fort had been permitted of it) was 'old-fashioned'. In this valuable book was the account of the royalist who took shelter in Upper Fen, his violent death and his hasty interment.

Mute wondered why, since Tomlinson already knew so much, he wasn't racing to get hold of the treasure, breaking into the crypt and so on. According to Fort, Tomlinson liked to take things slowly (Mute remembered 'Softly, softly, catchee monkey'). In any case, the black sheep seemed to be enjoying himself in the fen country. He spent time at Phoenix House. He stayed at the Lion Hotel in Ely. He had befriended a married couple in the city, or rather befriended a woman whose husband, he said, was a silly inventor. This was in addition to his friendship with Mrs Lye. According to Fort, Charles Tomlinson liked to refer casually to his 'harem', an allusion which Mute considered to be almost indecent.

So things went on for two or three months over the summer, with no action taking place and Tomlinson apparently waiting for the darker evenings of autumn before he began his treasure hunt in earnest. Eric Fort was primed to alert Mute when it looked as though things were about to begin. Mute rather enjoyed employing Fort in this surreptitious way. He felt that he was getting one over on Charles Tomlinson. It was like having a spy in the enemy camp. Even so he wondered whether the hunt for the Ely treasure was ever going to begin. He hoped it would be soon, since he was in need of funds for the scheme which was near fruition.

Then matters took a bizarre and worrying turn. By chance, Mute bumped into a young solicitor by the name of Will Evers at Willow & Son. Mute was there, partly to fish for gossip but mostly because he enjoyed the deference paid to him as the pseudonymous columnist for *Funereal Matters*. If ever he needed reminding that he was an individual of influence, he only had to drop into a funeral establishment. By contrast Will Evers was calling at Willow & Son on business, not pleasure. He was making some arrangements to do with the Abney Park funeral of one of the senior partners of Scott, Lye & Mackenzie of Furnival Street. A couple of mornings previously, Alexander Lye, a gentleman of advanced years, had died suddenly and unexpectedly in his own room.

Mute's ears pricked up at the name of Lye. Immediately he thought of the Lyes of Upper Fen. Were they by any chance related? It wasn't difficult to get Will Evers to chat once they left Willow & Son together. The difficulty would have consisted in getting him to stop chatting. Mute claimed he was travelling in the same direction, towards Holborn, and during a short walk and a longer omnibus ride, he picked up several pieces of information, some of them useful, some not. He learned that Will Evers was hoping to get married, and trying to pluck up courage to speak to the girl's father. That there were some decent fellows in the office where he worked, especially a chap called Tom Ansell who was married to a fine-looking lady who wrote 'stuff'. That old Alexander Lye had died following a sneezing fit, it seemed. That there was the question of a missing testament, which might possibly be mislaid out at some isolated country house and which that good fellow Ansell was going in search of . . .

It was fortunate that they were sitting side by side on the knife-board on top of the omnibus while Will Evers was slipping Mute all this information out of the side of his mouth. Fortunate because, if they'd been sitting face to face, Mute would hardly have been able to hide his surprise, even his shock, at a couple of things that the young lawyer was telling him.

They got off the omnibus near Furnival Street. It was easy for Mute to persuade the sociable, chatty Evers to join him for a spot of lunch in a nearby chop-house. Once they were indoors and eating, Mute attempted in a discreet way to extract more information. But it seemed that he'd obtained about as much as Evers knew. That there was an important document, which had gone missing in Ely, one linked to the Lyes of Upper Fen, and that his good friend Thomas Ansell was to go in search of it.

When he was back in the St Dunstan's Alley office, Mute allowed himself to grow increasingly agitated. Was it possible that others were after the Ely testament and the mysterious treasure? Yes, it was very possible. The presence of Thomas Ansell was a complicating factor. He would need to be kept an eye on as well.

Mute recruited Fort for this task. He decided to keep a closer watch on Charles Tomlinson himself and, to do so, took lodgings in Cambridge. This was close enough for Ely, where Tomlinson was spending much of his time, but not so close that Mute would run the risk of encountering his enemy unexpectedly in the street. To Eric Fort he delegated the tracking of Thomas Ansell and his wife. The undertaker's man's meeting with Tom and Helen at Alexander Lye's funeral was quite coincidental, but his dangerous encounter with them outside Liverpool Street Station was not since, in accordance with Mute's fresh instructions, he was on the track of the young couple. After the near-accident Fort continued to keep an eye on the Ansells once they were established in the Devereux Hotel, before reporting to Mute who was residing temporarily in a dingy house in a dingy Cambridge street.

Mute's fear was that the Ansells would somehow frustrate him in his quest for the Ely treasure just as the moment was drawing near. Fort told him that Tomlinson had instructed him, Fort, to come to Upper Fen on the Saturday evening, equipped with tools that would be useful for breaking into a house – or a crypt (jemmies, chisels). Mute's instructions to Fort were clear and simple: he was to assist Tomlinson to retrieve the treasure from St Ethelwine's, whatever it might be, but to make no attempt to take the item.

The next day – a Sunday – Fort was to convey to Mute two vital pieces of information. They were the nature of the treasure and Tomlinson's whereabouts. In fact, Mute expected Tomlinson to remain in Ely. There he planned to confront his old friend and enemy and, by subterfuge or force, to obtain the treasure for himself. How to guarantee that Tomlinson would not pursue him? Well, that would not be so difficult. He intended to deal with the Tomlinson problem once and for all. He'd been preparing for that eventuality all summer. Mute's hatred of Charles had not exactly grown but rather it had hardened during the summer months until it was like a crust over his soul, only to be broken by Tomlinson's death.

Mute believed that he had all his pieces in position, like a chess player about to check his opponent. Charles Tomlinson was doing the dirty work for him, Fort would bring him the information, and then he would swoop. But Eric Fort never materialized on the Sunday morning. Mute waited with growing anxiety in his Cambridge lodgings, the sound of the church bells a mocking accompaniment to the growing darkness of his thoughts. Had Fort betrayed him and sided with Tomlinson? Unlikely, thought Mute, since Fort was beholden to him and frightened of Charles. Had Tomlinson laid hands on the treasure, disposed of Fort and already boarded a tidal-express to catch a boat to the continent? That was not so unlikely, although it contradicted his earlier belief that Charles would stay in Ely for a time.

By the early afternoon Mute was too anxious to wait any longer. He took the train to Ely and went on the hunt for Charles Tomlinson. One way or the other, he meant to do for him.

David Mackenzie's Letter & Ernest Lye's Book

On the Tuesday morning before the Ansells set off once more for Ely, Tom received a letter from David Mackenzie. He thanked Tom for his letter of the day before, and for outlining the troubles besetting Ernest Lye. But his real purpose in writing was to say that the original reason for Tom's fenland visit had fortunately been overtaken by events. He and Ashley had unearthed a copy of Alexander Lye's will from the mound of documents, files and folios in his Regent's Park study. Their search succeeded in a surprisingly short time. So the senior partner did not die intestate and the reputation of Scott, Lye and Mackenzie was preserved.

After that, it was something of an anticlimax to read that were no irregularities in the way Lye disposed of his estate, which was to be divided equally between his sister Edith, and his half-brother Ernest. There were no belatedly acknowledged love-children, there were no mistresses tucked away in St John's Wood to be made amends to. Mackenzie said that he wasn't sure whether the difficulty over the will was a piece of mischief on Alexander Lye's part – Tom thought that 'mischief' was a kind way of putting it – in the same way that the contents of Lye's deed-box appeared to be nothing more than a heap of red herrings. In a final note, he added that Tom and Helen should stay in Cambridge or Ely for as long as necessary to assist Ernest Lye and his wife.

While Tom read the letter, Helen was browsing through Ernest Lye's history of Phoenix House and Upper Fen.

'It is unexpectedly interesting, Tom,' she said.

'How so?'

'The older house on the site of the present one was called Stilwell Manor. It was well known as a royalist outpost and before that as a place where Catholic priests might hide from their persecutors. There's even a legend that King Charles himself took shelter there when he was defeated at the Battle of Naseby.'

'I thought this region was all Cromwell's territory,' said Tom. 'He lived in Ely, didn't he?'

Helen referred to a page in the book on her lap. 'Mr Lye explains it here. He says, "As well as being the dwelling-place of the future Lord Protector, Ely was also the episcopal seat of Bishop Wren, who had been chaplain to Charles the First. The city was therefore a centre of royalist sympathies. When the Civil War broke out Matthew Wren set about the raising of forces for the king."'

Interesting details, Tom thought, but they could not have anything to do with their current business. Helen observed his look and held up her hand.

'Wait, Tom, there's more. It is to do with this legend of King Charles.'

She found a couple of paragraphs on the next page and read

aloud, "'From generation to generation the denizens of Upper Fen have handed down a story of how King Charles the First, fleeing from the rout at Naseby, sought refuge in Stilwell Manor, on the site of which Phoenix House presently stands. History, in the person of the great Clarendon . . ." Who's Clarendon?'

'He wrote a history of the Civil War, I think,' said Tom.

"'History, in the person of the great Clarendon, tells us that Charles actually escaped from Naseby towards the north-west, first to Ashby-de-la-Zouch and then to Lichfield. Members of the King's household as well as his private papers having already been captured on the battlefield, the pursuit of the fleeing royalists by Cromwell's horse was unrelenting. With the scent of triumph in their nostrils, they must surely have been hoping for the supreme prize of the unhappy monarch himself.

"'It may be that Charles' counsellors devised a stratagem whereby the Parliamentarians might be tricked into the belief that the King was escaping perhaps in disguise and in a quite contrary direction to the one he actually took. This is the probable reason for the persistent story (a story which prudent opinion might more rightly term a fable) that King Charles sought shelter east of Naseby in the fen country and at Stilwell itself, where he might depend on the loyal welcome as well as the silence of sympathizers. As regards the further tale that the escaping King was carrying a prize of great value, a true treasure, the present writer is unable to resist the thought that once a hare has been started there is no saying how far or in what direction it will run."'

'Starting hares? What does he mean by that?' said Tom.

'Mr Lye is saying that he does not believe in the stories about King Charles or the treasure of Upper Fen,' said Helen.

'The Treasure of Upper Fen, eh? Sounds like the title to a story. Old Lye's history is interesting enough but I can't see it has any connection to the murder of Tomlinson, or of Eric Fort.'

'Mr Fort told us he'd been involved with Tomlinson in doing things he regretted.'

'Yes.'

'He never said exactly what those things were. But he did mention being up to no good with Tomlinson somewhere outside Ely. Which could describe Upper Fen.'

'So you think their activities have something to do with this story about King Charles, who was never there in the first place, and a – what was it? – a "true treasure" which is also a legend?'

'It's not impossible.'

Tom smiled, then he shrugged. He thought it was almost Helen's duty as a writer to think up implausible ideas, to start hares and see where they'd run to.

'We can mention it to Inspector Francis, I suppose,' he said, wondering what that very practical policeman would make of it all.

The Murderer's Story, Part Two (Sunday, 19th October)

It was an easy matter to track down Charles Tomlinson, much easier than Mute expected. Not only was his enemy in Ely but he was still staying in the Lion Hotel. Or rather he was on his way back there from somewhere, not very steady on his feet and about to enter the hotel via the stable entrance from Market Street. It was drawing near the end of the Sunday afternoon and the weather was as overcast as Mute's mood.

'Tomlinson,' he called from across the street. 'Wait!'

Tomlinson peered round uncertainly. He squinted as Mute approached but did not recognize the other man until he drew nearer. Tomlinson's expression registered surprise but no great pleasure.

'Why, if it isn't my good friend Mute.'

Mute was pleased to see how battered and disreputable Tomlinson looked. He was unshaven and his eyes were bloodshot. He carried no stick, he wore no gloves or hat and his hair was dishevelled. Close to, Mute could smell the liquor coming off him. Tomlinson's coat not only seemed even more threadbare than usual but it was dusty and smeared with some kind of chalky substance. Seeing this, Mute thought of the crypt in St Ethelwine's church.

'What the devil are you doing here in Ely?' said Tomlinson.

'I am here to claim my investments.'

'What investments? Oh those ones.'

Tomlinson wafted his hand through the air to dismiss the whole business and made as if to walk off into the stable yard but then he paused. A more cautious look came into his face. He stroked his chin.

'Can we talk about them inside?'

'You're staying here?' said Mute, though he already knew the answer to the question.

'I find it more convenient to approach by this route instead of through the lobby,' explained Tomlinson, as they crossed the stable yard and, after weaving their way through mounds of crates and barrels, into the hotel through one of several small doors. 'I can come and go unannounced, which is what I prefer.'

Had the two men looked round as they entered the building, they might have seen a clerical gentleman riding into the yard. It was the Reverend George Eames, the old college friend of both Tomlinson and Mute. And if Eames had been looking hard at the rear quarters of the hotel he might have spotted the backs of his one-time fellow students. He might even have recognized them from their backs alone, since none of them had changed very much – backs or fronts – over the years. But they did not turn round and Eames was distracted by looking out for an ostler to take his horse. Once he'd found his ostler the cleric from Upper Fen set off on foot in search of Tomlinson, but it was Mute who'd found him first.

Tomlinson led Mute up narrow stairs to an upper floor. He seemed in conciliatory mood.

'I must apologize for my somewhat mean accommodation,' he said as he unlocked a door that gave on to a rectangular little room, with a rug covering warped floorboards and, at the end, a threadbare curtain drawn back to give a view over the backs of other buildings. It had the appearance of a servant's room rather than somewhere a guest would be put up.

'I have an understanding with the housekeeper of this place and she, in turn, has an understanding with the manager, a chap called Salter, and so what with one understanding and another, the arrangement is that I am to be given a room here in the Lion whenever I want it.'

Mute wasn't surprised to hear any of this. Tomlinson was just the man for 'understandings' and 'arrangements', especially where a woman was concerned. Tomlinson gestured for Mute to sit on the room's single (hard) chair, even as he sank with a sigh on to the single bed, probably just as hard. He drew his flask out of his pocket.

'Let us have a little libation to . . . to celebrate your arrival in Ely,' he said, making a half-hearted offer of the flask.

'Thank you but I've brought my own,' said Mute tapping his pocket, which gave off a dull, metallic sound.

'You have? Oh good. Because I do not think there is enough left in here.'

Tomlinson raised the flask and tilted his head back. Mute observed his Adam's apple bobbing, helplessly. He had his stick with him, and he was tempted for an instant to deal a slashing, sideways blow across the other's throat. He visualized the hip flask flying from Tomlinson's grasp, the momentary look of shock in his eyes, the mouth gasping for air. Mute reached for his stick then stopped himself. Not now, not here.

Unaware of any of this, Tomlinson lowered the flask and tucked it back in his pocket. He wiped his hand across his mouth. The bed was low and he sat slumped while Mute perched in the chair a few feet away and with his back to the wall. Because he was slightly higher up, and because of the broken-down state of the other man, Mute experienced something that was very unusual in his dealings with Charles Tomlinson: a sense of superiority.

'So you've come for your investments, Mute. I must say it is good to see you again. Where'd we last meet? Up the Monument, wasn't it?'

'Yes,' said Mute, remembering that that was the occasion when Tomlinson said he was paying for his company and his conversation. The memory reinforced his cold anger against the man on the narrow bed. Aloud, he said, 'Where is Mr Fort?'

'Who? Oh, little Mr Fort. 'Course, I forgot you know him too. Where is he? I don't know.'

'He was with you last night.'

'How'd you know about that? Well, yes, he was with me. But where he's got to since, I do not know.'

'Where is the treasure you were after last night, in company with Eric Fort?'

Tomlinson put both his hands on his knees and looked at Mute. The light in the little room was poor but, even so, Mute was conscious of the other's dark stare.

'You're well informed.'

'I have been keeping an eye on you.'

'Do you know what, Mute? I am almost tempted to think of you with an ounce of respect.'

'Remember, Tomlinson, you promised me a share in whatever you found.'

'You're welcome to a share of nothing. How much of it would you like?'

Mute hadn't expected anything different. He did not disbelieve Tomlinson. There was dejection, there was failure, written in the other man's posture. If Charles genuinely had unearthed anything in the St Ethelwine's crypt he would most likely still be drunk, but there'd be more than the usual swagger and confidence to him.

'You found nothing then?'

'How slowly do I have to speak in order for you to understand, my dear Mute? Yes, I found nothing, yes, I came away empty-handed.'

'What about the Ely testament?'

'Oh that,' said Tomlinson. 'I should have left it where I found it.'

'Where did you find it?'

'Fossicking around the old quarters of an old house, in a place where no one had ever looked. It doesn't matter anyway. It is nothing. A female fantasy.'

'That's not how you talked about it before.'

'Well, that's how I talk about it now.'

The only item of furniture in the room apart from the bed and chair was a little table on which stood a water jug and a bowl for washing and shaving. The table, which stood near the window, was fitted with a drawer. Mute noticed Tomlinson's eyes several times darting towards the table, and the area of the drawer, while he referred to the Ely testament. He guessed that the drawer was where the item, the Ely testament, was tucked away.

'Still, all is not lost,' said Tomlinson. 'I have some other irons in the fire here in Ely. I say, did you mention you had a flask with you? In your pocket.'

Mute said nothing but shook his head. He wasn't ready yet.

'There is a man who shares our interest in all things funereal,' continued Charles Tomlinson after a moment. 'A fellow called Chase. He lives near here, in Prickwillow Road. A house called *Mon Repos*. He has a wife who . . . well, never mind. Anyway, he has invented a device for a security coffin, a sort of spinning bird – what's the matter?'

'I've mentioned it in my column,' said Mute. 'I didn't realize you were involved, Tomlinson.'

'I'm not involved, not directly, although I may have referred to the coffin-bird on one of my visits to Willow & Son. Perhaps I gave the impression it was my own idea. But I do have access to the device. At the bottom of his garden this fellow has a workshop, and the workshop has a door, and the door has a padlock, and I have the key to it.'

Tomlinson fumbled in his waistcoat pocket and drew out a key and held it up for Mute to see. Then he looked at it as though wondering what it was he was holding before attempting to return the key to his waistcoat. It fell from his fingers and on to the floor. Tomlinson paid no attention but extracted the hip flask once more, shook it helplessly and looked at Mute.

This time Mute took out his own flask and passed it to Tomlinson. The other weighed it in his hand for a moment, pleased to realize that it was full or nearly so. He unscrewed the cap and took a good swallow, then a second and a third. He tried to replace the cap, gave up and passed the flask back to Mute, less readily than he'd taken it.

'Aren't you thirsty?'

'I want to keep a clear head,' said Mute.

'Why the devil do you want a clear head?'

'Because it is such a complicated story you're spinning.'

'Let's go for a walk,' said Tomlinson.

'No,' said Mute. 'Stay here.'

'You do what you like, but I'm going. It is very close in here.'

He pushed himself up from the bed and made for the door. Mute went after him. He closed the door behind them. Tomlinson did not think to lock it. They left the hotel by the same route, down the narrow stairs, through the stable yard and out into Market Street. Mute's plan was to steer Tomlinson away to an open area of town, perhaps to the meadows and parkland below the cathedral, but it did not seem as though there'd be time for that.

The light was beginning to go and the mist to gather. They passed the front of the Lion and then struck off at a diagonal towards Palace Green. Luck was still with Mute. The rawness of the afternoon meant that there was almost no one to be seen, despite the fact that Evensong must soon be starting in the cathedral.

'My throat is burning,' said Tomlinson. 'That is a fiery liquor in your flask.'

Mute peered urgently through the gloom, looking for somewhere secluded. There were a few trees on one side of the green, together with a couple of elegant houses, while on the other side stretched the wall of the bishop's palace. Not a living thing was visible on the green apart from a handful of ducks sitting, incongruously and innocently, on the grass. Almost in the centre of the open area was positioned a cannon which, Mute thought, had been captured at Sebastopol.

He was walking beside Tomlinson, close enough to grasp him. He kept glancing sideways as if fearful that the other man might suddenly topple over.

'Do you want me to die?' said Tomlinson. His voice was loud but strained, as if it cost him an effort to speak.

'No,' said Mute.

'Lie,' said Tomlinson.

His companion said nothing.

'I think I'm going to shoot the cat,' said Tomlinson.

For an instant, Mute thought he meant the words literally before realizing that Tomlinson was announcing he was about to vomit. He did not move away, and after a moment Tomlinson brought himself back under control. They were still walking, slowly, and by now were in front of the cannon. They stopped by its black mouth, and faced each other. Mute's eyes darted about. There were a few people at the western entrance to the cathedral but they were dozens of yards away and the light was fading.

'What have you done to me, Mute old chap?'

'Nothing, Tomlinson. I swear it.'

'That's a lie,' repeated the other. 'You have done something. I cannot feel my feet.'

'I expect it's the drink. You keep away from me!'

Tomlinson was staggering towards Mute, his arms stretched out in front of him and the fingers of his hands crooked as if he were going to seize the other round the throat. Mute raised his stick, fumbled with the ivory handle and a six-inch spike shot out from the bulbous tip of the thing. He pointed the stick in Tomlinson's direction. Mute had not handled the flick stick in anger (or fear) before, but he had frequently practised with it since purchasing the implement earlier in the year from a swordsmith's in Hanover Street.

He was still frightened of Tomlinson, even of a dying Tomlinson, and he wielded the stick more to ward off the other than to injure him. He was panicky and oblivious to witnesses now. By a lucky stroke he caught Charles Tomlinson across his brow, and blood began to well up from the deep gash almost straightaway. Tomlinson may not even have been aware of the injury until the blood was dripping into his eyes. He raised a hand and inadvertently smeared it down his face, then he looked at his reddened palm in confusion. Again Mute jabbed at his old friend with the tip of the flick stick, and then for a third and fourth time.

But these blows were partly warded off by Tomlinson's waving arms and Mute succeeded in inflicting only small wounds in the region of Tomlinson's neck. The blows were sufficient to keep him at bay, though, before he abruptly sat down on the grass and then started to scrabble his way under the barrel of the cannon, frantically using his elbows and heels. It was as if he were seeking shelter.

Tomlinson came to a stop when the back of his head struck the crosspiece of the undercarriage of the cannon. Gurgling sounds emerged from his throat, and his legs twitched. Mute stood, stooping slightly and watching him for a few more moments. He glanced up towards the western face of the cathedral. There were still a handful of people around the porch. Were they looking in his direction? Had they heard any sounds? Had there been any sounds to hear, apart from the dying man's gurgles which were now shifting into wheezes? Mute was in such an agitated state that he could not be certain whether these bystanders were aware of what was happening or not.

What was certain was that he couldn't stay here. He believed that Charles Tomlinson was done for; he thought he must be done for. Mute twisted the bulbous end of the flick stick so that the spike retracted. Then he took off, going at a fair lick, in the reverse direction from the one he'd walked with Tomlinson only a few minutes earlier. He needed to get back to the Lion Hotel and up to Tomlinson's room before a general alarm was raised. He needed to get his hands on the Ely testament which, he was sure, was in the table drawer. He remembered also the key that Tomlinson had been brandishing.

What about the others though? The others who, like the pseudonymous Mute, had gone to Ely that Sunday afternoon in search of Charles Tomlinson? Any one of them might have killed him, if he or she had had the means and been ready to seize the moment. Someone taking a bird's-eye view over the town centre and able to penetrate the gathering mist might have seen Bella Chase making her way into the cathedral via the western entrance, at the moment when the man she had briefly fantasized about as a lover was breathing his last under the Sebastopol cannon. The same bird – not one of the ducks still squatting on the Palace Green but perhaps one of the gulls that haunted Ely docks – might almost simultaneously have glimpsed Ernest Lye as he walked, almost unaware of his surroundings, through the Dean's Meadow. At one point, Lye scraped his hand against a rusted gate and the blood that came as a result left a stain on his cuff.

As for the other two suspects, they were out of sight, invisible to any bird. Cyrus Chase was in the workshop at the bottom of his garden. He was contemplating his security coffin. He was wondering whether there'd be any response from Willow & Son to the letter which he had written pointing out – in quite moderate tones, he thought – that Charles Tomlinson was not the creator of the coffin-bird but that he had purloined the idea from him, Cyrus Chase. Cyrus' mood was not, in fact, quite as grim as it might have been. Already his thoughts were moving beyond the coffin-bird to another more advanced device that would be a safeguard against premature burial.

The third man who had cause to hate Tomlinson, and who

had actually ridden over to Ely with the intention of confronting him, was George Eames, the perpetual curate of St Ethelwine's. He too was out of sight, tucked away at the back of St Mary's and on his knees, in prayer. His actions that afternoon were exactly as he'd described them to Inspector Francis. He had gone through a change of heart. He had been directed by his better angel and abstained from a terrible sin. Once he finished a lengthy period of prayer and contemplation he sought out the most obscure, the lowest area of the town and took lodgings for the night with the landlady who had reddish hair.

And Lydia Lye? She had no motive to hate her cousin Charles, none at all. She enjoyed his company and, like almost everyone else, had been diverted by his traveller's tales. She might even have entertained dreams that he could relieve her of the boredom of her life with Ernest in Upper Fen. While her husband was wandering about the town, she remained behind in the warmth and comfort of the Lion Hotel, ignorant of the death of her cousin a few hundred yards away. There is no reason to include her in the list of suspects except that it sometimes happens in this sort of thing that the least likely person has done it.

So not one of these five – Mr and Mrs Lye, Mr and Mrs Chase, the Reverend Eames – had any part in Tomlinson's murder. The responsibility and the guilt belonged solely to Mute, at present scurrying back through the gloom, his flick stick at his side.

Summer, 1645

*A*larmed by the smoke and the shouting, the guards and Trafford and Mr Martin and the strangers from Ely came running out of the little office, and Loyer came in their wake. Seizing his opportunity – they had not bound him or tried to constrain him in any way, perhaps out of some residual respect for what they believed was his royal status – he broke away and darted across the hall. Anne was by the front door, where she'd retreated after starting the fire. Swathes of smoke billowed across the hall. She was terrified by what she had done. Some of the household were already attempting to put out the flames in the priest-hole, with blankets, buckets of water. It was all confusion.

Loyer saw Anne by the door, and hesitated. She gestured towards the dark outside.

'Run!' she mouthed.

But Loyer fumbled at the locket about his neck and pressed something into her hand.

'Take it,' he said. 'The King gave it to me but I have no use for it now.'

He slipped through the door, cloak flapping behind him, hat on head. Mary stumbled down the stairs. By this time the other soldiers were alerted and they set off in pursuit of Loyer. The fugitive was making for the church, or the outline of its tower on this fading summer evening. He scrambled over the drystone wall into the churchyard. But another group of armed men, by now familiar with the lay of the land, had circled round and were ready to intercept him by the church gate.

Loyer hesitated and turned back. Too late. He was encircled by the men. It was the lank-haired Trafford who finally cut him down, stabbing at him repeatedly with a pike. Loyer staggered away, hoping for sanctuary in the church, but the whole band entered St Ethelwine's and finished him off on that sacred ground. Anne and Mary stood, petrified with horror, watching the spectacle. Behind them smoke issued from their home.

The Murderer's Story, Part Three
(Monday, 20th October)

Early on the afternoon of his death, Eric Fort called on Mute in his little rented house in the little side street in Cambridge. At this point Fort had no idea of Tomlinson's fate. The last time he'd seen that gentleman was in the St Ethelwine's crypt, from which Tomlinson emerged dusty, frustrated and empty-handed. Then the undertaker's man underwent his change of heart during the long night in the crypt before making his 'confession' to George Eames. Now he was fulfilling his obligations towards Mute. He was doing so with reluctance because the only report he was bringing was of a failed search.

As we know, the columnist for *Funereal Matters*, growing tired of waiting for Fort to bring him news on the previous day, had gone off to see (and murder) Tomlinson for himself. So he was already aware that the search of the crypt had been fruitless. But, after committing his first murder, Mute got hold of the so-called Ely testament from Tomlinson's room in the Lion Hotel. The little leather-bound volume was in the drawer of the table. He had also picked up from the floor where the drunken Tomlinson had dropped it the padlock key to Chase's workshop. He wasn't sure why he'd taken the key. Perhaps he was curious to see for himself the coffin-bird to which he had made reference in one of his columns.

Eric Fort was relieved that Mute was not angry or particularly despondent over the news that Tomlinson retrieved nothing from the crypt. It was almost, he thought, as if the other man already had the information. Encouraged, he raised the subject of payment.

'What for?' said Mute. 'You haven't brought me any good news.'

'Don't you want me to go on keeping an eye on Mr and Mrs Ansell?'

'That won't be necessary.'

'The fact is,' said Fort, 'I am in need of a little cash and cannot wait.'

'Then go and see my uncle, as they say. You must have something to put in pawn.'

Sensing he would get no further on the money front, Fort explained to Mute that he was resolved to live a better life in future and that he really wanted nothing more to do with Tomlinson. He also meant that he wanted nothing more to do with Mute, though he didn't quite have the nerve to say this to the man's face.

'I don't think you will be having anything more to do with Charles Tomlinson.'

'Has something occurred?'

'No, no,' said Mute quickly. 'Not that I am aware of.'

'I have received a request from our London friends at Willow & Son,' said Fort. 'They have asked me to visit a Mr Chase in Prickwillow Road in Ely. He has made a complaint that involves our mutual friend, Tomlinson. It seems that I cannot get away from the man.'

'Is the complaint to do with a mechanical bird and a security coffin?'

'Why, yes, it is. You are a veritable mind-reader.'

'I am familiar with the situation, Mr Fort.'

'Are you sure that nothing's happened to Mr Tomlinson?'

'Would you be sorry if it had?'

'Not altogether.'

'Well then, we can rest easy.'

The two men were silent for a moment. They were sitting in the shadows in the front room of the little terraced house. The curtains were drawn so that only a narrow gap was left in the middle. This was not to ward off the sun or to protect the meagre furniture – it was overcast – but because in his present mood Mute apparently preferred the gloom. It was cold inside the room as well. It seemed to Fort that there was something different about Mute. He wondered whether, like himself, the other had experienced some sort of change of heart. If so, it might not be a change of heart for the better.

Fort was no fool. He was aware that something undesirable had probably happened and that it involved Charles Tomlinson. At once, he wanted to get away from Mute. He stood up.

'Where do you think you are going?'

'I told you. I am going to Ely to see this man Chase and to hear from him the exact nature of his complaint.'

'I'll say goodbye to you then.'

Mute accompanied him into the narrow hallway. He picked up his stick from the hallstand as if he was intending to go outside with Fort. He toyed with the ivory handle and seemed about to say something further but, in the end, he simply stood aside to allow Fort to open the front door and go.

Once Eric Fort had gone, Mute remained in the hall. Several times he twisted the handle of the flick stick and, by the light that came through the smeared fanlight, observed the satisfyingly prompt emergence of the spike. It was soundless and deadly, a beautiful mechanism, as the Hanover Street swordsmith had promised him. It amazed Mute that less than twenty-four hours previously the spike had helped in the killing of a man. The spike and the hip flask together. These facts amazed him but they did not frighten or oppress him.

Mute was not suffering from any pangs of conscience. When he finally returned to the little house on the previous evening, with the Ely testament in his pocket, he even had the appetite to prepare a small supper for himself. After eating, he slept soundly. He woke up at his usual time and it took a moment before it occurred to him that on the day before he had killed a man.

Now he was asking himself whether a second murder might be necessary. Putting on his hat and coat and tucking his stick under his arm, he left the house. There was only one direction Eric Fort could have gone in if he was heading for the railway station and, sure enough, when Mute reached the main road he saw the figure of the undertaker's man in the distance. Yet Fort did not turn right at the junction which led to the station but continued walking towards the centre of town.

Mute took care to stay at a distance. As they drew nearer the heart of Cambridge, the streets grew more crowded. At one point, Fort came to a stop outside a pawnbroker's and gazed fixedly at the window. Mute noted that he'd taken the advice to visit his uncle. He observed him from afar. Despite the gap separating them, and the passing people and traffic, he could sense the other man's reluctance and hesitation. Indeed, after a few moments, Eric Fort walked on without entering the pawnshop. Mute trailed him for another few hundred yards. They were in the older and grander area of the city now, among the great colleges with their noble chapels and spacious lawns. All at once Mute saw a woman he recognized on the other side of the street. She was walking with a man. He ducked into the lodge of the nearest college. He thought for an instant. Then he emerged, almost with a spring in his step. He practically ran across the road.

'Mrs Ansell! Mrs Ansell!' he cried.

Introductions followed. He said, 'It is a pleasure to meet you, Mr Ansell. You are a toiler in the snares of the law, I believe?'

Less than two hours later, Mute (or Arthur Arnett, to give him his full and proper name) was waiting on the platform of the Cambridge railway station. Like the Ansells, he was expecting the Ely train. He was at one end of the platform, his coat collar turned up and his top hat tilted down so as to conceal as much of his face as possible. He had removed the tinted spectacles which he wore as Arthur Arnett, editor – he liked the academic, slightly mysterious look that they provided – but which his eyes did not require. In addition, Mute must have found the imminent arrival of the Ely train a fascinating prospect for he kept his gaze turned away from the station buildings and down the track on which it was due to appear.

Meanwhile Tom and Helen Ansell and Eric Fort were talking together. Or rather Mrs Ansell and Fort were talking, and Mr Ansell was listening like a dutiful husband. The principal thing was that they were unaware of his presence, and therefore they were not asking themselves why he, Mute or Arthur Arnett, was about to board the same train. When the train came in, Mute climbed into the last carriage, a third-class one, while the other three got into a second-class nearer the front. He had deliberately chosen to ride third-class.

After meeting the Ansells on King's Parade, Mute had almost come to the decision not to murder Eric Fort. He changed his mind again when he happened to pass the coffee-house where he had talked with Mrs Ansell. Now he spotted the three of them inside – the Ansells and Eric Fort – in earnest conversation. At once he became afraid that Fort was somehow going to betray him, to reveal their mutual links with Tomlinson.

He determined to deal with the undertaker's man, and to deal with him very soon. He regretted not having got rid of him in the hallway of the little house, then realized that it would hardly have been prudent to quit a house which he was renting under his real name, and leave a corpse in his wake. Nor could he assail Fort while he was with the Ansells in the streets of Cambridge. At a discreet distance, he trailed the trio to the Cambridge station. The first problem lay in separating Eric Fort from the Ansells. Surely they were not all on their way to visit Mr Chase?

The problem was solved on their arrival at Ely when the young couple got into a cab without Fort. Mute, hanging back behind a column in the porticoed entrance to the station, could not be certain but thought that he heard Ansell tell the driver to go to the police-station. Eric Fort, meanwhile, set off on foot in the direction of the town centre. Mute knew where the undertaker's man was going, to call on Mr Chase in Prickwillow Road. It was fortunate that he was saving his pennies by not taking a cab.

A plan formed in Mute's head. Really, he was surprising himself with how quickly he was capable of forming plans under the pressure of events. He took a cab himself and was put down to the north of the cathedral. From there he walked rapidly to Prickwillow Road and found the house with *Mon Repos* engraved on the gatepost. The afternoon was dull and growing duller, and there was a glimmer of light from an upstairs room.

Mute unlatched the gate. Moving confidently, as if he had every right to be there, he walked towards the front door then veered off to one side. Soon he was dodging among the trees and shrubs of the back garden and then he was standing outside Cyrus Chase's workshop. He had the key that Tomlinson had dropped in the room at the Lion. He undid the padlock, opened the door, and swiftly inspected the interior. He noted Chase's security-coffin on the work table. Perfect, he thought.

The next twenty minutes passed with the smoothness of a dream, although they should have been a nightmare. Out into Prickwillow Road to intercept Eric Fort, who was by now tired and out of breath following his walk up from the station and who was, to say the least, surprised and perhaps alarmed to see Mute. Then round the side of the house and back again to Cyrus Chase's workshop – all the while unobserved! – on the pretext that the inventor would be arriving in a moment. The offer of Mute's hip flask, accepted. The manoeuvring of Fort's body into the coffin as the contents of the flask began to take effect, although when Fort started to struggle Mute had to keep him down by jabbing at him with his flick stick, a process which drew some blood. A deal of blood in fact.

The whole time Mute might have been interrupted but he scarcely considered that, just carried on with his job of finishing off Fort. Then at the end when Fort was twitching and his life almost departed, Mute heaved the coffin lid, with all its cumbersome apparatus of bell and bird, back into place.

Finally, out into Prickwillow Road once more. Mute thought he discerned, in the distance, Mr and Mrs Ansell walking together. The Ansells, joint contributors to *The New Moon*. He turned in the opposite direction, and soon passed a graveyard. With a professional eye, he noted the newness of the headstones and monuments and concluded that it must be a municipal cemetery, built in the last few years when the old churches could no longer accommodate the city dead. With another part of his mind, he thought, I've got away with it! Like a cuckoo laying an egg in another bird's nest, he had perpetrated a murder in another man's property, and done so without being observed, let alone apprehended. He laughed out loud then looked about as if fearful of being heard. Against the grey sky, the darker shape of the spire and belfry of the cemetery chapel stood out.

Mute asked himself whether he was going mad. He concluded not. The things he had done, the murders of Tomlinson and Fort, had been rational deeds, acts of self-preservation. Murders carried out with the aid of his trusty flick stick and his hip flask, among the contents of which was arsenic. Mute considered the use of arsenic as just the thing – almost à la mode, one might say. Arsenic was also easy for him to obtain since it was widely employed as one of the ingredients in embalming fluid. Those visits to Willow & Son had been productive in many ways.

It was true that with all this murdering, Arthur Arnett had wandered rather far away from his original plan, which was to share with Tomlinson the 'treasure' he obtained from Upper Fen, to realize its cash value and to use the money to fund his magazine, *The New Moon*; the magazine which had been his ambition all the while he'd been working at the *Funereal Matters* office. But the straightforward need for cash had been warped by his growing detestation of Tomlinson, and his decision not to share in the fruits of his old friend's labours but to steal them from him. Then would-be theft had turned to actual murder. Or murders. And they had been less difficult than Mute might have believed.

Wicked acts, perhaps, he thought, but rational. Leaving the municipal cemetery behind him and walking in a wide loop, he made his way back to the lower part of the town and the railway station, where he caught the next train back to Cambridge. Before he boarded, he checked to see whether he had marks of blood on his clothes. He couldn't see any.

Upper Fen

Tom and Helen were driven out to Upper Fen in company with Inspector Stephen Francis. They arrived at the police-house in Ely only to find the senior policeman in the lobby and about to depart for the village.

'Why are you going to Upper Fen, Inspector? Not to see Mr Ernest Lye, I hope,' said Tom, considering Ernest to be almost a client of his firm.

'No, sir. I have more or less cleared Mr Lye of any involvement in this tangled affair. I have other fish to fry. In the meantime I am going to look at a church, and to talk to the incumbent.'

'That would be the Reverend Eames,' said Helen.

'How do you know?' said Francis with real surprise.

'We have information to give you.'

'Then you'd better accompany me now and tell me later.'

They walked to the yard behind the building, which also housed the assize court. In the yard their transport awaited: a two-horse wagonette, uncovered and furnished with longways benches. From the hardness of the seating and the generally dilapidated state of the vehicle, it could be employed only for police purposes. Or perhaps agricultural ones, since the driver was wearing patched labourer's clothes. Francis addressed him as William.

The discomfort of the seats was exacerbated by the poor condi-tion of the road to Upper Fen. Tom and Helen jolted about on one side and opposite them were Inspector Francis and Constable Parr. This was the constable to whom Tom had talked at the scene of Tomlinson's murder, the one who'd claimed they did not enjoy much murdering on the Isle of Ely. The constable gave a courteous good morning and a smart salute to the Ansells as they clambered on board the wagon. His presence was explained when Francis said that PC Parr's brother was the sexton at St Ethelwine's.

The noise of the little wagon would have made conversation difficult between the Ansells and the policemen on the other side even had there been much to say, so Tom and Helen gazed out across the flat, black-earthed countryside. Indicating the great cathedral, Helen said to Tom that it was like a great ship riding on the fens. Tom smiled at his wife's poetic language. Thinking of her way with words made him also think of Arthur Arnett, the editor fellow they'd met on King's Parade. A boyish, enthusiastic individual, punctuating his remarks with little jabbing motions of his walking stick. Yet Tom had not taken to him much, for all that he'd more or less solicited an article from him on – what was it? – the byways of the law, for that magazine of his.

By now they were approaching the outskirts of Upper Fen. The Inspector told the driver to pull up by the small cottage where Tom had noticed the mason at work a few days before. Constable Parr got down and rapped on the door. The lad who answered was the driver of the dog cart from Tom's previous visit. Parr asked him something that Tom couldn't hear and the boy nodded his head in the direction of the church, whose stubby tower was visible from where they sat. The policeman gave some instructions to the boy and, after a moment's hesitation and an apprehensive glance at the individuals in the wagon, the lad took to his heels towards the village. Parr boarded the wagon again.

'That your nephew, Parr?' said Francis.

'Yes, sir.'

'Where is your brother?'

'Gabriel's at the church. I told Davey to go and get him.'

'Let's meet him halfway.'

Francis gestured to William to move on, and the wagonette lumbered up the road towards Upper Fen. They passed a turn in the road which led towards Phoenix House. Tom pointed out the roof line of the large house to Helen. They passed a few scattered dwellings whose gardens were mostly given over to vegetable plots and, in one case, a pigsty, before drawing up at the lych-gate of the church. A man watched them arrive, while leaning against the gate with arms folded. The boy Davey was hanging back at a distance.

Tom recognized this person too as the man who'd been working on the headstone. There was a remote similarity to Constable Parr, not exactly in any particular feature but as in two objects cut from the same block of wood. Once again, Constable Parr got down. The brothers, policeman and sexton, nodded at each other but said not a word of greeting.

'Can I help you, Inspector?' said Gabriel to Francis, who stayed seated in the wagon. Since he wasn't addressing his employer, the St Ethelwine's sexton spoke without the deference of his brother.

'We need to see the church, Mr Parr. We need to see inside the crypt.'

'Mr Eames has the keys.'

'You don't have a set?'

'That's as may be but you'd better see Mr Eames first. You'll find him over there.'

Gabriel Parr tilted his head towards the parsonage, which lay on a patch of slightly higher ground and beyond a high beech hedge. Inspector Francis unlatched the gate at the back of the wagon and jumped down. He was surprisingly nimble. He approached the sexton, who continued to lean, unmoving, against the lych-gate.

'True enough, we had better see Mr Eames first,' Francis repeated in a reasonable tone. 'Let us do all of this properly and without irregularities.'

'You'll find it quicker to go through the graveyard.'

Gabriel did not unfold his arms but with a flick of a finger indicated a beaten track of grass that ran among the headstones and towards a gate in the hedge. While this conversation was going on, Tom and Helen climbed down.

'Very well,' said Francis to Gabriel, before turning to his constable. 'You are to stay here with William, Parr. No doubt you'll welcome the chance to exchange family news with your brother.'

'Sir,' said Parr. The constable took up position, hands behind his back. Francis said, 'Mr and Mrs Ansell, are you coming with me?'

Tom and Helen were curious to meet Mr Eames, if only to see

the victim of the long-ago jape involving a stuffed monkey. But now that they were in Upper Fen they decided to call on the Lyes first. Tom felt some responsibility towards Ernest, so recently arrested on suspicion of murder. Helen had glanced through Mr Lye's volume about the house and village and she wanted to make some complimentary remarks to him, for cheering-up purposes.

Gabriel Parr directed them to Phoenix House by a different grassy path, one running south of the church. On the far side of St Ethelwine's the Ansells came to the road leading to Phoenix House.

'It's a handsome place although I'm not sure I'd care to live somewhere so remote,' said Helen, gazing at the facade. In front of the house were a dilapidated stone wall and a pair of rusty iron gates, set open.

'Isn't that Mrs Lye's opinion too?'

'I believe so.'

For an instant they halted and looked back at the sweeping stretch of countryside that ran south and east, before walking towards the house again. The front door opened and two men and a woman emerged, and came towards the iron gates. They were dressed as if for an afternoon stroll.

'Why,' she said, 'isn't that . . .?'

Mr and Mrs Lye were easy to recognize, the shortish man in late middle-age and his taller, younger, elegant wife. One might expect to see the owners of the house coming out of their own front door. More surprising was the appearance of the individual who was walking with them. He was carrying a stick and, as they approached the entrance, he raised it to point at something – perhaps the tower of St Ethelwine's – in a querying sort of way.

'Yes,' said Tom, 'it is Mr Arnett.'

'What is he doing in Upper Fen?'

The Lyes and Mr Arnett noticed the Ansells. Arms were waved, hats tipped. The five of them met just outside the entrance of Phoenix House. Quite a bit of explanation was required once it had been established that everyone already knew everyone else and that no formal introductions were needed. What were Tom and Helen doing in the village? And how did Arthur Arnett know the Lyes? That mystery was easily solved by the editor himself. He was eager to explain.

'I was at college with Charles Tomlinson, and we recently renewed our acquaintance after his years of global peregrination. I was most shocked to hear of the violent demise of my friend and so have come to offer Mrs Lye my sincere condolences.'

'You are very kind, Mr Arnett.'

'It is no more than my duty, Mrs Lye. Charles often talked of you – and of Mr Lye of course.'

'We're about to show Mr Arnett the village, or rather the church,' said Lydia. 'As an antiquarian, he is particularly interested to see St Ethelwine's.'

'An antiquarian, Mr Arnett?' said Helen.

'Why yes. It is another string to my—'

'Lyre?'

'I was about to say bow, but lyre is better. Very good, Mrs Ansell.'

'Everyone seems to be interested in the church,' said Tom, deciding he couldn't match his wife's quickness.

'Everyone?' said Mr Arnett.

'Inspector Francis of the Ely force certainly is. We have come to Upper Fen with him.'

'The police are here?'

This time the editor of *The New Moon* spoke so sharply that the other four looked at him. Tom was pleased to see him put out. However, Arnett recovered himself quickly, smiled and said, 'One would not suppose that the local constabulary had anything much to attend to in such a tranquil and sequestered spot as this.'

'What does Inspector Francis want, Mr Ansell? Do you know?' said Ernest Lye. These were almost the first words he'd spoken and he was anxious.

'I'm not sure,' said Tom, 'but I don't think it's anything to do with the . . . with that recent business.'

He meant, I don't think it's to do with you and Tomlinson's murder. Tom wanted to reassure Ernest Lye that the finger of suspicion was moving away from him but this wasn't the right moment. Besides, there was something odd about this meeting that he couldn't quite pin down. Something odd about Arnett too. Why should the fellow be going out of his way to offer his condolences to a cousin of Tomlinson's whom he'd never met? For that matter, the very fact of Arnett's friendship with Tomlinson was, well, not so much odd as unexpected. And why was he so startled to hear that the police were in the village?

These thoughts, half formed, flashed through Tom's mind. He glanced at Helen. She was regarding Arnett with a look that he recognized; quizzical, doubting.

'Would you like to accompany us to the church, Mr and Mrs Ansell?' said Lydia Lye.

'Yes, why not?'

They set off the way they had come, skirting St Ethelwine's on the south side. Arthur Arnett hung back, as if slightly reluctant to make up one of the party. Helen said some nice things to Ernest Lye about his *Annals of a Fenland Village* and he visibly brightened. Tom, who was walking behind with Lydia Lye, gave her his own condolences on her cousin's death, which he had not had the opportunity to do before.

'Thank you, Mr Ansell. I was much affected at the time but I believe that it was more the shock of the event than anything else. I did not know Charles well. He was almost a stranger to me. How ridiculous to suppose that Ernest might have had a hand in his death! Look at him. How could a man like my husband be capable of murder?'

Lydia sounded quite benign when talking about her husband, as if his inability to murder was a positive attribute. Ernest was walking next to Helen, glancing at her with pleasure and approval for the things she was saying about his book. You had to admit that Ernest Lye did not have the appearance of a murderer, whatever a murderer's appearance ought to be. Yes, if you were searching for a murderer, you might more plausibly find him elsewhere.

For no good reason Tom looked behind him. Arthur Arnett quickly averted his eyes. He had been staring hard at Tom and Lydia. Now he started to swing his stick through the grass as he walked, as though searching for an item concealed there.

Near the lych-gate was the police wagon, with William the driver still in his seat and the horses restless in their traces. The Parr brothers, constable and sexton, were in the postures they'd been occupying when Tom and Helen left. Gabriel leaning against the gate, Constable Parr standing at a little distance and with hands clasped behind his back. Tom wondered what family news had been exchanged or whether the two had uttered even a single word to each other. The sexton's boy, Davey, was also on the scene, loitering among the headstones.

Tom was curious to observe Arthur Arnett's reaction to a police uniform but, rather than paying attention to the group of men, the editor was peering up at the overcast sky. Then, as though this arrival of one and all was by prearrangement, through the parsonage gate in the beech hedge there came two men followed by two women. Two by two, they began threading the path between the headstones. The younger woman was wearing housemaid's clothes; the other, older woman might have been a housekeeper. They kept a suitable distance behind the men, one of whom was Inspector Francis. Constable Parr, seeing his superior on the way, became alert. He brushed past his brother and went through the lych-gate. Gabriel too roused himself and turned into the churchyard. Helen and Ernest Lye, together with Tom and Lydia, followed behind so that there was quite a little crowd assembling among the graves.

The other man with Inspector Francis was presumably the curate of St Ethelwine's, George Eames, the stuffed-monkey man. Tom had a lazy picture of a typical country clergyman as a red-faced, rotund figure, likely to spend more time thinking of his stomach or his hounds than his parishioners. But this individual was slight, with a pallid face that didn't suggest much appetite for pleasure. To the sexton the reverend Eames said nothing. To the Lyes he gave a nod that was half friendly, half deferential. The perpetual curate looked curiously at Tom and Helen. Then Eames' eyes flickered towards the lych-gate. His casual glance became a gaze which turned into a stare.

His look was so fixed that the others turned to see what had caught his attention. It was nothing much, only a man coming through the lych-gate. But this individual was advancing with a peculiar reluctance as if summoned to his own funeral. It was Arthur Arnett, of course, the last of the little party out of Phoenix House. Somehow, and without apparently wishing it, Arnett was making himself the centre of attention and provoking everyone to look at him. Scattered among the gravestones and monuments were the brothers Parr and the boy Davey, the two women from the parsonage, Ernest and Lydia Lye and the Ansells, the Reverend George Eames and Inspector Stephen Francis. The latter said, 'Good day to you, sir. And you might be . . .?'

'Arthur!'

This was George Eames. Arnett's first name was not uttered cheerfully. The curate was speaking through clenched teeth. His formerly pale face was now suffused with a dull red. Arnett seemed surprised to see Eames but he spoke in an oddly placid way.

'Why hello, George. What are you doing here?'

Arnett came to a halt a few yards from everyone. He waggled his stick slightly in greeting. Helen Ansell said to Tom in a whispered aside, 'Of course, they must know each other. Mr Arnett said he was a university friend of Mr Tomlinson and that gentleman there was the victim of Tomlinson's prank at college. They are old friends.'

'But not new friends,' whispered Tom. 'Look at them.'

It was true. Eames was standing with his arms held out from his sides, his hands clenched. Arnett was trying to smile but failing. No one moved. Inspector Francis coughed to draw attention to his presence. He said, 'I ask again, sir. Who are you?'

'I am Arthur Arnett, editor of the forthcoming periodical *The New Moon* and the author of a column in a distinguished journal. You may have heard of it. You may even have heard of me, under the pseudonym which I employ to cloak my activities. It is appropriate that we are meeting in a graveyard since you are looking at Mute of *Funereal Matters*.'

Helen recalled the name of the journal being read by Cyrus Chase. But it seemed as though Arnett lacked for readers among the group.

'Well, Mr Arnett, I can't say I'm familiar with your work though it sounds most interesting. I am Inspector Francis of the Isle of Ely Constabulary. It seems that you know Mr Eames?'

'Yes,' said Eames, answering for the other man. 'Arnett was a friend of mine once. He was a friend of Tomlinson too.'

'Of Tomlinson? Were you, sir?'

'I knew him, Inspector.'

'And from your choice of the past tense, you are evidently aware that Mr Tomlinson is dead.'

Arnett looked mildly surprised, not so much at the fact of Tomlinson's death but perhaps that a police inspector should know there were such things as past tenses.

'I have come to Upper Fen to offer my condolences to Mrs Lye there, as his cousin.'

'That's true, Inspector,' said Lydia.

Tom glanced at Helen. Both could sense the tension in the air. Everyone was hanging on the exchanges between Arnett and Francis, as if it were the last minutes of a melodrama.

'Well then,' said Arnett. 'I have offered my condolences so that is that. I'll be on my way now.'

'Didn't you say you wanted to look at the church, Mr Arnett?' said Helen.

'Another time perhaps.'

He tucked his stick under his arm and made a half-turn. Inspector Francis gestured to Constable Parr to move towards the lych-gate. His intention was obvious: to prevent Arnett from leaving. The wagon-driver, William, drawn by the prospect of some excitement in the churchyard, had climbed down from his perch and was already standing inside the entrance.

'A moment, Mr Arnett.'

'Yes, Inspector?'

'I have some questions for you.'

'Perhaps we can meet later, at a time of mutual convenience.'

'Now would be better.'

Francis walked a few paces down the slope towards Arnett, who glanced indecisively between the lych-gate, where Constable Parr was established, and the Inspector advancing towards him. He fiddled with the ivory handle of his walking stick. The others in the churchyard formed an impromptu semicircle, like an audience, waiting to see what happened next. Inspector Francis spoke quietly but because he was still standing at a distance from Arnett – perhaps wary of a swipe from Arnett's stick – he spoke clearly enough for his words to carry.

'Can you tell me where you were late on this Sunday afternoon, sir?'

'I was in Cambridge, I believe.'

'Not with Mr Tomlinson in Ely?'

'No.'

'That is strange, Mr Arnett. A witness who works in the Lion Hotel saw two gentlemen leaving the stable yard together in the late afternoon. One of them he knew as Mr Charles Tomlinson. The other he did not recognize but he was able to provide a description, a good description. Clothes, and the rest of it. And a characteristic motion of his stick; jabbing gestures as he walked.'

Arthur Arnett's assurance was visibly leaving him. He stood, head down, not meeting Francis' gaze. His stick hung limp at his side, with no give-away jabbing motions. He seemed to be pondering how to reply. This might have gone on for some time were it not for an extraordinary interruption. Out of the corner of his eye, Tom was aware of a blur of movement. A small figure ran towards Francis and Arnett. For an instant Tom thought this must be the witness mentioned by Francis, coming out on cue. But it was not an employee of the Lion Hotel. It was Davey Parr, the sexton's son. He stopped a few feet away from both men.

Davey looked fixedly at Arnett. He said, 'You did it! I saw you. Like this, you did it.'

Davey mimed an up and down stabbing movement, in the manner of a man wielding a knife. He was seeing a murderer standing in front of him, though it was not the murderer of Charles Tomlinson and Eric Fort. It was the figure who'd stabbed, repeatedly, at the fugitive royalist, in the vision which Davey witnessed while he crouched close to his mother's grave. A murder occurring more than two centuries earlier.

In any normal circumstances, someone might have tried to stop the lad. His father or his uncle would have stepped forward, to deliver a clip round the ear accompanied by some words of apology. Don't you pay any heed to him, sir. The lad lives in his head. Doesn't know what he's saying.

But these weren't normal circumstances. No one stepped forward to ask Davey what he was talking about. No one rebuked him for his nonsense. It was left to Arnett to answer for himself.

'You can't have seen me,' he said to the sexton's son. 'You can't have seen me because you weren't there.'

His response was instinctive. At almost the same instant he realized the fatal significance of what he'd said. So did Inspector Francis. With a flick of his hand, Francis summoned the constable from the lych-gate. The policeman advanced towards Arnett on a diagonal. Francis pushed Davey back, firmly, as if to move the boy out of harm's way.

'You really will have to come with me now, Mr Arnett.'

Francis' voice remained low and reasonable. Arthur Arnett looked around. Behind him was the bulk of St Ethelwine's. To his left were Constable Parr and William the wagon-man. In front of him were ten other individuals, their expressions showing accusation or apprehension or simple confusion at the turn of events. The editor might have made a run for it to his right, but there were too many obstacles for a race through the graveyard. Instead he stepped a few yards back towards the steps leading to the crypt.

'I'd rather not go with you but elsewhere,' he said.

'I don't advise it, Mr Arnett.'

'I'd also like to apologize.'

'Apologize for murder?'

'No, no. Apologize to Mrs Ansell over there. I do not think I will be in a position to publish her piece in *The New Moon* now.'

While the onlookers were distracted by turning towards Helen, as if they expected her to reply (she did not, though her hand flew to her mouth at being singled out), Arthur Arnett brought his walking stick into play. By some quick manipulation of the handle, he caused a metal spike to spring out from the tip.

Arnett held the flick stick in front of him like an awkward fencer, as if daring anyone to come near. With his free hand he fumbled in his pocket and the gesture caused a collective tremor among the bystanders as though he might produce another weapon, a gun perhaps. But Arnett brought out into the open what looked like a hip flask. Inspector Francis held up a restraining hand, directed more at his constable and the others than at Arnett. But there was no rush to overcome the man. The murderer edged backwards with stick in one hand and flask in the other and then, using a strange sideways movement, he went down the steps of the crypt.

Francis gestured again, towards Gabriel Parr this time. He raised his eyebrows, made a turning motion, key in a lock. No answer was needed because they heard the creak of the crypt door. This time Francis spoke, low but still calm.

'Is there another way out of there?'

Gabriel shook his head.

'Then we shall wait him out. Mr Eames and Mr Lye, perhaps you would like to accompany the ladies and take them indoors.'

Quite willingly, George Eames retreated with the two women from the parsonage, and with more reluctance Lydia Lye went off.

Ernest remained behind, however. Tom looked at Helen. She shook her head.

'No, I shall stay,' she said to Tom. 'There are plenty of men here for protection. Besides, I consider that I have a personal interest in Mr Arnett and what becomes of him.'

'The gallows is what will become of him,' said Tom.

'I shivered when he mentioned me by name. Why has he done these terrible things?'

Meanwhile Inspector Francis had obviously changed his mind about waiting for Arnett to emerge from the crypt and was in discussion with Ernest Lye, the Parr brothers and William. Or rather he was telling them what he intended to do next. Davey hovered on the edge of the group but was shoo'ed off by the policeman, who now looked in Tom's direction. The look said, are you game for this? Tom nodded. Gabriel Parr went off. Ernest Lye walked to where the Ansells were standing.

'Inspector Francis was asking me whether there was anything hidden in the crypt. Only a collection of bodies, I said.'

'Isn't there a story of some treasure?' said Helen. 'You refer to it in your book.'

'A legend merely,' said Lye. 'But, now you come to mention the subject, I remember Charles Tomlinson referring to it once or twice.'

'Perhaps that's what they're all after,' said Tom.

By now Gabriel Parr had returned with a lantern and a couple of spades, not for digging but for use as weapons. His brother had already drawn his police baton. The sexton handed Inspector Francis and Tom a spade each. Parr himself produced what looked to be a tool for engraving stone.

'Be careful, Tom,' said Helen.

With Francis in the lead, the group advanced on the steps to the crypt. Looking down, he could see that the door was open. Holding the spade by the haft, Francis trod down the worn steps, followed by Constable Parr and his brother. Tom was next while Ernest Lye took up the rear. They crowded together at the bottom of the steps, trying to see into the dim interior.

'Mr Arnett,' said Francis. 'You might as well come out now.'

There was no sound from within. Francis gestured to Gabriel for the lantern. Holding it aloft in one hand and grasping the spade in the other, he stepped inside the entrance to the crypt. The others pushed through after him. The smell of mould hit Tom's nostrils.

They filed into a larger area, with coffins arrayed on stone shelving. To one side was a broken-down stretch of wall. Francis once more held up the lantern so that they might all see the contents of this smaller chamber, so small that it was little more than a cupboard. Inside was another coffin, the wood of which was black and disintegrating. It contained a skeletal form wrapped in a yellowing shroud, although the bandages had been torn away in the region of the neck. Next to the coffin lay the corpse of Arthur Arnett. Unlike the skeleton, he was newly dead, still warm, frothing slightly at the mouth. To one side was his lethal flick stick. In his hand was the flask from which he'd taken his final draught.

And also in Arnett's possession was found the Ely Testament, a black-bound journal that explained everything – or almost everything. The story told in it, handwritten by Mary Stilwell, was of a terrible day in the midsummer of 1645 shortly after the Battle of Naseby. Mary was the younger daughter of the house and her parents were confirmed royalists who had agreed to give shelter to a man fleeing in the guise of King Charles while the genuine monarch sped in the opposite direction.

The plan worked, to a point. Soldiers arrived and searched Stilwell without success, and then apparently departed. Later on the same day Mary's sister Anne – 'always more venturesome than I' she wrote – discovered the individual, whom for some reason they called Loyer, on the edge of the grounds of the manor. But almost straightaway he had been taken prisoner by the soldiers, whose departure had been a feint. When they found out that they had been deceived, their fury knew no bounds, particularly after the fugitive made an attempt to escape. Under the gaze of the horrified sisters (there was no mention of the whereabouts of their parents at this time) Mr Loyer was cut down in the churchyard and, although he took sanctuary in St Ethelwine's, he was murdered inside the church itself.

Shortly afterwards, the soldiers slunk away as if ashamed of their sacrilegious violence. Mr Loyer's body was interred in the crypt but the villagers, fearing further discoveries and reprisals either from the Royalists or the Parliamentarians, walled up the body in an alcove in the crypt, hastily erecting a crude plaster wall. Almost as an afterthought, Mary Stilwell added that Mr Loyer had been in possession of a diamond, which he wore in a silver locket and which, she believed, had been buried with him since no one apart from her sister and herself knew of its existence.

Mary wrote the story many years afterwards, when she was an old lady with grandchildren and wished to put the tale down in black and white. Her sister Anne had not been so fortunate. She was more affected by Loyer's fate than Mary. Indeed, she had even started a fire as a diversionary tactic to help the aristocrat escape. The flames had swiftly been extinguished – it was not the same fire that destroyed parts of Stilwell Manor, which occurred many years later – but Anne continued to feel deeply her responsibility, her guilt, in the death of the gallant royalist. Unlike her sister, she never married but eventually entered a convent in the Low Countries.

There was other material in the Ely Testament, which Tomlinson had undoubtedly discovered on an early visit to Phoenix House while he was, as he would have put it, fossicking around in its older parts, perhaps in the top floor room where Tom Ansell had searched in vain for Alexander Lye's will. But it was the story of the diamond that he seized on. The skeleton in the alcove was indeed wearing a locket on a thin silver chain, which was now blackened with age, but the locket was empty. If the locket had ever held a diamond, no one knew what had become of it since neither Tomlinson nor Arthur Arnett (or 'Mute') could have laid hands on the thing. The assumption was that one of the village burying party had taken the precious stone more than two centuries earlier.

What About the Other Characters?

What happened to some of the other characters in this story? Mr and Mrs Chase were not involved in the climactic confrontation in the churchyard of St Ethelwine's. They learned

later of the death of Arthur Arnett – a person who meant nothing
to Bella and was known to Cyrus only under the guise of Mute
in *Funereal Matters* – and his responsibility for two murders. Bella
grieved mildly for Charles Tomlinson's demise but, as she heard
more about his rackety background, she began to think she'd had
a lucky escape from a more intricate involvement with him.

Cyrus more or less abandoned his work on the coffin-bird. It
was tainted by Tomlinson's interference, and the security-coffin
itself had been the site of Eric Fort's murder. In any case he was
developing a fresh device for averting the horror of premature
burial, a device more in keeping with the forward-looking spirit
of the century. What if, he asked himself, the man or woman
trapped underground was able to communicate directly with those
on the surface by means of a telegraphing mechanism, a Morse
code apparatus? Such a machine would have the advantage of
occupying little space in the coffin, and if placed next to the
supposedly dead person it could be operated merely with one or
two fingers.

A message could be sent with a real assurance that it would be
answered. There could be no error in understanding the straightforward appeal produced by a repeatedly pressed buzzer. For those
who had mastered Morse code a more elaborate communication,
perhaps I HAVE BEEN BURIED ALIVE, would be possible. Nor
would the system be expensive to operate. An entire cemetery, a
whole city's worth of cemeteries, could contain coffins equipped
with telegraphic machines, each of them linked to a single office
where one man – one single man! – might be on duty (with
another available for the night-time, of course). True, there were
problems involving dynamos, generators, coils and wires but Cyrus
felt certain that these could be overcome.

Cyrus continues to work on his transmitting device in the
workshop in the bottom of his garden. From time to time he
remembers that a man was murdered in this very place, an unfortunate individual named Eric Fort who was on his way to see
Cyrus when he was waylaid by Arthur Arnett. Fort seems to have
been a decent enough individual, a toiler in the funereal field like
himself, though at a less elevated level. Cyrus thinks that perhaps
he ought to commemorate Fort's passing in some way but he is
not quite certain how to do this.

He has already invented a name for the telegraphic machine. It will be called 'The Chase Communicator'. He believes that his father would be proud of him and he relishes the echo of 'The Chase Coupler' in his choice of name. He feels that a public statue, enshrining his contribution to mankind's well-being (and well-dying!), is not such an absurd prospect after all. He even strikes statue-like poses every now and then in the privacy of his workshop.

Mr and Mrs Lye stayed together at Phoenix House in Upper Fen. Lydia, who was more sensible than Bella, remembered her friendship with her Tomlinson cousin with a slight shudder. The idea that he had cultivated her acquaintance partly to have a pretext to search for some non-existent treasure was unsettling. So Lydia looked more affectionately at her husband, a good man if not a very effectual one. Her attitude towards Ernest was coloured slightly by the fact that shortly after his step-brother's death, he was also plunged into mourning for his step-sister, the aged Miss Edith, who fell asleep one afternoon during teatime and never woke up again.

Ernest was therefore the beneficiary not only of Alexander's eventually discovered will but of Edith's estate too. He gained the house in Regent's Park as well as enough capital (in stocks and bonds) to afford the cost of repairs, even renovation, on Phoenix House. Possession of the Regent's Park house provided that 'little place in town', in fact quite a big one, for which Lydia had always hoped. Ernest is happy enough to accompany Lydia on their stays in London. He doesn't do a great deal while she goes out and about, but he reads widely and contemplates writing a book about the folklore of the fens.

As for the Reverend George Eames, he too stayed on in Upper Fen. He did not rejoice at the violent deaths of his old enemies, Charles Tomlinson and Arthur Arnett, although in his more indulgent moments he believed it might be an instance of higher judgement. The way Arnett had eliminated Tomlinson, and then himself, brought to mind the words of Psalm 37, specifically that verse (the twentieth) which describes the wicked as being like the fat of sacrificial lambs since 'they shall consume; into smoke shall they consume away.'

Mr Eames had other and happier matters to occupy him. Within a few months of that unfortunate business in the St Ethelwine's crypt he was surprised to find himself married. There'd been a wife on his doorstep all the time. Or rather, inside his door. It was either the widowed Mrs Walters or the young and shy housemaid Hannah. You may take your pick as to which he chose. Or which chose him. The result is that he is much more content. His sermons may not be gentle but they are less severe on human failings. In fact, he no longer toils over his sermons as he used to. He is even growing to like the backwater which is Upper Fen.

Nobody lost a great deal by the murders and the suicide. Eric Fort, the man who ran errands for Willow & Son, had no dependants or family, apart from his recently deceased wife. The ring that he put into pawn in Bartle & Co. in Cambridge is still there. Alfred Jenkins, the editor of *Funereal Matters*, was both excited and alarmed to discover that his popular columnist Mute had committed murder twice over. But all the bad publicity caused a temporary rise in the circulation of *F.M.*, and he was able to pen a couple of articles along the lines of 'The Murderer Dwelling in Our Midst' for the more sensational papers.

Of course, the magazine *The New Moon* never appeared, and so Helen Ansell was deprived of the chance of publishing a portrait of Cambridge or Ely. She was not too troubled, however. The idea of having been commissioned, if unknowingly, by a murderer was disturbing. Besides, she had other things on her mind as Tom found out on Christmas Eve, when he made some casual, commiserating remark to her about it being a pity – in a way – that they would never see an issue of Mr Arnett's periodical *The New Moon*. Helen, who was looking blooming, said, 'Never mind, Tom. There is another issue I'm looking forward to seeing.'

'Oh yes?'

'One that takes only two authors. I expect it to come out around next July. It will be a summer issue.'

'It will? What's it called?'

'Tom, you are very slow sometimes. I don't know exactly what "it" will be called. The authors have yet to decide. But part of his name – or hers – will be Ansell.'

Summer, 1645

*A*nne *paused by the edge of the fen. She looked at the diamond as it lay in her palm. As vivid as the object before her eyes was the sight of Mr Loyer fleeing from Stilwell Manor, stumbling over the wall, being surrounded in the churchyard and then cut down by the brutish Trafford. Anne shuddered. She wanted nothing to do with the precious stone that he had pressed into her hand, even if it came from King Charles. She wanted nothing more to do with worldly things. She closed her hand, raised her arm and threw the thing — a crystal which flashed red or blue or green wherever it caught the light — so that it arced through the air and landed somewhere, out of sight, gone for good.*